ESCAPE FOR THE

By

Ruth Saberton

Copyright

Also by Ruth Saberton

Escape for Christmas

Dead Romantic

Hobb's Cottage

Weight Till Christmas

Katy Carter Wants a Hero

Ellie Andrews Has Second Thoughts

Amber Scott is Starting Over

The Wedding Countdown

Runaway Summer: Polwenna Bay 1

A Time for Living: Polwenna Bay 2

Winter Wishes: Polwenna Bay 3

Writing as Jessica Fox

The One That Got Away

Eastern Promise

Hard to Get

Unlucky in Love

Always the Bride

Writing as Holly Cavendish

Looking for Fireworks

Writing as Georgie Carter

The Perfect Christmas

Chapter 1

You have insufficient funds to complete this transaction

Please contact your branch

The neon letters dancing across the cashpoint screen couldn't have looked more complacent if they'd been flicking V-signs and pulling moonies. Although it was a sweltering June day, the kind when Londoners go mad picnicking in Hyde Park, Andi Evans was glacier cold. As the man queuing behind her cleared his throat irritably and the hot sunshine beat down, she stared at the screen in disbelief, her blood freezing from her insides out and spreading a chill of dread to the tips of her fingers and toes.

Insufficient funds? How on earth could there be *insufficient funds* in her personal account? Andi was always in credit and, unlike her sister Angel (who was probably single-handedly to blame for the economic downturn), she was never overdrawn. Not even as a student and certainly not now as a fully paid-up member of the adult world with rent and bills to pay, as well as supporting an actor boyfriend who rested so frequently he could double for Sleeping Beauty. No, Andi Evans always kept on top of her finances. She *had* to.

So what on earth was going on?

Fearfully she glanced back at the screen just in case she had been mistaken. Maybe the pressure of work and an evil boss was getting to her more than she'd realised? That must be it. The strain of working so hard and this morning's big row with her boyfriend, Tom, had all been too much. She was seeing things.

Whipping off her sunglasses, Andi gave her eyes a quick rub – but when she returned her attention to the screen the message was still there, a baleful lime rebuke that made her feel sick.

You have insufficient funds to complete this transaction

Andi shook her head. There was no way she could possibly be overdrawn. Today was payday and her salary, together with the five-hundred-pound buffer she always kept in the account, meant that she had more than enough cash. Add to this a thousand-pound over-draft facility and it was impossible that she didn't have any money. What was going on?

With a growing sensation of dread she pressed the *balance only* key and, seconds later, had to clutch the ATM for support.

Over two grand in the red?

WTF?

Andi's every cell was paralysed with disbelief. Had somebody cloned her card? Or hacked into her account? Maybe the cashpoint had made a mistake? Even machines were allowed off days, weren't they?

"Excuse me, love, but some of us would actually like to use that machine before we die of old age."

The impatient words snatched her back to the present. Mistake or not, she couldn't spend the next hour staring at the ATM. Apart from the fact that this wouldn't explain the mystery of her missing money, Andi only had thirty minutes before she was due back at her desk and slaving over the latest bunch of recalcitrant figures. She didn't dare be so much as a nanosecond late back either, because then Zoe, her boss from hell, would have even more of an excuse to make her day a misery. There was no way Andi wanted to give her any extra ammunition. She wasn't sure what she'd done to make her new boss hate her so much, but from the first day Zoe had tottered into the office on her skyscraper heels and with her Cheddar Gorge cleavage on display, she'd gone out of her way to make Andi's life a misery. Fortunately Andi enjoyed her job, which made it bearable; accounting might sound dull to most people, but there was a simplicity and beauty to balancing figures that she found hugely satisfying. The other thing keeping her sane was the fun email friendship that she'd struck up with one of her latest clients. She'd been dealing with the finances for the flotation of the Internet security company he worked for, so they'd been in touch regularly. She didn't know his real name only his title at the firm, which was Project Manager B. Similarly he only knew her as AE, but it didn't matter though; Andi enjoyed chatting with him online and PMB's funny emails just about compensated for the endless sarcastic comments from her boss. It was rather sad that talking online to a total stranger was the highlight of her day, but Andi preferred not to dwell on that thought too much.

"Quit," was always Angel's answer whenever the topic of Andi's unhappiness with her boss was raised. "Tell the silly old cow to stick it up her bum, and do something else. Take a chance."

But Andi didn't dare take a chance. Or more accurately she couldn't afford to take a chance. She needed her job. Tom hadn't worked since an episode of *Holby City* six months previously (he'd played a demanding patient, with alarming ease) and somebody had to pay the rent on the flat in Balham. And if that someone was her at the moment then she knew it wouldn't be forever. Like Tom always said, his big break was probably only just around the corner. Just what and where this corner might be was something of a mystery, though. Andi had a nasty feeling that it could well be a corner very far away. Maybe Australia? Or perhaps on the moon? She was beginning to worry…

"I said, are you going to stand there all day, or what?" The man behind was really impatient now. "Some of us do have other things to do, you know!"

Muttering a hasty apology, Andi cancelled her transaction and retrieved the card. Maybe she'd accidentally used the wrong one? Perhaps Tom had placed his in her purse for safekeeping or something and because she was so stressed she'd used it by mistake? That would make sense. It wouldn't be unlike Tom to have an overdraft that made the National Debt look small.

And neither would it be the first time he'd kept this from her…

Andi stepped aside and let the man behind take her place. Then, slowly and hopefully, she turned the card over. Please, please let it be Tom's. They shared a PIN – to make things easier, Tom had argued. She lived with him, after all, and she loved him, didn't she? Then what was there to worry about? Didn't she trust him?

The sun was hot on her pale skin and heat rose from the pavement, but Andi remained icicle cold. Of course she trusted Tom. They'd had a row this morning, just a silly row because yet again he'd forgotten to pay their rent, but it hadn't meant anything. He said he'd left the cash in a taxi and that people made silly mistakes all the time, which was fair enough. Look at her right now getting their cards confused. It was an easy mistake to make. She'd laugh about it in a minute.

Or at least she hoped she would.

The card lay flat in her palm. *Miss Miranda Evans*, it read. There was no mistaking it: her name was emblazoned right across the plastic in raised metallic letters. This Maestro card was undoubtedly hers, as was the emptied bank account.

Andi had the hideous sensation that she was descending very fast in a lift. This couldn't be happening. She was good with money. Stingy and mean, Angel called her, but then Angel could afford to have a more carefree attitude when there was always a big sister on hand to bail her out. Who was there to rescue Andi if the rent was due and she'd blown it on a handbag instead? Or if she'd maxed out her credit cards and couldn't make the minimum payment? Their father, Alex, lived abroad with his wife – he had sold the family home shortly after Andi and Angel's mother had died – and couldn't be expected to stump up money whenever Angel got economically sidetracked by a designer frock or the latest must-have shoes. Save a postcard or two, their father was pretty useless at keeping in touch. Not that this was anything unusual. He'd been exactly the same when his daughters were in boarding school. Holidays had been spent with housemistresses or the pitying mothers of friends; plays and prize-givings had seldom been attended, and birthdays had been rather sad affairs. Such was the life of children of a globetrotting diplomat. Andi and Angel's father had paid the school fees, bought the tuck and then carried on as usual, moving from one glamorous embassy to another. No wonder she had, as Tom had put it earlier, "control issues" when it came to money.

Do I have issues with finances? wondered Andi. If she'd had any money left, a few sessions in The Priory might have helped answer this question. Now was probably not the best time to start thinking about her father. The point was that she only had herself to rely on. Nobody else was ever going to appear and bail her out; that was for certain. Unlike Angel, whom people seemed to fall over themselves to help,

Andi had always been seen as the grown-up one, the sensible big sister who could always be relied upon. It made her feel about as exciting as a paint-drying test run in the Dulux factory, but old habits died hard. Today she had only taken a break from the office, and the huge pile of work that was going to take her half the night to complete, because Angel had phoned in floods of tears. Her latest credit card had been refused, Angel had told her, and she desperately needed some cash just to tide her over until payday. She was going to sell her Gucci lookalike bag on eBay tomorrow! She could pay Andi back by next week. *Please? Please!*

As usual Andi had caved in. She'd promised her sister she'd help, just this once more, and had left her desk – much to the displeasure of Zoe who, pointedly eating her wrap at her desk, had warned Andi that she needed to be back on time. Running down the Haymarket in the blazing heat had been almost enough to give Andi a heart attack, but add to this the stress of finding all her money vanished into the ether and she was now a near-certain candidate for the local casualty department. Angel might have to wait. Normally the Bank of Big Sis was pretty reliable but today it was unexpectedly closed for business. Maybe she'd check once more just in case it was a technical error?

Stepping back into the queue, Andi wondered whether Tom would know what was going on. Tom was charming and silver-tongued but he was as much use with finances as chocolate was for making teapots. In fact he was so ostrich-like when it came to ignoring calls from Barclaycard and hiding bank statements that she was considering buying him a pile of sand and suggesting he just stick his head in for a bit while she paid the bills again and cut up his cards. Fishing out her mobile from her leather satchel, Andi attempted to reach him, but her call went straight to answerphone. Typical. He was probably deep in *Loose Women* and oblivious. She'd try again later.

Andi sighed. Between them her sister and her boyfriend left her juggling everything. She was so good by now that Cirque du Soleil could have snapped her up, which was a far cheerier prospect than spending hours in the office with Zoe making snide comments and giving her the most difficult clients. Most of the time Andi credited herself with doing a pretty good job of holding everything together, but sometimes it might have been nice just to lean on somebody else and ask them to share the burden.

"All yours again," said the man who'd stepped in front. He was stuffing twenties into a wallet. Andi's heart plopped into her shoes. So the machine *was* dispensing money then. There went the vain hope that it was broken.

Tucking a stray curl of red hair behind her ears, she forced herself to take a deep breath and to start again. In went the card and with shaking hands Andi punched in her PIN. One balance request revealed exactly the same information as before; this was followed by a swift checking of her savings account and then her credit-card balance with paper slips, just to put the awful truth into writing.

Andi leaned against the wall to stop herself from falling over. It was at times like these she wished she hadn't been such a swot at school, preferring to bury her nose in the library; if only she'd slunk around the back of the PE huts with Angel and the others to read illicit Jilly Coopers and learn to smoke. Andi had never had so much as a drag in her life but right now she could have killed for a nicotine hit.

Right. Standing here worrying wasn't doing any good. She had to find out what on earth was going on. She checked her watch. Twenty minutes until she had to be back at her desk. Just enough time to nip into the bank and talk to somebody. Standing out here stressing wasn't going to achieve anything. She was more than capable of sorting this out. It was bound to be a silly admin error on the bank's part, that was all – nothing that a twenty-nine-year-old, (moderately) successful career woman couldn't resolve.

Glancing in the shiny glass of the huge swivel doors, she caught sight of her reflection and was quietly satisfied. She looked every inch the professional with her neat ponytail and smart trouser suit, cut loosely to hide curves that would have been distracting somewhere as buttoned up as Hart Frozer Accounting. Her eyes were the same green as Cornish rock pools and she wore no make-up except for a sweep of mascara over her lashes and a subtle pink stain on her full lips. Why Zoe gave her such a hard time, Andi really had no idea.

Taking a deep breath she stepped into the revolving doors. It was probably just a clerical error, and putting it right would only take a matter of minutes.

Wouldn't it?

Chapter 2

While her sister was facing a financial meltdown, Angelique Evans was tuning out yet another rollicking from her long-suffering supervisor, Dawn. As the other woman's voice droned on, her glossy lips opening and shutting like a Botoxed goldfish, Angel found herself wondering what on earth had possessed her to call in sick because of a broken nail. In retrospect this had turned out to be a very bad idea indeed, even though it had seemed such a reasonable explanation at the time.

Angel couldn't really see what Dawn was making such a song and dance about. She worked as a beautician at one of Knightsbridge's most expensive and exclusive salons. WAGs and celebs were regulars, the wives of Russian oligarchs seemed to use it as a social club, and once even Pippa Middleton had graced the place with her presence. Standards had to be maintained at all times, surely? And snapping one of her acrylics would have meant Angel appearing at work looking well and truly below her glossy and groomed best. What sort of impression would *that* give the clients? And imagine if Pippa Middleton had chosen yesterday to reappear with her sister in tow? Then what?

Really, thought Angel resentfully, her boss should be thanking her, not giving her a bollocking. Some people just had no sense of gratitude.

"This is the third time I've had to warn you about your attitude," said Dawn, fixing Angel with a stern look. The girl was impossible. She was consistently late to work, spent more time on her lunch break than she did with the clients and had her nose buried so deep in *Heat* that it was little short of a miracle her pretty face wasn't permanently covered in newsprint. If it wasn't for the fact that Angel was actually very good at her job, when she put her mind to it – not to mention that she was popular with the clients and her model looks added to the overall glamour of the salon – Dawn would have given the girl her marching orders months ago.

"I'm going to have to give you a final warning, Angelique," Dawn told her. "Any more sickies, late arrivals or silly errors and we're going to have to let you go. Do I make myself clear? Mrs Pamapov wasn't very happy with her nails."

Angel pulled a face. "I thought she said she loved red."

"No, what she said was her mother was *dead*. She was going to a funeral, Angel. The last thing she wanted was bright scarlet acrylics."

Angel felt most hard done by. She'd spent hours on those nails and she'd thought they looked brilliant. Why were people so picky?

"Her accent was really hard to understand," she said sulkily.

"Then I suggest you listen more carefully in the future," Dawn replied sharply. "You've got Mrs Yuri this afternoon for a facial. You know how particular she is and how sensitive she is about her mole. Whatever you do, don't look at it. And for God's sake, don't mention it."

Angel groaned. Of course, she wouldn't be able to look at anything else. Mrs Yuri, the wife of one of the richest men on the planet, had a huge mole on her chin, complete with a curly hair reminiscent of piano wire. Angel had only seen it briefly and had been mesmerised. Why on earth the woman didn't pluck it out or even have the darn thing removed was anyone's guess.

"I'll do anything rather than deal with her," she pleaded. "Tell Angie I'll do that Hollywood wax she's dreading if she'll swap."

Hollywood bikini waxes (where everything came off) were every beautician's worst nightmare – apart from dealing with Mrs Yuri, it seemed. Nobody was willing to swap and so Angel was stuck with the sensitive client. She didn't have anything against demanding Russian women, which was fortunate since the exclusive salon depended on them, but she'd had a horror of moles ever since her mum had died of skin cancer. How on earth would she manage to ignore this whopper?

"Not a single glance or so much as a comment," warned her boss. "Believe me, you won't want Mr Yuri after you if his wife is upset."

She wasn't wrong there. Mr Yuri looked like a pig squeezed into a suit and overcoat, and always reminded Angel horribly of Napoleon from *Animal Farm*. Nope, Mr Yuri, one of the wealthiest men alive and rumoured to have links to the Russian mafia, was not a person she would care to upset. She'd be at the bottom of the Thames before you could say "Siberia".

"So, mind on the job please, Angel. Any more errors and you'll be looking at your P45. Do you understand how serious this warning is?"

Angel widened her eyes and thought very hard of the saddest thing she could possibly think of. At this point in time that happened to be the beautiful pink patent-leather Chloé bag she'd set her heart on, which had been left dangling out of reach in the designer section of Selfridges just because her latest credit card was maxed out. Having had a rather good education – which she did her hardest to conceal because, after all, nobody on *TOWIE* ever mentioned the Classics – Angel felt like a modern version of Tantalus, albeit one with waist-length blonde extensions and false lashes. True to form, the tears began to pool in her eyes. God! She *loved* that bag so much! If Andi were any sort of a big sister she'd lend her the money. It was only a few hundred quid after all. Andi was such a tightwad with her cash; she was bound to have some spare. But if she didn't, somebody else might buy the bag and then it would be lost – forever!

At this thought a tear really fell in earnest, rolling down her peachy cheek like a perfect diamond and splashing onto the polished wooden floor.

Brilliant. Tears were one of the few things that had never failed Angel in twenty-seven years. Parents yes. Boyfriends definitely. But tears? Never. Angel might not have Andi's economics degree but she was well aware of the effect that her looks and tears had on people. And so far, so good.

"I'm sorry," she said, looking up through her double layer of Eylure's best, in what she hoped was a winning Princess Diana manner. "I promise it'll never happen again. I'll come to work no matter what I look like. Even if my nails all break. Or my extensions fall out. Or I come out in boils or—"

"Yes, yes, Angel, I get the gist," said her supervisor hastily, before Angel could continue any further.

Oops. Had she laid it on too thick? Used a shovel rather than a trowel? Making a mental note to ask her actress best friend Gemma for some emergency drama lessons, Angel crossed her slender fingers behind her back. Much as she craved fame and fortune, wanting nothing more than to sashay across a red carpet or have her own reality show, Angel needed her job. For now, at least. Her big break was just around the corner, she knew it, but since this morning's post had brought with it two red credit-card bills, a thinly veiled threatening letter from her bank manager and a rejection from the latest series of *Signed by Katie Price*, painting toenails and waxing unmentionables would have to continue for a little bit longer.

As Dawn, predictably softened by tears, proceeded to tell her exactly what was expected of an employee of Blush, Angel zoned out again. Although her eyes were widened and she was nodding attentively, in reality she was a world away – somewhere where she wore designer clothes rather than her cleverly purchased eBay fakes, and ate at the finest restaurants in town. She went shopping with Posh, dined out with Jamie and Jules and had been socialising with Peter Andre. Well, why not? He only lived in Brighton, for heaven's sake, and if those pesky security guards on the private estate – the only men she'd ever met who'd been immune to her charms – had let her through, Angel knew she would have had a brilliant time at his last celeb-filled bash. An agent would have been bound to sign her on the spot, if only she hadn't been caught trying to scale the fence. She'd been plucked off it with absolutely no ceremony whatsoever. As if that hadn't been bad enough, insult had been added to injury today when a sternly worded letter from the estate's management had been delivered by hand, politely but firmly telling her to stay away unless she wanted to face legal action.

Lecture over, she returned to work and the demanding Mrs Yuri. As she prepared the treatment room for her latest client, Angel wondered whether dropping out of her degree had really been her smartest ever move. Sure, the lectures had been torturously dull and the other students about as exciting as watching the Sky Planner screen, but asking pampered women about their weekend plans was hardly thrilling either. And as for the razor-wire stabs of jealousy when they told her about their latest skiing holiday or Maldives jaunt, well those weren't exactly pleasant either.

Oh God. She had to find a way out of this soon, surely? If Amy Childs could do it, then why not Angelique Evans? If only she and

Gemma could have afforded to rent in Chelsea rather than Tooting Bec. She could have got herself a part on *Made in Chelsea*. Or maybe even met Prince Harry! Maybe the next time that Pippa Middleton came in…

"Angel, Mrs Yuri is ready for you," Dawn announced.

Angel gritted her teeth, selected some relaxing panpipe music from the iPod docking station and checked that the products were all lined up and ready for action. Industrial strength cleanser to try to remove the caked-on foundation was a must, and a chisel would have been even more help. While Angel filled a bowl with water and laid out a heap of fluffy towels, Mrs Yuri shuffled into the room and heaved her bulk onto the treatment table.

Don't look at her mole. Don't look at her mole. Don't look at her mole.

"Good afternoon, Mrs Yuri. I'm Angel and I'll be doing your crystal scrub therapy facial today," she said chirpily.

Mrs Yuri grunted. Not a talker then. Fine. Angel actually preferred it when her clients didn't want to chat. It gave her more thinking space to figure out a way to find fame and fortune. Concentrating very hard, she began to massage dollops of cleanser into the jowly face.

Don't look at her mole. Don't look at her mole. Look at her mole. Look at her. Look at her mole.

Oh bollocks.

Angel couldn't help it. She was looking at the mole. It was pretty impossible not to, really. She was just about to drag her gaze away when something caught her eye and made her heart bump painfully. Hang on. That looked awfully familiar. Was it the light in here, or was that mole looking a little sore around the edges? It seemed swollen too, and not just in a usual mole type way but as though it was changing size.

"Vat are you looking at?" hissed Mrs Yuri. Eyes like boot buttons glinted beneath fleshy lids and she pinned Angel with a stare that the KGB would have envied. This was the point where Angel should fib and make something up about pores and indulge in some bland beautician jargon – but she couldn't bring herself to do it. Instead, horrible memories were flashing across her mind's eye. Drips, clumps of hair falling to the floor, the smell of antiseptic… The last time Angel had seen a mole that looked as irritated as this had been on her poor mum. How could she possibly lie about something she knew had the potential to be life threatening?

"Your mole," Angel confessed. "It looks very sore. Does it itch? Has it been like this for long?"

"You are looking at my mole? How dare you be so insulting, you bold girl?" Mrs Yuri hissed.

"It's not because it's big or anything," Angel said hastily, wanting to kick herself as the client went puce with rage. Great. Top marks there for tact. Why not just say it was the biggest, grossest mole ever? She took a deep breath. "I hardly noticed it! Honestly! It's just that if a mole is sore or changes shape it could be an indication that there's something changing or of melanoma."

"Melanoma?" screeched the client. "What is this you call me now? Some new insult?"

Oh God. This wasn't going so well. Why hadn't she just kept quiet?

The answer was, of course, because if somebody had spotted Natalie Evans's mole earlier on, Angel's mother might still be alive. Angel tried again.

"Of course not. Melanoma is another word for skin cancer."

"You are saying I have cancer?" Mrs Yuri screeched.

"No! No, of course not! I just think it would be worth getting a doctor to check it over. These things can be easily removed."

Mrs Yuri leapt off the table as though scalded. "You tell me I should get my mole removed? Nobody in my whole life haff ever insulted me so much! Vait until my Anton hears about this!"

Her shrieks continued to increase in volume. Possibly they could even drown out the sound of the planes taking off at Heathrow. In any case, they were certainly more than loud enough to alert Dawn and several other beauticians who came running.

"What's going on?" demanded Dawn.

"I just mentioned that the mole looks a little sore," explained Angel desperately. "No harm done."

"No harm done?" Despite being Botoxed to almost lethal levels, the client managed to show her shock. Rounding on Angel, she hissed, "You are rude bitch! You haff insulted me! Do you know who my husband is?"

Angel gulped. She'd be feeding the fishes in the Thames by teatime. And that was if she was *lucky*.

Dawn was clearly having very similar thoughts.

"Mrs Yuri, I am so sorry! I can't apologise enough!"

The furious client spun around. "Your apologies are meaningless! Vat do you sink my Anton will say when he sees how this girl has upset me? Personally insulted me?"

Angel dreaded to think – and so did her boss, judging by Dawn's white face.

"He will sue you," continued Mrs Yuri, warming to her theme. "Then he will want to personally speak to the owner of this pitiful excuse for a salon. Unless—" she paused for dramatic emphasis and pointed a gore-red talon in Angel's direction. "Unless you have rid of this useless imbecile of a girl. At once!"

"I was trying to help!" cried Angel desperately. "The mole looks sore. You really should see a specialist just in case!"

"How dare you!" Mrs Yuri squawked in outrage. "There's nothing wrong with my mole! How dare you say I need to see doctor?"

Rounding on Dawn she added, "Are you going to let her speak to me like that? I haff never been so insulted! My Anton, he will be furious! Are you going to do nothing to compensate me for being so insulted in *your* salon?"

"Of course not, madam! We'll do anything to make up for Angel's appalling lack of manners. Whatever you wish!"

Angel felt faint. This was it. River time.

Mrs Yuri shot Angel a look of triumph.

"Either she goes, or I do! And my friends, of course! We do not come here to be insulted. My Anton vill make sure this salon closes for good."

Now Dawn had a face that was an exact match for her starched white uniform. Angel's heart plummeted into her sparkly Skechers. Mrs Yuri was exactly the kind of loaded and bored customer on whom the salon depended. Along with her friends, yet more pampered and glamorous wives of small ugly Russian oligarchs, she probably spent more in one visit to Blush than Angel earned in an entire year.

P45 here she came.

Maybe I should get a job as a psychic instead of being a beautician, thought Angel miserably, as less than five minutes later she stood on the pavement with the contents of her locker in a carrier bag. She'd been ejected so fast that her head was reeling. While just about every beautician in the place raced to pamper Mrs Yuri, she'd been frogmarched out of the building and told never to return. Honestly, she'd only been trying to help. That mole had looked very suspicious and Angel was sure that it needed medical attention. There was no need for such a ridiculous overreaction. Some people just loved to make a drama.

Mind you, it would have made a fantastic scene for a dramality show. If only she'd had a film crew in tow...

But unfortunately for Angel she didn't have a film crew following her every move. Flipping her long blonde hair back from her face and hiking up her skirt an inch or two just in case a millionaire came cruising by and fancied offering her a lift, Angel plucked her iPhone from her bag and set off along the street.

In a moment she'd call her sister, just to make certain that Andi had got that money out for her. Angel was definitely going to buy that bag now.

After the day she'd had, it was the least she deserved.

Chapter 3

"You told me she was a size fourteen! I specifically requested a girl who was a size fourteen for this job! Not one who's a sixteen on a good day, breathing in and wearing granny pants!"

Gemma Pengelley, she of size-sixteen curves that today were possibly billowing to an eighteen after a weekend spent comfort eating and mainlining vodka, felt her face turn into a giant Edam of humiliation. Standing in a freezing studio and wearing nothing more than a deeply unflattering minimiser bra while two Twiglet-like women poked her fat bits and squabbled over the size of her thighs was not top of her list of favourite things to do. It didn't even make it to the bottom of that list.

"Does it really matter?" Gemma's agent, Chloe, was saying hopefully. "She's modelling control pants anyway. Surely the whole point is that they should hold her in? Won't it look better to have them modelled by the type of girl who might actually need to wear them?"

"She's supposed to look slim so the consumer thinks that these briefs really work. They're meant to hold a tummy in. Not work miracles!" The creative director of the shoot for Trim Tums looked at Gemma with disgust. "How on earth are we supposed to hide that overhang? Call in Kevin McCloud?"

"What about Photoshop?" Chloe said helpfully.

The creative director shook her head. "If we wanted to use Photoshop we could have just hired another slim girl and made her look bigger. We wanted somebody slightly on the larger side, not somebody fat! Didn't you read the job spec we emailed you?"

Chloe was mortified. "Of course I did. I just haven't seen Gemma for a few months. Work's been quiet for her. Let me assure you that the last time I saw my client she really was a size fourteen. Weren't you, Gemma?"

Gemma nodded miserably. As if it wasn't humiliating enough to be stripped down to her knickers in a room so cold that her goosebumps had goosebumps, now she had to have all her squishy bits poked and prodded in full view of all the other stick-insect models. Even though she'd fixed her gaze firmly on the studio floor, Gemma could tell that the other, slimmer girls were sniggering and enjoying every minute of her humiliation. Oh God, she *knew* she should have turned this job down but her agent had insisted that it would be, in her words, "a nice little earner". So, being perpetually broke, usually because her flatmate Angel had failed to make the rent, Gemma had taken the job, albeit against her better judgement. Acting work had been thin on the ground lately and so she'd taken her eye off the ball a bit with her weight, choosing to treat herself to a Snickers when she didn't get a call back or grabbing a quick Maccy D's on the way home from yet another fruitless casting. Somewhere in her wardrobe, stuffed full of clothes that ranged from twelves up to voluminous size eighteens, there were garments she could squeeze into which bore the legend *14*, so technically when Chloe had asked her what she size she was she hadn't really been lying.

I'm an actress anyway, not a bloody model, thought Gemma resentfully while her agent and the creative director continued to bicker and prod her flabby bits. In the cold studio lighting her cellulitey legs were the same colour and texture as the porridge she'd shovelled down before she'd left the house that morning. Well, porridge was good for you, wasn't it? Everybody knew that. *But maybe without the huge dollop of condensed milk and the three big spoonfuls of sugar?* whispered the Diet Angel, who often liked to perch on Gemma's shoulder. Fat lot of use she was;

Gemma hadn't heard from the Diet Angel for weeks. She thought it must have been squashed flat by the Diet Devil, who seemed to be in permanent residence, urging her that one more slice of pizza wouldn't hurt and murmuring *Go on, you've eaten one biscuit; you might as well just finish the packet.* However, the Diet Devil didn't have to parade around in her knickers in front of a group of girls who made Bambi look chunky.

Gemma sighed. Maybe on the way home she'd pop into her local Greggs? They always saved her a cheese swirl or two. That would cheer her up.

"I don't know why you're sighing," hissed Chloe as, with her bony fingers biting into Gemma's fleshy shoulder, she propelled her client across the studio. "You're not the one who's just been made to look like a total and utter dick. In fact, worse than that! An *unprofessional total and utter dick!* You told me that you were a size fourteen!"

"I am a size fourteen. I think these pants are probably cut on a bit on the small side," protested Gemma, trying to conceal her billowing body with a wrap.

Chloe, in her early forties and funky and slim, shot Gemma a withering look. Dragging her client to a full-length mirror and whipping away the wrap, she said sharply, "Look in that mirror and tell me what you see! Is that a size fourteen? Seriously?"

Gemma gulped. There was a lump in her throat the size and consistency of one of the rock cakes she'd baked the day before. They'd been lovely too, just the right mixture of crusty on the outside but soft and fluffy and curranty on the inside. Gemma loved to bake, especially when she was feeling low – which seemed to be most of the time just lately. The problem was that she also liked to eat what she'd baked. She was already looking forward to going home and polishing off the rest of the batch. Preferably all alone in her bedroom, where nobody could have a go at her.

"Don't, Chloe!" she begged, when her nose was practically rammed into the glass. God, but Gemma hated mirrors. Really hated them. In fact Dracula was probably happier to tuck into a clove of garlic than Gemma was to look at her reflection. She managed to avoid mirrors most of the time, or full-length ones in any case, which was some feat for somebody who shared a house with Angel, the girl who'd have trampled Narcissus on her way to a spot of pool-gazing.

"Don't you dare look away!" warned Chloe when Gemma tried to avert her eyes. "This is called tough love, Gemma! No matter what Christina Hendricks might say, nobody wants to hire a fat actress. Now look in the mirror!"

So Gemma looked, and a plump blonde, all natural honey curls and eyes the same bright blue as hyacinths, peered back at her. Those were the good bits, but the face, blurred by weight and with the suggestion of a double chin, wasn't quite so great. The pink control underwear sliced into her flesh like cheese wire, sucking lumps and bumps in for sure but not quite able to contain them when they made a break for freedom. Completing the picture were dimpled arms bristling with goosebumps, a tummy like a Michelin tyre and patchy fake-tanned legs that chaffed at the top.

Oh God. She looked like one of those "before" shots that they took of fat celebrities to sell their fitness DVDs! If only she could now magic herself an "after" shot. How on earth had this happened? Tears blurred the hideous image.

"Gemma," said Chloe, meeting her eyes in the glass, "I've been your agent for six years and I have to be honest. Unless you make some pretty major changes you won't be getting any work at all. Don't you want to act?"

Gemma nodded. Her throat was too tight with tears to speak. Of course she wanted to act! It was the only thing she'd ever wanted to do – apart from to be with Nick, of course. Six weeks ago he'd dumped her again; the last time she'd seen him had been at their local, where he was wearing some skinny brunette like a chest bandage and giving a good impression that they were Siamese twins joined at the tongue. Gemma had turned around and gone home via Waitrose. That night she'd enjoyed a threesome with Ben and Jerry, the only men she'd rely on in the future.

Chloe sighed. Gemma was a lovely girl and, when she had been successful in auditions, she'd always managed to impress the people she worked with. With her curves and blonde curls and mouth like an unpopped fuchsia bud, she was a dead ringer for a Botticelli angel who'd gobbled just a little too much ambrosia. It was pure bad luck she'd been born a few centuries too late. Even icons like Marilyn Monroe would struggle to find work in the body-obsessed twenty-teens. There was only one way Gemma could possibly pick up roles now, and that was to lose some weight – and pronto. Chloe, who existed on a diet of Marlboros and fresh air, found it hard to be sympathetic, especially now that today's commission was in serious danger of going down the drain. You had to suffer to be beautiful, right? And Gemma clearly hadn't been suffering. At all.

"I have had work," Gemma protested, through the rock-cake lump. Her voice sounded odd, glass fragile and as though it might shatter at any moment. A bit like her self-confidence, in fact. "I was in *EastEnders* and I—"

"And you asked Phil Mitchell if he had a light," interrupted Chloe, rolling her eyes so much that Gemma almost expected them to roll right out of her head, across the studio and down the street. "That was *two years* ago! It's been *two years* since you had a proper television role. Since then you've only had a couple of voice-overs, that Shakespeare play for schools – where you were fantastic as Ophelia, I know – and a few adverts. Unless you up your game you'll be left behind. Babe, I can't afford to carry any dead wood!"

Gemma stared at her. "What's that supposed to mean?"

Her agent exhaled slowly. "That I'm going to have to let you go unless you sort yourself out, lose the weight and find a way to get yourself out there. Flick through *Closer* or *Heat* – they're full of *TOWIE* people and soap stars; you should be right up there with them. You *can* act, Gemma, but unless you start marketing yourself slightly more seriously I'm going to have to remove you from my books."

"You'll drop me?" Gemma couldn't believe what she was hearing. "After all these years? Because some stupid lingerie people thought I was fat?"

Chloe shrugged. "Let's face it: you're not exactly earning me any money. I do have kids to feed, you know."

She shouldered her Mulberry bag and considered Gemma thoughtfully. The girl had potential, she really did. She'd graduated from the BRIT School as one of the most promising students in her year, but somehow she'd just never managed to fulfil that promise. Maybe she was just too kind? Too easy-going? Too undisciplined? All qualities that the world of the media hardly valued, preferring to grind people like this into the dirt. Maybe Gemma Pengelley would have been better off staying in the West Country, filling her face with pasties and scones?

Either way, a kick up the ample backside was most definitely what she needed.

"Please don't take me off your books," Gemma whispered. "I'll lose weight. I'll get myself in the papers. I'll do whatever it takes, but please, please, don't stop representing me."

"Then sort yourself out," Chloe said sharply. "I don't know what's been going on but you look a state." Pulling out her BlackBerry, she scrolled through the calendar and punched decisively at the keys. "We'll meet again at the start of September and regroup. If by then you seem committed and have been proactive, then I'll continue to represent you and be more than willing to put you forward for any roles that may be suitable. But if not..."

The words unsaid hung heavy in the air like something out of *Harry Potter*. Gemma nodded. It was fair enough, she reflected miserably as her agent stalked off, leaving her to continue the shoot in the revolting underwear. She had let herself go, hadn't she? While she posed as best she could, stomach in and chin out and horribly conscious of the comparison she made to the other skinny models, Gemma thought how unfair it was that she had always struggled with her weight. Even as a child she had only to look at a saffron bun to be pounds heavier. Add to this a mother who was a fantastic cook and who dished out huge stews and buttery mash to her strapping sons and husband when they came home after a hard day's graft on the family farm, and it was no wonder she'd always piled on the pounds. Gemma loved to cook too and adored the magic of throwing ingredients together that resulted in flavours bursting across her tongue. The only problem was that she didn't adore the subsequent bursting waistbands quite so much.

"Turn left, love; cover your belly with your arm," called the photographer. Woodenly, Gemma obeyed. No more just thinking about it, even if it was the thought that counted: she'd go on a diet when she got home, she really would. Once she'd finished up all the goodies in the fridge first, obviously. There were those rather scrummy rock cakes and last night's lasagne too. It would be wrong to bin that lot. Mum would have a fit at such waste. Along with the Diet Angel and the Diet Devil, her mother also spent a great deal of time in Gemma's head.

Once the shoot was over – it hadn't escaped Gemma's notice that she'd spent most of it draped on a chaise longue with her fat bits disguised by gravity and a cunningly draped shawl – she retreated back to the cramped changing room. A gaggle of models hogged the mirror, dabbing at their make-up with cleanser and elbowing each other out of the way as they jostled for pole position. Sinking into a corner and hoping to stay off the radar, Gemma wrestled herself out of the control pants and slumped on a chair while her internal organs rearranged themselves. All this humiliation and pain for a measly few hundred quid? Maybe she should just cut her losses and look for a normal job?

But what about her ambition to be an actress? All those childhood dreams couldn't be wasted just because she was a greedy pig. Maybe when she got home she'd borrow Angel's laptop and check out Weight Watchers? All you had to do was count the points, apparently, so maybe you could have all your points consisting of chocolate and vodka? That was Gemma's idea of a balanced diet – a Dairy Milk held in each hand. At this thought she instantly felt much more cheerful. That was Project Weight Loss sorted. By September she'd be a size ten if it killed her. All she had to do now was find a way of raising her profile. Short of shagging a Premier League footballer though (which wasn't likely, as they didn't tend to hang out in the Dog and Rabbit off Fulham Broadway), she was a bit stumped. Maybe Angel would have an idea? Gemma perked up at this thought. Yes, Angel was always good for an idea. After all, hadn't she nearly managed to gatecrash Peter Andre's party?

Gemma's plotting was cut short by a flurry of excitement at the far end of the room. Looking up, she noticed that one of the models, a tall brunette with collarbones that could take someone's eye out, was shrieking excitedly into her iPhone while the other girls twittered and squeaked. At first Gemma ignored them; during the shoot the brunette had made some particularly bitchy comments about Gemma's weight. But after a moment her curiosity got the better of her, especially when she heard the word *Cornwall.* Pretending to be engrossed in teasing her hair into an updo, she sidled up to the mirror for a good earwig.

"Oh my God! You lucky cow, Emily!" one of the girls said enviously. "You seriously get to spend the whole summer in Rock *and* you get paid for it? I'm well jel!"

Emily flipped her silky tresses back from her face and pouted at her reflection. "The filming starts next week and you should see the house the production team has hired! It's lush!"

The other girls twittered excitedly, but only Gemma really knew just quite how lush this house would be. She came from the less glamorous town of Bodmin, famous mainly for its gaol and its beast, but she'd visited the upmarket holiday destination lots of times. Although she'd yet to bump into Wills or Harry, Gemma was always struck speechless by the stunning properties facing the estuary, the superyachts bobbing on the pontoons and the endless four-by-fours driven by women as glossy and highly strung as thoroughbreds. Rock was the playground of the rich and famous, that was for sure. With Rick Stein's just a boat ride over the Camel Estuary and Jamie Oliver's a few miles away at Watergate Bay, it was a kind of Chelsea on Sea: the likes of Gemma could just about afford a latte at one of the stylish new coffee bars, and that was only on payday. Still, expense aside, Rock was one of Gemma's favourite places and her ultimate dream was to be a famous movie star, buy a house there and bake lots of yummy cakes in her luxury kitchen.

Err, she meant go running and eat salads. Or something like that anyway. Emily, who probably got full just staring at a lettuce leaf, would fit in perfectly.

"But to film with Callum South," breathed another model enviously. "You're so lucky, Em! He's smoking hot!"

Emily shrugged her skinny shoulders nonchalantly, enjoying every moment of having a captive audience. Everyone knew that ex-Premier League star Callum, who'd battled against and conquered his booze and junk-food addictions in a blaze of red-top glory, was the hottest thing on reality TV. His last two shows had pulled in over six million viewers and now you could scarcely go a day without seeing his handsome face plastered across a billboard or in a magazine. Gemma had had a secret crush on him for years.

"So what's this show about?" asked another model. "I liked the one where he did a boot camp for six weeks. It was hilarious."

In spite of herself Gemma nodded. She'd loved that show. Callum South's ongoing battle of the bulge was well documented in the tabloids and his stint at an army-style fat camp had been compulsive viewing. She'd genuinely felt for him when he'd first arrived and been bullied over the assault course. And when his calorie-counted supper arrived she'd shared his pain so greatly she'd been forced to call for a Domino's.

"It's some get-fit thing again," Emily said dismissively. "He's got to spend the summer doing all sorts of water sports, losing weight and competing against members of the public who've been picked to take part. He's a right lard-arse at the moment, so he might as well work it off and make some money. *Fat Camp for the Famous* is what they should call it!"

The others tittered sycophantically. Gemma's hands curled into fists. Still raw from the photo shoot from hell, she couldn't stand to hear somebody else criticised for his weight. What was it with these bloody diet and exercise Nazis?

"That's a mean thing to say!" she said hotly.

Emily's top lip curled. "Why? Because it's true?"

"No! Because it's a horrible way to speak about someone!"

Gemma's heart was pounding but Emily just laughed, with the shrill screech of a hyena about to go in for the kill. Too late, Gemma realised that she'd laid herself wide open. So much for keeping her head down. Maybe next time she'd wear a helmet?

"Touched a nerve has it?" sneered Emily. "Don't think we didn't notice they had to shoot with a wide-angle lens today! Well, I tell you what, if you feel sorry for Cal why don't you take a leaf out of his book and join him? You could call it *Fat Camp for Failures!*"

While the other girls shrieked with mirth, Gemma racked her brains for a witty comeback, but by the time she'd collected her thoughts Emily and her cronies had long since shuffled their UGG boots out of the room. The brunette clearly thought she'd won the day – but if she'd turned around she'd have seen that, rather than tears, an expression of excitement was spreading across Gemma's face.

Oh my God! For such a brainless bimbo Emily was a genius. Gemma could have risked being skewered by a hipbone and hugged the girl! That final cutting comment, designed to wound in the worst possible way, had had exactly the opposite effect. It had given Gemma the most fantastic idea and maybe the solution to all her problems!

Gemma dug her mobile out of her bag and began to text Angel. There was no time like the present…

Chapter 4

By the time Andi arrived at the office she was running horribly late and was none the wiser for having spent twenty minutes with the bank manager. All she'd managed to discover was that although all of her available funds had been withdrawn, none of her security had been breached. Whoever had managed to make the transactions had done so by using all her online passwords. This only meant one thing: whoever withdrew the money was either some kind of online evil genius or somebody she trusted. Andi didn't need her economics degree to figure out who that might be.

As she rode the elevator to her office, Andi chewed her nails and tried to quash her growing sense of panic. The conversation she'd had with her bank manager played on a loop through her mind.

"I really don't understand this at all," he'd said, leaning forward and frowning at his computer screen. "According to our records all the transactions have been authorised by you."

Andi had shaken her head. "I haven't been near my accounts or my credit cards! You've let somebody else withdraw my money!"

"If that has happened then I can't apologise enough," the bank manager had said with a grave expression. "I assure you we take our customers' security very seriously indeed. However, according to our system you made the withdrawal of funds yourself using your Internet banking access codes." His brow had crinkled. "This is very strange: you appear to have gone through the three highest levels of security and used the correct PINs and passwords too. That isn't standard practice at all for card cloning."

Andi had had the horrible sensation that she was whizzing down to earth even faster than Jeb Corliss in his wingsuit.

"My money was taken over the Internet?"

He had nodded. "It's very unusual for this to happen. Is it possible that somebody could have got access to your security? Could anyone else know your PINs? A family member, maybe?"

Andi closed her eyes. There was only one person she'd trusted with those details. Not a family member – if Angel had had access to any of her money she'd have done a trolley dash round Gucci before you could say "credit card" – but there was one person, one person she'd trusted totally...

"My boyfriend," she'd whispered.

The bank manager had stared at her. Incredulous didn't come close to describing the look on his face. "I'm sorry, for a minute I thought you said your boyfriend had access to your online security?"

Andi had nodded miserably. "I'm at work a lot and Tom's at home. He does a lot of our shopping online." He also did the lion's share of their poker playing and porn viewing too, which had been the cause of this morning's enormous row. Tom had thought her most unreasonable; what else was he supposed to do all day? Andi had almost suggested getting off his backside and finding a job, but had stopped herself just in time. After all, she knew how sensitive Tom was to any suggestion that his career as an actor might have to be reconsidered. He was convinced that it was only a matter of time before his talent was spotted. Andi was all for matters of time, but just how *much* time was starting to become something of an issue. Was he talking weeks? Months? Or, as she was starting to fear, aeons?

Talking of time, maybe it was time she called exactly that on their relationship? She wasn't happy and it wasn't working. The fact that she believed Tom could steal her money spoke volumes.

While her thoughts had raced, the bank manager had taken off his glasses and sat pinching the bridge of his nose. He'd looked like a man on the brink of nervous collapse.

"So you're telling me that you have given your boyfriend permission to access your accounts? Then it isn't a case of theft, Miss Evans." The words *it's a case of stupidity* had hung in the air like subtitles. "This really isn't the bank's fault, is it?"

What could Andi possibly have said to that? She had fled from the bank feeling so stupid that she wouldn't have been surprised if the Oxford English Dictionary's definition of the word had been *Miranda Evans*. She tried calling Tom but he wasn't answering and was pointedly ignoring her private Facebook messages.

The lift doors hissed open and Andi somehow managed to make her way to her desk. The office clock glared down at her, balefully announcing that she was over forty minutes late. Her heart sank even further when Zoe stalked over. So much for hoping to come in undetected. What was she thinking to even imagine that would be possible? Zoe was a bloodhound when it came to sniffing out office misdemeanours.

"You're late," Zoe said when she reached Andi's workstation. The air was instantly choked with the cloying scent of Poison, which made Andi feel queasy. She took a deep breath and prayed she didn't hurl all over her line manager's Kurt Geiger shoes.

"Sorry, Zoe, it won't happen again. There's been a bit of a problem with my bank account and—"

But Zoe was holding up her hand and looking bored.

"I don't need to hear any excuses, Andi. Time is time, remember? And what does time cost?" She fixed Andi with a pebble-eyed stare.

"Money," said Andi dully. This little mantra was one of Zoe's favourites.

"Exactly!" Zoe agreed, triumphant. "So you can explain that to Ms Clark, can't you, seeing as she asked to see you at 2 p.m.?"

Andi's stomach lurched as though she was in a plane that had suddenly lost altitude. Leeza Clark was the boss of her division. Normally she didn't stir from her glass-walled office, but just recently she'd taken to calling various employees in to see her. Like the old song about the spider and the fly, those who ventured into Leeza's lair were seldom seen again.

OK, she thought as she watched Zoe's narrow frame returning to her own desk, *I mustn't panic. Being summoned to see the boss isn't necessarily bad news.* It was time she started thinking more positively. Wasn't that what all those career-building seminars said? Andi would bet all the money she had lost that Alan Sugar never sat at his desk quaking and chewing the end of his ponytail. Not that Lord Sugar had a ponytail, but still. He wouldn't be trembling behind his computer, would he? No way. He'd be far too busy striding around looking grumpy and firing people.

"Andi? Has Leeza asked to see you too?" Andi's colleague Jen peered over the top of the computer monitor. It wasn't the dodgy office lighting that had turned her the exact hue of mushy peas.

Andi nodded.

Jen's hands were shaking so hard her bangles rattled like castanets. "What am I going to do if they're making redundancies? Mike was laid off last month. If I lose my job there's no way we can make the mortgage repayments. We need my income. What do you think's happening? Why do they want to see us?"

Andi took a deep breath. Jen's terror was contagious and unless she made a real effort they were both only seconds away from drowning themselves in the office loo.

"No idea, but I'm sure it's nothing to worry about," she said, crossing her fingers, toes, eyes and anything else crossable. "They probably just want to tie off some of Safe T Net's loose ends."

Jen exhaled slowly. "You're right. Their CEO was only on the phone a minute ago. I'm just so paranoid at the moment. Everyone I know seems to be losing their jobs."

Jen wasn't wrong. It seemed that hardly a day went by lately without news of another firm going bust or another company being streamlined. It felt as though there was no end in sight. Andi often woke up in the night worrying about it all – unlike Tom, who slept the deep and untroubled sleep of a man whose girlfriend worked her butt off.

Andi was just trying to think of something cheerful to say when Alan Eades, the office creep, perched his bony backside on her desk.

"Have you two been summoned as well?" he asked, legs at right angles as he treated both girls to a view of his groin.

Andi had heard it said that one of the great things about life was having new experiences, and being pleased to see Alan was certainly a first. Normally she tried her hardest to avoid being anywhere near him; those clammy hands had a habit of wandering just a little too close and it was amazing how many lint specks and stray hairs he managed to find in need of flicking away from her chest. Merely breathing the same oxygen as Alan was enough to make her want a shower, so having to work with him on the Safe T Net accounts had been a nightmare.

Sloths were more proactive than Alan: she'd lost count of the amount of times she'd had to stay late triple-checking the figures because of his sloppy mistakes. Most days Andi felt like ripping off his head and beating him to death with the soggy end. But today he was a blessing in disguise, albeit a blooming good one, because if he'd been called to the boss as well it must be because the team was being assigned to a new account. Alan was useless, whereas Jen and Andi were Sabatier-sharp with figures. There was no way the bosses would lump them in with him. No way at all.

"Any idea what it's about?" Jen asked.

Alan shrugged. "There was some talk about cost-cutting and redundancies. Recession this, downturn that, blah blah blah. Well, if they sack me they're making a big mistake. There aren't many accountants of my calibre about."

"You're not wrong there," Andi said fervently.

Still looking worried, Jen returned to her desk. After Andi prodded him with the sharp end of her pencil, Alan pushed off too. That made a very welcome change: for the last few weeks she'd hardly been able to get rid of him. Andi had caught him lurking around her desk several times and yesterday he'd even had the cheek to be working at her computer terminal. He'd muttered some excuse about his needing defragging, which may or may not have been true – but, even so, it didn't explain why he was using her login or why he minimised the screen so quickly when she tried to peer over his shoulder. Andi didn't need to be good with figures to know that something didn't add up.

Hey! Was it possible that Alan had managed to access her personal data? Had she been too hasty in assuming Tom was to blame? How could she find out?

Pondering this thought, Andi waited for her computer to boot up. Honestly, you'd think the thing was on flexitime. While it beeped and buzzed to itself she wandered to the dingy broom-cupboard kitchen in desperate search of caffeine. As the kettle wheezed away, Andi scraped the cold dregs of her coffee into the least mouldy mug she could find and tried to concentrate on doing some slow yoga breathing. Not that she'd ever made it to yoga, but Tom was always glued to some fitness DVD – supposedly to work on honing his pecs, although Andi suspected he was actually perving over girls in Lycra. *Essexercise* and *The Jordan Workout*? Seriously?

"Ooh! Are you making coffee, Andi? Can you do one for me?" asked Cally, the office junior, who never had her own milk/coffee/mug (delete as appropriate).

Swallowing a sigh, Andi doled out another spoonful. In the general scheme of things, what was another cup of coffee?

"You're a star," said Cally gratefully. "Just two sugars, ta. I'm cutting back."

While Andi stirred in lumpy sugar, Cally chatted away about everything under the sun. Andi wished she could be more like her. The younger girl was a little sunbeam in high heels and a Top Shop suit. She just didn't seem to be able to shake off a feeling of heaviness. Was this the reality of approaching thirty, with responsibilities weighing you down like concrete boots? As Cally nattered away, Andi wondered what it must be like to be nineteen and free from worries. No bills, no wrinkles and no gigantic rent payments...

Nope, it was no good. She couldn't imagine it for the life of her.

"So I said to Chloe, phwoar! *I* would! He's well fit! I would! Wouldn't you, Andi?"

Andi dragged her thoughts back to the kitchen, where Cally's tiny bum was perched on the minuscule counter. The office junior was waving a copy of *Cosmo* under Andi's nose in the fashion of a Victorian administering smelling salts.

"Would I what?" Andi asked. God, she must be getting old because she hadn't a clue what Cally was on about. It was official: Andi no longer spoke teen.

Bugger. That ruled out the teacher training option if all else failed.

"Shag *him*!" Cally thrust the magazine at Andi and stabbed at the paper with a scarily long acrylic nail. "He's number one most eligible bachelor because he's going to be worth gazillions when his company floats on the stock market!"

Andi glanced down. To be honest the closest she got to shagging these days was walking past an Ann Summers shop on the way to work. Her sex organs were practically retired. She wasn't quite sure when this became the norm but she supposed it was another of the joys of nearly hitting thirty, a bit like having to wax her upper lip and worry about wrinkles. Tom was always out at some acting thing in the evenings, and by the time he arrived home Andi had usually conked out. She still fancied him, of course she did, but she was just so tired.

So shagging? Andi thought she could just about remember it.

"Isn't he just sex on a stick?" gushed Cally, practically gobbling up the page while Andi looked on blankly. "Come on, Andi! You must know! That's Benjamin Jonathan Teague? The CEO of Safe T Net. You've only just spent the last few months getting his company ready to go public!"

Reaching forward, she grabbed the magazine and began to read aloud, like a primary teacher with a particularly dim pupil. "'Benjamin J

Teague, 31, is the genius behind Safe T Net, the Internet security company. Hailed as Britain's answer to Bill Gates, Teague is set to become one of the UK's wealthiest men when the company floats on the stock market. In his spare time Teague enjoys extreme sports like wakeboarding, flying and racing his speedboat.' And it says he's single! Apparently he's just split up with someone and is back on the market!"

Andi gave the page a cursory glance. A man smiled up at her from the glossy paper. Eyes hidden by expensive shades, he lolled against a red sports car with his designer suit crumpled in an *I'm such a normal guy* pose. She supposed he was good-looking in a rich city boy way, but everything about him, from the immaculate haircut to the snowy whiteness of his shirt, screamed expense and self-satisfaction. Two champagne flutes dangled from his hand, drawing attention to the chunky watch on his wrist – which was clearly some kind of status symbol, if only Andi had the knowledge to recognise it. She was more of a £4.99-watch-from-Argos kind of girl, so it didn't mean much to her. Anyway, that car was a giant phallic symbol if ever there was one. He may just as well have been waving a sign saying *I have a huge willy!*

And *this* was the person she'd spent the last few months slaving her guts out for?

"Maybe he'll visit?" said Cally hopefully, hugging the magazine to her chest.

And maybe George Clooney will pop in too and whisk me away? thought Andi. *Then perhaps Brad Pitt will dump Angelina and fight George for me?* But until that happy day dawned, it was probably best she got back to her desk before Zoe pounced again.

Murmuring something non-committal, Andi left Cally to her coffee and daydreaming. Back at her workstation, the computer had finally decided to boot up, but it was still so slow that Andi felt like nipping to Starbucks and getting it a double espresso. Across the open-plan office Jen was typing busily and Alan was stalking people on Facebook. Situation normal, then.

Beyond them, Leeza's door opened and her PA peeped out in her tortoise-like fashion to beckon to Jen, who turned the same grey shade as the office carpet. To distract herself, Andi opened Outlook and reread the latest emails from PMB. Opening his mails had been the highlight of the project, and it certainly made a change to work with a guy who wasn't sleazy but appreciated her as a professional. Maybe the fact that they only used their initials had helped? In any case, he had said that he was so impressed with her work that he would make sure her line manager knew. Andi exhaled slowly. Maybe this was what it was all about?

She was on the brink of drafting an email asking PMB what he thought of his boss appearing in *Cosmo* when the office door opened and Jen lurched out. Her eyes were red and swollen and she was swaying as though the floor was moving beneath her.

"Miranda Evans?" called Leeza's PA, before Andi could so much as step forward and give Jen a hug. "Ms Clark will see you now."

Zoe's face was a study in gloating. Andi's stomach went into free fall. Something told her no amount of positive thinking would help now.

Chapter 5

Andi didn't need to be psychic to know that this meeting wasn't going to end well: Jen's sobs as she crammed her belongings into a box had been a bit of a giveaway, as had the pitying looks from their colleagues.

None of this made any sense. Jen was good at her job. Better than good, actually. She was brilliant. As was Andi.

Andi glanced around her boss's office in the hope that there might be one friendly face, but no such luck. The door had shut and she was stranded on a plastic seat, floating on a grey carpet sea with nobody to throw her a lifebelt.

"Thanks for coming in, Miranda," her boss said coolly and as though Andi had a choice in the matter. "I should imagine you have a fair idea what this is all about, so I won't make things any more difficult. Times are tough at the moment, as I'm sure you're aware. I'm afraid we have to let you go."

Andi stared at her boss. Let her go? What? Like a hot-air balloon? She had a sudden image of herself swelling to mammoth proportions and floating up over the city, treating everyone to a view of today's red and white spotty knickers. Laughter bubbled up inside her like a geyser. *Help*. She was getting hysterical. *Get a grip!* she told herself sharply. She was about to lose her job in the middle of a double-dip recession and on the very day all her money had vanished. It was hardly a laughing matter.

"But I'm good at my job," she managed to squeak once her vocal cords got it together. "I work really hard! Ask anyone!"

Leeza Clark couldn't quite look her in the eye. "Rest assured, we will give you an excellent reference."

Andi hated to be ungrateful but the last time she went shopping Tesco's didn't take references as a method of payment, excellent or otherwise. And Tom might be amazing at spouting Shakespeare soliloquies but annoyingly her bank baulked at accepting those as legal tender. Unless she could come up with something fast, she was stuffed. There had to be a reason to keep her on, something, other than her coffee-making skills, which made her unique to this company?

Then inspiration struck.

"What about the Safe T Net flotation? That all went really well. They were pleased, weren't they?" She was on the edge of her seat now, her hands clinging onto the plastic chair just like she was trying to cling onto this job.

Leeza Clark nodded.

"Zoe tells me that Alan Eades did a fantastic job, and I'm sure you played a part in it too."

Andi's jaw was practically swinging on its hinges. Alan did a fantastic job? Err, in what parallel universe was that exactly? On Planet Earth, which is where she'd lived until about five seconds ago, he was about as much use as a papier mâché umbrella. She'd spent hours clearing up his basic mistakes!

"Safe T Net was my project," she whispered.

"We know all about Safe T Net and who did what," hissed Leeza, shooting Andi a look of utter loathing. "The CEO of Safe T Net was very clear that we should recognise Alan's efforts. At no point, Miranda, was your name mentioned."

Andi glanced around the office in case this was someone's idea of a prank. Ha ha, everyone. Hilarious! Not. But nobody leapt out shouting

"Gotcha!" And her boss wasn't laughing either; rather, she was looking at Andi in a very disapproving manner.

"Here at Hart Frozer we take a very dim view of people who take credit for their colleague's work," continued Leeza Clark icily. "People who succeed here do so on their own merits. Zoe Symonds has mentioned your lack of team spirit on several occasions."

Andi stared at her, stunned by the unfairness of this statement. She'd put in hours of her own unpaid time to get the Safe T Net accounts ready in time for flotation. She'd taken personal pride in it! For at least the last three weeks she'd never been home before nine o'clock.

"I'm afraid our decision is final," continued Leeza, mistaking Andi's stunned silence for acceptance. "We have to let staff go and, frankly, you've been underperforming. You'll have the salary you're entitled to paid into your account by close of play today and we'll provide you with a reference. Now, if you would clear your desk, Gareth will escort you from the building."

Andi goggled at her. Head of Security Gareth made Arnold Schwarzenegger look weedy. She'd never met anyone with *love* and *hate* tattooed on his face until she met Gareth. And now he was going to escort her from the building like some kind of criminal? Seriously?

With her brain still struggling to take all this in, Andi returned to the main office. While Alan was summoned she tried to log onto her computer, only to discover that her access had already been blocked. Bloody hell, that was fast. A cardboard box had also appeared on her desk. Numbly, Andi started to fill it with all the detritus of her working life: a picture of Tom in guise as Hamlet, a faded summer snapshot of her and Angel on a pontoon in the Cornish town of Rock a lifetime ago, her pencils and pens, a cheese plant. Oh. Was that it? That wasn't a lot to show for two years of slavery.

She paused, fighting back tears. It was a pretty sobering thing to realise that your working life amounted to nothing more than a few pieces of tat in a box. Jen's desk was already cleared and it was as though she'd never even existed. What exactly had she been working so hard for?

Just as she was contemplating this depressing thought, the office door opened and Alan sauntered out. It was a bit odd that he was grinning. It was even odder that he was shaking hands with Leeza Clark and kissing Zoe on the cheek. Now he was moving his stuff to Jen's old desk, which was the best one by the window. What on earth was going on?

"I've been promoted," Alan gloated when he saw Andi glance over. "They're so impressed by my work on the Safe T Net account, you see. Even their CEO was singing my praises."

Andi's chin was almost on her desktop. Alan had to be the worst accountant she had ever worked with. She did everything while he did sweet FA; in fact he just did FA because there was absolutely nothing sweet about it! How unfair could life get? Why on earth had they promoted him?

Then the penny didn't so much drop as plummet to earth and wallop Andi on the head. *That* was what Alan had been up to when he'd been messing about with her computer. Never mind pinching her money; it was a thousand times worse than that! He was taking credit for all her hard work!

Of all the sneaky, sly, underhanded gits!

Andi couldn't help it; she didn't have red hair for nothing. Moments later Alan was wearing her pot plant as a hat, his computer had toppled over and she was yelling at him while he just smirked.

"Prove it!" he sneered.

"Don't you worry, I will!" Andi promised. It was lucky for Alan that Gareth grabbed hold of her at that point, otherwise Alan would have been wearing his gonads as earrings. The next thing she knew, she was being bundled out of the office and, moments later, unceremoniously deposited on the pavement with only her cardboard box to keep her company. Andi supposed she'd better hang on to it; if the worst came to the worst she could always sleep in it.

"What about my reference?" she called after Gareth's retreating figure, but he didn't reply. Andi guessed she could wave goodbye to that now.

She bent to scoop up her belongings. The unfairness of it all was staggering. In spite of her brave words, how could she ever prove what Alan had done? The simple answer to this question was not by sitting on the pavement close to tears. She needed an emergency caffeine injection to get her head together.

Once in Starbucks Andi ordered a latte and tried not to wince when it cost nearly three pounds. It'd be instant coffee in a flask until she found another job.

While she waited for her drink, Andi chewed the end of her ponytail (a bad habit, she knew, but it was free and better for her than smoking) and thought about whom she could call for some sympathy. Tom still wasn't answering, PMB's true identity and Safe T Net email address were locked into the company system and she was ignoring Angel after the earlier begging email.

It looked as though she was on her own.

Chapter 6

Being unemployed was not all it was cracked up to be, Angel decided. Once the novelty of reading magazines and drinking coffee while her colleagues toiled wore off, she was at a loose end and bored. It was one thing having all day to herself if there was a limitless credit card to play with or a luxury spa to enjoy, but another thing altogether when she had about twenty pence to her name. By lunchtime even she was tired of admiring all the designer bags in Selfridges. What was the point? It was so unfair; shopping was no fun at all when she had as much chance of flying to Mars as she did of owning one of those beautiful Chloé bags. And what was the point of trying on all the gorgeous clothes when she had absolutely no hope of seeing them wrapped up in tissue paper and lovingly placed in a shiny yellow carrier bag? Angel longed to feel the weight of those black cord handles cutting into her fingers, almost as much as she longed to be heading off for lunch at The Ivy before being interviewed by *Heat* magazine about her latest TV show...

Until that happy day dawned, though, she was penniless and unemployed and actually pretty hungry. Checking her purse only confirmed that she really was skint. Maybe she shouldn't have blown her last twenty on that MAC lippy? But it was such a gorgeous colour and exactly the same one that Katy Perry was wearing in this week's *Grazia*. Angel checked her reflection in the shop window and knew she'd made the right decision. The slick gloss, the exact hue of ripe cherries, made her full lips look pouty, plump and totally kissable. In terms of an investment in Project Rich Guy it was a wiser choice than lunch.

At the thought of food, Angel's stomach rumbled. Times were hard when a girl had to choose between lipstick and a bagel. God, she was operating on less cash than Kerry Katona! Maybe this was evidence of that recession Andi was always going on about?

Unable to even stretch to a packet of crisps, Angel contemplated going back home. Gemma was a fantastic cook and there was bound to be something delicious in the fridge or a bar of chocolate hidden in her flatmate's room. Angel had never met anyone with such a complicated relationship with food before. Gemma professed to be constantly on a diet but was always finding excuses to cram food into her face. No wonder she was several stone overweight. Turning sideways, Angel scrutinised her own figure in the shop window, her blue eyes narrowing critically as she looked at her waistline. Although a trim size eight with a toned stomach and curves in just the right places, Angel sometimes wondered if she ought to make a bit more of an effort and get herself down to a six. After all, didn't they say that being on the television added ten pounds? Maybe it wouldn't hurt to skip a few lunches? Then when she was discovered she wouldn't look out of place with all the *TOWIE* and *MIC* celebrities.

Pleased with this idea, she ignored her hunger pangs and the delicious aromas drifting on the breeze from the Italian restaurants lining the side roads that fanned away from Oxford Street. Project Rich Guy and fame it was!

All she needed to do was figure out a way of getting herself into the right place, Angel decided as she rode the escalator down into the bowels of the Tube. If she could only get herself an invite to a place where the rich and beautiful people hung out she knew it would just be matter of time before somebody noticed her. Then she'd be made.

Quite what she was going to do until then was a little vague, but Angel thought she could figure that out when the time came. Apart from her beautician skills, she didn't have any outstanding talents. She couldn't sing, she couldn't dance and she wasn't particularly good at acting either, unless you counted crying on demand, so there wasn't an obvious talent to get her noticed. Still, that had never stopped lots of other celebrities, had it?

What Angel did have in spades was charm, good looks and, buried beneath her fake tan and extensions, a razor-sharp brain. Angel had left school with four straight "A"s at A-level and an IQ score worthy of Mensa. She kept very quiet about this, though, because as far as Angel could tell being brainy didn't get you very far in life. Look at Andi, for instance, with all her qualifications. Where exactly had being brainy got her big sister? All Andi had to show for her years at uni was a dull job slaving over numbers, a wardrobe of identikit sludge-coloured clothes, a flat in the grotty end of Clapham and that waste-of-skin boyfriend.

Angel was still musing about her sister as she hopped onto the Tube. It was the middle of the day and for a moment she allowed herself to luxuriate in the novelty of being able to take her pick of the seats rather than being crammed into someone's stinky armpit. When she was rich and famous she would never, ever ride the Tube again, unless it was for a photo opportunity just to prove how *normal* and how *unchanged* she really was. As the train slithered its way beneath the city, Angel allowed herself the luxury of another little daydream where she posed in Sienna Miller style boho chic, her long blonde hair sexily bed-mussed and her large statement bag slung casually over her arm. Then, once the paps had pushed off, her Bentley would collect her, sweep her away from the skittering litter and fuggy Tube air and off to lunch at The Savoy with an impossibly gorgeous man.

Yep. That was what using your looks rather than your brains could get you. Why anybody would settle for a mundane job and an average life was beyond Angel. Take her sister, for example. Why Andi continued to toil away in that hideous office – it must be afflicted with sick building syndrome or something because Angel always felt nauseous just thinking about the place – was a mystery almost as huge as why she put up with Tom.

Angel dug her iPhone out of her (fake) Louis Vuitton bag and scrolled through her picture roll until she settled on a shot of her sister with her partner. Her blue eyes narrowed. Tom was good-looking, there was no denying it, but his were the kind of good looks that wouldn't last long. Already his blond hair was looking a little thin and he had a habit of sweeping it aside nervously in an attempt to hide the sparse patch at the crown. He worked out religiously but there was a blur of a double chin and Angel suspected the moment his efforts stopped he would puff up like a peony. Her sister had better be careful she didn't go to bed one night with Brad Pitt and wake up with Gollum! And talk about self-absorbed. The word *me* ran through him like a stick of Brighton rock. Her sister could do so much better.

Angel scrolled to another photo, this one just of Andi. It was a rare shot where her sister was glammed up – or Andi's idea of glam anyway, which was to pop her contacts in, slick some lipstick on and tug a brush through her hair. It had been lunch at Cliveden House the last time their father had been in the UK, and for such a sumptuous setting even Andi had managed to drag herself out of the office and put on a frock. In the picture Andi was leaning on a balustrade, with the formal gardens behind her falling away to the glittering ribbon of the Thames. Against the vivid green of the spring lawns her hair was a fiery red mane of glossy curls spilling over her shoulders to her curvy chest. As someone who could only fill a B-cup (on a good day, and with the wind behind her), Angel was deeply envious of her sister's figure. She guessed she could get a loan and sort out her own chest but, like the boobs, her sister's slender waist, long coltish legs and wide green eyes were all Andi's own. There was no way Angel could fake those. Angel, who *might* sometimes have a little bit of help from L'Oréal with her own tresses (because not only was she worth it but she was actually a closet brunette), simply couldn't understand why her sister insisted on camouflaging her assets with dull trouser suits, scraped back hair and an unmade-up face. Angel thought her sister was stunning. She just wished Andi would think the same. In Angel's opinion, useless lazy git Tom should be on his knees thanking God her sister even noticed him, not taking the total piss on a daily basis.

Angel shook her head. If there was ever a way to remove Tom from the scene she would take it. Actually, a solution had occurred to her when Tom's hand had found its way to her knee last Christmas. Although Tom had laughed it off as too much sherry, the look in his eyes and his still-full glass had told a different story. Angel trusted him about as much as the Road Runner trusted Wile E Coyote, and for a split second she'd been tempted to blow his cover once and for all. Only the thought of how much this would hurt her sister had stopped Angel – but she was biding her time. Tom could wait. Besides, she had her own suspicions about her sister's low self-esteem. Their father had a lot to answer for. Good-looking, charming and totally unreliable Alexander Evans had swanned in and out of his daughters' lives for years. Sometimes he had showered them with attention, theatre trips and trolley dashes round Hamleys; on other occasions weeks would go by without so much as a phone call. Their mother had never said much, but sometimes the expression on her face had mirrored the disappointment in her children's eyes.

"Talk about parents fucking you up," muttered Angel to herself. Honestly, Freud would have had a field day with the Evans clan. They had more Big Issues than their local high street. No wonder Andi had been drawn to Tom. It was that old familiar striving to please a man thing, wasn't it? An impossible task, since nobody had ever managed to please Alex Evans – not even their beautiful mother.

Well, bugger that. She, Angel Evans, was only going to please herself!

Angel sighed. Tucking the phone away, she decided to take a detour out towards Balham – sorry, Clapham – and see if Andi was working from home. She sometimes did and Angel, whose rumbling stomach was loudly protesting against her size-six master plan, figured that she might as well grab a bite to eat from her sister's fridge. Anyway, didn't Gemma say that diets always started tomorrow?

As the train drew into the next station, Angel tidied her hair in the blurry glass, craning her neck to avoid the reflections of adverts for Match.com and tooth-whitening products getting in the way of her own image. She hoped her sister was in. They could watch afternoon telly and drink tea. That had to be better than going back to the flat.

Angel grimaced at the thought of the flat she shared with Gemma. It was a pigsty right now and in serious need of mucking out. When she'd left that morning the place had been strewn with Gemma's underwear, a downpour of pants, thongs and Spanx as her flatmate had frantically hunted for an outfit that would fit. The detritus of a late-night Chinese had sat congealing on the coffee table, gloopy MSG doing awful things to the French polish and probably sounding the death knell for any hope they'd had of seeing their deposit again. The floor had remained littered with crumbs and dust bunnies since their last vacuum cleaner had choked out its death throes. Neither Gemma nor Angel had the cash or the inclination to buy another one, so instead the flat was sliding gradually into Dickensian squalor. Angel would hardly have been surprised to come home one evening and find Miss Havisham ensconced on the sofa, while the dust fell softly through the air and the London grime continued to block the daylight out.

Outside the station the glare was dazzling; above the crawling traffic and leaden rooftops a fried-egg sun blasted down onto the pavements and turned the windows of shops into liquid gold. Fishing out her oversized Gucci shades, Angel turned her attention to scrolling through her missed calls and text messages, feeling slightly alarmed when she saw that there were three from Gemma. Oh God, she hadn't left her straighteners on again, had she? Last time the firemen had been really sweet about it, and one of them had even slipped her his phone number, but Angel wasn't sure they'd be quite so amused a second time. Or would this be the third? She'd better call her flatmate.

Crossing the street and leaving Clapham South Tube station behind her, Angel meandered towards the common, pretending that she hadn't noticed the attention that her long Fake Baked legs in their miniscule denim cut-offs were attracting. God, she loved the summer! Wearing skimpy vests rather than sweaters and drinking wine instead of tea. It was heaven! If only she could spend the summer somewhere *slightly* more glam than South London, though, like St Tropez or Marbella for instance. Clapham Common was all very well, and there was no shortage of fit young guys out running or flexing their muscles as they fooled around with Frisbees, but there was a distinct lack of superyachts and eligible millionaires. A cute guy with shaggy blond hair and a six-pack you could bounce rocks off threw a grin her way but Angel chose not to notice. She was twenty-seven now, and the dreaded thirty was only three years away, so there was no time to fritter on guys who were wasting weekdays in the park! Millionaires were too busy making serious cash to have fun in the sun, after all.

Flipping her long blonde hair over one shoulder and pretending to be absorbed in her phone, Angel wove her way through the picnickers scattered over the grass and found herself a shady spot under a horse-chestnut tree, all green leaves and white candles. The sun played havoc with skin, everyone knew that, and right now she was too poor to start a Botox habit. Angel leant back into the grass and stared up at the blue flecks of sky peeking through the shady canopy. Stretched out like this, her stomach looked pancake flat. Maybe once she got to Andi's she could indulge just a little? In the meantime she'd text Gemma back and find out what the latest trauma was. Taking a deep breath, and praying that her friend wasn't knee-deep in firemen, Angel began to dial.

Chapter 7

By the time she arrived home Gemma knew the premise for Callum South's new show off by heart. As she trudged along Tooting High Street, dodging puddles and narrowly missing having her eye poked out by an old lady's brolly, she was willing to swap the traffic and leaden skies for golden sand and sharp Cornish air right there and then. She was sick and tired of recession gloom – why else would she have spent the day freezing her butt off in an arctic studio – it was time to try something else, time to be a little bit creative.

Sod it. Things in London weren't exactly working out the way they were supposed to. A dramatic change was needed, or she'd still be modelling granny pants when she really was a granny.

With Emily's taunts still ringing in her ears, Gemma stood in the queue for the 219 and scrutinised her reflection in the bus shelter. She'd avoided mirrors for so long that it was something of a shock to see what she really looked like. Lord. She wasn't that big surely? Her stomach didn't really stick out that much, did it?

Gemma gulped and looked away. Either she had reverse body-dysmorphic disorder or else the Perspex was distorting her reflection. Yes, that was probably it. And her coat was quite padded; to be fair, it had never really done up properly across her boobs. Sizes just weren't that accurate, that was the trouble. Weren't they modelled on women from the 1950s who were still skinny from all that rationing?

Gemma sucked in her cheeks. Phew! Her cheekbones were still there; they'd just got a bit buried, that was all. A few days of calorie counting and they'd be sharp enough to ski off. That 5:2 diet was meant to be brilliant. How hard could it be to fast for a couple of days a week? Not hard at all if you knew you could eat whatever you liked for the remaining five days. Simples!

And her bum wasn't big: it was just… curvy. Curvy butts were really fashionable; just ask Pippa Middleton! Gemma twisted round to get a really good look and decided that what was good enough for the future queen's sister was certainly good enough for her. Hey, if her plan came off and she got famous, maybe she'd even get to meet Prince Harry? You never knew…

For a few wonderful minutes Gemma was lost in a daydream where she floated through Westminster Abbey while the nation looked on in admiration at her stunning dress and backside. "Princess Gemma" certainly had a ring to it and was a million times better than being saddled with "Ginormous Gemma". Yep, thanks for that one, parents.

Gemma was so lost in her daydreams that it was a surprise to find the bus pulling up. Catapulted out of her sumptuous wedding breakfast at Buckingham Palace – there was no way she was calorie counting on her wedding day – and back into rainy Tooting, Gemma clambered on board and squeezed herself into the aisle. London buses in rush hour were always a nightmare. Once she was a TV star she'd be chauffeur driven everywhere and never play sardines on a crowded bus again. Ten years of living in the capital and travelling with your face wedged into a stranger's armpit was more than enough for anybody. Cornwall was looking like a better option with every second that passed.

It wasn't that she was greedy, thought Gemma sadly as she clambered on board and the bus splashed its way through the sodden streets: she just had a slower metabolism than lots of other people. It was pure bad luck. Lots of people ate way more than she did and were pencil thin. Take Angel's sister Andi, for example. She was always eating yet had the kind of figure models envied. Gemma had asked Andi what her secret was and Andi, without missing a beat, had replied "Stress."

Stress? Gemma wasn't buying into that. She was very stressed herself, actually. Every time she opened a bank statement she nearly passed out, and her last game of cashpoint Russian roulette was definitely responsible for her first grey hairs. So if Andi's theory was correct, Gemma should be a size zero.

Maybe she should dig out one of her exercise DVDs? Gemma had an impressive collection ranging from *Essexercise* to Davina's workouts. She'd watched them all, just to get the idea of what was required – after all, these things had to be taken seriously – and she'd thought long and hard about which one to do. It was the thought that counted, after all. But somehow she'd never quite got around to doing any of them. *Davina Fit* currently made a very useful coaster, while *Zumba Challenge* was propping up the wonky coffee table. But not for much longer. The time for change was nigh!

As the bus crawled through the traffic, Gemma took her phone out and looked up *Callum South* again. There it was in all its Googled glory: the outline of his new ITV2 reality show. Gemma read it over and over again, and with every word she felt more excited. Her imagination was full of sunshine and seafood and gorgeous twinkly-eyed Callum. Even though she was soaked through to her size-sixteen knickers and her sodden hair was plastered against her head, Gemma hardly noticed. Neither did she notice the traffic swishing by, headlights turning the puddles into diamonds. Even the soggy pigeons and trundling buses vanished. Instead of Tooting Broadway, Gemma saw the wide estuary of the Camel River, all glittering sapphire water and gleaming powerboats, and her heart skipped a beat.

This new get-fit reality show had her name written all over it! Hadn't Chloe just told her to lose weight and get herself onto the telly? If she could only win a role on this show she could kill two birds with one stone. She'd soon be a size ten and she'd be on the television too. It was perfect!

Finally the bus drew up at Gemma's stop just off Fulham Broadway. With relief she gathered up her things and soon was splashing through the puddles.

Catching sight of her reflection in the bakery window made Gemma sigh even harder. It was another unwritten universal rule that depressed fat girls should never look in bakery windows. Such an activity never ended well...

See, here she was already pushing open the door and walking into the pastry-scented fug as though tugged in by an invisible Star Trek style tractor beam. There was no hope for her diet now. Those cheese straws were already making her mouth water. And the iced buns looked delicious. Just one wouldn't hurt, would it? And there were strawberries on the meringues, which surely counted towards one of her five a day?

"Hello, Gemma love! We wondered where you were. Have you been working today?"

OK, thought Gemma resignedly, when you were on first-name terms with the bakery staff it was a sure sign there was a problem. As was the fact that they had already put aside two sausage-and-bean melts for her. She'd have to buy them now. It would be ungrateful not to. Anyway, if *Heading South* was based on transforming blobs into stunning babes, then surely the blobbier she was the better? When Angel had called her back just now, she'd thought the idea was blinding and was all for throwing her lot in with Gemma.

"It's like a sign from God!" she'd squealed when Gemma had tentatively sounded out her plan. "I've been sacked, so there's nothing for me to stay here for. Why don't we go together?"

Once Gemma had commiserated and they'd enjoyed a mutual bitching session about Mrs Yuri, they got down to the practicalities. The lease on their basement flat was up at the end of the month, so it was the perfect time to move on. Gemma knew a family friend with a caravan just outside Rock; although it didn't have the glamour of one of the sugar-almond-hued cottages in the town, it would at least be within their budget. Surely the two of them together would be able to pick up some seasonal work, split the rent and have an awful lot of fun! At this thought Gemma's heart rose like the loaves in the bakery oven.

"I used to love Rock when I was a kid. It would be a blast to go back," Angel had carried on, sounding more and more excited with every word. "Mum and Dad…" She'd paused and Gemma had just let the silence remain because Angel rarely mentioned her family. Then her friend had shrugged and continued.

"Anyway, before Mummy was ill they always rented this gorgeous house overlooking the river. We used to spend every summer there and we absolutely loved it. We'd play on the beach all day and we spent hours catching crabs off the pontoon. Andi used to like the boats best and she'd spend hours just watching them out at sea. In the evening we'd have chips right out of the paper. Nothing ever tasted so good."

Gemma had nodded, her mouth watering at the thought of chips. She too had spent many sunburned days on the beach at Rock and gone home salty, sleepy and full of food. The place had changed a bit since then though: the chips would be hand cut these days, organic and served with slithers of expensive fish. Jamie, Rick and Hugh had certainly put their stamp on the South West.

"It's changed though," she'd said. "The place is really upmarket now."

"Good, that's *exactly* what we want," Angel had replied decisively. "Project Rich Guy isn't going to happen in Tooting bloody Bec, that's for sure. If Rock is where the rich and famous hang out for the summer then it's time we got ourselves down there too. You can get yourself a role on Callum's show and I'll find myself a prince or something. Simples!"

Was it really that easy? Gemma wasn't so sure. She hated to be the one to rain all over her friend's parade, but experience had taught her that life was often a bit more complicated.

"Rock's expensive," she'd warned. "We'll have to really be careful with our money. I only have a few hundred quid left in savings."

"That's a few hundred more than me," Angel had said cheerfully. "I'll borrow some off Andi. That'll tide us over for a bit. In the meantime there's bound to be oodles of work. Just think of all those rich women who want facials! Summer in Cornwall! I can't wait!"

Angel had rung off, en route to find Andi and blag a loan, and Gemma had made her way to the bus stop. Just the thought of a summer back at home, waking to the call of the gulls rather than the wail of sirens, perked her up. She could hardly wait for Angel to get home so that they could start putting their plan together. The idea of lemon sunshine, sharp salty air, glittering water and watermelon slices of beach made Gemma tingle with excitement. She hardly dared hope that in just a few days' time she could be back in Cornwall.

Two sausage-and-bean melts and one doughnut later, Gemma let herself into the basement flat. There was no sign of Angel. Only a trail of glossy magazines and plates evidenced that she had been in at all. Gemma sighed; her friend was terribly messy. Angel left more devastation in her wake than the most severe hurricane.

She shrugged off her wet gear and stomped into the kitchen. After one hot chocolate and four rock cakes she felt ready to boot up her laptop and embark on some research for their brainwave.

So it wasn't Shakespeare or the dazzling film career that she had once dreamed of, but it was a start. If her dad's farmer friend still owned that caravan just outside Rock then maybe, just maybe, things were going to change for both her and Angel. Feeling hopeful, she composed an email to him and then sent it into the ether with a prayer.

There, it was done – and Gemma sensed that this was the start of something good.

Chapter 8

Andi was so lost in thought that she didn't quite know how she made it home. One moment she was in Starbucks, and the next she was back in Clapham, surfacing from the Tube as though awakening from a dream. Not that she really lived in Clapham anyway; no, strictly speaking it was Balham, although Tom would rather poke his eyes out than admit that. She'd tried arguing this point once and he'd sulked for days. As sure as Andi was that Coventry was a lovely place, she'd no wish to live there and had finally cracked. Now she agreed that they lived in Clapham, even if it was the tatty end near the gasworks, and everybody was happy. Or at least until the astronomical rent was due.

At the thought of rent, her stomach lurched. How the hell was she going to pay it if her account really was empty? Tom had better have a bloody good explanation.

That was strange: the curtains were drawn at their attic window. Was Tom poorly? Or maybe he'd gone out and had forgotten to open them? Or maybe he was still in bed? She hadn't worked from home since the Safe T Net job had started. He could sleep all day for all Andi knew.

"Tom?" she called, ditching her keys in the fruit bowl and heading for the kettle. "Tom? It's me!"

Odd. There was no reply. He wasn't due anywhere, not as far as she could remember. It was only Monday and he hadn't got a casting until Thursday. Their flat was so small you couldn't swing a gerbil in it, so he had to be in the bedroom. The kettle was still warm. He'd probably made a cup of coffee and gone back to bed. They were going to need to have a serious heart-to-heart now about his finding work. Any work.

She flicked the kettle back on and lobbed a tea bag into a mug. A hit of PG tips was definitely required if she was going to tackle the important question of *Where the bloody hell was her money?* There were even bigger questions too, which she knew she'd ignored for far too long. It was time now for total honesty.

While the tea brewed Andi wandered across the flat to the bedroom, stopping only to scoop up some washing draped across the back of the sofa rather than folded up, the way she always left it. So she was a bit of a neat freak? It wasn't a crime!

Hang on, though, this was odd laundry. Tom's tee shirt didn't smell very clean and she sure he was wearing those Ralph Lauren shorts when she'd left for work that morning. And Andi didn't recognise that bra...

There was a loud whooshing in her ears and the laminate floor dipped and rolled like a stormy sea. Andi clutched the sofa for support and for a hideous moment she thought she might pass out. That bra was hot pink and frilly. Andi's head could fit in one of the cups, maybe even her entire body.

With a thudding heart she stepped forward and flung open the bedroom door.

"Andi!" gasped Tom, when he caught sight of her over his shoulder. "This isn't what you think!"

Andi couldn't help it. She laughed. Unless this was a game of naked Twister and they'd forgotten to fetch the board, she was pretty certain it was *exactly* what she thought. Tom looked ridiculous with his boxers around his ankles and his naked buttocks poised in mid-air like peeled hard-boiled eggs. Beneath him, Gina from the flat below turned the same colour as her abandoned bra. She'd come home from work unexpectedly and caught her boyfriend shagging a girl with boobs as big as her head and the IQ of a lettuce. What a pathetic, sordid, obvious cliché.

Tom, scrabbling to his feet, hopped after Andi while attempting to yank up his boxers.

"Babe! Wait! Shit! Ouch!" In his haste he cannoned off the bedside table and head-butted the wall. Andi hoped it bloody well hurt. "This isn't what it looks like!"

Andi whipped round. Suddenly the laughter subsided, replaced by a blast of anger as white hot as the reactive core of Sellafield. How dare he? She'd been slaving her guts out and having to tolerate slimes like Alan and bitchy Zoe just so that her boyfriend could hone his art in so-called Clapham – and in return he was screwing the neighbour, in between *Loose Women* and the lunchtime news.

"It's exactly what it looks like! How long have you been shagging her?"

A hurt expression settled across Tom's features.

"Babes, I know you're not going to believe me but this is the first ever time. I swear it!"

He was right. Andi was not going to believe it.

"God, you're pathetic," she said.

"Come on, don't be like this!" Tom finally tugged on his boxers. Gina was totally forgotten. "It's a mistake! It doesn't mean anything! What can I say to prove it means nothing?" He widened his eyes beseechingly before brightening visibly as an idea occurred. "I know! Of course! What else? Andi, sweetheart, I love you. Will you marry me?"

Was he totally insane? Who on earth got caught cheating and then proposed? It was like something from a bad soap opera. Then Andi remembered he'd been preparing for an *EastEnders* audition. Talk about method acting. In a moment he'd be telling her that they could go for a right old knees-up in the square and have a chat with Dot Cotton. Maybe they could even have a wedding reception in the Vic? Oh dear God. Had the last eighteen months with Tom been based on nothing more than him *acting* the part of her boyfriend?

"Get up, Tom," Andi said wearily. "You're being ridiculous. Of course I won't marry you. I've just caught you screwing another woman."

"But can explain! It doesn't mean anything!"

There was a lump in Andi's throat because it meant something to *her*. She balled her hands into fists, the nails digging into her palms as she fought to keep control. She knew things hadn't been going well but nothing had prepared her for this.

"How long has it been going on?" she asked.

For a moment Tom paused, teetering on the brink of a lie, then he exhaled slowly. He could tell there was no way he could talk his way out of this one.

"A couple of months. Four? Maybe five? Since you started that Safe T Net job. I never saw you once that began. You never have time for me these days, do you? All you care about is work."

Andi felt like he'd punched her in guts. She'd been working for *them*! Every hour that she'd sweated over her computer had been about putting money towards their future. How deluded was she? Or perhaps Tom was a better actor than she'd given him credit for?

"And what about the money?" she demanded. "Don't try and deny that you've cleared my accounts, either. You were the only person who knew those passwords."

Tom shrugged. "I needed some funds quickly, babe. Den – you know Den, he has the garage near Penge – he's got this Audi TT come in. It's only a year old and it's an absolute bargain. If I hadn't been quick I would have missed a great deal. You'll love it, babe. It's bright red and a soft top."

Andi stared at him. "Let me get this clear. You blew all my money and our rent on a *car*?"

Tom tilted his head in a winsome way. In fairness to him it was a look that had always worked in the past, but right now Andi could have cheerfully kicked him all day long.

"It will be great for the summer," he continued, as though he hadn't just been caught cheating and swindling. "I needed it too: taking cabs to all my auditions costs a fortune."

Andi thought she was about to combust with fury. Tom's taxi habit was already a bone of contention. Why he insisted on taking cabs when they lived practically in the sodding Tube station was a mystery. And now he'd stolen her money to buy a car? Who was going to tax it and insure it?

Muggins. That was who.

"I want my money back," she said coldly.

Tom shrugged. "Cash deal, babe. You know Den. Don't look like that. I'll pay you back."

"I need that money! It's my money!" Andi couldn't believe that she had just caught her boyfriend cheating and yet was more worried about the lost money than his infidelity. If she'd had the time to pause and think about it, this realisation would probably have made her feel a whole lot better.

"Car's in my name." Tom jingled a set of keys under her nose. "Prove it's not yours."

Behind them the door clicked shut, and seconds later Gina's heavy tread thumped downstairs. Was she one of many? A sensation of dizziness threatened to swamp Andi and suddenly nothing mattered so much as getting him out of her space. The money could be dealt with but right now just the sight of him was suffocating.

"Pack your things and get out," she said wearily.

Tom curled his lip. "You can't kick me out. I live here too, remember?"

"It's my name on the rental contract," Andi shot back. "It had to be, remember? You have a worse credit rating than Greece."

Tom couldn't argue with this. Instead he gave her a pitying look. "You're making a big mistake. Come on, baby, we've been together for ages now. Don't throw it all away."

Andi's hands were on her hips. She didn't think she'd ever felt this determined. "I didn't throw it away: you did."

He rolled his eyes. "Don't overreact. Anyone can make a mistake. It was just a shag. I'm a man. I have needs. And let's be honest, you hardly ever show any interest. All you ever do these days is fall asleep. What else am I supposed to do?"

Andi was working twelve hours a day to keep Tom and his Clarins habit. Of course she fell asleep when she got home. She was knackered.

But Tom, mistaking her outraged silence for agreement, was into his stride now. "Have you any idea of the pressure I've been under? It isn't easy being an actor, you know. All you do is work and all you want to talk about is bloody Safe T Net. At least Gina's interested in what I have to say rather than going on about work or the sodding bills all the time."

Andi was speechless.

"So in lots of ways this is your fault." Tom sauntered to the sofa and picked up the Sky control. The arrogance of this gesture was compounded by his following words. "Be honest, Andi, if you'd been more committed to our relationship this would never have happened."

And then Andi saw red: glorious, bright, furious scarlet. How dare he blame her? How dare he! Almost before her brain could figure out what was happening she was diving into the cupboard under the sink and pulling out bin bags. Seconds later she was in the wardrobe stuffing Tom's designer gear into them. Turnbull & Asser shirts rubbed shoulders with Gaultier jackets, while Hugo Boss boxers were given a good kicking by Tommy Hilfiger socks. Then she stormed into the bathroom, swept all his products into the mix and dropped his new TAG Heuer watch down the loo. As far as Andi was concerned money down the bog was exactly what that latest ridiculous status symbol represented.

"What the hell are you doing, you crazy bitch? My bloody watch!"

Tom charged past and plunged his hand into the toilet bowl. Andi stood back and watched as he swirled his hand around in Bloo loo freshener. When he surfaced he looked like an extra from *Braveheart*.

"Pack your things," she ordered. "Anything you don't take I'll put out for the dustmen."

"Don't worry, I'm out of here with pleasure," Tom snarled as he crashed around the flat stuffing his belongings into bags. "I should have left months ago."

Andi resisted pointing out that he wasn't leaving so much as being thrown out. Packing finished, Tom dithered by the front door just in case she might have a change of heart. No such luck. He'd smashed that into pieces long ago.

"You're making a big mistake," he said.

Andi held out her hand for his door keys. Her biggest mistake was wasting nearly two years of her life on him and thinking they might have a future. Men only ever let you down. She wouldn't ever make that error again.

"Face it, Andi," Tom called over his shoulder, as he lugged his bags out of the door. "You'll never find anyone like me again."

"I hope you're right," Andi said fervently. "To meet two lying, cheating narcissists in one lifetime would be very bad luck indeed."

Tom's features twisted into an ugly expression. Why had she never noticed just how close together his eyes were before? Were his lips always so thin? Who was this man?

"You'll regret speaking to me like that," he spat, as with eyes narrowed and glinting with malice he humped his bags through the doorway. "And don't think this is the end of it, either. I've got a few things up my sleeve, or rather on my hard drive, that I'm sure you'd rather stayed there. I'm not afraid to show everyone what you're really like, Miss Oh-So-High-and-Mighty Perfect Accountant!"

Something in his tone of voice scraped a cold finger of unease down Andi's spine.

"What's that supposed to mean?" she demanded.

Tom smirked. "Wouldn't you like to know? Maybe I'll let you find out in my own time? Let's just say I have some very happy memories of our time together."

Andi gripped the doorframe so tightly her knuckles glowed through her skin. If he was alluding to what she *thought* he was alluding to, then Tom was even lower than the worms.

"That was between us," she whispered. "That was private!"

"And the operative word there is *was*," Tom laughed, a harsh mirthless sound. "After all, Andi, like you say, it's over. You've thrown me out without even giving us a second chance." He shrugged. "Well, it's your loss. Without me you're nothing! Just a pathetic, boring, crap-in-bed accountant who lives in Clapham. And that's all you'll ever be."

And with this parting shot he was gone, sauntering out of the apartment block without so much as a care in the world.

How dare he? When he had cheated and lied and ripped her off and threatened her? Andi was furious!

"I'm not an accountant anymore!" she yelled at his retreating back. "I've been made redundant and guess what? I'm going to do something different. I'm going to go somewhere new and start again. And," she added with a sudden flash of inspiration, "this isn't even Clapham, you moron! It's bloody Balham!"

And Andi couldn't wait to see the back of the place.

Chapter 9

As far as Andi was concerned today had gone as heinously as any day could possibly go. So far she had been set up by her git of a colleague, made redundant from the job that was keeping the entire pack of wolves from her door, caught her boyfriend cheating and had her bank account emptied. And it was only early afternoon.

Since Tom's departure she'd been very busy tearing round the flat like the Tasmanian Devil, ramming any of Tom's leftover bits into bin bags. Hurling them down the stairs was extremely cathartic. She ripped the sheets off the bed and stuck them on the hottest wash possible and played "I Will Survive" at full volume. All she needed to do now was get a radical haircut and lose a few stone and she'd have exhausted every broken-hearted cliché going.

Not bad going for one hour's efforts.

Andi had to keep busy because if she thought too hard about everything she'd go into meltdown. The problem was that the flat was so small that tidying it only took ten minutes – and there was only so long a girl could watch daytime telly before she seriously contemplated sticking her head in the microwave. So, there was only one thing for it. Andi was going to have to start drinking until she didn't care anymore or passed out; she really wasn't fussed about in which order.

Right. What did she have in the kitchen? Some ancient red that she sometimes used for cooking. It smelt a bit rough and could probably double for paint stripper, but broken-hearted beggars couldn't be choosers. There wasn't very much left though. What else was there? She flung open the fridge and tra da! Hiding behind a heel of tired-looking Cheddar and a wilted bag of Florette was a bottle of white wine. It needn't think it can hide there, thought Andi as she reached in, not when there was a woman in need of oblivion in the kitchen!

The Christmas Baileys from the back of the cupboard soon joined her haul, as did a bottle of ten-year-old malt Tom had overlooked in his speedy exit. Andi lined her spoils up on the worktop and then fetched a mug. Today was not a day for faffing about with glasses. It was time to get stuck in.

Andi was just in the process of making a lovely concoction of red, white and whiskey – which would hopefully do the trick – when there was a knock at the door followed by non-stop sounding of the buzzer. She ignored it. It was probably Tom coming back for another game of Fish the Watch out of the Bog. Well, he could ring all day and all night! There was no way she was opening up.

Andi was deliberating whether or not to add a splash of Baileys to the mix just to help her on her way when there was a knock on the door. Typical. Where was solitude when a girl needed it to drink herself silly?

"Go away!" She shouted, sloshing the Baileys into a mug having decided that she may as well do this properly. "I never want to see you again!"

"Charming," replied a voice huffily. "Be like that then. If that's how you feel then I'll go."

Andi nearly choked on her drink. Not only because it was disgusting but because it was Angel at the door. This was unusual for two reasons: the first was that Angel seldom left Tooting unless she really wanted something, and the second was that she should be hard at it waxing and plucking and tanning in the beauty salon where she worked. "Worked" in the loosest sense of the word, that was. Angel hadn't been in the queue when the work ethic was handed out; she'd probably been lying in after a heavy night out clubbing. So to find her sister banging on the door in the middle of the afternoon did not bode well. With a horrible "beware the Ides of March" sensation, Andi went to let her in.

"About bloody time," muttered Angel, trotting into the lat and flopping onto the sofa. "Tea would be nice, Andi Pandy, and a biscuit if you've got one. I'm starving. I've had such a bad day."

Andi shut the door slowly. The day was only halfway through; surely it couldn't get any worse?

"Ooo! What's this?" Angel's big blue eyes clocked the drinks on the kitchen counter. "Cocktails? Yummy! Can I have one?"

Without waiting for a reply she was pouring herself a tumbler of Andi's special Misery Mix, which she knocked back like it was a tequila shot.

"Bloody hell, sis! That's strong! How much of this have you had?"

"Not nearly enough," Andi said grimly.

Angel's nose crinkled. "It's got a right kick to it. Beats Jägerbombs. Can I have some more?"

"No you can't," Andi said. She knew her sister. If she wasn't careful Angel would guzzle the lot and then how could she get roaringly drunk?

"You're so tight. I only wanted a little drink." Angel pouted but, unlike those who usually succumbed to Angel's ploys, Andi was not a man and was therefore totally unmoved.

"Step away from the alcohol," she said. "And if we're playing crap-day trumps, yours cannot possibly be worse than mine."

"Bet it can," said Angel airily, opening up the fridge and screwing up her perfect nose at the lack of contents. "No food? But I'm starving! And I've lost my job."

That was a big surprise, rather on a par with being told that the Pope is a Catholic. Nevertheless Andi felt herself going into big sister mode. She just couldn't help it. After years of looking out for Angel this was Andi's default setting.

"Oh Angel! What happened?"

Angel shrugged. "Nothing really. It was silly. Mrs Yuri just took something I said really personally."

"Not Mrs Yuri, wife of the oligarch?"

Angel nodded her blonde head. "Yep, the one who looks like a pig in a suit? Oink oink! She's got this mole on her face. It's huge and hairy but she seems fine about it and we're all meant to ignore it. But today it looked different, a bit pink and sore, and I had to say something." She paused. "If somebody had pointed out Mum's mole things could have been very different, couldn't they?"

Andi swallowed. Even after all these years the loss stabbed her speechless.

"Anyway, before I could finish explaining it was only because I was worried it looked suspicious, I was on the pavement with my P45." She looked most hard done by. "I was only trying to help."

"Of course you were," said Andi firmly. "Maybe she'll actually go away and think about what you said?"

Angel pulled a face. "I doubt it. She's probably organising a hit on me right now. Anyway, never mind her. This arrived this morning too. I'm really not very happy."

She delved into her Chanel bag, scattering old lippies, tattered celebrity magazines and fluffy Tampax all over the just-cleaned floor, and pulled out a thick and official-looking envelope. Thrusting it at

Andi, she said, "Some guy handed it to me just as I was leaving the salon. It's bang out of order, don't you think?"

Andi tugged the letter out of the heavy envelope and skimmed the words. Even though they were phrased in eloquent legalese, the meaning couldn't be any clearer.

Trespass again, you lunatic, and we will sue your ass.

For a second her sacking, the missing money and even Tom's betrayal were totally forgotten. What on earth had Angel done now?

"Nothing! It's all a silly fuss," said her sister when Andi pressed her on this. "Some people have absolutely no sense of humour."

"I may be one of them today," Andi muttered. "Have you tried to gatecrash another party?"

She already knew the answer. It was practically one of the laws of physics; Stephen Hawking probably had an equation for it.

"Oh come on, Ands, where's your sense of adventure?" said Angel, now readjusting a false eyelash by peering at the microwave door. "If I hadn't been caught trying to sneak into the private estate I know it would have all worked out," she sighed. "Gemma thought it was a great idea."

At the mention of her sister's flatmate Andi rolled her eyes so hard they almost fell out of her head and rattled across the kitchen floor. Gemma was so flaky you could stick her in a 99. When she wasn't driving everyone mad with fad diets she was busy coming up with some madcap scheme to get on the telly and make her fortune. In Andi's opinion Gemma was a seriously bad influence on her sister. They were both as fame obsessed as each other. And she was so messy! Any self-respecting pig would balk at spending time in Gemma's basement hovel.

"Don't look like that," said Angel. "Gemma's all right once you get to know her."

Andi considered telling her that getting to know Gemma Pengelley wasn't top of her bucket list, but she decided to keep quiet. Actually, she didn't decide at all; it was more a case that she couldn't speak because she was far too busy reading about how her sister had been pulled off the private estate's fence and carried away by the security team, probably totally amazed to meet men immune to her long tanned legs and tearful pleas. Apparently the estate management didn't tolerate trespassers.

"Trespassers? Of all the cheek!" spluttered Angel when Andi read this bit aloud. "I don't think I've ever been so insulted in my entire life!"

"So, until you are famous, what are you going to do for work and money?" Andi asked.

"Chillax, sis, that's all sorted," Angel grinned, flipping her blonde extensions over her fake-tanned shoulders. "Gemma and I have decided to get out of London for the summer and head down to Cornwall to get some sun. What have we got to lose? She's not working and I'd had enough anyway even before Mrs Yuri and her silly old mole. Apparently Callum South's filming his reality show in Rock. Rock, Andi! Remember how we loved it there?"

Andi didn't reply and Angel sighed wearily.

"At least try and look excited for us. Who knows, maybe we'll get picked to appear on Cal's show? It'll be like Cornish *TOWIE*! I love Callum South, don't you? He's well fit!"

Andi grimaced. Callum South, the ex-Premier League footballer, was more famous these days for his battle of the bulge than his once glittering career. He was pretty much everywhere you looked, from billboards to magazines, and even she had seen bits of his reality series in which he'd had to lose weight by trying out extreme sports. No holds were barred and she had to admit it was compulsive viewing. Once, revoltingly, they even filmed his colonic irrigation. However attractive Callum South might be with his melting Malteser eyes and sexy Irish accent, it was a bit depressing if appearing on his show was the height of her sister's ambitions. The entire idea smacked of Gemma Pengelley. It was *exactly* the sort of hare-brained scheme she always hatched.

"Stop pulling faces; you'll get stuck," warned Angel. "Cal's well fit and I think it could be fun. Anyone who's anyone spends the summer there. London's practically empty. Who knows who we'll meet and what could happen?"

"Rock's really expensive," Andi said doubtfully. "How will you afford it?"

"Stop looking for all the negatives!" Angel shook her head. "Sis, you need to chill. We're not about to sleep on the streets! Gem's from Bodmin, remember? She knows somebody with a caravan in Rock we can have really cheap. We'll get summer jobs and have a right laugh." She paused and her face went all dreamy. "You never know, Prince Harry might be about! Maybe he'll take me to Rick Stein's?"

Andi laughed in spite of her despair. "Or perhaps he'll just moor his superyacht next to the windsurfing school, catch one look at you in your wetsuit and fall head over heels in love?"

"That's exactly it! Of course he will! Oh Andi, you should come too! It's about time you had some fun. You'd love it! We had some good times in Rock, didn't we? Before Mum died?"

Andi nodded. She didn't tend to look back much – it was too painful – but when she did think of those endless summers they were framed in her mind like golden snapshots of another life, a life before illness, grief and the misery of boarding school. She wasn't sure how she'd feel about going back. There were too many memories there, some happy and some painful. Her past wasn't so much a foreign country as another planet entirely.

"Stop being such a stick-in-the-mud," said Angel dismissively when Andi didn't jump at the offer. "I'll get a tan, do some wakeboarding and meet some hot guys." She grinned at this before adding as an afterthought, "Anyway, enough of me going on. Why weren't you in the office? Are you bunking? Or are you ill?" Her blue eyes narrowed suspiciously. "You look bloody awful."

That was hardly surprising because "bloody awful" was exactly how Andi felt – but Angel was so optimistic about her summer plans that Andi couldn't bear to start banging on about her own woes. Anyway, Angel had drunk most of the misery cocktail and if Andi lost her composure now there'd be nothing to blot out the pain. Maybe she'd go to M&S and buy a great big slice of Death by Chocolate instead? There were worse ways to go.

"It's nothing," Andi said.

Her sister gave her a hard stare. Angel knew Andi inside out. Nothing bonded sisters more than losing a parent and having to survive a concentration camp of a boarding school.

"Honestly, I'm fine," Andi fibbed.

Angel snorted. "You're a worse actor than Tom. By the way, why is he outside with his arm down the drain?"

Andi half sobbed, half laughed at this image. "It's a long story."

"I don't have to be anywhere," her sister said firmly. "I'm officially unemployed now, aren't I?" She sat on the sofa and patted the space next to her. "Come on, spill."

So Andi spilled. She took a big gulp of her revolting cocktail and proceeded to tell her sister all about the money going missing, Slimy Alan and losing her job – while Angel spat "bastard" and "git" at suitable intervals. But when Andi got to the part about Tom cheating, Angel was so incensed she snorted sludge-coloured liquid all over the sofa and Andi had to slap her hard on the back.

"I can't believe it! He was shagging fat Gina in your bed? And then he had the nerve to try and blame you?" Once she had got her breath back Angel shook her head in disbelief. "What a tosser! He stole your money *and* he was cheating on you? Bastard! What on earth did you ever see in him?"

Andi swallowed back tears. "I've no idea, but from this point on I swear to God that the only man in my life is Mr Kipling."

"I blame Gemma," said Angel. "If she hadn't introduced you in the first place none of this would have happened."

Andi smiled. "I don't think we can pin this one on Gemma. Messy flats and bad-for-us food, maybe, but she didn't force me to go out with Tom."

"Hmm." Angel was unconvinced. Andi had met Tom at one of Gemma's famous parties where the booze flowed, food was piled high and the most eclectic mix of people tended to appear and socialise. Gemma was a brilliant hostess: generous, warm-hearted and so sociable that people she randomly met at the bus stop or in the shops soon felt like treasured friends. They flocked to her like she was a partying Pied Piper. Tom had worked with Gemma on *Heartache High*, a teen school soap that had lasted for one season. He had ended up at one of her parties, where he'd made a beeline for Andi. The rest, unfortunately, was history.

"Don't blame me!" Gemma had wailed on the countless occasions when Angel berated her for inviting him in the first place. "I hardly knew the guy. He was only in two episodes and he played a teacher, so I didn't have any scenes with him. Anyway, I'm sure he wasn't such a tosser back then."

As far as Angel was concerned the jury was out on this one. In fairness to her friend, Tom had been working steadily in the early days of his relationship with Andi. But as the roles had dried up he'd taken to pitying himself and hanging out with a dope-smoking crowd who modelled themselves on *Withnail and I* – although when it came to work ethics they actually had more in common with the characters in *Shameless*. Angel had been to enough parties where she'd seen Tom stoned and maudlin to have made up her own mind about him. Maybe he had been talented once. Maybe not. In any case, the talent was draining away and all Angel saw was a parasite making her tender-hearted sister feel guilty. How many times had she heard him tell Andi that he'd given up his flat to move in with her and put his career on hold so that they could be together? Far too many times, was the answer, and it was all nonsense.

Angel might have been the younger sister but sometimes she felt about a hundred years older than Andi. Andi still believed in fairy tales and happy endings, whereas Angel was a firm believer that a girl made her own luck. That was why she was so excited about Gemma's plan to go to Rock.

"Well done for flushing that watch down the bog," she said admiringly. "Shame you couldn't stick Tom's head down after it and hold him under until the bubbles stopped."

Andi laughed in spite of herself. "Have you been hanging out with Mr Yuri?"

Angel grinned. "There's more to being a beautician than just giving facials! You'd be surprised what I've learned." She jumped up and, grabbing Andi's wrists, pulled her sister to her feet. "And one of the things I do know is that when a man does the dirty on her, the last thing a girl should do is sit and mope! Revenge is needed! Can't we dump tonnes of manure on his doorstep or something?"

Andi smiled. "Nice thought, but if he's at Gina's we share the same doorstep!"

"OK, bad idea," Angel agreed. "Here's a better one. How about we tip this disgusting drink down the sink, go to the pub and get hammered? Celebrate losing our jobs and having new adventures?"

Andi shook her head. All she wanted was to be left alone and allowed to have a good cry in peace before she started to rummage through the rubble of her life. There was a landlord to appease, a bank to plead with and an employment agency to call. The last thing she could afford to do, literally or metaphorically, was go on the lash with Angel.

"I don't feel like going out."

Her sister put her hands on her hips and fixed Andi with a determined look. It was the same look that over the years had seen Andi part with her dolls, do Angel's homework and, lately, dish out money. "There's no way I'm leaving you here breaking your heart over a knob-end like Tom. You've given him nearly two years. He doesn't deserve another second."

It was a valid point. Besides, what was left of Andi's misery cocktail was curdling in the jug. Goodness only knew what it was doing to their stomachs. Suddenly the idea of a cold glass of white wine was very appealing.

"Maybe just one then," she agreed.

"Fantastic!" Angel said. "Grab your purse, sis: I'm skint. I'll text Gemma and she can meet us. I think it's time we all put our heads together. Look on this as your lucky day – how do you fancy joining us in Cornwall?"

Andi stared at her. Could she really do it? Leave London and the flat, and step away from everything for the summer? At the thought of going back down to Cornwall her heart rose like a paper lantern. A break by the coast promised mental elbowroom, bright light and the sting of sea salt against her skin.

"Come on," urged Angel. "You know you want to be a Rock chick!"

Andi's bank account was empty, her boyfriend had left and she'd lost her job. Why on earth not? What did she have to lose? At that moment a Rock chick was *exactly* what she wanted to be.

Chapter 10

"Oh my God! Oh my God! I can see the sea!"

Angel's shriek in Andi's left eardrum was just about enough to make her weep. Her head was already pounding from listening to Gemma's Lady Gaga CD all the way from London to Cornwall; now it was ready to explode. By the time they'd joined the M4 Andi already knew the lyrics so well that she was confident she could put on a meat dress and double for Gaga should the star ever require a break; by the Tamar Bridge she was starting to wonder whether it was a new kind of torture. Death by "Poker Face". Add to this the roaring Beetle engine only inches behind her backside and the constant squeals and giggles from Angel, and it felt like a pneumatic drill was boring into Andi's brain. She'd popped so many painkillers she was in danger of developing a Nurofen addiction.

"The sea! The sea!" echoed Gemma, bouncing up and down in the driver's seat and craning her neck to glimpse the small slice of glittering blue nestling between hills that resembled Jordan's boobs.

"I can't believe we're nearly there!" Angel cried. She pogoed in her seat, the glimpse of Atlantic blue whizzing her back to her six-year-old self faster than you could say "tardis". Andi couldn't help but smile even though her neck was aching and she probably had deep-vein thrombosis. It was hard to move when you were sharing the back seat of a car with three suitcases, a hatbox and more pairs of shoes than you could count. And that was before she added in the endless chocolate wrappers, empty cans and sweet papers that had been constantly lobbed into the back seat. It had been like sitting in a skip for five hours.

Turning to her, Angel said excitedly, "Oh my God, Andi! We're back after all this time! Can you believe you're going to be in Rock for the whole summer?"

The short answer to this question was a resounding and heartfelt *no,* because Andi couldn't quite believe that she was in Rock. Normally on a Wednesday morning she was sitting at her desk, frantically hoping Zoe would leave her alone for just one day and trying to wrestle figures into submission. By lunchtime she would be cross-eyed from staring at the screen and only able to make it through the day by emailing PMB for a chat. Andi wondered who had taken over her role and whether PMB would miss chatting to her? Probably not, she told herself sternly. He probably had a life. She hoped Zoe hadn't told him that Andi had been sacked for taking credit for another colleague's work. That thought made her skin prickle with mortification. Apart from the fact that it was untrue, she couldn't bear the idea of him thinking badly of her. Somehow she had to clear her name. Maybe once she was away from the city and had some thinking space she'd come up with something? At the moment, though, her brain felt as if it had turned to cottage cheese.

As the car began the descent towards the seaside town, Andi thought about how her life had taken a very odd turn. A week ago she was an accountant at a prestigious company, working on the figures for Britain's answer to Microsoft and living with her long-term boyfriend in a small but comfortable flat. Fast-forward a week or so and here she was, suddenly homeless, penniless, unemployed and on her way to Rock to share a caravan with her sister and her sister's bonkers friend.

Even Russell Grant couldn't have seen this coming.

Andi was just contemplating, for the umpteenth time, the horrifying and gut-churning discovery that Tom had not only cheated physically but also emptied all her accounts and maxed out her credit cards to boot, when Gemma slammed on the brakes with such force that several bags flew off the parcel shelf and walloped Andi on the head.

"Ouch!" she gasped. There was something really hard in that fake Louis Vuitton holdall. There was probably a dent in her skull now. Maybe she had concussion too? She could hear a really weird buzzing sound...

"Gemma! Don't look at the sea! Look where you're going!" cried Angel, her hands over her eyes. "We've got all summer to look at the view!"

"Oops! Sorry!" giggled Gemma. She ground the gears; the Beetle kangarooed forwards and another bag smacked Andi on the head.

"I can hear buzzing," Andi said, wrestling the holdall back into position. "Either I have a head injury or else your electric toothbrush has been set off."

Gemma chuckled. She caught Andi's eye in the rear-view mirror and winked.

"I hate to break it to you, but that is not my *toothbrush*!"

Andi recoiled from the bag as though scalded while her sister and her best friend cackled with mirth. She felt about a hundred and ninety. She was thrilled to be back in Cornwall, and the moment they had crossed the Tamar her stomach had pancake-flipped with excitement – but for the life of her she just couldn't summon up the exuberance and energy that fizzed from the other two. Andi supposed this was hardly surprising. She'd just broken up with her long-term boyfriend, and although she wasn't breaking her heart over him she was bound to be a bit flat.

Andi had never seriously intended to join the girls on their westerly pilgrimage to find sunshine, fame and millionaires. It had been a wonderful slice of escapism for a few hours on that blackest of black Mondays to listen to Gemma and Angel planning their summer and how they would be bound to find Callum South in one of the cafés or maybe running along the water's edge. As the white wine had flowed and the pain of the day had begun to blur around the edges, Andi had almost believed that she too would be journeying westwards and spending the summer by the ocean. In her mind's eye she'd seen herself wearing frayed denim cut-offs and deck shoes, her hair caught up in a simple knot at the nape of her neck; she'd be sitting on the edge of the pontoon, bare legs dangling as she watched the flotilla of boats bobbing on the estuary. She had almost felt the warm sunshine on her skin and heard the slap of waves against hulls. But of course reality was different. Deep in her heart Andi had known that she would have to wake up the next day, take two Alka-Seltzers and then deal with the car crash of her life. She'd ended up moving in with Gemma and Angel because she'd shortly afterwards discovered that landlords didn't take "my cheating bastard boyfriend stole all my money" as a valid reason for not being able to pay the rent.

Living with the girls had certainly been an education. Slugs roamed free in the kitchen, dirty plates festered in the sink and all Andi could find in the fridge was nail varnish and rotting veg. When she lay on the sofa at night, alternating between sobbing over her finances and worrying about Tom's threats, she could practically hear the listeria and E. coli having a chat from the sticky work surfaces. After a week with the girls Andi felt as though she needed to bathe in disinfectant and dreaded to think what they'd do to a caravan. Public Health would probably condemn it after a week. But she didn't have a choice.

Andi had no money and no job. Tom had been given access to her banking details, so the bank wasn't obliged to compensate her – and there was no hope of ever seeing a penny back from him. It was a truth universally acknowledged, that a young woman in possession of sod all must be in want of a place to live. Andi couldn't afford the Balham/Clapham flat, Tom had nicked her cardboard box on his exit, and so she had ended up on the sofa at Angel and Gemma's place. A bed of nails would have been more comfortable, but at least she'd had somewhere to go while she attempted to decide what to do next.

Andi sighed. It had probably been easier for Einstein to figure out his theory of relativity. At the moment she couldn't see much further than either panicking or ranting or, when she wasn't engaged in those activities, eating all the cakes Gemma insisted on baking. For a girl who was always on a diet Gemma had some very odd ideas about what was healthy. Andi was pretty certain that carrot cake couldn't really be classed as one of your five a day. Still, there was no doubt about it, Gemma Pengelley was an amazing cook and Andi had enjoyed comfort-eating every calorific mouthful. She figured she deserved a lot of comforting. She might as well add getting fat to her list of woes. Maybe Callum South could hire her for his show? Andi smiled in spite of herself: if you couldn't beat them, join them.

Anyway, now Angel and Gemma had quit their flat and were out of Tooting on their wild goose chase to Cornwall. Andi hadn't really any choice but to throw her lot in with them and come too. She had contemplated contacting her father for some help but the thought of his silent disappointment seeping down the phone line had frozen her finger every time she almost called him. Andi had spent the past twenty-nine years feeling as though she was a big letdown to her father. No matter how hard she tried, she was never able to please him. She hadn't achieved the A-level grades he'd expected; she hadn't followed in his footsteps to Magdalen College in Oxford; and her job, although steady, wasn't something he could boast about at embassy soirées. If she asked him for help he would probably loan her some money, but Andi knew she'd be paying it back in more ways than one. Sharing a caravan with Angel and Gemma was definitely the lesser of two evils. At least she could keep an eye on Angel. Surely her sister couldn't get up to much in a quiet Cornish seaside town?

The car breasted the top of a hill, then coasted downwards – and suddenly they were in Rock. The road dropped away steeply to the turquoise ribbon of the Camel Estuary twinkling in the sunshine and braided on each side with egg-yolk yellow sand. Moored boats danced on the tide, Padstow glittered across the water and a RIB zipped by, leaving a paper-doily wake across the shimmering surface. To her left and right, chunky Range Rover Sports, BMW X5s and Porsche Cayennes lined the streets while impossibly skinny women with golden tans, tortoiseshell hair and huge shades meandered along the road. There wasn't a clapped-out banger or scruffy person in sight. Suddenly conscious of her own lank hair and soggy jeans, Andi sank back into the seat.

Talk about hitting Rock Bottom. She was practically ready to dig.

Andi *knew* she was no good at positive thinking. Here she was, arriving in one of the most beautiful seaside towns in Britain, and she was still moping. She couldn't possibly have any more tears left to shed, surely? She had to get a grip and try to make the most of being here. She was bound to find some kind of a job; in the meantime, she could work out a way of getting her money back from Tom, a way that didn't involve threatening to chop off his bollocks as Angel had so temptingly suggested. She could live cheaply here and get herself together for a bit.

"We're here! We're here!" Angel chanted, her eyes big blue saucers of excitement. Turning around she cried, "Look, Andi! There's Ocean View! It's hardly changed!"

Sure enough, there was the beautiful old house where, until their mother had died, the Evans sisters had spent every summer. Ocean View was one of Andi's favourite places in the world. Rented by her father for the whole summer break, long before the royals and the Hooray Henrys discovered Rock, it was a higgledy-piggledy New England style affair, all weathered clapboard and turrets and widow's walk. Perched high on the hillside, surrounded by ancient cedar trees, it overlooked the sparkling Camel Estuary and gazed dreamily towards the Atlantic. Over the years various owners had added to it and decorated it, but in Andi's imagination it remained as it had always been, a rather tatty and beloved family haven filled with powdery sand and children and happy sunshiny memories.

"We have to stop!" Angel ordered Gemma. Already she was pulling on her shades and gathering her things up into her bag. "Let's get a coffee in The Wharf Café and see what's going on!"

Gemma didn't need asking twice. "Callum could be about. I saw on Twitter he's been spotted there and his Facebook Fan page says he was at the Ski School yesterday. Let's check it out."

Somehow she squeezed the car into a minuscule gap between a Lotus and a convertible Mini. Andi stumbled out of the car and onto the pavement, her legs coming back to life in a gush of pins and needles. Since Gemma drove as if the motorway was her own personal game of dodgems, Andi felt like kissing the tarmac, Pope style. She had survived the journey! Maybe this was positive thought number one?

"You guys go ahead," Andi said when her sister tried to nudge her towards the café, all funky chrome and glass and where Andi knew her final ten pounds in the world would not last long. "I want to stretch my legs."

Angel looked doubtful. She'd practically been on suicide watch since Empty Bank Account day. "Are you sure?"

Andi nodded. "I'll catch up with you in a bit."

Angel and Gemma headed off into the town, fake designer shades firmly perched on top of their artfully tousled hair, and Andi wandered back up the main street to the newsagents. Unlike her sister, whose nose had been buried in *Heat* for most of the journey, she had a burning and very square urge to buy a copy of the *FT*. She might not be working at the moment, but she still liked to keep up to speed with everything. Like the Safe T Net flotation, for example. From what she'd read it had gone phenomenally well and for a ridiculous amount of money too. Aston Martin man was now worth the kind of crazy money Bond villains used to ransom the world for. One gazillion dollars! Mawahahahaa!

Right now Andi would be happy with twenty quid...

The shop was quiet and cool. It was late afternoon and everybody was either on the beach or waterskiing. Andi browsed the newspapers for a while before selecting the local one, (with the vague hope that she might find a job) as well as the last copy of the *FT*. She was just reaching out to scoop it up when a man beat her to it.

"Oh, sorry! Did you want that?" he asked, turning to her. Eyes the same turquoise hue as the sparkling water outside met hers and he smiled apologetically.

Andi found herself thinking that if life was one of Angel's pink books with shoes on the cover, this was the point where her stomach should turn into melting ice cream and her heart should start to flutter at his shy lopsided smile. Then she'd notice the sharp planes of his face and the perfect bone structure of his skull beneath the moleskin-short haircut, before her eyes drifted down to take in a muscular, tee-shirt-clad chest and strong legs below board shorts. Yes, in the world of Angel's books Andi would probably fall head over heels in love. But because this was the real world and right now she liked men about as much as Superman liked Kryptonite, all she could think was *Step away from my* FT, *buster!*

"Please, you take it," he said, offering her the pink sheets. "My brother-in-law asked me to pick it up but he's supposed to be having a break from work. To be honest, I've no idea why he needs the *FT* when he's on holiday. Kicking drugs must be easier than quitting the world of business!"

Andi laughed in spite of herself. "To be honest I don't need it either. Please take it."

The man shook his head. "If Mel catches Simon working while he's supposed to be on the family holiday she'll probably file for divorce! You'll be doing my nephews a favour."

The paper was held out. Andi touched the pink pages tentatively. "Really?"

He nodded. "Really. Or else it will all be your fault when they get divorced and the boys have a broken home."

Andi couldn't have that on her conscience.

"I'd better have the paper," she agreed.

Leaving *FT* man flicking through a copy of *Closer* – this issue with a red-faced Callum South plastered all over the front – Andi made for the till, only to discover that her purse was totally empty. For a few dreadful seconds she ransacked every possible pocket and hiding place where a shy tenner could lurk, but no luck. Her final ten-pound note, all the money she had in the world, had vanished – and Andi had a good idea where to. Angel must have swiped it and her change when she borrowed Andi's purse to buy her magazines.

Andi felt as though she was under water. It really had all gone to hell in a handcart now that the sum of her worldly goods could be spent on *Heat*

"I'm sorry," she said to the shopkeeper, feeling dangerously close to tears all of a sudden. "I seem to be out of cash."

"We have a cash machine here, my love," the shopkeeper said helpfully. "And we take cards."

Andi thought she'd probably have more luck going down to the beach and coaxing blood out of the pebbles than getting her Visa card to play ball.

"I'll have to leave it," she said, her throat tight. "I'm really sorry."

Abandoning the paper on the counter, Andi dashed out of the shop. Once outside in the bright sunshine she blinked rapidly and tried to slow her jagged breathing. This was just a blip. Things could only get better – or at least she bloody well hoped they could. Taking a deep breath, she squared her shoulders and started to walk down the main street towards The Wharf Café. Once she'd found her sister and wrestled her money back, Andi was going to buy herself a big glass of wine and drown her sorrows. And if that failed she could always hurl herself in the estuary.

"Excuse me! You forgot this!"

It was the man from the shop. He caught Andi up and was brandishing the *FT* at her.

"I didn't pay for it," Andi said awkwardly. "I forgot my money. You'd better take it back."

He smiled and she noticed how his eyes crinkled at the corners. He must smile an awful lot. "Don't look so worried; I haven't nicked it. I bought it for you."

Andi stared at him. Why would he do that? Why was he being kind? Was he some sort of nutter? It would be just her luck to meet the local loony only minutes into her stay.

"I promise I'm not a crazy stalker," the man said hastily, accurately reading her expression. "It's just that I can see how much you want that paper and how upset you seemed when I nearly took it. Look, if it makes you feel awkward, how about we share it? There's a little boatyard up the road that has a café. It's not posh, I'm afraid, but we could get a coffee and you can read the paper. Then I'll take it home."

"I can't let you do that," Andi said, flustered. "Besides, I thought your sister would file for divorce?"

He laughed. "I doubt she means it, Mel's been bossing Si around since they were teenagers. She'd be lost without him to nag. Still, I'm prepared to take the risk. How about you?"

He paused expectantly. The paper hovered above her fingertips. Then, as though it had a mind of its own, Andi's hand took it.

"Phew!" he said, miming mopping his brow. "My ego was in serious danger there! I'm Jonty, by the way."

"Miranda," she told him. "But everyone calls me Andi."

"So, Andi, what do you say? Will you let me buy you a coffee?"

She paused. Down the hill Gemma and Angel would be posing in The Wharf Café, Angel tossing her hair extensions and waiting for a celebrity or millionaire to wander past. Andi supposed she could join them and ruin things by sitting there like a black cloud or she could go for a quiet coffee with this kind stranger, her knight in shining newsprint.

It was one coffee, that was all: one coffee, which she couldn't even afford to buy herself. Coffee and a read of the financial pages. So why on earth not?

After all, what had she got to lose?

Chapter 11

"How brilliant is this?" Angel asked, raising her coffee cup at Gemma. "Here's to our summer! Cheers!"

"Cheers," Gemma echoed, chinking her cup against Angel's. She took a sip of ice-cold Chardonnay and could have wept with happiness. Honestly, it hardly seemed real that only this morning she'd woken up to the rumbling of traffic and beneath a leaden sky and now she was sitting on a roof terrace with nothing but the cry of the gulls in her ears and a light southerly wind lifting her curls.

Although it was a midweek afternoon the terrace was rammed with people, all of whom had that rosy glow that came with endless days spent on the water and middle-class wealth. Bright Seasalt-branded bags sat bulkily below the metal-legged tables, Mulberry satchels were slung casually over the backs of chairs and an array of prints by Joules, Cath Kidston and White Stuff prints were jumbled together in a laughing and glamorous patchwork. Tanned feet, as smooth and as brown as butterscotch, were thrust into expensive deck shoes and Gemma instantly wished she wasn't wearing her stinky old Skechers that had seen better days. She'd forgotten how Rock had its own look, a curious blend of the shabby but expensive, and she suddenly felt self-conscious in her elasticated-waistband jeans and George hoody. Everybody looked so ridiculously glam and thin! She seriously had to diet.

Gemma pushed her packet of hand-cut salt-and-balsamic-vinegar crisps away. She really needed to get her eating under control and this was the time to start. For a moment her hand hovered over the packet before she caved in. It had been ages since lunch and they didn't have any food for supper. Until she went to Bodmin's branch of Asda, these crisps were all she had. It would be silly to waste them.

As she munched away Gemma noticed that although Angel also stuck out like a sore thumb in her tight white jeans, glittery pink vest and sky-high wedges, she seemed totally oblivious. Sipping wine and scrolling through the contact list on her iPhone, Angel was every bit as at home among the moneyed, nautical set as she was trawling the boutiques of Kensington. Fake tanned, false eyelashed and sporting a full face of make-up, she was glammed up to the nines and pretending not to notice the admiring glances thrown her way by practically every guy in the place. Project Rich Guy was clearly go.

Gemma sighed. She may as well as have been wearing Harry Potter's invisibility cloak. That was what being fat did for a girl. If only she could chance upon Callum South's production crew, or even the man himself. This was the key to solving all of her problems, she was sure of it. Unlike Angel, Gemma had no hopes that Prince Charming was about to roar by on his Sunseeker and sweep her off her feet. She was so heavy she'd probably sink his boat. No, for Gemma the path to fame and fortune was not going to come from being beautiful. She was going to have to get herself noticed in a different fashion. She was going to have to be creative.

Angel drained her skinny latte and set it down with a resolute thump.

"Right, there's nobody in here worth hanging about for," she said dismissively. "Just lots of day trippers and holidaymakers. How about we shoot across to Padstow and see what's going on at Rick Stein's?"

Gemma, tired after her long drive, didn't think she could face queuing for the ferry and then fighting her way through the hordes in Padstow. Besides, she'd promised to check in with the Tregartens, the owners of their caravan, before it got too late. She knew that as soon as Angel was in Padstow she'd be tweeting selfies outside the world-famous seafood restaurant and updating her social network site non-stop with pictures and micro blogs. Then she'd probably hit the shops for another few hours before settling herself down prettily at the harbour side in case a passing millionaire showed up to give her a lift back to Rock on his superyacht. Having a fat friend in tow was only going to cramp her style.

"I think I'll go and check out the caravan," she began – but was swiftly cut off.

"Ssh! Are you crazy! Don't mention that here! Or anywhere, in fact."

Gemma was confused. "Mention what?"

Angel lent forward. "The C word," she whispered. "Caravan. We don't want anyone knowing we're living in a caravan."

They didn't? This was news to Gemma. "Why not?"

"Because we want to fit in. Look around you. Do you think anyone in here is staying in a *caravan?*"

Gemma glanced around. The café crowd, groomed and glossy as corn-fed ponies, looked as though they had stepped out of the Fat Face catalogue, via Boden. Most of them would be staying in the stunning second homes strung out like charms on Pandora bracelets, along the coast from Rock to Daymer Bay. These people had probably never been in a caravan in their lives.

"The point is," Angel continued, her eyes taking on the kind of glint more commonly associated with religious fanatics, "that we *look* as though we are *exactly* the same as them. If we make sure we're eating in the right restaurants, even if it's just a starter at Jamie Oliver's or chips from Rick Stein's takeaway, then we're going to be mingling with the right crowd. If I wanted to hang out with people who go camping I'd have gone to bloody Glastonbury!"

Gemma wasn't convinced. "I thought we were here to get on Callum South's show?"

Angel flipped her new blonde extensions (the end result of yet another maxed-out credit card) back from her shoulders and scooped them up onto her head in an untidy updo that was instantly the pinnacle of messy chic. If she lived to be a hundred years old, Gemma knew she could never pull off that kind of skinny grunge glam. Feeling a familiar stab of despair she crammed another handful of crisps into her mouth and munched hard.

"Babes, that's more your thing than mine, being an actress and everything," Angel said kindly.

"You mean you're already skinny and I'm a fat lump," said Gemma thickly through her crisps.

Angel sighed. "No, I mean because you have your heart set on that show. I'm looking for something different, something for me. I'm not sure what that's going to be yet but I do know I won't find it sitting in a café eating carbs. I need to be seen in all the right places. The kind of guys I'm hoping to meet won't be in here all day any more than they'll be at Butlins. They'll be out in their boats, eating at Stein's and cruising around in supercars. I need to make sure that's where I am too. Even if I'm just having a glass of fizzy water in the yacht club then at least I'll be in the right place."

Gemma stared at her. "So let me get this right. You're only here to look for a rich man? Forty years of feminism and it's come to this?"

Angel shrugged her slender shoulders. "It was good enough Kate Middleton." Her smooth brow pleated. "Maybe I was too hasty dropping out of uni?"

"You were at UCL, not St Andrews," pointed out Gemma.

"True. Anyway, I'm not saying that I'm not looking for love either." Angel crossed her fingers under the table. The last thing she needed was love. That only complicated things, as far as she could see. Look how much her mother had adored Alex Evans – it hadn't exactly done her any favours. And Andi was as bad, breaking her heart over that bloody Tom. No, as far as Angel was concerned it was Project Rich Guy all the way from now on in. If he happened to be a pop star or even a footballer that was fine by her. She wasn't going to be totally fussy. "But it's time I set my sights a little higher. Besides, I think if I try to break into any more private estate I'll end up doing time!"

The girls laughed. In the corner of the café, just in the shade and sitting alone, a slender man with long floppy hair the colour of treacle looked up. Catching Gemma's eye he smiled and raised his glass. A chunky watch sat snugly on his wrist and designer sunglasses were pushed back into his hair. Angel was seemingly oblivious, but Gemma felt herself start to do a beetroot impression. Oh God. She was simply hopeless at all this flirting and impressing stuff. In fact, Gemma decided, she actively hated it. She much preferred it once you were actually settled into a relationship, when all that insecurity had vanished and you both knew exactly where you stood. Then you could cosy up on the sofa watching DVDs and eating curry to your heart's content, wear your pyjamas and not worry whether or not somebody liked you. In the morning you'd wake up all snuggled up together before wandering into town hand in hand to have a bacon sandwich or maybe a pastry.

Oh God. No wonder she was so fat. Even her romantic fantasies involved grub. Maybe she should just get off with the Little Chef and be done with it? It was just as well she was here to try and get herself featured on a weight-loss show.

"Anyway, probably best you do stay around," Angel said, fishing change out of her Radley purse. "Andi won't be far away and I don't like to think of her being on her own at the moment. She's having a tough time."

Gemma nodded. She didn't know Andi that well but she sympathised with her and had been trying really hard to cheer her up the best way she knew how – by cooking delicious cakes.

"She knows where we're staying," Angel added, "but if I know my sister she'll probably be trying to get a signal on her BlackBerry and figure out what the FTSE's doing or something. Let's hope she can kick back a bit here or else we're all in trouble."

Having settled the bill, the girls parted: Angel headed down to the beach to hop on the water taxi while Gemma meandered back through the town. It had been several years since Gemma had last visited and she was surprised by how many new buildings had appeared. Several old timber-framed houses had vanished and vast glass and wood structures had sprung up in their place, their windows blinking in the late afternoon sunshine like bright eyes enjoying unrivalled views over the town. Outside them on immaculately raked gravel drives Aston Martins nestled next to Range Rover Sports and funky new Beetle convertibles, the Rock teenage driver's weapon of choice. Warmed by the sun and charmed by the views that met her at every turn like a living tapestry, Gemma spent a happy couple of hours wandering through the town. Not once did she bump into Andi, which surprised her because the town wasn't very big. Gemma had heard Andi crying quietly the night before and she really felt for her friend's sister. She'd soaked a few pillows herself when Nick had dumped her. It wasn't nice. Maybe Angel's practical approach did make more sense?

Gemma was just about to retrace her steps to the car, via the beach again just in case Andi was there, when the smell of pasties stopped her in her tracks. For a second she was transported back to her mother's kitchen, doing her homework at the old oak table while Demelza Pengelley fried up onions, swede, potato and beef in an ancient skillet. Just the thought of how the golden pastry rose in the Aga made her mouth water. Oh God. A real Cornish pasty! Not one of those limp and pallid imposters they tried to fob her off with in London! Gemma's stomach rumbled. Maybe she should buy one just as a welcome-back-to-Kernow treat? One wouldn't hurt, would it?

It was as though her feet had a life all of their own. Before she even knew what she was doing Gemma found herself following the meaty aroma through the main street and up a tiny side road, so small and narrow that she might have overlooked it if she hadn't been so intent upon her quest. Up the street she walked, her strides gaining a pace that Davina, Josie and Jordan's workouts had never inspired. At last she saw it: a shop with a small steamed-up window and faded awning shimmering in the evening sun like a mirage.

Rock Cakes.

Cakes, buns and sausage rolls; Gemma didn't care about those right now. All she knew was that she had to get to those pasties! She had to sink her teeth into the soft pastry, feel it crumbling and flaking against her lips, gasp when the hot air puffed against her tongue.

Who needed men when there were pasties in the world?

Like an Olympian only seconds from the finish line, Gemma picked up speed. Nothing mattered now except getting her hands on those pasties. She'd buy one each for Andi and Angel too. That wasn't being greedy: it was finding dinner.

If Gemma could diet half as well as she could make excuses she knew she'd be a size zero by bedtime…

Three steps, two steps, one step and she was there! Almost giddy with relief, Gemma launched herself at the door, seconds away from her goal and fuelled by a ferocious hunger. In seconds she would be biting down into pastry…

But unfortunately Gemma's pasty vision stopped her from actually looking where she was going. Just as she shoved the bakery door open a plump man was stepping out of the shop, his arms filled with fat sweating packages and boxes of cream cakes. The door slammed into his stomach with such force that the goodies he was holding flew into the air. Sausage rolls, saffron buns and éclairs rained a calorie shower; cream splattered the floor and pastry drifted like flaky autumn leaves.

It was carb carnage.

But it wasn't the mess that made Gemma cry out in horror. If the only problem were the mess she would have been fine. No, it was worse than that. Much worse. The man she had crashed into and covered in food was none other than Callum South.

Chapter 12

"Here we go! Two bog standard coffees and a couple of slices of carrot cake."

Jonty placed two white mugs, a packet of biscuits and some huge wodges of cake onto the weathered picnic table and motioned at Andi to take a seat. This was easier said than done because the splintering wood was smattered with seagull droppings, but eventually she managed to find a fairly safe patch. Once seated, she wrapped her hands around the chunky ceramic.

"Believe me, this is great," she told him with a grateful smile. "Any coffee, bog standard or otherwise, is more than welcome. And the cake looks great too, so thanks."

He smiled back. Although his eyes were hidden behind shades, Andi could already tell that they were crinkling and twinkly. Jonty, *FT* angel, seemed to smile a lot.

"My pleasure. But you've probably already gathered there's nothing much on offer here that isn't bog standard," he said, swinging his tanned legs over the bench and then reaching for the sugar bowl. "There's nothing posh like a latte, I'm afraid."

He was right: Andi had already gathered this. The café was, as Jonty had warned her earlier on, basic. They had walked a little way out of Rock, leaving behind the more stylish establishments with their distressed tables and chairs and loops of shabby-chic bunting, and climbed the hill to an industrial estate. Jonty wound his way between the units, chatting easily about the small boatyard they passed and filling her in on which royals had been taught to waterski by the tousle-haired owner who waved cheerily at them. Angel would love to hear all this,

Andi thought, but she wouldn't have been quite so impressed with the ex shellfish-packing unit – still complete with eau de seafood – that now served as workman's café to the marine engineers and ski instructors. A tea urn, a chiller cabinet with a few exhausted ham sandwiches, and some plastic tables completed the look. Outside, two ancient picnic tables had been abandoned on a patch of grass at such an acute angle that they listed drunkenly.

They did have a sign up advertising a vacancy for part-time staff though. Andi had made enough cups of coffee for her office colleagues in the past to feel confident that she could cope with the job. She'd make an enquiry before they left. *You never know*, she thought, *maybe I'll be able to pick up some work?*

In the meantime Andi was eternally grateful to Jonty for the coffee and cake. Several calls to Angel had gone unanswered and until she found her sister she was penniless. Any coffee, unsophisticated or otherwise, was very much appreciated. Lattes were out of her budget for the foreseeable future; that was for sure. As were food, rent and basic survival, unless she managed to get her act together somehow. This carrot cake would have to last her until Angel or Gemma went shopping. Since Angel existed on thin air and Gemma would guzzle all the food before it even reached the fridge, Andi was very happy to see that cake.

"Honestly, this is great," she assured him.

Jonty had helped himself to several packets of sugar. Ripping each packet open with strong white teeth, he tipped the lot into his mug and swirled the liquid around with enthusiasm. "I really like it here. It's honest, you know? Real. And you don't need to remortgage just to buy a couple of coffees. I'm working on my boat at the minute too, so I'm up here a lot. To be honest, I probably don't have blood anymore – I just have Nescafé flowing through my veins!"

Andi laughed. She'd felt similar when she'd been wrapping up the Safe T Net accounts. At one point she'd almost contemplated bypassing the water altogether and just spooning the coffee granules straight into her mouth. What a waste of all her efforts that project had turned out to be.

"What sort of boat is it?" she asked, determined not to spoil the sunny afternoon by dwelling on Alan and his lies.

The boatyard they'd passed had been crammed full of all types of watercraft, from graceful yachts with glowing wooden decks and sweet little portholes to huge gleaming powerboats with fuel-guzzling engines and propellers that were bigger than she was. All status symbols of course; after all, this was Rock and what did any wealthy holidaying exec need to broadcast his success more in this town than a flashy boat?

"Nothing very glamorous, I'm afraid," Jonty told her, pushing his sunglasses back onto his head. His turquoise eyes were bright with enthusiasm. "She's just a little fibreglass boat, called a Glastron, about fourteen feet long. She's hardly a gin palace but she's the perfect size for scooting around the estuary and popping out to sea on a calm day. Or rather she will be once I've finished working on her."

What Andi knew about boats could fit on a postage stamp, and there'd still be room left over. She liked looking at them though. When they'd been in Rock as children her father had spent one summer tearing up and down the estuary on a speedboat, the latest in a long line of intense and short-lived passions. Andi and Angel had loved every adrenalin-filled second and had been bitterly disappointed when Alex sold it.

"Is there a lot to do?" she asked politely. Quite what you did with a boat Andi had no idea. You didn't really come across that many in Clapham.

He laughed. "You could say that! I found her in a garden where she'd been for about six years. She'd made a lovely container for geraniums. She's ten years older than me but I figure that with a bit of TLC she'll be able to return to her former retro glory. I bought her a few years back as a project but work kind of got in the way so she's just been sitting in a shed, looking more like a plant pot than a boat. I'm lucky Rock in Bloom haven't pinched her!"

"So you're not working?" Andi asked and then could have kicked herself. Who knew better than her about how sensitive an issue this could be? She'd assumed that he was just a bit of a beach bum, spending the summer tinkering with boats and topping up his money with a spot of bar work. His tan suggested that he spent time outside rather than in the office and his clothes weren't designer garments. Talk about making assumptions. For all she knew Jonty could have been laid off too. Luckily he didn't seem worried by her question. Instead he was busily dunking digestives into his mug.

"I'm kind of between jobs at the minute," he said through a mouthful of biscuit, "so I thought I'd finish an old project before I get my teeth into a new one. I'm having some time out and my brother-in-law, the workaholic one I told you about, is letting me crash in the pool house for the summer. I'll do a few bits and pieces about the place and take the kids out wakeboarding and skiing. Knowing my sister, I'll probably end up walking the dogs and doing the shopping too! Mel loves to organise everybody."

"So the doing up the boat will be an escape." Andi knew all about life with a demanding sibling. She had the empty purse and grey hairs to prove it.

Jonty looked bashful. "Look, you can laugh if you like at this, but having one of these boats has been a dream of mine ever since I saw *Live and Let Die* when I was a kid. Back when Bond was about a bit more than Daniel Craig's swimming trunks, I watched that speedboat leap out of the river and I knew when I grew up I had to have one. It's just taken a little longer than I'd imagined."

"So I'm having coffee with James Bond?"

"This coffee is definitely stirred not shaken," he joked. "Besides, aren't all men James Bond in their heads?"

"I'm the last person who could tell you what goes on in a man's head," said Andi darkly.

Jonty raised an eyebrow Roger Moore style. "I sense issues?"

"No more than anyone else." There was no way Andi was going to be drawn into discussing her personal life with a total stranger, even one who was easy to chat to and had bought her an *FT*. To change the subject she said, "So when you're not being a secret agent, what do you do?"

Jonty shrugged. "It's very boring to be honest. I used to work in ICT. Real nerdy stuff. I'm not nearly so glam as my brother-in-law. He does all sorts of exciting things. You might have heard of him? Simon Rothwell? Last week he was overseeing the merger of two major television companies, and the last I heard he'd been asked to be the chairman of Mermaid Media."

Andi was impressed. No wonder Jonty's brother-in-law had wanted the *Financial Times*. Mermaid Media was huge. Not only did they own

television and film companies but they also owned Vidz and Gamz! –
Britain's biggest video-games chain store. She'd seen their share prices
rocket over the past eighteen months.

"In that case he'd better have this back," she said, sliding the *Financial
Times* back across the picnic table.

"Christ, no!" Jonty looked horrified. "I told you earlier: Mel will go
mental if she catches Si working when they're supposed to be having
family time. That's the whole point of them being down here for the
summer. He's promised her that he'll take some time out. Anyway,
don't you need it? You seemed really frantic earlier on."

Earlier on Andi had been frantic. Now with the late afternoon sun
warming her face, and with cake filling her stomach, she didn't feel
quite as hysterical. If she was offered some work at the café then that
sickening, lurching sense of panic might subside too.

"It's fine. To be honest it was more habit than anything else. I'm just
so used to reading the *FT* for work that it's become second nature."

"You're on holiday. Leave all that behind. There's more to life than
work."

This was easy for him to say, Andi thought bitterly. Crumbling a
piece of cake between her fingers she stole a look at him from behind
her fringe. With his golden tan, cinnamon dusting of freckles and
sprinkle of dark stubble, Jonty was certainly the typical Rock guy. The
town was full of men like him – a bit surfy and a bit boaty. They
dropped out and did bits and pieces all summer, cut a dash zooming
across the estuary on their waterskis, tinkered with boat engines for
some cash in hand, chatted up the tourists in the bars and claimed the
dole all winter. No, for guys like Jonty there probably was a lot more to

life than work. Right now though Andi couldn't quite imagine for the life of her what this might be.

"I'm not on holiday exactly," she said.

Jonty didn't reply, perhaps sensing that she had more to add. Andi pushed a lock of hair back behind her ear and sighed. Oh sod it, what did it matter? She'd probably never see him again anyway.

"I lost my job," she explained. "I'm a casualty of the recession, apparently. My sister and her friend are here for the summer so I've tagged along. The master plan is that I can get a summer job and buy myself a bit of time. A bit like you, I'm working out what to do next."

She pushed her plate away and stood up. Suddenly, sitting chatting and scoffing cake seemed like the most ridiculous, indulgent luxury when she had to find work. "In fact, there's no time like the present, is there? I'm going to go and ask about the vacancy here."

Jonty reached out and put a hand on her arm. His fingers were strong and suntanned against her own pale skin.

"Christ! Don't do that! Angie's a tartar! You'd have an easier time working for Attila the Hun! Honestly, I'm not exaggerating. The last girl who worked here lasted about twenty minutes."

Andi pulled a face. "Beggars can't be choosers."

Jonty's hand was still on her arm. Awkwardly he removed it.

"Look, tell me to get lost if you like, but you certainly don't strike me as a beggar and I don't think slaving over a tea urn is your great calling in life either. There's got to be something else you can try? What do you usually do, when you're not drinking coffee with strangers you've practically wrestled to the ground for their *FT*?"

Andi laughed in spite of herself.

"That's more like it," he said. "Come on, sit down. Chill for a bit. Believe me, that job will still be there tomorrow. Nobody else in Rock would dream of working for Angie. What exactly do you do?"

For a split second she almost told him everything, all about Hart Frozer and Alan and the unfairness of losing her job. Then, luckily, her brain engaged and stopped her tongue in time. There was no way she was blabbing about it all to a total stranger. Besides, Rock was supposed to be her fresh start. Neither was she was admitting to being a qualified accountant, not when Jonty's brother-in-law was such an eminent one, the Harrods to her Primark of accounting. Hart Frozer may well have been one of the UK's premier accountancy consultants but it hardly compared. There was no way she wanted to admit that she'd been fired. However unfair and untrue it was, mud had a nasty way of sticking.

"I'm a bookkeeper," she said, sinking back onto the bench and pretending to find the splintering tabletop fascinating. "I do a bit of everything really, from accounts to odds and ends for my boss."

Jonty stared at her thoughtfully. "A bit like a PA?"

Andi liked this idea. She'd been Zoe's bitch, after all, which was practically the same thing.

"I guess so."

"A PA who does accounts and who reads the *Financial Times*?" Jonty said slowly. "Andi, this is a bit of a long shot, and it might not come to anything, but would you mind if I mentioned you to Simon?"

Andi was confused. "Mention me to your brother-in-law? Why?"

His brow crinkled thoughtfully. "I just think he might have some work for you."

"Walking dogs and babysitting?" Andi guessed anything was worth a try. She'd never seen herself as the Mary Poppins type but then again she'd never imagined that she'd be thrown out of Hart Frozer either.

"I think that's more what Mel has in mind for *me*!" grinned Jonty. Andi liked the way that laughter lines fanned from his eyes. "No, I was just thinking that you could be the answer to another of my sister's problems. Remember how I told you that she was fed up with Si working non-stop?"

"If he brought the *FT* home then it was divorce?" she recalled. "I thought that was a joke?"

"It was a bit of an exaggeration maybe, but the truth is that Si does work too hard and Mel's getting fed up with it. He's totally up against it with work and family, but I know my sister and when she makes up her mind about something there's no going back."

Andi said nothing. There was a twisting, churning sensation in her stomach that felt dangerously like hope.

"Si does lots of work with buyouts and companies going public," Jonty continued. "He's in the middle of taking Pasties Drekly public and he's going to be really up against it to put the deal to bed and manage to have quality family time. Especially if Mel holds him to his promise. I tell you what; it makes life very difficult when your sister marries your best friend. Divided loyalties hardly covers it. If I agree with Si then Mel will play the blood's-thicker-than-water card; if I side with her, who will I play *Grand Theft Auto* with?"

"I feel your pain," Andi deadpanned.

He pulled a face. "You can mock all you like. A man needs his Xbox buddy! Seriously, though, if Si had somebody like you on hand here to help him that would really take the pressure off. He might only need a few days a week but I bet he'd jump at the chance of hiring you. Would it be OK if I mentioned you to him?"

Andi hardly dared to hope it would be OK. If she could get some proper work then she'd be able to save up some money, pay off the huge credit-card debts that Tom had run up in her name and hopefully get her finances back on track.

"Say something?" Jonty urged when she didn't reply. "I haven't been too pushy have I? It just seems as though you've fallen out of heaven!" He blushed right to the roots of his short dark hair as soon as the words were uttered. "Oh God, sorry. That sounds like a really terrible chat-up line. All I'm trying to say is that I think you could be exactly what Si needs. Would it be all right to take your number and ask him to call you?"

"Of course it would," Andi said. Her heart was doing an excited lambada against her ribs but she hoped outwardly she looked calm and professional.

"Brilliant!" His face split into a big grin of delight. "In that case I think we should toast a potential future work partnership with a couple more of Angie's famous bog-standard coffees. What do you say?"

Andi grinned back. Jonty's enthusiasm was infectious and for the first time in what felt like aeons hope was fizzing throughout her nervous system like lemonade. Maybe, just maybe, Gemma and Angel's crazy plan wasn't quite so crazy after all?

"I think it's a fantastic idea!" she told Jonty.

And it wasn't just a second coffee she was referring to.

Chapter 13

Angel had been having a lovely afternoon in Padstow. The pretty seaside town was teeming with summer visitors, all intent on making the most of the glorious sunshine while it lasted. Girls in skimpy vests and tiny shorts held hands with their sunburned boyfriends and drifted through the streets while yummy mummies pushed Bugaboo strollers to Rick Stein's café for afternoon tea. High above the higgledy-piggledy rooftops seagulls wheeled and shrieked in a cloudless blue sky before dive-bombing unsuspecting tourists for their ice creams and pasty crusts.

Angel treated herself to an ice cream, which she ate slowly while dangling her legs over the quayside. Across the shimmering sand and the water ribbon of the Camel Estuary, Rock was only a smudge on the horizon, but the place still made her stomach knot with excitement like the tangled fishing gear piled up alongside the trawlers. The sense of all the possibilities just there for the taking was overwhelming. Whatever was she doing just sitting around eating ice cream? There was so much to do.

Lobbing what was left of her cornet to the squabbling gulls, Angel continued to explore Padstow. It must have been at least ten years since she had last visited. Her mother had adored the town, much preferring Padstow to its more upmarket sister across the water, and had regularly taken both girls across by boat. Andi and Angel had loved exploring the gift shops, but most of all they'd been fascinated by the lobsters on sale at the wet fish shop. Angel smiled to herself as she remembered how they'd loved watching the strange and almost prehistoric creatures floating around their shallow tanks with their claws firmly secured with rubber bands. She'd always wondered whose job it was to try to get those on!

The fish shop was still there but it, like the rest of the town, had undergone a transformation. Now it was Stein's Fisheries; it was housed in a smart building of mellow timber and steel next door to Rick Stein's Fish & Chips shop. Roughly opposite was another structure that seemed more in keeping with the South Bank than the South West: the National Lobster Hatchery. Angel vaguely recalled Andi telling her all about this, something to do with sustainable fisheries, yada yada, but she hadn't really listened. Her sister was so intense sometimes; in fact Angel was starting to think that Andi actually cared about all this environmental stuff. To be honest the only lobsters Angel was interested in were the kind served in Rick Stein's exclusive restaurant and accompanied by gallons of champagne. The tricky bit was finding a way to get herself into the restaurant in order to sample all these treats. Figuring it was time to crank her social media profile up a gear, she opened the Twitter app on her phone and typed:

in Padstow can't wait for dinner #Steins

Seconds later her tweet was safely logged in cyberspace and Angel's work was done. It wasn't strictly a fib anyway. She *was* in Padstow, she *was* looking forward to her dinner and she *was* only a pebble's throw away from the world-famous restaurant. If everyone wanted to read her tweet a certain way then that was hardly Angel's fault. That was semantics!

Deciding that she'd return to book herself a table there once she had some money and was dressed up, Angel retraced her steps, dodging the hundreds of cyclists wobbling towards the Camel Trail, and back through the town. It had been a good afternoon, she felt, and another positive step in moving Project Rich Guy forwards. Already she could see that this side of the water was pretty much catering for families and, unless there was a wealthy single father about, that wouldn't really be much help. On the other hand, there were several restaurants and exclusive bars, which in the evenings would attract a very different crowd. She would return and, when she did, she would be eating something much better than ice cream and wearing some of her designer eBay bargains instead of jeans and a vest. Yes, in terms of a research trip Padstow had been very positive, Angel decided cheerfully. She only hoped that Gemma had had as much luck sorting out their caravan and finding supplies.

The tide was right out by the time Angel reached the beach and the water taxi that was operating from the furthest jetty. Although it was late afternoon and shade was climbing over the hillside, the sand still basked in the light of the sun that had slipped from the narrow streets. Families with checked picnic rugs and gaudy windbreaks were sprinkled across the sand like hundreds and thousands, and shouts of excitement drifted from the water's edge. Recalling that sand was an excellent natural exfoliant, Angel kicked off her Gina sandals and strolled along the shore. The water was warm from the sunbaked sand and she sighed with pleasure. How many hours had she and Andi spent on this very beach? Hundreds probably. They'd loved nothing more than spending an entire day by the water; they'd always returned home to Ocean View salty and sandy and heavy with that almost drugged exhaustion that came from spending hours in the fresh air. Yes, they'd been regular beach babies back then. What a shame it had all had to end so abruptly...

Angel rolled up her jeans and splashed her bare feet in the shallows as though trying to scatter the memories away like the sunlight that was flickering over the waves. Some things were better just left in the past. Instead, she focused on the sand beneath her feet and the joy of having nothing more pressing to do than walk along the coast. Luckily, nobody here knew her yet, so she wasn't ruining her image by doing something as uncool as paddling. There would be plenty of time to walk along the jetty in Rock all decked out in her designer best. For today she was content to just enjoy herself.

The ferry was put-putting its way across the estuary and Angel was just about to head towards it when an agonised wail pierced the laughter. Amongst the kaleidoscope of inflatables and splashing children, a small boy had sunk to all fours and was sobbing uncontrollably. Every time he tried to get back up to his feet he collapsed again and cried even harder, his small face tight with pain. Angel cast her gaze across the beach for a distraught mother or horrified au pair racing over to attend to him, but there was no sign of anyone.

It looked as though he was all alone. She couldn't leave him, not when he was this distressed. Children weren't really Angel's scene – their hands were far too sticky and, anyway, how could you like people who could stuff sweets all day long and never put on weight? But she couldn't leave this little chap to cry by himself. Besides, she already had a strong suspicion as to what the problem was.

"Hey, hey, don't cry." She crouched down next to him and put a comforting hand on his shoulder. "I'm Angel and I think you've hurt your foot. I bet it really hurts. Am I right?"

The little boy was too busy sobbing to speak but he nodded and raised his left leg out of the water. Angel wasn't surprised to see several sharp spines sticking out of his sole; she'd already suspected as much. The poor little mite must have trodden on a weever fish. It wasn't unusual along this bit of coastline, and Angel and Andi had both learned the hard way that it was best to wear wetsuit boots when wading out into the deeper water. The small fish loved to bury themselves in the sand, their needle-sharp spines invisible to the eye but torture for bare feet. Treading on them was excruciating.

"It's OK," Angel said gently. "I know it hurts awfully right now but I promise in a little while it'll feel much better. Can I take a look?"

The child looked up at her with big dark eyes. "Are you really an angel?"

"Of course," she said firmly. "And who are you?"

The boy gulped back a sob. "Dmitri Vassilly Alexshov." He pointed to an enormous Sunseeker moored at the estuary mouth. "That's my papa's boat. He and Mama went to the shops."

More wealthy Russians. Angel hoped Mr and Mrs Yuri weren't here too, otherwise a weever sting would be the least of her worries.

Managing to scoop Dmitri up, drenching her own clothes and covering herself in sand in the process, Angel carried the little boy up the beach. Once he was sitting on a rock she managed to remove the spines from his foot, which was easier said than done given that he flinched every time she tried to tug at the poisoned spikes. When that task had been achieved, she blagged a plastic bucket and a flask of hot water from a nearby picnicking family and coaxed the little boy into putting his foot into the makeshift footbath. It was funny how quickly all this came back to her, but then after seven summers spent in

Cornwall Angel had become something of an expert in treating weever-fish stings.

Once Dmitri's foot was soaking in the bucket, his tears began to subside a little. It would still hurt, Angel knew, but at least this offered a little bit of relief.

"Can I have a plaster? A Peppa Pig one?" he asked hopefully.

Angel laughed. The kid's dad owned a Sunseeker and he was excited about a plaster?

"I'm afraid not. There's some nasty poison in that foot and it needs to drain out. A plaster really won't help very much. You've been very brave though. I expect there's probably an ice cream in it for you somewhere."

He brightened visibly. "A green one? With chocolate bits?"

"Definitely a green one with chocolate bits," she agreed.

So while her little patient soaked his foot, Angel found herself visiting the beach café and spending her final couple of quid on an ice cream. OK, so it was technically Andi's money, but they were sisters and sisters were supposed to share. Anyway, as soon as she had any money Angel fully intended to help Andi out. Starting by paying for a hitman to sort that Tom out. Tosser.

Lost in a very pleasant *Kill Bill* type daydream where she single-handedly kicked the stuffing out of Tom whilst simultaneously looking hot in a red leather catsuit, Angel was surprised to discover on her return that Dmitri was surrounded by a posse of very scary-looking heavies. She gulped. They all looked worryingly similar to Mr Yuri. She hoped it wasn't concrete boots time...

"You!" boomed a big bear of a man. "Have you put my son's foot in this water?"

Angel gulped. This guy was so huge he'd make The Rock look weedy.

"I know the water's hot but, honestly, this is the best way to ease the pain," she began.

But the man wasn't interested in hearing any explanations. Instead he stepped forward and engulfed Angel's non-ice-cream-holding hand in an enormous paw. At the end of the paw was the biggest Rolex Angel had ever seen in her life. Wow. She had no idea you could get them in solid gold.

"Then you have saved my son's life!" exclaimed the bear, pumping her arm up and down until Angel feared it might snap off. "Thank you! Thank you!"

"It was nothing, really," Angel said awkwardly. Goodness, this man was so big she practically had to crane her head back ninety degrees to even look at him. With his thick mane of inky hair, monobrow and glinting gold fillings it felt at bit like being greeted by an early Bond villain. He probably had a lair in a volcano somewhere. "I did what anyone would have done."

"No. It's not *anything*. You saved him." The man was adamant. "My son has told us what happened. My wife and I cannot thank you enough. Isn't that right, Vanya?"

An excruciatingly thin woman with long honey-coloured extensions and a tan like yacht varnish was sitting next to Dmitri and stroking his hair back from his tear-stained cheeks. Her twiggy arms rattled with what looked like half of the Pandora bracelet collection and her fingers dripped with diamond rings. The woman may have been wearing only a bikini and a kaftan, but Angel instantly clocked the Chanel labels.

Blimey, with all that money you'd have thought they could have bought their son some Crocs!

"I am Vassilly and this is my wife, Vanya," the bear continued, still shaking Angel's hand so hard that her fillings rattled.

"I'm Angel Evans," she said, although it was hard to be heard above the jangle of all the bling he was wearing.

"So you really are an angel!" Vassilly flashed a broad grin and Angel gulped nervously. His teeth were so sharp and white it was a bit like being smiled at by the Big Bad Wolf. Like Mr Yuri, this was the sort of man you didn't cross or say no to. She sent up a fervent prayer that the hot water hadn't scalded the kid's foot.

Once her hand was released and Dmitri was happily guzzling ice cream, Angel retold the story of the weever-fish sting and explained very carefully what they should do next.

"He should be fine," she finished. "Just keep the wound clean and keep an eye on his temperature. His foot doesn't look too sore but it might be an idea to pop him up to the doctor just to make sure."

Dmitri's father was nodding. "Of course, of course. We will do so straight away. In the meantime we must make sure you are rewarded."

"There's no need for that," Angel said awkwardly. "I only stuck his foot in hot water. It wasn't a great deal. Anyone would have done the same."

"You knew what to do and you looked after him," Dmitri's mother said firmly. "To us this very great deal indeed. I blame myself: I was shopping and he run away from his minder again."

Vassilly scowled. "I have spoken to you about this, Dmitri! See what trouble you cause when you disobey?"

Dmitri looked mutinous. "I hate being stuck with Sergei! He never lets me play in the water."

Sergei, Angel assumed, was one of the black-clad heavies surrounding them, each of whom looked as though they could chomp on a small beautician for breakfast and pick her bones clean for lunch. They didn't exactly look like the types who'd enjoy splashing around in the shallows with a rubber ring, that was for sure. Angel was intrigued. She hadn't a clue who Dmitri's father was, but to have security that made the royal family look relaxed, he must be somebody pretty important in his home country.

"Enough talking," said Vassilly with such force that everyone fell silent, even the seagulls. "Miss Angel, my wife and I would like to invite you to have dinner with us this evening, as a token of our appreciation."

Angel glanced down at her damp jeans. The rest of her clothes were bundled up in the back of Gemma's Beetle and she was hardly suitably attired for dinner. "That's really kind of you but I'm not exactly dressed for it."

"You can borrow something of mine and bathe on board," Vanya insisted. "Please, we really want to thank you. Dmitri is our only child and you have been so kind."

Both Vassilly and Vanya were obviously not used to people saying no to them. For a moment Angel dithered, torn between checking out their impressive yacht and going back to Rock to help Gemma and Andi settle into the caravan.

Hang on! What on earth was she thinking, hesitating like this? Dinner on a superyacht versus eating a Pot Noodle, or whatever else they could just about afford, in a grotty caravan? Angel could have walloped herself over the head, and hard. Hadn't she come to Rock for the express reason of mingling with the super rich and seeing what opportunities came her way? She hadn't come here to sit in a caravan and listen to Gemma moan about her weight. Angel could have done that in Tooting Bec – and without the sodding caravan!

No, it was time to grab whatever opportunities life chose to throw at her, with both hands. Just think, last week she had been doing beauty treatments for rich Russians; now she was going to dine with them. And you never knew who else they might have on board! A count, perhaps, or maybe even a prince? There were loads of princes in Russia, weren't there? Or at least there were in Tolstoy novels.

Angel smiled at her new friends. It was time to take a chance and roll the dice.

"Thanks," she said warmly. "I'd love to dine with you."

Chapter 14

It was a good indication of how embarrassed Gemma was that even after three hours, one major food-shopping trip and a recce of the caravan her skin was still crawling with mortification. Another very significant pointer was that she couldn't face eating a thing. As soon as she'd realised that she'd covered Callum South in cream buns and pastry, Gemma's appetite had vanished. It was still AWOL now. Even her trip to Asda – usually an exercise in willpower that defeated her as soon as she saw the family packs of iced buns – hadn't held any appeal. There had been nothing on the shelf that she'd remotely wanted to cram into her mouth.

Gemma had no desire to eat. It was most unusual. She supposed this was because she felt so sick with horror.

Actually, at the time it had been difficult to say who was more aghast, Gemma or Callum. At first she'd had to do a double take because although the guy wiping cream out of his hair and dusting flaky pastry from his trackie bottoms looked *like* Callum South, his features were blurred and puffy, as though somebody rubbish at Photoshop had been messing around with the smudge and liquefy tools. On the television, too, she was certain his eyes were brighter and his hair much thicker. Maybe it wasn't him after all? Didn't Angel say that television added ten pounds? Not at least twice that? But this guy was much larger than the reality star whose face was everywhere. Even the fat picture of him in Angel's latest copy of *Heat* was slender in comparison.

"Jaysus, will you stop staring at me and help clear up this mess?" the man snapped, his lilting Irish accent instantly dashing any hope that she'd been mistaken. Oh God! It really was him! Gemma knew she'd been desperate to come to Rock and bump into Callum South, but she hadn't meant literally! Why did these things always happen to her?

"Sorry, sorry!" She dropped to the floor like a paratrooper and started scooping up the remnants of his food. Quite what she thought she was going to do with it she had no idea, but at least she was making an effort. As she picked up pasties and sausage rolls, Gemma tried frantically to think of a way she could introduce herself, but her tongue felt as though it had turned into a pretzel and it was hopeless. If only she could be more like Angel. Her best friend would probably have batted her eyelids, laughed it all off and had Cal licking choux pastry and cream off her slim fingers by now.

Callum South made no attempt to help. Instead he was desperately pulling up the hood on his Quiksilver hoody and backing away from the shop window. When his phone shrilled he swore under his breath and switched it off.

"This is all I fecking need," he muttered.

Gemma sneaked a quick look up at him from under her blonde fringe. The star was dressed for exercise in his expensive sports gear, comprising state-of-the-art trainers and a designer tracksuit – a look that was at odds with the bag of cakes and sausage rolls he'd been carrying. Or rather, it would have been at odds to most people's way of thinking, but to Gemma it made perfect sense. Once you'd burned a few calories, rewarding yourself with a few thousand more only seemed fair. Callum didn't need to look so awkward about it. Anyway, he was famous for his love of food. Surely it wasn't a problem for him? Gemma would have bet that nobody had ever asked Callum to wear control pants and told him his career was over if he didn't shed the pounds. Hadn't he made a fortune from doing exactly that? Men in the media were allowed to gain weight and still have a career. It was unfair, but since when had that made a difference?

"I think that's all I can save," she said, apologetically offering him the salvaged food.

"Just leave it," he snapped. "I don't want it anyway."

"But you've paid for it," Gemma said. She felt terrible. Reaching into her rucksack she pulled out her purse. "Let me buy you some more. Please. It's the least I can do."

"I said, leave it." Callum glared at her so angrily that Gemma shrank back. That glower could have frozen fire. Blimey. This wasn't the easy-going guy she'd seen on the telly. TV Callum was always full of humour and happy to laugh at himself. This version was more like Heathcliff in sweatpants.

"But it's your food. You must be hungry."

He shrugged. "Yeah, well. I'm always hungry. Sure, you get used to it."

"Really?" Gemma found this hard to believe. She never had.

Cal sighed. "No, not really. But you've probably done me a favour. I shouldn't be eating all that shit anyway. My trainer would pop a blood vessel if she saw the calorie count in that lot. It's probably a week's worth; hell, more like two at the moment."

Gemma paused in the middle of trying to cram some squashed éclairs back into the box. "But you've just been exercising. Surely you deserve a treat?"

Cal laughed bitterly. "What's the point of running six miles if I just pig out again? Sure, I may as well have stayed indoors and saved myself the bother."

"Poor you," said Gemma with feeling.

He shrugged. "Yeah, well. It is what it is."

"But dieting sucks!" Gemma cried. "People should be able to enjoy food. Life's miserable otherwise."

Cal was peering over her shoulder, down the street both ways, his head bobbing like the Churchill Insurance dog.

"Try telling that to my manager," he grimaced. "And if my personal trainer had seen me in here my life wouldn't be worth living. I'm here to get fit, otherwise I'm screwed. My manager says diet and I diet: that's how it is."

Gemma nodded sympathetically. If Chloe had had her way, Gemma knew she would have been booted off to fat camp years ago. How much worse would it have been to have had the nation watching her sweat off every pound?

"I'm always on a diet myself," she told him. "People are always making digs about my weight."

Cal sighed wearily. "Tell me about it."

"In fact," Gemma continued, as she scraped up pastry and cream as best she could, "I shouldn't even be here now. I've practically been told that if I don't lose a few stone I'll lose my job."

"Jaysus. That sounds familiar," he said with feeling. A second or two passed by before he added hastily, "Anyway, you're not overweight."

Gemma said kindly, "That's very sweet of you but I think we both know that's blatantly untrue. Isn't this the point where you should say that I have a pretty face?"

He stared down at her, his Galaxy Minstrel eyes holding hers. Gemma could see herself reflected in the dark depths, looking pale and distinctly chubby. God. What a state. What was she doing in a cake shop?

"Sure, and you do have a pretty face," he agreed thoughtfully. "A very pretty face. And if—"

He paused, looking as though he was trying to put some profound point into words. Well, Gemma knew exactly what was coming next.

"And if I lost weight I could look really good?" Her shoulders slumped. "Don't worry, you can say it. It's nothing I haven't already heard."

But Cal was shaking his head. "That wasn't what I was about to say. I was going to say that if people are genuine then they won't care about what you weigh, so they won't. The weight bollocks, it's all superficial."

Gemma stared at him. This was a bit hard to take, coming from a man who made his living from losing weight.

"But on your show you always say how much better you feel when you are slim," she pointed out.

"I know, I know; I can talk." Cal shrugged. "If I took my own advice I'd probably be a lot happier. Jaysus, I couldn't be any more miserable. This fecking show is driving me mad."

While Cal watched the street, presumably for a lurking pap or maybe a fan armed with a camera phone, Gemma toyed with the idea of talking to him about his show and the possibility of getting herself onto it. After all, wasn't that why she was here? Perhaps this was her moment now? The golden opportunity she'd been waiting for? She had to be brave, take her chance and put her brilliant plan into action.

Screwing up every drop of courage she possessed, Gemma said timidly, "Look I've seen your show and I really love it. Maybe if people knew how you really felt—"

Cal spun around from the window. "If I see so much as a word of what I've just said repeated in a newspaper anywhere, my lawyers will be onto you so fast you won't know what's hit you! We never had this conversation and you never saw me here. Got it?"

He glowered down at her and there was such fury in those dark eyes that Gemma quailed.

"Got it?" he repeated.

She couldn't speak; instead she just nodded. What on earth had she done to make him so angry? Only seconds earlier he'd been pouring out his heart to her.

"Good." Callum South tugged his hood down even lower over his face and shoved past her to the door. Then the shop bell tinkled and he was gone, running down the road and out of sight; her thudding heart and a trail of cream and pastry footsteps were the only evidence he'd ever been there at all.

Every time Gemma replayed this episode she felt more and more embarrassed. Not only had she trashed his cake-shop haul and plastered him in cream and crumbs, but she'd also behaved like some star-struck fan. Which she supposed she was. It was true that Gemma had adored Callum South for years. Even now her mum still bought Gemma his calendar at Christmas. She sighed. Even carrying the extra weight and with all the social graces of a bout of diarrhoea, he was still Callum South, once the toast of the Premier League and owner of a six pack that would have made Peter Andre weep. Beneath the layers of fat those once-sharp cheek bones were still lurking; his tall frame still had an athletic grace, and as for those big brown chocolate-button eyes... Gemma reckoned they had the power to make her melt – when they weren't glaring at her, that was. And, when he wasn't shouting, that Irish accent was very sexy too.

What a shame he'd turned out to be such a knob. She really shouldn't be surprised. Most celebrities Gemma had come across were so up themselves they were practically inside out. She'd just thought that Callum was different. On his show he always seemed so self-effacing and so genuine. Gemma guessed this was just an act for the cameras. It was all very disappointing. So much for getting herself onto his show as one of the weight-loss victims. Cal had looked as though he'd like to have stabbed her with the cheese straws. She was going to have to rethink. Once she got over the embarrassment, obviously.

Luckily Gemma had been very busy shopping and sorting out the caravan, which helped to take her mind off the incident a little. Their new home was a rather elderly static, considered far too tatty for a campsite that a farmer friend of her parents had bought for a nominal sum with the intention of making a bit of extra cash letting it to tourists. Unfortunately for him the type of visitor who came to Rock didn't want to slum it in a caravan that had shared its heyday with Joan Collins. The wealthy Rock crowd, whose Mecca consisted of the water-sports facilities, beaches and restaurants, had their pick of interior-designed holiday cottages and luxury hotels with spas and sweeping coastal views. For those who wanted to attempt to "rough it" Rock style, there was always glamping, complete with fire pits, organic produce and snug yurts. The caravan at Trendaway Farm had stood unloved and uncared for since the day it had arrived. No wonder Gemma had been able to rent it so easily and so cheaply.

After several hours spent cleaning the caravan, Gemma reckoned the smell of damp was slightly less overpowering. She'd evicted countless spiders, scrubbed off the black mould and generally given the place a good airing. With some flowers on the table in the living area, a few generous squirts of Febreze onto the mattresses and seats, and a lamp switched on, it was looking much more homely. The bathroom left a lot to be desired, but at least they had a hot shower and a loo that worked. Peeling lino and a window that didn't shut weren't ideal – but compared to her initial fear that they might not have running water connected, this was the height of luxury.

There were only two minuscule bedrooms, more like cupboards really and with built-in beds topped with cheap mattresses. Gemma claimed the double bed for herself. Andi and Angel were sisters and could share the room with two singles, Gemma reasoned as she crammed her clothes into the tiny wardrobe space. Since she was paying all the rent until the other two found work, it only seemed fair. She opened the window and instantly the sweet evening air, heavy with honeysuckle and salt, drifted in and filled her with happiness. So she was tired and still stinging from the afternoon, but who cared? She was back in Cornwall. She was home!

Gemma had done the lion's share of the work but to be honest she didn't mind because it gave her something to think about rather than dwelling on how spectacularly she had mucked things up with Cal. She even thought about doing some baking because that was always good therapy. Hey! Maybe she could bake Cal a cake as an apology? At this thought Gemma brightened. She knew exactly what she would make for him: one of her famous sponges, light as air and cushioned by cream and fresh strawberry jam. The farmer sold both in his shop, alongside free-range eggs with the yellowest yolks imaginable. They would make the sponge the most amazing colour. Maybe she could even buy some real strawberries to decorate it with?

Fired up by this brilliant plan to put things right with Cal, so that she could make a new start and persuade him that he really did want her on his show, Gemma abandoned the bedroom for the tiny galley kitchen. There were pots, pans and a small cooker which, once cleaned, she knew would be more than up to the job. All she had to do was stock up on baking equipment and, even more importantly, find out exactly where Cal was staying. Once he'd seen and tasted what she could bake he was bound to forgive her and sign her for his show.

Gemma could hardly wait to get started.

Chapter 15

"Are you sure it's all right to speak to your brother-in-law right now?"

As she strolled with Jonty through the town and out towards the coastal path, Andi was starting to worry about turning up unannounced on Simon. "He's on holiday, after all, and he must be really busy with his family."

Jonty gave her a sideways look. "Is this a genuine worry, or are you having second thoughts?"

"It's a genuine worry. I'd hate to interrupt a family supper."

He grinned at her. "There speaks a girl who's never met my family. Their idea of a family supper is a race for who can get to the microwave first or a dash to the chippy. There's no way Mel's going to cook when she's on a break. Anyway, I told you, Si's really keen to meet you. It was his idea we came up straight away. Like I said, you are the only one who can save his marriage!"

Andi relaxed a bit. She was shocked to find herself on the way to meet the chairman of Mermaid Media. That certainly wasn't what she'd expected to be doing this evening. Still, it was hard not to be swept up by Jonty's enthusiasm. She'd only known him for a couple of hours but already Andi realised he wasn't the kind of man to let opportunities slip away. Once Jonty had an idea in his head, that was it: he ran with it. Take this idea of her working for his brother-in-law, for example; no sooner had Andi agreed than he was on his mobile and had arranged for her to meet Simon. Now they were on their way to Simon's house and Andi felt a ripple of excitement spread through her entire body. Could her luck be about to change at last? Could she really be fortunate enough to have found a job this quickly?

As they walked through Rock, Jonty gallantly positioned himself at the kerbside. It made a lovely change; Tom would have willingly shoved Andi under a juggernaut to save his own skin, she now realised. On the way, she and Jonty chatted easily about the town: he liked to spend most of his time at the boatyard or out on the water, whereas Andi had always headed for the beach or spent her time reading in the garden. They both agreed that the town had changed hugely over the past few years, though.

"Take this house here," Andi said, pausing to point up at Ocean View. The house lay before them, reclining on manicured lawns like a sultana on her cushioned throne and turning golden in the sunset. It had certainly been smartened up since those long-gone days of her seaside memories. "That's the one that we always used to rent for the summer. Back then it was a piece of faded splendour. The paint was peeling, the floorboards creaked and the garden was a wilderness, but we absolutely loved it." She paused, shading her eyes against the bright light. "It looks like it's been spruced up and extended too, which is a bit of a shame. It's like something out of a magazine now, whereas before it was real. I expect it's probably had the designer seaside makeover inside too, for some rich city boy who sees it for a week a year."

Jonty cleared his throat. "Uh, Andi? I think I ought to tell you now – that's Simon's place."

Andi blushed to roots of her hair. Why hadn't she had her tongue removed at birth?

"Oh," was all she could say.

"Oh," agreed Jonty, but his eyes were crinkled and full of mirth. "So, will I tell Mel to reconsider the decor? Or shall I leave that to you?"

Andi swatted him on the arm. It was strong and muscular and she drew her hand back quickly.

"I think the less I say the better," she told him.

The old wrought-iron gate that Andi remembered had been hanging on one hinge and always opened with a creak and a thud. As she recalled those noises, a flood of nostalgic memories came back to her, as striking and diverse as an Instagram page. That gate was long gone now, replaced by a smart pair of high wooden ones, which swung open easily. The old path that snaked its way through a maze of tangled rhododendrons and elderly azaleas crunched underfoot with freshly raked gravel and had been widened to allow cars to pass. The view, though, was unchanged; it was still a vast living picture of scudding clouds, white-tipped waves and fields of golden wheat beyond the river that rippled in imitation of the Atlantic below. It was so achingly familiar that Andi could almost believe that at any moment her mother would shout for her to come in for supper. Even after all this time the knowledge she would never hear that voice again still felt like a punch to the guts.

"Are you OK?" Jonty asked as she came to a halt. "Is it weird to see it again?"

Andi took a deep breath. The place looked different, that was for certain. There had never been parking outside before and neither had there been a deep blue infinity pool perched on the edge of a smooth green lawn. Wow. It made her feel as though she could dive into the cool water, then down and down into the town below.

"It's just changed a little," she remarked tactfully.

"I think it's been pretty sympathetically done," Jonty said, and he was so hopeful as he spoke that her heart went out to him.

"Don't take any notice of me," she told him. "I'm being nostalgic. It's just that this house always meant something special to me. I think it's probably the place I've been the happiest."

"The happiest in your childhood?"

Andi couldn't really think of another point in her adult life where she'd been as effortlessly happy as she'd felt here.

"I think at any time," she told him thoughtfully. "I spent a lot of time here with my mother just before she died. We never came back afterwards, but I thought about it a lot."

Jonty's eyes didn't leave hers. "I'm sorry. That must have been tough."

Tough hadn't come close. Still, there was no point dwelling on it now, no matter how easy to chat to and sympathetic he was. Jonty was a total stranger and, besides, some things were better left in the past.

"It was a long time ago. Definitely before that little cottage was built."

He didn't push but let her change the subject, and Andi liked him for that. There was nothing worse than people who wanted her to spill her guts like something from *The Jeremy Kyle Show*.

"That's the pool house where I'm staying. That's new, but they've made a real effort to build it in the same style. It's a great place to crash for the summer. It even has a wood burner for those blazing warm August nights!"

Andi thought the pool house was sweet. It stood where there had once been a large and ugly asbestos garage. Not all changes were bad; she had to make sure she remembered that. The pool house was built of wood and made to look like a New England cottage, so that it resembled a miniature one-storey version of the main house. There was a deck complete with a rocking chair; ivy and dog roses trailed up the walls and a battered old Defender was parked at a wonky angle by the three steps leading to the duck-egg-blue door.

"It's really pretty," she said, and was rewarded with a smile of such sweetness that she had to look away. There was something about Jonty that invited confidences and made her tempted to open her mouth and pour out all her secrets – which was so not a good idea. Tom already knew enough of her secrets, and that did not make for a good night's sleep.

The inside of the main house was pretty much as Andi remembered it, but it had undergone the obligatory seaside-chic makeover. She was pleased to see that many beautiful old features of the house still remained, though – from the carved newel posts of the winding staircase to the wooden floors, which shone with beeswax. Ocean View felt the same as it always had, peaceful and still, as though it was slumbering in the late evening sunshine.

Odd. It felt like home still, even after all this time.

"Si will be in the kitchen," Jonty said. "That's where everyone hangs out when they're here."

Sure enough, when they entered the huge kitchen, complete with duck-egg-blue Aga and giant American-style fridge, a lanky figure was slumped at the kitchen island, several empty lager cans lined up next to him while he tapped away on a laptop. When Jonty slapped him on the back he jumped so hard he nearly fell off his stool.

"Shit, Jonty, do you have to creep up on me like that?" he gasped, raking a hand through thinning sandy hair. "I thought you were Mel come back early. You know what she thinks of me playing *Warcraft* when I'm supposed to be working."

So this was what captains of industry got up to in their spare time? Pretending to be orcs? Andi supposed it was one way of releasing the pressure.

Jonty introduced them; then, while he fetched a couple of Buds from the fridge, Andi turned to Simon.

"The house is lovely," she said warmly.

"It is great isn't it? We're so lucky to be able to stay here," Si agreed. "I can't take any of the credit for it though—"

"Where's my big sis?" Jonty interrupted, leaning against the butler's sink as he necked his beer. Muscles rippled in his tanned throat and his tee shirt rode up, revealing a taut, tanned stomach. Andi looked away.

"She's taken the kids to Wadebridge to see a movie," Simon replied. "I'm supposed to be having a bit of a catch-up on Pasties Drekly while they're out. I have to finish tonight because we're having a day out tomorrow." He smiled at Andi. "I think this is where you might become my new best friend! Jonty tells me you're an amazing bookkeeper?"

Andi blushed. "Jonty is very kind."

Simon grinned. "No, Jonty is very honest. If he thinks somebody is worth paying attention to, then he's generally right. Although, come to think of it, there is one exception to that rule – and talking of the lovely Jax, she's left two messages on the answerphone today, mate. She's certainly persistent."

Jonty groaned. "Don't start, Si. I'll speak to her."

Simon winked at Andi. "I've heard that before." To Jonty he added, "She's not giving up easily. Maybe it's because of—"

"Mate, lay off." Jonty's tone of voice said that he wasn't going to be argued with. "I mean it. I don't want to talk about *any* of that stuff."

Simon held up his hands up in mock surrender.

"None of my business, fam," he said quickly. "My lips are sealed."

Andi looked from one to the other. There were more undercurrents flowing here than the riptide beyond the river. Jonty had a hunted expression on his face and Simon just looked embarrassed.

"Jax is my ex," Jonty explained to Andi when an awkward silence fell. "It's a long story and not one I'll bore you with right now."

Nobody knew better than Andi about long stories and exes. The Tom saga made *War and Peace* look like a comic. So that was why Jonty was hanging out in Rock for the summer and living with his family: he had broken up with his partner. Suddenly everything made a bit more sense.

"Aren't they always?" was all she said.

Simon finished his beer and wiped his mouth with the back of his hand. With his baggy jeans and faded tee shirt, Andi thought he looked more like an overgrown teenager than one of the most powerful men in media, and this made her relax.

"Let's have a chat about this job," he suggested.

"I'll leave you guys to it," said Jonty, finishing his Bud and lobbing the bottle into the bin. He smiled at Andi and mouthed *good luck*. "I'll be in the pool house, guys. Give us a shout when you're done."

Once Jonty had left, Simon and Andi chatted about work. Any nerves she may have had were quickly dispelled because Si was so easy to talk to and soon put her at ease. Before long they were chatting away about her previous experience. Although she didn't mention Hart Frozer or Safe T Net, Simon was still impressed by the companies she had worked for and her first-class degree. The more she chatted, the more confident Andi felt. She knew she could take some pressure off him and hopefully learn a lot too in the process.

"How about we give this a trial run for a couple of weeks and see how it works out?" Simon said finally. "You seem really well up on it all. No wonder you wrestled Jonty for my *FT*."

She smiled. "Force of habit."

"Well, it was worth sacrificing my paper to find somebody as well qualified as you," said Simon with feeling. "I'll call your referees first thing tomorrow and if that's all in order how about you start here on Monday? Three days a week, eight hours a day, at twenty-five pounds an hour? What do you say?"

Andi did the mental arithmetic and nearly fell off her stool. That was six hundred pounds a week, before tax. More money than she had dreamed of being able to make in Rock! She'd be able to start making inroads into her debts in no time.

"I say yes!" she told him.

"I think you must be my guardian angel or something," Andi remarked to Jonty, later on that evening when they drove back through the town. The night was falling in earnest now, the last crimson fingernail of the sunset slipping into the inky sea and twilight seeping over the rooftops while shadows pooled in the streets. Out on the estuary, lights twinkled from the cabins of boats that had called in and anchored up for an evening at the restaurants and bars. Stars speckled the sky like glitter on a Christmas card, and across the way the lights of Padstow trembled in the water like jewels. It was so pretty, and Andi felt that at long last maybe her luck had started to turn. "I owe you one."

Jonty shrugged. "Not at all. I was just helping out. This way Mel and Simon actually get a holiday; they'll spend some time with the kids and I'll not have to be a free babysitter. You see: I'm not all heart. It was motivated by a selfish desire not to have to play *Guitar Hero* non-stop!"

The Defender was cruising slowly along Rock Road. It was a balmy evening and the town thronged with people dressed up for dinner and teenagers on their way to a beach party. Jonty pulled up at the jetty and together they watched the boats bobbing gently on the swell of the tide. It was a world away from London; Andi felt her pulse start to slow for the first time in days.

Jonty pointed out to sea at a powerboat tearing in at breakneck speed. "Look at that," he said. "It's the tender for that huge Sunseeker out there. Rumour has it that's owned by Vassilly Alexshov."

Andi was none the wiser. "Vassilly Alexshov?"

"The oligarch? He's just bought Dukes Rangers FC."

"Isn't that Callum South's old team?"

Jonty looked at her, surprised. "I didn't have you down as a footy fan."

"Believe me, I'm not." Tom's passion for the Premier League – which tended to involve sitting around swilling beer and hogging the telly – had driven Andi round the twist. "It's just that my friend Gemma is a big fan of Cal's. She's rather hoping to get herself onto his show."

He raised his eyebrows. Andi found herself thinking that she liked the way Jonty's emotions flickered over his face like sunshine and shadows over the landscape. There was an honesty there that was very refreshing.

"Good luck to her!" Jonty said. "He's renting Valhalla, that carbuncle of an overgrown greenhouse that's next door to my – or rather, I should say Simon's – place. I see him most mornings out pounding the pavement and looking fed up to the back teeth with it. He was out on the water yesterday trying to ski. It wasn't a pretty sight. His camera crew were wetting themselves."

Andi felt sorry for Callum. It couldn't be much fun to be ridiculed, no matter how much money it earned him.

They stood in companionable silence for a bit watching the small boat slicing through the water towards the shore. Once it was moored up by several uniformed crew members, a stunning blonde in a grey lace Versace dress alighted. Her long hair rippled over shoulders as smooth and brown as toffee and her dress clung to her curves like a second skin. She teetered precariously across the jetty in the most enormous glittery sandals and eventually had to be carried to the shore, her laughter tinkling in the evening stillness. Several people at the water's edge were watching this spectacle, including a tall man with high Slavic cheekbones, a hawklike profile and a long mane of treacle-coloured hair. He watched the girl intently as he leaned against his Aston Martin and drew on a cigarette, the red sparks fantailing towards the estuary as he flicked the butt away. He seemed absolutely mesmerised.

Moments later a black Bentley pulled up and the girl stepped inside, to be chauffeured off into the summer night. As it purred past the girl gazed out, a broad smile on her pretty face.

Andi gasped. No way! It couldn't be! It was impossible.

"Andi," said Jonty gently. "I don't want to make you feel awkward but why are you gripping my arm?"

Andi's mouth was dry. She was still taken aback by what she'd just witnessed. "That girl," she said slowly. "The one who just came in from the sea?"

"From the Sunseeker? Yes, I saw. Pretty hard to ignore really! Why? Do you know her?"

Andi nodded. "You could say so. That was my sister, Angel!"

Chapter 16

Angel was on top of the world. Not only had she just had a fantastic evening drinking champagne and eating delicate crab thermidor on board the most sumptuous powerboat imaginable, but Vanya had insisted she keep the designer dress and shoes she'd been loaned for the evening. The moment her feet alighted on the gleaming deck, Angel had been transported into another realm, and it was one in which she very much wished to remain! From soaking neck-deep in a bath of Floris-scented bubbles to sipping Cristal beneath twinkling fairy lights, Angel knew this was where she was meant to be. The girl who had stared back at her from the illuminated mirror as a maid tweaked her hair into an elaborate chignon – the girl who was wearing designer clothes and shoes – was glossy and groomed and already had that wealthy glow about her.

That girl did so *not* belong in a caravan!

Unfortunately for Angel, though, for now a caravan was exactly where that girl did belong. Once the Bentley purred away into the night she slipped off her Louboutins – there was no way she was risking scratching those iconic red soles – and hobbled up the stony path to the decrepit static. God, what a skip! Even in the dark Angel could tell that the caravan was ancient and smothered in a thick layer of green slime. Was this really the best that Gemma could come up with? Thank goodness she'd already drilled her friend not to give their address away to anyone! Angel made a mental note to do the same with Andi, although she had a feeling her sister wouldn't be nearly as obliging. Andi would be totally confused as to why appearances mattered so greatly. Things like this didn't register at all on her radar; she simply didn't get it.

It was just as well one of them did, Angel decided, otherwise this entire exercise would be a waste of time. She was pretty pleased with her own achievements, and all in less than twenty-four hours too! So far she'd made friends with the Alexshovs, enjoyed dinner on a superyacht and, when Vanya discovered that Angel was a beauty therapist, been offered oodles of work. OK, so going back to waxing and plucking wasn't *quite* part of the master plan, but it would pay some bills and hopefully put her in the right places. Angel was under no illusions about the importance of giving the right impression, and her arrival into Rock in a crewed tender and sporting designer clothes had been a real coup. She may have given the impression of nonchalance but inside she'd been shrieking with excitement, *Look at me!* And they had looked too!

She paused on the piled-up paving slabs that doubled as a step for the caravan, reluctant to break the spell of her amazing evening. Once inside, the Bentley would be a pumpkin, the suited waiters mice and her stunning dress jeans and a vest. And as for the handsome prince...

Angel wrapped her slender arms around her body and shivered with delicious anticipation. Of course there was a handsome prince, that went without saying, but she didn't think she would have identified him quite so soon or that he would have been quite so gorgeous. She'd noticed him earlier on that afternoon when she was in The Wharf Café with Gemma but had deliberately played it cool because it never did to show your hand too soon, did it? She'd felt his gaze burning into the back of her neck, so hot that on a trip to the Ladies she'd caught herself checking for scorch marks. On her way back to their table she'd checked him out from behind the safety of her Oakleys, running through her mental checklist. Expensive watch, check. Designer shades, check. Glass of champagne, check. Decked out head to toe in Hugo Boss, check. LV man bag, check. So far it had all been so good. The fob for his car keys was Montblanc but she couldn't decipher the brand of car without craning her neck and being totally obvious. What she had noticed though was the small crested signet ring he wore on the little finger of his right hand.

Titled? Rich? Possibly. In any case it was looking very promising. But something else made her heart pick up pace. She hugged her arms closer and allowed herself to dwell on his features for a little longer: the sharp cheekbones, the thick sweep of toffee-coloured hair, the soft skin of his neck...

One thing was for certain: he was gorgeous, whoever he was.

Still, there was more to Project Rich Guy than looks, so she had studiously ignored him, even to the point of leaving the café and going to Padstow. But, as luck would have it, when the tender had dropped her back to shore he happened to be parked up by the slipway in the sexiest Aston Martin convertible imaginable. It had taken every ounce of self-control Angel possessed not to look in his direction when every cell in her body was frantic to drink in a glimpse of his haughty hawklike profile. When the Bentley pulled up she had swept past him as though oblivious, a feat of willpower that she hadn't even known she possessed.

Thank God he hadn't seen the reality of her life in Rock, Angel thought with relief as she leaned her shoulder against the sagging door and shoved her way inside the caravan. A sex-on-a-stick loaded guy like him wouldn't be seen dead with a girl from a trailer park, that was for sure. And Angel knew that, whoever this guy was, he would want to see her again. Men always did. It was practically a law of physics.

If Angel had felt like Cinderella beforehand, entering the caravan really did make her feel as though the clock had struck midnight. Gone were the ankle-deep carpets, gleaming mahogany woodwork and trembling notes from the baby grand piano: they'd been replaced with curling lino, peeling plastic and the blast of Pirate FM. The living space – which was a contradiction in terms, since there was barely enough "space" to swing a gerbil – was piled high with their suitcases and bin bags; the kitchen sink was overflowing with dirty washing-up and the work surfaces were liberally dusted with flour. In the midst of all this chaos stood Gemma, oblivious to her friend's arrival, putting the finishing touches to an enormous sponge cake. It was oozing with thick yellow clotted cream and luscious strawberry jam; Angel's arteries were hardening just looking at it.

Angel groaned. She was used to Gemma's cooking frenzies and the destruction to the kitchen that followed. Angel was generally fine with all of that because Gemma was a fantastic cook and her cakes were to die for, but this wasn't the point of being in Rock! The whole purpose of their visit had been to make a fresh start. For Gemma this meant going on a serious diet and losing a good couple of stone. That she was baking already, and only within a few hours of arrival, was a very bad sign indeed.

"Angel! You made me jump!" Gemma gasped, spinning round and placing a hand against her ample chest. There was a smudge of flour across the bridge of her nose and her thick golden curls were piled up on the top of her head and secured with a rubber band. The telltale glimmer of sugar around her mouth suggested that, as always, Gemma had been sampling her cooking. "Wow," she added when she took in Angel's new attire. "You look amazing! Where on earth did you get those clothes?"

"Long story," Angel told her, plopping herself down on the couch and leaping back up when a spring skewered her bottom. "Ouch!"

"Oh yeah, watch that seat," Gemma said apologetically. "It's a bit knackered."

"So's my bum now," said Angel. Sitting down gingerly, she curled her long legs underneath her. "Gem, what's going on here? I thought you were going to diet?"

"I am," said Gemma, with her back to Angel as she returned her full attention to carefully positioning strawberries on the top of her masterpiece.

Angel raised her perfectly plucked eyebrows. Talk about being in denial! "So what's with the cake?"

Gemma turned round. Her face was bright with excitement. "This isn't for me! It's for Callum South."

Angel stared at her. "Callum South? But isn't he supposed to be on a major health kick?"

Gemma nodded. "Yes, but it's making him miserable. What he really wants is cake, and lots of it."

"Have you been drinking?"

Gemma laughed. "Only Diet Coke, I promise. You're not going to believe this, but I have had the craziest afternoon."

As she continued to decorate the cake Gemma told Angel all about her meeting with Cal. With every detail that passed her friend's lips, Angel felt more excited. What were the odds of this meeting happening? She could hardly believe Gemma's good luck. As far as

Angel was concerned, this was even more proof that their summer adventure had been an inspired move.

"We'll have to track him down," she said firmly. "Once we know where he lives you can take the cake over. If he likes grub as much as he seems to, there's no way he'll resist a cake like that. You'll be made!"

"I already know where he's staying." Cake completed, Gemma stood back and admired her handiwork. "One of the ladies in the bakery told me. They had no idea who he was, can you believe it, but they did know that he was staying in that big glass place off the Rock Road. Do you know the one I mean?"

Angel nodded. A brand new architect-designed pile, all ceiling-to-floor windows with breathtaking views of the estuary, it was pretty hard to miss.

"I thought I'd pop over tomorrow and apologise," Gemma explained. "At least then I'll have done my best to make up for knocking him flying. Then I'll give him the cake as a thank you. But enough of me, what on earth have you been up to?"

Angel smiled. "Pour us both a glass of wine and I'll tell you all about it."

So Gemma ignored the washing-up, stowed her cake in a brand new Tupperware box and fetched a bottle of white from the fridge. It was passably cold and soon they were busy working their way through it while Angel told Gemma all about her day. Gemma's face was a study in disbelief.

"Honestly, there's one rule for the beautiful people, who fall on their feet at every turn, and another for the rest of us, who keep tripping up!" she said, when Angel finally came to the end of her story.

Angel laughed. "Tripping Cal up is probably the best thing you could have done! At least now you've had an introduction."

Gemma wasn't convinced. "Even if he hates me?"

"Of course he doesn't hate you," said Angel. At least, she hoped he didn't, because that would seriously bugger up Gemma's chances of reality TV stardom. "Anyway, at least you've made an impression."

"Even if it's a bad one?" Gemma looked doubtful.

"At least he knows you exist," said Angel firmly. In her book it was always a good thing to be noticed. Going undetected was her worst nightmare. "That's the first hurdle over. Now you've figured out that cake is the way to Cal's heart it'll all be plain sailing!"

"I hope so," Gemma said. If not, she could kiss goodbye to her agent and her career.

"Now all we need to do is get Andi sorted," Angel concluded. "Which may be easier said than done."

There was a sudden flare of brightness as full-beam headlights swept up to the caravan, illuminating every inch of tired lino and faded upholstery. A car door slammed and the murmur of voices broke the stillness. Pulling aside a grimy net curtain, Gemma peered outside. Then she turned back to Angel, her eyes wide with surprise.

"Sorting Andi may well be easier than you think," she said.

Angel stared at her. "Really?"

Gemma nodded excitedly. "Really. You won't believe this, Angel, but your sister has just rocked up and she's not alone. She's with one of the hottest guys I've ever seen!"

Chapter 17

When Andi woke up the next morning it took her a few moments to work out where she was. A beam of bright sunshine sliced through faded yellow cheesecloth curtains and filled the room with lemony light, while a breeze sweet with summer grass kissed her cheeks. The incessant rumble of city traffic she was used to had been replaced with the cry of gulls, and for a split second she was thirteen again and tucked up in her attic bedroom at Ocean View with days and days of school holidays ahead of her. The leaping of her heart when she realised that she really was in Rock – and that Tom, London and the whole hideous mess had been left behind – was on a par with that start-of-the-summer joy.

Andi stretched luxuriously in her narrow bunk, bathing in the sunshine like a cat and loving the cool breeze that swept in beneath the curtains. Although the mattress was hard and the covers a little on the damp side, her sleep had been sweet and heavy, as though the salty air had drugged her. As she stretched and yawned she realised that this was the first night for a while that she hadn't woken up with her heart rate doing a tango. Getting away had been the right thing to do. Andi just hoped that this was the start of her being able to sort her life out.

Across the small room a shape huddled under the blankets muttered and sighed to itself: Angel was fast asleep and, Andi knew from experience, dead to the world for hours yet. Checking her watch she saw that it was only half past six. Still, the day outside was far too beautiful to waste in bed. With a feeling of excitement fizzing inside her like shaken-up Coke, she grabbed her clothes from the neat pile by her bed and headed for the bathroom.

She might as well have been trying to shower in a wardrobe, and the water was just a half-hearted lukewarm trickle, but in spite of that Andi soon felt refreshed and ready for anything the day had to offer. Dressed in cut-off denims and a green vest top, and with a coffee in hand, she perched on the caravan step and raised her face to the sunshine. Although early, it was already warm and the sky was deep blue and brimming with the promise of a hot day. Andi sipped her drink and enjoyed the birdsong. Honestly, she couldn't believe their luck in finding such a tranquil spot. It had been pitch black when Jonty had dropped her back at the caravan and, once the girls had finished interrogating her about him, she'd almost passed out from exhaustion. She certainly hadn't been able to explore her surroundings. Now that the sun was up and the other two were still sound asleep it was a different matter.

The caravan was certainly past its best but the setting for it couldn't have been more idyllic. Tucked away behind a tumbledown farmhouse, it sat in an overgrown meadow brimming with daisies and buttercups, and sheltered from the wind by a small orchard of gnarled ancient apple trees. At the end of the meadow, fields of wheat and barley rolled gently down towards the town, edged with a ribbon of blue where the estuary met the sea. Andi drank her coffee and listened to the chirruping of a little wren and the trembling call of a wood pigeon. Her pulse slowed. A more private and healing spot she couldn't imagine. Gemma had done them proud.

Fetching her phone from inside and an apple to keep her suddenly ravenous hunger pangs at bay, Andi settled back onto the step and began using the organiser to list all the things she needed to do. Angel always laughed at her for making lists, calling her anal and a control freak, but Andi liked to be organised. Lately the only things she'd had any control of had been her endless lists (*Ten ways to kill Tom/Things I need to do/Ways I can make some money*), so Andi felt she could be forgiven for hanging onto them. Hey, if she were a superhero she would probably be List Girl! Today's list involved finding somewhere with Wi-Fi so that she could email Simon Rothwell her resumé; next was a visit to the bank to see if her redundancy money had been paid in. Jonty had suggested meeting up for a coffee later on if she was free but Andi wasn't sure. He was a nice guy and she knew that he was just being friendly, but to be honest at the moment she just wanted to be by herself. She needed to sort herself out.

Andi paused from her typing and stared out to sea. Yesterday had certainly been crazy, that was for sure. Much as she was thrilled with the idea of having found a potential job, she wasn't counting any unhatched chickens just yet – and so she added *visit the job centre* to her list of tasks. Unlike Angel, who seemed to have fallen yet again on her well-pedicured feet and claimed to have more beauty work than she could handle (and new designer clothes to boot), Andi was cautious by nature. She guessed a psychologist would probably say her trust issues were down to her father walking out on the very day they discovered her mother had cancer. Maybe so. And maybe Angel was constantly searching for a replacement father figure who would protect her? Cod psychology made Andi's head hurt and it was far too nice a day to dwell on the past. She'd gone against all her instincts and trusted Tom and look where that had got her. From now on, Andi was determined that she was only going to trust herself. However genuine and helpful Jonty seemed, he was still a man and therefore programmed to let women down. If the job with Simon came off, then brilliant. If it didn't... well, she was an independent woman and had taken her future into her own hands. She was going to be like that Beyoncé song!

Angel hadn't been at all impressed once she'd learned that Jonty wasn't a holidaying millionaire but merely the brother-in-law who lived in the pool house and did some chores in return for his rent. All interest had vanished quicker than their bottle of Chardonnay.

"You spent all afternoon with a guy who tinkers with boats and mows lawns?" she'd wailed. "Ands! You didn't need to come to Rock for that: you could have done it in Clapham!"

"There aren't many lawns in Clapham," Gemma had said helpfully, but Angel had quelled her with a look.

"We're here to make a new start," she'd continued slowly, as though explaining this to the local village idiot, a post for which Andi was actually starting to feel well qualified. "That means making the most of all the opportunities that come our way. Babes, thanks to Wanker Tom you're brassic. If you're going to hook up with a guy, couldn't you at least find a rich one? It's not as though there's a shortage here."

Andi had felt herself colour. God, she hated being a redhead sometimes.

"I haven't *hooked up* with anyone," she'd said hotly. "It was just a coffee and a chat. It was nice just to talk to somebody who doesn't know all the ins and outs of what's happened."

Talking to her new friend had been fun and uncomplicated. There had been no sleazy overtones and definitely no agenda. Jonty had just been lovely company, nothing more and nothing less, and she'd certainly not thought anything more of it. Besides, he was getting over a broken relationship too and had probably sensed her *not interested* vibes.

"It wouldn't matter if you did hook up with him," Gemma had argued, scraping up the remains of the whipping cream with a spoon and dolloping it in her coffee. "Rich or poor, who gives a toss? He was gorgeous."

Angel had looked as though she was about to weep with despair.

"Will you drag yourself out of Mills and flipping Boon, the pair of you?" she'd groaned.

Unable to take another lecture from her sister, Andi had made her excuses and retired to bed. There she'd spent a cramped hour unpacking her bag and trying to squeeze the few clothes she did have into the tiny wardrobe. Then she'd climbed into her narrow bed, pulled the chilly sheets up to her ears and tried to ignore Gemma and Angel discussing Project TV Show. Although the walls were little more than cardboard, the Cornish air had done its job and she'd quickly and mercifully dropped off.

The sun was climbing higher in the sky now and there were sounds of life coming from inside the caravan. Andi threw the dregs of her coffee onto the grass and ventured back inside. It was time to get going, she decided, and start ticking off some of the items on her list.

The time for sitting back and just letting things happen to her was over.

Chapter 18

Angel was not overly thrilled to be dragged into Wadebridge on such a sunny day. She'd planned to have a shower and then plaster herself in fake tan before slipping on her Victoria Beckham jeans and Chloé top and wandering into town – once the tan was dry, obviously, and that total bore John Humphrys had stopped jabbering on. Why her sister insisted on listening to him when there was Radio One on offer Angel had simply no idea, but then Andi was weird like that. It was like the fuss she'd made because Angel had spent her sister's *FT* money on *Heat* magazine. Why would anyone want to read the *FT*? There were no celebs in it at all, unless you counted Richard Branson – and even he was a bit past it for Angel's taste.

While she'd lain in bed listening to Andi and Gemma chatting, she'd screwed up her eyes to block out that annoying sunlight and had run through her mental itinerary. Today's plan was simple: find some money – she'd already sent her father a text begging for funds – and have lunch somewhere kick-ass. Then in the afternoon she'd go for a run and this evening she'd hit the bars with Gemma. Vanya wanted a manicure at some point too, which would mean popping up to the enormous house overlooking Daymer Bay that Vanya and Vassilly were renting for the summer. Busy, busy, busy! She really ought to get up and think about straightening her hair. Angel hadn't even been in Cornwall for twenty-four hours yet, but already the damp air was playing havoc with her hair and it was starting to curl. She'd better find a Boots ASAP and pick up some Frizz Ease before she ended up looking like her sister.

So, it was only her pressing need for styling products that had persuaded Angel to deviate from today's plan and take the bus with Andi to Wadebridge. The bus! Angel had almost died with horror. What if somebody saw her getting on? That would undo all the good work she'd achieved yesterday in approximately thirty seconds flat. She may as well just go round wearing a sign that read *Poor!* She'd tried her hardest to persuade Gemma to drive them to town, but for once Gemma was proving impossible to talk round; when even the suggestion of a cream tea somewhere had failed to persuade her friend, Angel had known she was doomed. For some reason Gemma was off her food – which was unheard of – and determined to stomp around Rock with her cake. Although in principle Angel approved of the whole Callum South plan, she wasn't one-hundred percent convinced that giving him a cake was the smartest move (the guy was filming a weight-loss show after all), but Gemma wasn't having any of it.

"You should have seen his face when he left his food behind," she'd said when Angel had mentioned this. "Honestly, the guy was devastated. I just know a cake is exactly what he needs to cheer him up."

Angel had opened her mouth to suggest that Gemma's food issues were starting to affect her brain and that the last thing a dieting celeb needed was a ginormous cream sponge – particularly when pictures of him looking fat had only just been splashed across the red tops. However, the look of fervent determination on Gemma's face stopped Angel in her tracks. Gemma was generally more pliable than Blu Tack, but once she set her mind on something there was no changing it. She'd no more listen to Angel than her sister would swap hanging out with odd-job men for spending time with multimillionaires.

Honestly, Angel had thought in despair as the bus had trundled into Wadebridge, there was absolutely no hope for either Andi or Gemma; they both seemed totally set on sabotaging their chances. She'd pulled her baseball cap down over her face, pushed her shades up her nose and sighed. It was time to face the harsh reality: it was all down to her. The other two just didn't have a clue. Look at Andi, for example: she was ridiculously pleased to be on a bus and kept trying hard to point out the views along the way. Anyone would have thought she'd never seen the sea before. Didn't Andi realise that if anyone saw Angel on *public transport* it was game over? She glanced across at her sister, who was chatting away to an elderly woman, and groaned. Of course Andi didn't realise and even if she had, she wouldn't care. Her sister simply didn't get it. Well, if Andi was happy to hook up with odd-job men and grannies then that was her lookout, but as far as Angel was concerned there had to be more to life.

Wadebridge was busy. Although it was a weekday the town was packed with tourists keen to set off along the Camel Trail on hired bikes or to explore the shops. Leaving Andi to visit the bank – just the thought of her black-hole overdraft was enough to make Angel sweat through her several layers of Sure deodorant – she hotfooted it to the nearest Co-op, where she dove into the Ladies and spent a good fifteen minutes repairing her hair and make-up. Once she was satisfied that she looked immaculate and that her false eyelashes weren't crawling down her cheeks like AWOL Incy Wincy spiders, she doused herself in Coco Mademoiselle and headed into the town. Her baseball cap was rammed into her fake Chloé Paddington bag and she'd swapped her ballet pumps for the Louboutins. Angel admired her reflection in a shop window. Those sandals looked brilliant with her skinny jeans and a

Diane von Furstenberg wrap dress! With her huge shades, waterfall of hair and designer bag she totally looked the part. Now it was time to hit the shops.

Unfortunately for Angel, hitting the shops was easier said than done when your bank account was empty. When her card was declined for the second time in Boots she had to wave goodbye to all her products; with cheeks flaming, Angel left the store, wishing a thousand plagues on her father. Honestly, what sort of parent was Alex Evans? It wasn't like he was short of cash either. Would it really have been asking too much to just bung a couple of hundred quid into her bank account? It wasn't as though he'd done much else for Angel.

Feeling very hard done by, she wandered back towards the bank. Andi had mentioned going there to talk about her finances and to check to see if her redundancy money had been paid in. Angel shuddered at the mere thought of discussing her finances with a bank manager. The last time she'd tried this, an attempt to get a loan to buy the most gorgeous Missoni coat, she'd been sent away with a flea in her ear and with the stern advice that she should spend less money in Boots. Angel shuddered at the memory. It was not an experience she wished to repeat in a hurry. If Andi's money had come through then her sister could lend her a couple of hundred, just until Vanya paid her. Angel was due to do a manicure for her after lunch and she was sure that once the Russian woman saw how brilliant she was at acrylics all her friends would want Angel to do theirs too.

The bank was quiet when Angel entered. A couple of customers were queuing at the counter and there was no sign of her sister. Taking a seat in the enquiries corner, Angel checked her iPhone just in case there was a message, but the screen was clear. Andi must be in with the manager then.

Angel was just contemplating slipping on her flats and walking along the Camel Trail back to Padstow then hopping back to Rock via the ferry, when the door to the manager's office opened. Angel looked over just in case it was her sister and her heart did a base jump when none other than her gorgeous stranger walked out. She looked away hastily. Close up he was even more beautiful than she'd realised. She could imagine the royals skiing down those cheekbones, and his skin was as bronzed and smooth as peanut butter. She suddenly had an insane urge to lick him.

"Thanks for your time," the stranger said, shaking hands with a small man in a suit. His voice was clipped, the pronunciation unmistakably upper class. "I'll get back to you."

He shouldered his LV bag and headed towards the door. He was even taller close up, at least six foot three, and there was something about him that commanded the attention of everyone in the place. Determined not to be like everyone else, Angel pretended to be totally absorbed in her iPhone. He'd think she was busy scrolling through her oh-so-important emails, when in reality she was checking her reflection in the mirror app. She knew he'd notice her, but there was no way she'd let him know she'd clocked him too. That was not how the game worked.

His Kurt Geiger loafers were drawing closer. She could smell his aftershave too: Montblanc, unless she was very much mistaken. Angel's heart was racing. Any moment now he was going to stop and speak to her, she just knew it. Every cell in her body was on red alert.

"My Lord! You've left your sunglasses behind!"

The bank manager came scuttling across the foyer, a pair of Ray-Ban Aviators clutched in his hand. Angel looked up; she simply couldn't help herself. The bank manager had uttered the magic words "My Lord". Hadn't she just known all along that this man was something extra special? Seriously. She must have some kind of super power when it came to guessing these things!

"Thanks," said the mysterious aristocrat, taking them and perching them on the top of his thick mane of hair. "It would have been an absolute bore to have to drive all the way back from Kenniston Hall for those."

Angel's ears were on elastic. Sending up a quick prayer of gratitude to the God of Wi-Fi, she typed *Kenniston Hall* into Google and very nearly squealed with excitement when her search revealed a picture of a massive Palladian mansion, complete with rolling parkland and enormous lake.

Jackpot alert!

It was time to roll the dice…

Looking up from her phone Angel caught the man's eye and threw him her brightest smile. It was so high wattage it made searchlights look dim – and, of course, he smiled back.

"Bank managers who retrieve sunglasses," she remarked. "I'm impressed with Wadebridge."

"It's not exactly Coutts," the man said thoughtfully, "but the service isn't at all bad. I lose count of how many pairs of shades I mislay, so it's good to have these back."

Coutts? This was music to Angel's ears. She slipped her iPhone back into her bag and rose gracefully to her feet, flipping her long hair over her shoulders. Angel didn't need L'Oréal to tell her she was worth it: she already knew she was.

The man held out his beautifully manicured hand. Even his arm looked aristocratic. A chunky Rolex sat above his slender wrist – although the time was wrong, Angel noticed.

"Laurence Elliott," he said. "Viscount Kenniston."

She let him take her hand. His was cool, the fingers soft and strong. Angel was instantly reassured. These were not the hands of a labourer. Laurence Elliott was the real deal. His index finger skimmed across her palm and deep inside her a pulse quickened into life, although whether this was from his touch or his title Angel wasn't certain.

"Angelique Evans," she said, tilting her head so that she could smile up at him. Goodness, but his eyes were grey. "But my friends call me Angel."

"That's because you look just like one?" he asked. Then, looking at the expression on her face, he groaned. "Christ! How cheesy was that? Can we start again?"

"You're not going to ask if I fell out of heaven?" she deadpanned.

For a moment he stared at her. Then when she started to giggle, a crescent-moon dimple appeared in his left cheek and he began to laugh.

"Sorry, sorry! Look can we start over? I don't think that went so well," he said. "I'm not normally quite so gauche. I've seen you in Rock a couple of times and I've been thinking of ways to introduce myself. Can't say I'd imagined ballsing it up quite so spectacularly!"

He'd been thinking about her? Angel wanted to punch the air. Yes! Ignoring the good-looking guys always worked; they weren't used to it and couldn't bear it. Still, it didn't do to give her jubilation away, so she just widened her blue eyes and made an o of surprise with her mouth. She'd practised this a lot in the mirror and she knew it looked cute.

Viscount Kenniston certainly looked as though he thought she was cute.

"Listen," he said, still holding her hand and gazing down at her with those stormy sea eyes, "my finances are just about able to support us going and having a glass of fizz together. Have you got your chauffeur with you or can I drive you back to Rock?"

Angel could safely say that she hadn't got her chauffeur with her, which wasn't a lie – Gemma was far too busy with her urgent cake delivery.

"I just asked to be dropped off," she said. "I think a glass of champagne and a lift home would be just wonderful."

Laurence jingled his keys. At the thought of that stunning Aston Martin, Angel's stomach flipped with eager anticipation. Andi, the bank and their money worries were instantly forgotten.

This was why she'd come to Rock!

Chapter 19

The sun was already high in a cloudless blue sky when Gemma pulled up outside Valhalla. She was glad she'd decided against walking to Callum's house because the day was hot and she didn't think the heat would have done any favours for her gorgeous cake. Safe in its Tupperware box it sat tucked in pride of place on the front passenger seat, a work of art with its careful cream piping and beautifully arranged berries. Gemma was sure that as soon as Cal tasted a mouthful he'd forget to be angry with her. They'd get talking and before long he'd understand how much she needed to be on the show. It was all going to fall into place; she just knew it.

In the meantime, though, Gemma had to work out just how she was going to get the cake to Callum, something she hadn't really thought about until she parked the Beetle outside a pair of the most enormous electric gates she'd ever seen. Nearly ten feet tall and topped by elaborate wrought-iron spikes and razor wire, they wouldn't have looked out of place on Buckingham Palace. The security cameras, which instantly swivelled in her direction, were like something from Bond, and a thick and impenetrable privet hedge ringed the entire property. Flipping heck, Cal's security people weren't messing about, that was for certain. This place made Fort Knox look half-hearted.

Carrying her cake, Gemma made her way to the giant intercom. All those cameras trained on her made her skin prickle with nerves. Invisible eyes were watching her every move and this made her feel very uncomfortable indeed. Gemma couldn't help wondering how she must look on the CCTV. TV added at least ten pounds and at the minute she could hardly afford to put on another ounce. Much as she loved the summer, Gemma dreaded the inevitable baring of flesh that accompanied the warm weather. It was all very well if you were slim and leggy like Angel and Andi, but no fun at all for those who were slightly more generously proportioned. Already she could feel the tops of her thighs chafing beneath her shorts and her bra biting into her back, making odd bulges appear, alien style, beneath her vest. Gemma wasn't even going to think about what her dimpled arms and legs looked like in black and white; they looked horrific enough in colour. Maybe she could pinch some of Angel's fake tan? Having a tan was supposed to be slimming.

Anyway, if today went according to plan none of this would matter. She'd soon be signed up for the show and losing loads of weight. Buoyed by this thought she tucked the cake box under her arm and pressed the intercom.

"I'm here to see Callum South," she said. "I've got a delivery for him."

There was crackle and a pause at the other end. With her free hand Gemma tugged her vest down over her stomach. Were they watching and wondering who the fat girl at the gate was?"

"One minute, we'll be with you."

There was a buzz and a click and, as though by magic, the vast gates swung open. Gemma gasped. Beyond was a stunning garden, all jewel-bright azaleas and smooth emerald lawns leading to the house itself. She was sharply reminded that Callum was more than just the plump guy from the bakery – he was a Premier League star with the dizzying wealth and status that came hand in hand with this.

And she'd brought him a *cake?* What the hell had she been thinking? This wasn't a good idea at all! This was lunacy!

She was contemplating turning on her heel and making a break for it when a tall man appeared at the gate. He was smartly dressed in chinos and a mink-coloured shirt and was wearing mirrored shades that reflected her round face in all its pink and sweaty glory. There was a walkie-talkie in a holster at his hip, which for a second she'd thought was a gun. Bloody hell. Callum had serious security. No wonder he was so keen to sneak off to the bakery when he was undetected.

"Can I help you?"

Gemma gulped. She doubted it. She was beyond help, possibly certifiably insane.

"I've brought a cake for Callum." She held out the box hopefully but the man didn't make any move to take it. Rather, he just stood there until, feeling foolish, she tucked the cake box back under her arm.

"A cake?" He said, sounding astonished. "Is this some kind of a joke?" He stepped forward and loomed over her. Gemma gulped nervously. She hoped to goodness that *was* a walkie-talkie.

"Are you from the press?" he continued. "Is this another bloody tabloid wind-up?"

Gemma shook her head. Did journalists regularly visit Callum South with cake?

"No. Definitely not. I bumped into Cal by accident and I knocked his shopping over."

The man stared at her. "His shopping?"

"In the bakery? I knocked his cakes and pasties everywhere. This is my way of trying to make it up to him. I've made Cal a cake to apologise. Seeing as I ruined his, it felt like the right thing to do."

She had to admit that said out loud it sounded crazy, even to her own ears. Last night this had seemed a brilliant idea, the logic so sound that even Mr Spock would have been awed. In the cold light of day, however, her plan suddenly seemed to have more holes than the trawl nets on Padstow quay.

The man removed his glasses and pinched the bridge of his nose hard. If she had to describe the expression on his face, Gemma would have said it was despair.

"You think you met Callum in town?"

"I did," Gemma insisted. "In the bakery!"

The man exhaled slowly. "The bakery. That's just great. The one time he goes running on his own he's in the sodding bakery. I *knew* we should have sent the team out with him. God only knows what he's eaten. This could set us back weeks."

"He dropped it all," said Gemma. "I don't think he got to eat any of it. But surely that's up to him?"

He fixed her with a very sharp look. "I'm Mike Lucas, Callum's manager, and he doesn't do anything first that he doesn't run by me. *Anything.* Not when we're on a shooting schedule this fucking tight, and especially not when he's signed a contract with ITV2. What was he eating? I need to know everything he had! *Everything!* Do you understand? "

Gemma understood far too well. Oh crap. She'd just dropped Cal in it, well and truly. He was filming a weight-loss show and was probably under some heavy contract not to eat a carb or so much as sniff at a cream bun.

"You have seen the press this week, I take it? Callum stuffing his face in KFC? PR disaster," Mike Lucas continued. "Does he look like a man who needs any more cake?"

In Gemma's opinion everyone needed cake; it was just that some lucky people could get away with eating more than others. She was just about to make her excuses and do a runner when the sound of pounding trainers and the rasp of heavy breathing announced the return of Callum from yet another jog. Today, however, he wasn't alone but was accompanied by a film crew and none other than Emily, the spiteful brunette from Gemma's disastrous last photo shoot.

Sometimes Gemma really wondered what she'd done wrong in her previous life to deserve all the crap constantly being hurled at her in this current one. Whatever it was it must have been something very bad indeed, because here she was looking like a Beryl Cook character, her hair all frizzy in the heat – and hot and bothered from just carrying a cake several feet – while Emily looked amazing in her teeny tiny running shorts and crop top, with her hair pulled sleekly in a long swingy pony tail. Cal appeared much the same as he had the day before. Those sun-kissed curls and the sleepy downturned eyes were instantly recognisable, but the doughy body and rippling chins made it seem as though the golden boy of soccer was melting away into himself.

Oh God. How could Gemma have been such an idiot? The last thing Callum South needed was a cake. Cakes were what had got him into this state.

Callum's trainer – a Twiglet-like woman with no boobs, who was bouncing alongside him – was putting him through some final exercises. Callum appeared to be on the verge of collapsing. His face was puce and the back of his tee shirt was sodden with sweat. In contrast Emily looked as though she'd been for a stroll in the park. More proof, Gemma decided sadly, that skinny people were genetically engineered in secret labs and nothing at all like the rest of the human race.

"Come on Cal," barked the trainer, "put your back into it! We've only been for an amble along the beach. You used to outpace Beckham and run rings round Rooney!"

Callum grunted. As he bent, his midriff rippled and Gemma couldn't help thinking that the only rings he'd run around anyone these days would be doughnut ones.

"Suck the air into your lungs! Feel alive!"

Cal looked as though he was only just managing to resist giving her the finger. He didn't appear to be "feeling alive"; he seemed closer to expiring.

"God, if the rest of the lads at Dukes Rangers could see you now they'd piss themselves laughing," the trainer jeered. "Callum South, the golden boy of football, can hardly run along a Cornish beach without an entire sewing machine's worth of stitches in his side! It's pathetic! Now, stretch!"

The cameras were rolling and although she knew that a lot of this OTT boot-camp style drilling was purely for the benefit of making good telly, Gemma's heart still went out to Cal. His running kit might state that RefreshZing – Britain's number-one sports drink – sponsored him, but in reality he was a far better advert for Greggs the Bakers.

"Cut all that out for a minute," Mike barked. As if by magic, everyone stopped in their tracks. Cal, bent double and with his hands braced against his knees, looked up. When he saw Gemma an expression of abject horror flickered across his face.

"This girl claims she met you in the bakery yesterday," Mike said. He placed his hand in the small of Gemma's back and gave her a shove forwards. "She's here with a cake? Something about needing to replace your food? Is that true? Were you in that bloody bakery again?"

All eyes were on Gemma. The cameras too. She suddenly felt as hot as Cal looked.

"Oh my God!" squealed Emily. "It's Ginormous Gemma! What on earth are you doing here?"

"I'm bringing Cal a cake," Gemma said. Or rather she tried to. In reality she sounded as though she'd been inhaling helium. Turning to Cal, she added, "Look, I'm sorry about yesterday. I thought this cake might make up for it? Like an apology?"

For a split second Cal hesitated. His gaze rested on the cake and his eyes when they met hers momentarily lit up. Gemma's heart lifted. She'd known he'd like it!

But the moment was very short-lived and her hopes were soon dashed when Cal's top lipped curled in distaste and he shrugged.

"Mike, if you believe every crazy fan who turns up here claiming to know me, it's going to take a bloody long time to film this show," he said coldly. "Of course I haven't been in a bakery. I've been trying to shift the weight, remember?"

Mike regarded him through narrowed eyes. "So you weren't there at all? You didn't meet this girl?"

Cal rolled his eyes. "Of course not. Does she look like the sort of person I'd spend time with? When I could be hanging out with Gorgeous here?" He put his arm around Emily and drew her against his side. "Besides, do you really think I'd eat a cake that a fan has baked? I'd have to be mad: it could have anything in it."

Emily gloated across at Gemma.

"She's had a thing about Cal for ages," she told Mike. "The last time we met she was busy telling everyone how unfair it was he has to lose weight. She was off on one saying it was mean!" She sniggered. "God, Gemma, I can't believe you've come all the way to Rock just on the off chance of finding Cal. That's crazy! "

Gemma's face was a big Edam of humiliation. She waited for Cal to say something, to man up a bit and admit that actually he had been in the bakery and Gemma wasn't crazy, just a bit impulsive maybe; but he kept his mouth firmly shut. He couldn't look at her though. The tips of his trainers were suddenly extremely fascinating to him. Gemma didn't think she'd ever been so let down in her life. To her, Cal's feet looked like they were made of clay.

"At least you've made it onto Cal's show after all," sniggered Emily over her shoulder as she jogged through the gates. "The fat girl who thought she'd bring her hero a cake. Priceless!"

There was a horrible tight knot in Gemma's throat. Standing back, still clutching her cake to her chest, she watched as they all traipsed past. Callum didn't even glance back. So much for all that crap about understanding how she felt. It was just a line and, like an idiot, she'd fallen for it.

Gemma drove slowly back into Rock. This was for two reasons: her vision was blurred with tears of humiliation and the town was absolutely heaving. Tourists thronged the streets and packed the cafés as everyone sought to enjoy the glorious weather. RIBs zoomed up and down the estuary, frilling the water with lace-like foam while seagulls enjoyed a spot of parkour on the rooftops and dive-bombed children for their ice creams. Skinny women in skimpy bikinis waited on the pontoon for tanned guys in board shorts to collect them in their speedboats. Everyone was having a wonderful day at the seaside. Everyone, that was, apart from Gemma.

She sat in the car blinking back tears. Her idea, which had seemed so brilliant at the time, had turned out to be flawed to say the least. Of course Cal was never going to want her on his show. Why would he want Ginormous Gemma when there were lots of little stick-thin girls like Emily clamouring to be noticed? The Emilys of the world were much more camera friendly and looked wonderful on Callum's arm. If he had Gemma on his arm her sheer weight would probably dislocate it.

The cake sat on the front seat. It was her best friend and her worst enemy all rolled into one. Right at that moment Gemma wanted nothing more than to rip off the lid and break off a huge chunk, cram it into her mouth and munch and munch and munch. The sweet sponge, gooey jam and cream would taste so good that while she was eating it the humiliation of being denied by Cal and mocked by Emily wouldn't matter at all. Her hand stole to the lid and hovered there for a moment. *Go on!* urged the Diet Devil. *One slice won't hurt!*

The Diet Devil was probably right: one slice wouldn't hurt. The problem was that Gemma knew she wouldn't stop at one slice. Or two. Or even three. No, she would gobble the entire cake until she felt bloated and sick not just from the carbs but also from the overwhelming self-loathing. Gemma was probably halfway to being bulimic, she decided woefully: she had mastered the binging to perfection; it was the purging part she hadn't got round to. Ignoring the cake was going to be impossible. There was no way Gemma would have a minute's peace while it was anywhere near her. Taking it back for the girls wasn't a good idea either. She'd have good intentions of sharing it, but once they'd started one slice wouldn't be enough for

Gemma. And even if she threw it in the bin she knew it would only be a matter of time before she was rooting around to dig it out again.

So her options were to either scoff the lot now or get rid of the cake. There was no middle ground here. She started to prise open the lid but Emily's mocking words, "the fat girl who thought she'd bring her hero a cake", echoed in her ears. If she carried on like this, TV work or no TV work, than "the fat girl" was all she'd ever be. Maybe this move to Rock for the summer wasn't going to be so much about her career as making a few life changes? And the first one was going to be not eating that cake.

But for this to happen she had to get rid of it fast. Gemma knew the perfect way; not only was it effective, but it was also satisfyingly symbolic.

Fired up with enthusiasm, she drove back down the hill and to the small car park by the water's edge. Clutching the cake tightly, Gemma marched down Rock Road as fast as her chafing legs could carry her. She was going to throw the cake into the sea and she knew the very place, just off the pontoon and out into the estuary. Gemma had read several books on cosmic ordering and was convinced that this would signify to the universe just how serious she was about throwing away her old bad ways and embracing the new. She was going to lob that cake out into the water and not so much as a crumb would pass her lips.

Unfortunately for Gemma, Fate decided to flick her a V-sign at this point: the tide was miles out. She stood by the lifeboat station, which was packed thanks to some kind of charity fundraiser, and wanted to scream. That was the end of that bright idea. If Gemma could throw the cake into the water at low tide, the Olympic hammer-throwing coach would probably sign her on the spot. For a moment she dithered as to what to do. Maybe she could eat it and then be good afterwards? Polishing off the cake would be the last greedy thing she would do!

"Oh! What a wonderful cake! Is that for our fundraiser?" Almost before Gemma registered what was happening, an elderly woman had taken the Tupperware container from her and was gazing at the cake in awe.

Gemma had been in such a frenzy to get herself to the pontoon before she guzzled the cake that she hadn't noticed she was standing in the middle of the RNLI fundraiser and practically on the cake stall. She must have an inner homing beacon when it came to cake. She held out her Tupperware container and smiled. If this wasn't Fate then she didn't know what was.

"It's all yours," she said.

"Thanks, my love! That looks delicious, doesn't it, Dee?"

Another woman, in her early fifties and dressed in Crocs and Boden, had materialised and was now peering into the cake box.

"My goodness, yes that's beautiful! Where did you buy that?"

"I made it myself," Gemma told her.

"Goodness!" Dee looked impressed. "Then you're very talented, my dear – and I should know because I own a bakery here: Rock Cakes. If this tastes as good as it looks then I've got some serious competition."

Gemma laughed. "It's just a hobby, although I am unemployed at the moment. Maybe it's time I set up a business!"

Dee looked at her thoughtfully. "I think you should come and work for me rather than be a rival. Pop up one afternoon when you're not busy and we'll have a chat."

"Seriously?" Gemma could hardly believe that somebody was being nice to her. In fact, better than nice. They genuinely liked her cake.

Dee nodded. "Seriously. The season's here and I could do with some help. Only part time, mind! And it all depends on whether or not I like this cake."

Gemma had no qualms on this score. She had yet to bake anything that wasn't delicious. As she wandered back to the car a smile danced across her lips and something very odd happened: the pressing urge to eat had totally vanished.

And what was even odder? Cal's rejection and Emily's cruel words didn't hurt nearly as much as they had a few minutes before. Maybe she should visit Rock Cakes. After all, apart from several stone, what did she have to lose?

Chapter 20

It may have been only a week since her arrival in Rock, but already Andi's life was starting to move to a different rhythm. Each morning she woke up at six; but unlike in London, where her eyelids had been glued together and she'd practically had to mainline coffee in order to function, here with sunlight streaming through the faded curtains and the sounds of birdsong rather than traffic, she sprang out of bed.

Angel – a heavy sleeper at the best of times, and an even heavier one lately, as she was rarely arriving home before the small hours – continued to snooze. Andi suspected that there was a man involved somewhere. Angel's designer clothes and bags were certainly getting a good airing, but her sister was keeping her cards very close to her chest. Even Gemma wasn't privy to Angel's secret. Not that Gemma was around a huge amount either, having found herself part-time work in town. Her sister claimed to be doing beauty treatments for Russians, which explained the money suddenly filling her purse but not the late hours or the sparkle in Angel's eyes. Whoever this mystery man was, he was he was certainly agreeing with her sister. Gemma said kindly that they should be pleased that Angel was having fun, but Andi worried exactly what kind of "fun" her sister was having.

"He must be loaded, whoever he is, otherwise why else would Angel keep him away from the caravan?" Gemma had pointed out with faultless logic. She was probably right, but Andi would have felt a whole lot better knowing whom her sister was with. Rich or poor, it really didn't matter; all she cared about was that Angel was happy and safe.

After she'd eaten her breakfast and dressed in a floaty summer dress and DM sandals, Andi walked the mile into town before turning up

Rock Road towards Ocean View. Unlike her previous scurry to the Tube, head down against the rain and eyes firmly fixed on the pavement, here she loved every step of her commute. The lane leading from Trendaway Farm was leafy and green, with high banks foaming with cow parsley and starred with buttercups. Swathes of pink campion trembled in the breeze and daisies tumbled drunkenly over dry-stone walls. Once the route began the descent into Rock, this greenery thinned out as the road dropped away and instead a breathtaking moving picture opened out before her, like a Bruegel come to life. The town was splattered with umbrellas outside cafés and slow-moving supercars, the estuary clotted with boats and shimmering in the morning light. Further out to sea, white horses tossed their foamy manes and pranced across the deep blue water. By the time she reached Ocean View Andi felt more alive after thirty minutes of walking than she'd felt in years of London life. Dr Johnson, with his "tired of London, tired of life" nonsense, had clearly never visited Cornwall.

Yes, life in Rock agreed with her, Andi decided as she stomped up the steep path to Simon's house. The constant tramping up and down hills was like having a free multigym and already she was feeling so much fitter. She thought she looked healthier too. The sunshine had tanned her skin and brought out a dusting of cinnamon freckles across her nose. With her red hair and pale skin Andi knew she'd never achieve the Tangoed hue her sister favoured (not naturally, anyway), but at least she looked a little less like a lost member of the *Twilight* cast. She was sleeping really well too, probably from a mixture of the fresh salty air, hard work and the sheer relief of no longer having to stress about Zoe or Tom.

Andi paused halfway up the path to catch her breath and admire the glittering sweep of estuary below. She was still upset about losing her job and would have loved to find a way to clear her name, but strangely the whole affair no longer stung quite so much. Yes, Safe T Net had been her baby and she couldn't bear the idea that PMB believed she'd cheated a colleague, but none of this felt quite as much like the end of the world as it had a couple of weeks ago. Working for Simon, who was funny and driven and insisted on her sitting in the garden to work as much as possible, was doing her the world of good.

To be honest Andi could still hardly believe her luck at finding such a fantastic job. When Simon had phoned a couple of days after Jonty had introduced her, Andi's heart had been in her mouth. What if he didn't want her or think she was good enough? Or what if Hart Frozer had somehow managed to smear her name with her past employers and ruin any chance of a good reference? As it turned out, Simon had been thrilled with what he'd discovered about her and unable to believe his good fortune that such an experienced accountant was on hand. Within an hour of his phone call Andi was up at Ocean View and on a week's trial. Once Mel, Si's friendly and very chatty wife, had made coffee and insisted she ate a saffron bun, Andi was ensconced in the office and working her way through a massive pile of folders. Good Lord, how on earth did Simon manage to run such a successful business empire? She'd never seen such chaos in her life; it looked as though he just threw everything up in the air and let it settle. There was no order whatsoever and for a second she'd been overwhelmed. Then her inner neat freak had rocked up and Andi had got stuck in. By the time Si returned from swimming with his boys, pink-eyed with chlorine and looking frazzled, Andi had already organised his office and made a start on the paperwork. After that, Si said, there was no way he was letting her go. Jonty was right: she was exactly what he needed.

Andi smiled when she thought about Jonty. She'd bumped into him a couple of times over the past few days and his cheerful grin and easy conversation made him somebody very comfortable to be around. He tended to spend most of his time working on his boat, "channelling my inner 007" as he laughingly described it, or doing chores around the property. When he was indoors he was either chatting with his sister in the kitchen or entertaining his nephews. Andi was struck by how relaxed he was with them yet how much the boys respected him. Uncle Jonty was certainly a big hit and something of a hero to the children. Yesterday he'd taken his nephews wakeboarding on Simon's RIB and the excitement had been contagious. Even though she knew she'd probably look revolting in tight rubber Andi had found herself wishing she could join in.

"I'm useless," Simon had said ruefully, "but Jonty's an amazing waterskier. You'll have to get him to take you out sometime."

Andi had laughed. "I'd be rubbish. I think I'll stick to figures!"

Simon had pulled a face. "That's what I said, but nobody listens to me. Just accept it; Jonty will have you in a wetsuit before you know it."

Leaving her to it, he'd gone to join his family on the water. Andi had sat down to her work, but the office overlooked the estuary and she'd been distracted several times by the sight of the RIB hurtling along with small wetsuited figures trailing behind the foaming wake. It had looked like great fun. She'd felt pleased that Ocean View was a family home again, complete with laughter and sand and salty swimming costumes. The chatter and merriment of Simon's family filled the echoing space left by her parents...

Andi had worked on the Pasties Drekly accounts until the late afternoon. A couple of times she'd seen the RIB blast by again, the final time towing a wetsuited man who leapt through the air with the natural grace and ease of a salmon returning upstream. That had to be Jonty then, equally at home on the wakeboard as he was behind the wheel of the RIB. She'd watched for a moment, admiring his agility, before getting back to her figures. On their return the family had brought fish and chips home for supper. Insisting she left the office and joined them, Jonty had shared his portion with her. He'd peeled his wetsuit down to his waist, revealing a muscular stomach and strong shoulders that were tanned and broad from hours on the water. Droplets of water had glimmered on his eyelashes, all starry from the water, and a wide grin had split his face as he'd recounted the day's adventures. Mel had shooed all the soggy men outside to stop them dripping on the floor, so Andi had sat with Jonty and the boys by the pool, where they'd munched hot salty chips and dangled their legs in the cool water. They'd chatted easily about everything under the sun and she'd returned to the caravan feeling contented and full with food – and with another odd feeling that she couldn't quite identify.

It was only much later on that she'd finally realised that this odd sensation was happiness.

It was great to have a friend with no agenda, she decided this morning as she let herself into Ocean View. Jonty hadn't told her much about himself and Andi respected his desire to keep personal things private. After all, nobody understood better than her how some things were better not talked about. The ugly business with Tom was still an open wound and one she had no desire to prod. Even though he'd never mentioned it again, Andi had gleaned from cryptic comments made by Mel and Simon that Jonty was getting over a break-up, and she totally appreciated that he'd rather not discuss it. He certainly hadn't broached it with her, but then again she'd kept her past pretty much under wraps too.

"Morning!" called Mel over her shoulder when Andi entered the kitchen. Standing at the Aga, Mel was busy frying bacon while her children and the family dog watched and drooled. "I'm just making breakfast. Would you like some?"

Andi shook her head. Checking her watch she saw that it was already half past eight. "I'm good, thanks. I'll go through to the office and make a start."

Turning around, Mel pinned her with a stare. "You will not! Simon doesn't pay you until nine. I'm not having my slave-driver husband grind you into exhaustion. The least I can do is fix you a coffee."

Simon was the antithesis of a slave driver and Andi laughed. "One coffee then."

"And then to work," said Simon with a mock-stern face, miming cracking a whip. He leant to kiss the top of his wife's head. "I'm just going up to the boatyard with Jonty. I'll see you at the pontoon, sweetheart."

His wife brandished her spatula at him. "You'd better! No getting distracted by that ridiculous wreck of a boat. Why Jonty bothers with it when—"

She stopped mid-flow because Simon was kissing her.

"Eww!" and "Gross!" squealed the boys, but Andi smiled. Mel and Simon clearly adored one another even after years of marriage. It kind of gave you hope. When was the last time that Tom had kissed her (and by "kissed" she meant properly kissed, not just a peck on the cheek)?

Far too long ago, was the answer. Andi sighed. Maybe that part of her life was over? From now on she'd just concentrate on paying off her debts and getting everything sorted. And if the closest she came to sex was walking past an advert for Play Gel then that was probably for the best.

While Simon promised faithfully he would be on time and Mel dished up huge breakfasts for her boys, Andi sat down at the large scrubbed-pine table and let the warmth of their family surround her. It felt a bit like sinking into a hot bath. The Rothwells were noisy and squabbled and created a trail of havoc wherever they went, but the sense of fun and love that accompanied them was palpable. Had her family ever been like this? As though peeling back layers that had been superimposed over an original print, Andi saw her own mother cooking at that very Aga while she and Angel sat at the table with their father. This was where any similarities ended. Unlike Simon, Alex Evans had spent very little time with his family, preferring to read in the drawing room or drive back to London for meetings. She certainly couldn't recall him ever kissing her mother, but she could recall plenty of silences and a sensation of resentment so strong she could almost see it. And unlike the boys, who clearly adored their father, Andi and Angel had been in total awe of Alex. His moods were uncertain, and his presence was only granted now and again; the girls had always been trying to either please or placate him.

Yep. A psychologist would have a field day with her and Angel all right.

"Boys, it's lovely outside. Take your food out onto the terrace. Loopy! Down! You go out too." Mel chased her brood outside and then wiped her hands on her Cath Kidston apron. "My God, they're enough to put you off kids for life! Now, let's have that coffee now we've got some peace and quiet."

A state-of-the-art Gaggia had pride of place in the kitchen but Mel bypassed it, cheerfully lobbing Nescafé granules into mugs and sloshing water over them from a kettle.

"I'm probably a complete philistine but I much prefer the bog-standard stuff," she apologised. "Jonty's machine is too clever for me."

"That's Jonty's machine?" Andi was surprised it wasn't in the pool house.

"He gave it to us," Mel explained quickly. "It's great and all that, but to be honest I can't figure it out for the life of me." She put two steaming mugs down and smiled at Andi. "I hope this is OK?"

"This is great, thanks."

"Good." Mel beamed at her. "So, tell me Andi, what brings you to Rock?"

Since they'd first been introduced, Andi had been struck by just how intrigued Mel was by her. She supposed it was only natural; she was a total stranger in their house after all, and in the other woman's shoes Andi guessed she would have felt exactly the same. So far Jonty had been around to head off what he'd laughingly referred to as the Sibling Inquisition, but today he was meeting Simon at the boatyard so she was on her own.

"Don't let my sister grill you," he'd warned last night over their shared chips. "She's right a nosy parker when she wants to be and she's desperate to know more about you."

"Me? Why?" Andi had asked through a mouthful of chip.

"Because she's my big sister and thinks anything I do is her business! Besides, you're the first friend I've brought up to the house, which has really got her on red alert. She wants to check you out!"

The word *friend* had given her a warm, tingly feeling. The idea of being checked out, however, hadn't.

"And do you generally listen to what she says?" Andi had teased. When it came to her own sister, she generally took anything Angel said with a giant handful of salt.

Jonty had raised a hand to touch his short hair. "I cut my hair off a while back for a photo shoot. It was this silly work thing. Mel told me not to; she said I looked like the FA Cup with short hair. She tried to stick my ears down with chewing gum when we were kids. When I looked in the mirror I thought she was probably right. I almost asked her the fetch the Wrigley's!"

Andi thought his hair, now growing out in thick waves, suited him. She liked the way it exposed the shells of his ears and the tender skin at the nape of his neck.

"You could always get a beanie hat," she'd deadpanned.

Jonty had laughed. "I'll bear it in mind! But to answer your question, then yes. Generally I trust my sister. The times I have ignored her things haven't always gone so well."

Now, as she drank coffee with Mel, Andi recalled this conversation and smiled to herself.

"I'm here with my sister and a friend," she told Mel. "I'm between jobs at the moment so it seemed a good time to take a break. Gemma found a cheap caravan just outside the town, so we've come down for the summer."

"That sounds like lots of fun. Jonty's doing the same in a way by hanging out with us. Rock always chills him out."

"He seems a pretty chilled kind of guy to me anyway," Andi observed.

Mel nodded. "He is generally but he's had some heavy work stuff to deal with and he needs a break. It's not been easy."

Andi waited for her to elaborate but Mel seemed reluctant to say any more. "Anyway, there's enough here to keep him busy. And at least it means he's away from Jax."

"Jax? That's his ex?"

Andi couldn't help herself. This was a name she'd already heard Simon mention the first time she'd met him. Jonty had clammed up like a scallop, his usually sunny countenance all shuttered and drawn, and hadn't wanted to expand on the topic. Jax, whoever she was, was definitely not up for discussion.

"Afraid so," said Mel. "Total nightmare bitch from hell. She was his business partner too – which was bad enough, because she abandoned Jonty when his company was going down the tubes and totally left him to carry the can. He's such a gentleman that he sold his house to pay back what he owed her, even though it crucified him. Of course, she took the lot and left him totally in the shit. It was a double betrayal. As you can imagine, we're not her biggest fans in this house."

This was a story that Andi could identify with only too well. Her heart went out to Jonty. No wonder he wanted to hide out in Rock with his family.

"Poor Jonty," she said.

Mel stared thoughtfully at Andi. "He hasn't had the best time of it, that's for sure. I've no idea what he ever saw in the woman, to be honest. Big false boobs, tight clothes and a fast car I suppose. God, men can be thick."

Although she didn't know him very well, this didn't sound much like Jonty to Andi.

"I'm sure there was more to it than that," she said gently.

Mel sighed. "Yes, yes, of course. Jax is a very successful businesswoman so I guess he admired her. He was certainly wrapped up in her for long enough. I just hope that she leaves him alone now that..." She paused and shook her head. "Well, now that he's happier. I'd hate to see him hurt again."

Andi understood. She'd have done anything to save Angel from being hurt every time Alex had failed to pick them up from school or forgot a birthday.

"He seems very happy now," she observed.

Mel shot her a familiar turquoise-eyed grin. "Yes, he does and I can't think why! Anyway, ignore me, Andi; I'm paranoid. It's just that I trust that Jax about as far as I could kick a concrete block."

Their conversation ended abruptly at this point because the boys had returned to the kitchen and were clamouring for more food. Taking her cup to the sink, Andi thanked Mel and made her way to Simon's office. That Jonty had been hiding a broken heart made her own go out to him even more. No wonder they seemed to have such a connection. They were both in the same boat, even if his was more James Bond style than hers!

When a text buzzed through to her phone, with the message *Coffee at boat yard L8r? J*, Andi found herself texting back a yes before she'd even thought about it. Then she put her phone away, called up today's files and set about her work. As she wrestled with the figures she was still thinking about how wonderful it was to have a friend who totally got her. Even when the numbers became so tricky that she had to go right back to the very beginning, Andi was still smiling at the thought of meeting him later for a coffee.

Jonty, it seemed, was starting to have a very good effect on her.

Chapter 21

It was early evening at Rick Stein's Seafood Restaurant, that westerly Mecca for those who love fine food and exquisite service – an elegant grey-stone and red-brick building with large windows overlooking the estuary, which forms a perfect frame for exhibiting the exclusive clientele.

A select group of diners were in attendance this evening. As they were seated at their window table, which was a work of art in fine white linen, gleaming silver cutlery and sparkling crystal glasses, Laurence discreetly pointed out to Angel the good and great who had flocked to the restaurant. Some of them – like Richard and Judy, for example – were instantly recognisable and she had to dredge up every ounce of self-control she possessed not to look impressed. Although inside Angel was shrieking with excitement and gagging to ask the famous duo for their autographs (or did they have one and share it?), her perfectly made-up face didn't reveal so much as a flicker of interest.

"See the man in the corner, the one with his wife and wearing the linen suit?" said Laurence, sotto voce and leaning forward under the guise of passing her a chunk of sun-blushed tomato artisan bread.

Angel held her hand up, declining the roll even though the mere smell of it was making her drool. Carbs were a big no no. In Rock thin was definitely in and, judging by all the Arabellas and Mintys and Millys in Laurence's circles, even size eight was on the chunky side. She was going to have to really put her mind to it and get down to a six. Carbs were the devil and to be avoided at all times.

Peering over Laurence's Pierre Cardin-clad shoulder, Angel saw a very scruffy-looking man tearing into a crab like a dog worrying a bone.

Bits of flesh speckled his chin and dotted the tablecloth like pink dandruff.

"That's Rupert de Lacey, Earl of Russex," Laurence told her in hushed tones. "Sixth-richest man in England, I believe. Great shot apparently, but an absolute bore about hunting. Pa fagged for him at Eton."

Angel nodded sagely, although to be honest she didn't have the foggiest what Laurence was on about. Aristocrats, she was learning, had their own special language and half the time she was completely confused. They also seemed to operate in a very small pond; it was all Binky this, Dizzy that and Fatty the other. Everyone had rowed/been debs/hunted (delete as appropriate) together, and keeping track of it all was proving very complicated. Still, she was certainly impressed that Laurence knew all these people. When he'd mentioned Prince Harry she'd nearly passed out from sheer excitement.

"Dreadful bore old Rupe," Laurence confided, topping up her champagne glass with a flourish. "And his daughter looks like a horse. Ma had her lined up for me at one point. Believe me, I was not impressed. I like riding horses but I certainly drew the line at Arabella de Lacey!"

Angel giggled and flicked her golden tresses (another set of new extensions, courtesy of Vanya's hairdresser) over her shoulders. She knew that nobody could ever accuse her of looking like a horse, unless you counted a very pretty My Little Pony, all sweeping mane, long eyelashes and delicate features. Every penny she'd earned this week had instantly been spent on beauty treatments and new clothes; catching sight of her reflection in a spoon, Angel was certain it was money well spent. The floaty jade dress from Ghost was a perfect contrast to her blue eyes, and the expensive French pedicure looked perfect with her Gina sandals. So, Gemma had gone mental when Angel hadn't been able to produce her third of the caravan rent, but that was Gemma for you. She was just totally short-sighted. Angel had tried to explain that this was an investment for the future, but Gemma hadn't been convinced. Then again, thought Angel despairingly, Gemma was the girl who wanted to lose weight but had ended up working in a bakery. There was just no helping some people.

While Laurence entertained her with an amusing anecdote about what he'd got up to at William and Kate's wedding reception, Angel congratulated herself for approximately the millionth time on finding somebody like him. In all her wildest dreams she'd never imagined that within days of arriving in Rock she'd have met a viscount. And not the chocolate biscuit kind that Gemma was so well acquainted with, either, but a real live, genuine viscount. The Eighth Viscount Kenniston, actually of Kenniston Hall in Devon where his family had lived for centuries in their sprawling mansion.

She took a mouthful of champagne, loving the way the cold biscuity bubbles exploded across her tongue. This was the life! Unlike her sister – who seemed happy to drink coffee with an odd-job man who, good-looking as he undoubtedly was, lived in overalls and on his sister's charity – Angel was looking for the finer things in life. With Laurence she had certainly hit the jackpot. The Aston Martin, the fantastic house overlooking Daymer Bay and the Quink-blue blood were all right at the top of her wish list.

What Angel hadn't expected though, and what was actually a lovely bonus, was that Laurence Elliott was not only funny, with a sense of humour drier than the champagne she was currently enjoying, but also absolutely gorgeous. When he placed his hand in the small of her back to guide her across the street her nerve endings fizzed and her heart rate quickened. Yesterday, as they'd sunbathed on the deck of his huge *White Shark* and he'd rubbed Ambre Solaire across her shoulders, Angel had been possessed by the strongest urge to flip over on her back so that he could continue with the rest of her. Luckily Laurence wasn't a mind reader and she was able to hide her blushes beneath her sun hat, but Angel was certainly alarmed by the strength of her attraction to him. That was never part of the plan. At night she lay awake in her narrow bunk, unable to sleep for thinking about him, her body restless and her heart rate like something from *Casualty*. It was as though her sexual organs were plugged into the mains. What was going on here?

Just looking at him across the table now was enough to tie her stomach up in delicate knots. This was only their third date – or fourth if you counted the meeting in the bank and the drive back to Vanya and Vassilly's house – but already Angel was worried that she was becoming just a little addicted to those clipped tones, tangled dark lashes and searching pewter eyes. So far though, Laurence had been a total gentleman, not even so much as leaning in for a chaste kiss. She looked down at her starter, something elaborate and scallopy, and her tummy twisted with longing.

Oh dear. She had to play it cool. To feel like this was most unexpected.

Laurence raised his glass in his slim hand. His gaze took a leisurely trip over her face and Angel felt her cheeks flush.

"You look absolutely stunning," he said softly. "I must be the luckiest man in Cornwall."

There was a glitter in those grey eyes. Maybe, just maybe, this would be the evening when he made his move? Angel was not used to guys playing it cool. Normally that was her role, and to have it flipped was confusing.

She raised an eyebrow. "Just Cornwall?"

Laurence grinned. Goodness, but his teeth were white. "How very remiss of me to leave out the entire country, if not the world. I apologise. How can I ever make amends?"

Angel drained her glass. She didn't think she'd ever get used to drinking vintage bubbly like water. "Another bottle of this might help," she told him.

For a split second he hesitated. Had she gone too far, Angel worried? They were drinking the most expensive champagne in the house. If Andi had seen the price of it, she would have had a fit and started to lecture her sister about waste/paying off debts/being greedy, but Angel wasn't worrying. This was on Laurence, after all, and he was a viscount and seriously wadded. They probably bathed in the stuff at Kenniston Hall. She hoped she hadn't made some awful social gaffe by requesting more? She'd already ordered lobster, one of the most expensive things on the menu, so champagne was a must really, wasn't it?

But she needn't have worried, because Laurence was already ordering and moments later another bottle was cooling in an ice bucket.

"To you, Angelique Evans," Laurence declared as he poured another glass and toasted her. They smiled at each other across the table and her heart somersaulted. God, but he really was yummy. She just wanted to reach out and sweep that lock of hair out of his grey eyes. To distract her hands she turned her attention to her starter. To be honest Angel didn't really like seafood, which was a bit of a menace seeing as they were in Rick Stein's, but she did her best to swallow a couple of mouthfuls.

"So, Angel," he continued, those grey eyes, the irises circled with black as though an artist had drawn around them with a fine liner, holding hers, "we've spent some time together and I feel that I've talked far too much about myself and not let you have a word in edgeways."

Quite frankly, Angel was perfectly happy with this arrangement. She knew loads about Kenniston, Eton, Aston Martins and the Royals, which was fantastic. They'd talked about music and theatre and clubs they both enjoyed, but so far Angel had managed to shy away from any questions about herself. Whenever she'd met up with Laurence she'd made sure that either he'd picked her up from the Alexshovs' stunning house or she'd joined him down in Rock. If he'd assumed that she lived in that breathtaking architect-designed pile and that the beautiful chauffeur-driven Bentley was hers, then that wasn't Angel's fault, was it? Andi, who didn't have to meet certain standards to drink coffee with her odd-job man, might look disapproving – but technically Angel hadn't lied.

Laurence steepled his fingers beneath his chin. "Tell me about *you*."

She stabbed at a scallop. "There's nothing much to tell."

"Now, that I don't believe for a minute. You're a mystery, Angel Evans. So far I know where you live…"

Thank God he didn't. The mere thought of Laurence rocking up to her tatty caravan was enough to bring Angel out in a most unladylike sweat.

"I know your family has a penchant for Sunseekers…"

The Alexshovs were more or less her family, Angel reasoned. She worked for them, after all, which made them *her* family she worked for. It wasn't a fib.

"And I now know that you don't like scallops," he finished, reaching across the table and gently removing the fork from her grasp. "But apart from that, you are an enigma."

"You've summed me up," agreed Angel swiftly. "How were your mussels?"

But Laurence wasn't going to be put off that easily. "You already know that I'm an idle aristo happy to fritter away my inheritance," he continued, "but what do *you* do when you're not with your family? You mentioned your London pad. Where is it? Kensington? Chelsea? If so, I'm amazed they haven't snapped you up for *MIC*." He pulled a mock-sad face. "Apparently, I was far too wooden!"

Made in Tooting Bec hardly had the same ring to it. Crossing her fingers and hoping that the nuns at school had been wrong about eternal hellfire and damnation, Angel said, "Clapham, actually." Well, Andi had lived there, hadn't she? Even if it was in the crappy bit. Since they were sisters it was practically the same thing.

He nodded. "Up and coming, I know. That's a smart investment. And do you live with friends?"

"Just my flatmate, Gemma," said Angel. "She's a model."

Laurence looked suitably impressed. Angel just hoped he never met Gemma or came across that advert for control pants.

"And what about you?" he was asking. "Do you model?"

Although in her fantasies Angel did indeed give Lily and Cara a run for their money, in reality (which was sadly where she lived most of the time) she was far too short to model anything except stilts.

"I work in fashion and beauty," she hedged, which was almost true.

Laurence looked dangerously as though he was on the brink of asking her more about this, but a waiter glided over to clear their table and the moment was lost. Steering the conversation back into safer waters, Angel let him chat about Kenniston Hall and his mother. Laurence was totally devoted to both and as he described the antics of his forebears he became very animated.

"So the Fifth Viscount nearly lost the entire place on the turn of the dice," he finished. "Luckily for the family, his wife shot the cards off the table with a blunderbuss, or we'd have been homeless. He went down in history as the Elliott who nearly lost the family seat." A shadow flickered over his face. "Not a good legacy. Nobody wants to be the heir who loses the place. That's not going to happen on my watch."

"It must be quite a responsibility, inheriting a family seat," Angel observed.

A muscle twitched in his cheek. "You could say so. Sometimes I think it might have been easier to be a media mogul or a city boy. Still, enough of that. Here's the main course. And doesn't it look wonderful?"

Wonderful wasn't quite the adjective that sprang to mind. Angel stared at the enormous lobster, Katie Price pink and still complete with claws, antennae and beady black eyes, gazing resentfully up at her. While the waiter draped a snowy white napkin over her lap, all she could think was how the hell was she supposed to eat the thing? It was still in its bloody shell!

The truth was that Angel had never eaten a lobster in her life. She'd only ordered it tonight because it was a) expensive and b) the sort of thing she imagined wealthy people ate. The embarrassing truth was that the only fish Angel liked tended to be smothered in batter and served with big fat chips – which, Angel had decided, wasn't quite the chosen dish of a viscount's dinner companion. Angel felt close to panic. She'd assumed there would be somebody on hand to serve it up to her, but instead all she had was a small mallet and something that looked like a pickaxe.

Oh God. She'd wanted dinner, not a mining expedition.

"Is everything all right?" Laurence looked concerned when she didn't dive into the lobster. If in fact this was what she was meant to do? Angel didn't have a clue. Did she wallop it? Tap it? Call a vet?

She bit her lip. This was it. One lobster and her cover was blown. If she got this wrong, gorgeous, titled Laurence would realise within seconds that she wasn't quite the sophisticated seafood-eating woman she'd made herself out to be.

"That's a beauty, isn't it?" he said admiringly. "I adore lobster."

Angel almost asked him why, in that case, he'd plumped for goujons of lemon sole, grilled with sea salt and lime. Then she had a brainwave of such genius that she thought it a miracle Mensa didn't sign her on the spot.

"Then why don't you share it with me?" she suggested. "There's far more than I can eat. Besides, I'll struggle to even get into it with these!" She held up her brand new acrylics and waggled her fingers at him. Saved by her nails! Andi was wrong yet again: good acrylics really *were* an investment.

Laurence raised an eyebrow. "They look lethal. Fear not, I'd be delighted to do the honours."

He set about the lobster with all the deft skill of a surgeon in theatre while Angel watched avidly. So that was how it was done. Honestly, if only they had taught lobster dissection in school rather than all those theories and formulae. Angel had yet to come across a use for quadratic equations but couldn't help thinking that being able to disembowel a lobster would have been very helpful indeed.

Once the lobster was dealt with, dinner passed in a blur of ice-cold champagne and delicious white flesh, which Laurence fed to her. When his fingertips brushed against her lips Angel had the strongest desire to lick the entire digit. She tried hard to distract herself with walnut tart and crème fraiche, but nothing was working. By the time the bill arrived all she could think about was the smooth skin of Laurence's neck and how it might feel beneath her lips. He smelt wonderful too, of something spicy and oriental and expensive that was making her senses reel and her head spin. Or maybe this was the champagne? Whatever the cause, Angel was no longer worried. She just wanted Laurence to whisk her away to his beautiful house, sweep her into his arms, carry her up the stairs and...

One of waiters, who had been attempting a transaction with Laurence's flash platinum card, cleared his throat nervously. "I'm sorry, My Lord, but there appears to be a problem with your card."

Laurence raised his eyes to the ceiling in exasperation. "Not this again. I swear, the incompetence of these high-street banks is becoming a monumental bore. How many times do I have to pop into them and explain how estate finances work?"

Angel had no idea how estates finances operated either. To be honest her own were quite enough trouble to be getting on with, but she rolled her eyes and pulled a sympathetic face.

"How else would you like to pay, My Lord?"

"Washing-up?" Laurence joked wryly. At least, Angel hoped he was joking. Apart from the fact that she was sporting brand new acrylics, her sharp brain had just worked out that their bill must run to at least £400. That was a lot of washing-up by anyone's standards…

"Or might the amount be charged to an alternative card, perhaps?" suggested the waiter helpfully, glancing first at Laurence and then at Angel.

Angel nearly fell off her seat with terror. The last time she'd checked her bank balance she'd needed a stiff drink to recover.

Luckily, though, Laurence was equally appalled by the idea of Angel paying the bill.

"I'm afraid not," he replied. "And I wouldn't dream of asking the lady, in case anyone was thinking that," he added firmly.

The waiter looked as though he was thinking that the bill needed to be settled. Angel felt weak with horror. Why, oh why, had she insisted on ordering that sodding lobster and drinking expensive champagne? She was starting to wish she had never suggested they visit Stein's at all. Laurence had floated the idea of an evening picnic – which, romantic as it sounded, hadn't the kudos of being seen at an award-winning restaurant. Now, though, she was wishing she'd gone for the romance.

"Don't look so worried, Angel." Laurence reached across and gave her hand a reassuring squeeze. "Things like this happen when your funds come from a family trust." He reached inside his jacket and pulled out his BlackBerry. "I'll give my personal banker a bell. He'll move some funds around for me." He made eye contact with the waiter. "This chap and I will have a chat first and then we can sort it out. Here, there's still some champagne left. Why don't you relax with that while I call my banker?"

Laurence took the waiter aside, presumably to discuss the banking details, and then went outside to make the call. Angel, still a bit shaken by her close escape from scouring Rick Stein's saucepans, downed the remaining champagne in a swift and very unladylike manner. She caught a glimpse of Laurence through the window and frowned; he was shaking his head and gesticulating wildly as he spoke.

"Is everything all right?" she asked on his return.

Laurence smiled at her, a slow sexy smile that made her insides melt like the crème fraiche on her walnut tart.

"Of course. Nothing my banker can't sort. He's wiring money straight to the restaurant now, in fact." He sat back down opposite her, his long legs folding themselves beneath the snowy tablecloth, and reached out to take her hands in his. In a slow and measured movement he raised her fingers to his lips and brushed his mouth against them. Her pulse quickened. She didn't think she had ever felt like this before.

"So, beautiful Angel," he whispered, holding her gaze with those sea-storm eyes. "How about we take a taxi back to my house in Rock? If you'd like to, that is?"

If she'd like to? Angel was desperate to see Laurence's house. In fact she could hardly wait! And maybe once they were alone he would finally kiss her?

"Laurence," she said, smiling up at him through a double row of Eylure's finest, "I'd love to go back to yours!"

Chapter 22

Over the next few days following her calamitous encounter with Callum South and her slightly less disastrous meeting with the ladies at the RNLI cake sale, Gemma's life had taken on a rather surreal bent.

Angel and Andi were both busy with work (although in Angel's case "work" was a loose term), and after days of moping Gemma had started to find the caravan claustrophobic. She'd stayed in her bunk for an entire day, reliving her humiliation on a masochistic loop, drinking White Grenache and hanging out with the only man who never let her down – good old Mr Kipling. Gemma really could have done with having a good chat with Angel, who was usually brilliant at putting these kinds of things into perspective, but her friend was out all day and wasn't returning until the small hours. Without Angel's quips to cheer her up, Gemma was soon plummeting into a quagmire of despair and self-loathing.

"Don't dwell on it," had been Andi's advice when Gemma had retold the Cal incident for about the ninth time. "You'll only end up bitter and twisted."

Quite frankly, ending up bitter and twisted had been top of Gemma's list of things to do next – but if Andi, who had been seriously dumped on from a vast height by wanker-who-couldn't-act-for-toffee Tom, could manage to rise above it all and still have a kind word and a smile for everyone, Gemma supposed she ought to give it her best shot too. This attitude had lasted for about five minutes before she'd cracked. Surely there had to be a man out there who didn't think she was a joke? She'd almost weakened and sent Nick a text but luckily had stopped herself in time. Texts, after all, cost twenty-five pence each and she really didn't want to spend another penny on him. Besides, his new Twiglet-like girlfriend would probably just delete it. Instead Gemma had worked her way through an entire block of cheese and loaf of Mother's Pride, which swelled her billowing midriff like something out of a sci-fi movie and made her feel even worse. When she'd been delighted to see two Jehovah's Witnesses – lost en route to the farmhouse – Gemma had realised that she'd hit a new low, and decided it was time to take action.

Finally, tired of fermenting in a fug of wine and self-destruction, Gemma had showered and, with the help of Angel's impressive make-up collection, transformed herself from a pink-eyed, puffy-cheeked wreck into somebody who looked slightly less like the undead. Then she'd pulled on a pair of leggings and her favourite blue smock, which skimmed her fat bits, and set off for town. Almost as though they had a mind of their own, her legs had carried her up Rock Road and towards the quirky side street where Rock Cakes was situated. One latte, a saffron bun and a chat with Dee later, Gemma had found herself wearing a pinny and setting to work on a coffee cake.

"Your sponge sold out in twenty minutes," Dee told her as they sat in the small courtyard, sunning themselves in butterscotch-coloured light and munching delicious warm-from-the-oven buns. "We could have sold it ten times over. You're very talented."

Gemma flushed with pleasure. "I don't know about that. I just enjoy baking."

Dee gave her a stern look. "Don't put yourself down. That's not a quality that will get you anywhere in this life. What you need to do is smile graciously and say 'thank you'. Go on, try it."

She gulped. In her ears she could hear her mother's voice. "Don't be a show-off, Gemma. Nobody likes a show-off." Lord, but her mother's conditioning was a menace, especially if you wanted to be an actress and your entire career was based on what was essentially "showing off". No wonder she kept on screwing up.

"Come on," urged Dee. "What's wrong with standing up and being proud of what you can achieve?"

Gemma hung her head. "It just feels wrong, like showing off or something," she mumbled.

"Showing off?" The older woman looked despairing. "Is that how you really see it? Listen to me, I worked on the trading floor of a City bank for all for my twenties and most of my thirties, and if I hadn't learned to point out how bloody good I was at my job then all those City boys would have twanged their braces and stamped all over me."

Gemma stared at her. Dee, with her Joules frock, Crocs and neatly bobbed hair, looked nothing like Gordon Gekko – unless "greed is good" referred to cakes?

"So I had my chin up, drew attention to what I was good at and made a fortune," Dee continued. "When I was forty-two I was able to quit my job, divorce my useless husband and move with the children down here and set up my own business as a life coach. I did that for three years and then I decided I wanted a total change. Cake-making was my hobby and I was always making them for friends, so I evaluated my strengths and weakness, saw an enterprise opening and well, here we are. Two years ago we were appointed to make a pre-wedding cake for William and Kate and, between you and me, another royal christening one is on the cards too."

"Wow," said Gemma, impressed. This made running away to a tatty caravan in a field look a bit crap.

But Dee shook her head. "No, nothing 'wow' about it. Just hard work, determination and standing up for myself. If you put yourself down why shouldn't anyone else do the same? You've set the precedent after all. Independence, Gemma: that's the key for every woman. Independence and self-respect."

It all made perfect sense when put like this. If Gemma thought she was fat and stupid and not worth hanging out with, then who was going to argue? Not Chloe, not Nick, not Emily and certainly not Callum bloody South.

"Yes, I'm an amazing baker. Thank you," she said, and actually once the words were out they seemed to become solid and real and utterly believable. Wow. Maybe there was something in all that cosmic ordering stuff after all? She made a mental note to try it out at once.

Dee's smile was as wide as the Camel Estuary. "Fantastic! Keep that up and you'll soon be super confident. Every day, stand in front of the mirror, focusing on all your best features, and tell yourself just how amazing you are."

Gemma wasn't convinced about this for a couple of reasons: a) her horror of standing in front of mirrors was on a par with Dracula's; and b) she was struggling to think of a best feature in the singular, never mind the plural.

"I know it sounds crazy," Dee admitted, "but these positive affirmations really do work. And look at it this way, what have you got to lose?"

"Nothing, I guess."

"And everything to gain!" Dee declared. "And because you are indeed an amazing baker, I'd really like to offer you some work."

The older woman's admiration had been warmer than the sunshine and a balm to Gemma's wounded pride. Before long Gemma had found herself agreeing to work for Dee three days a week and had quickly settled into the rhythm of her new job. One week later and it was now second nature to get up at daybreak, walk the mile into town and get baking. It certainly beat festering in the caravan and torturing herself over Callum bloody South.

So maybe it wasn't the glittering acting career she'd been hoping for, Gemma thought that morning as she cracked six eggs into a large bowl and began to fold them into flour and sugar, but there was something therapeutic about beating ingredients together and creating light-as-air sponges. Piping icing into elaborate swirls was also very satisfying, and yesterday she'd delighted a six-year-old with a Peppa Pig cake. Just recalling the wide-eyed amazement on the little girl's face gave Gemma a thrill. Admittedly, it wasn't quite as highbrow as Shakespeare or Pinter, but there was creativity to this nonetheless which really appealed to her.

As she beat the cake mixture by hand – this was Gemma's secret to creating a fluffy melt-in-the-mouth sponge – she listened to the cheery strains of Pirate FM and the rich-as-clotted-cream Cornish accents of customers in the small shop, and her heart felt lighter than it had done for ages. She still wanted to act – that wasn't going to change – but stepping away from the pressure of having to look and behave a particular way was actually very liberating. Dee, who still slipped into Life Coach mode every now and then, was adamant that if Gemma wanted to act then she would find a way to do it. Acting didn't have to be about fame and fortune, she'd pointed out: it could also be for fulfilment and fun. Gemma thought it was very refreshing to look at it this way. For so long she'd been so busy pushing herself to win the roles that brought maximum exposure and money, that she'd totally forgotten just how much she loved the alchemy of slipping into a new character and exploring that person's hopes and fears. Whether she was playing Desdemona or Blanche DuBois in a big production, or just speaking two lines in a soap, the magic was still there. When had the fun gone out of it? Gemma wiped her hands on a tea towel and shook her head. The answer was obvious: the fun had vanished at exactly the same time the diets and control pants had appeared.

While she greased some cake tins, Gemma realised it was also strange but true that now she was in a cake shop and surrounded by all the mouth-watering, calorie-laden goodies her hungry little heart could desire, she no longer felt the need to guzzle them. In fact, being surrounded by cakes and pastries was having the opposite effect; she no longer fantasised about them twenty-four seven. It was all very odd. Gemma wasn't sure whether it was her imagination, but even her waistbands felt a bit looser...

Maybe this was what they meant by aversion therapy? If you looked at something all day then you no longer wanted it anymore? Gemma smiled to herself as she poured the cake mixture into a greased tin: in that case, she really wanted to cure her Johnny Depp addiction!

She was also trying very hard to say nice things to her reflection too, which was easier said than done when her naked body looked like cookie dough. This morning she had peered into the cracked glass and told herself that her clear, tanned skin was gorgeous. For a fat girl.

OK, so maybe she needed to work on this affirmation lark?

"Morning Gemma," carolled Dee, breezing into the kitchen. Pausing by the oven, she inhaled deeply. "Mmm! That smells wonderful. What's cooking?"

"Gingerbread for that replica of Lanhydrock the National Trust want." Gemma had been struggling for days with how to recreate a stately home out of gingerbread, but she thought she just might have a plan. "I was going to have a trial run this afternoon."

Dee nodded approvingly. "That all sounds very positive. But Gemma, it's your afternoon off. Shouldn't you be on the beach or with your friends?"

Gemma had as much desire to wander across Daymer Bay with her wobbly bits on display as a pig would wish to take a tour of the Wall's sausage factory. Besides, Andi was working and Angel had swanned off to Truro with her mystery man. Gemma was quite looking forward to a peaceful afternoon figuring out how to fix a bad case of gingerbread subsidence.

"I'm happy to do this," she said firmly. Then, a thought occurred and she blushed. "I wasn't hinting. You don't have to pay me extra or anything."

Dee fixed her with a hard stare. "Your time is valuable because *you* are valuable, remember? Of course I'll pay you. Besides, there's no way I want to try and make that bloody thing. Show me again what you had in mind."

While Gemma fetched her sketches of what the finished product ought to look like, Dee brewed coffee, which they carried out into the small sunny courtyard. The sky above was Ikea blue and seagulls cried and wheeled above the rooftops.

"By the way, I picked this up for you on my way through town." Reaching into her spotty Seasalt bag, Dee pulled out a tattered leaflet, which she passed to Gemma.

"Rock Players – looking to cast for their end-of-summer production of *Twelfth Night*," Gemma read aloud. Turning to Dee she said, "I really don't think so."

"Why ever not? You said yourself you love Shakespeare, so this would be right up your street. Besides, what better way to get you back into acting without the pressure?"

Gemma stared at the leaflet. Although it was a bit dog-eared, the setting it depicted in the grounds of a local stately home made her heart skip a beat. Momentarily she saw herself acting the part of Viola. Oh God, she loved that role so much! Viola spent most of the play eaten up with her secret love for Orsino and having to hide her true feelings away, and hiding your true feelings was something Gemma knew all about. For a split second she was seriously tempted, before she remembered that Viola also spent most of the play dressed as a boy and wearing the obligatory tights. The very idea of anyone seeing her sausagey legs filled Gemma with horror.

She offered the leaflet back. "No thanks."

Dee looked disappointed. "Well, keep it anyway and have a think? You don't have to make any sudden decisions, but I reckon you'd love it." She paused and then added nonchalantly, "And who knows what it could lead to? Rock's full of all kinds of media types. You could end up being spotted..."

Gemma laughed. "You should never have given up your life coaching. I promise I'll think about it, OK?"

Dee raised her hands. "Perfectly OK!"

The rest of the morning passed peacefully. It was just coming up to lunchtime, and Gemma was wiping her hands on her apron before taking a break, when Dee burst into the kitchen. Her eyes were wide and she looked more excitable than Gemma had ever seen her.

"Take those off and get yourself into the shop," she ordered, whipping off Gemma's apron and cap, and giving her a shove in the direction of the shop.

Gemma scooped handfuls of curls out of her eyes. "What's going on?"

"There's a man here who says he's come to see you. Apparently he's taking you out for lunch!" Dee was breathless, but then pushing twelve stone of Gemma through a doorway was easier said than done.

"You've got the wrong person," Gemma protested. "There's nobody due to take me anywhere. Besides, nobody knows where I'm working."

"Well, somebody must have done their detective work, because he's definitely requesting you," Dee replied. Her voice had her *I won't be argued with* tone, so reluctantly Gemma allowed herself to be frogmarched out of the kitchen. It was all a waste of time anyway, because there wasn't anyone she knew who would want to take her for lunch – and even if there had been, she was hardly dressed for it in her flowery gypsy top, tatty Skechers and saggy leggings with perished elastic. No: the man standing in the doorway, his back to her and little more than a silhouette against the bright sunshine, wasn't really looking for her. She wasn't Cinderella, was she? More a case of Pastry Gemma.

Then the man turned round and Gemma's mouth fell open.

"Hello, Gemma," said Callum South softly. "Can we start again please?"

Chapter 23

Gemma was all for turning around and marching back into the kitchen. There was absolutely no way she was going to have lunch with Callum South. Firstly because the sight of him made her so angry she couldn't have eaten a thing and secondly because wasn't he supposed to be on some calorie-controlled macrobiotic diet? The last thing she needed was his manager and trainer and bloody Emily bawling her out for a second time.

"I don't think so," she said so coldly it was a miracle a glacier didn't slide by.

Cal was pulling off his cap and sunglasses. Behind him the midday sun turned his trademark corkscrew blonde hair into a halo, but Gemma wasn't fooled: he was no angel.

"Sure, Gemma, I don't blame you for being angry," he said apologetically. "What can I say? I behaved like a total prick. I feel terrible about it, so I do."

Gemma said nothing. He couldn't feel half as bad as she had, clutching a cake and looking like some kind of deranged stalker. Just the recollection made her skin feel prickly and hot with shame.

Cal twisted his baseball cap in his hands. "All I can say is that I panicked and I behaved appallingly. Please, let me make it up to you? And explain? Lunch as an apology?"

"Why? Because you think I'm a greedy, cake-munching lump that'll be won over by grub?" she snapped, and heard Dee groan.

Oh dear. So much for all those positive affirmations.

Cal looked horrified. "No! Of course not! I just thought it might be a nice thing to do. I had somewhere in mind: a friend's place, outside of

Rock where I can eat and chat to you without a manager nagging me or some pap trying to get a double-chin shot."

"Are you trying to make me feel sorry for you? Because it isn't working." Her floury hands on her hips, Gemma glowered at him. Typical self-obsessed celeb.

"Jaysus, no!" He ran a frantic hand through those boingy curls. "I was just trying to explain, but I'm fecking it up. Like I do everything. It's just lunch. That's all."

Gemma tried to avoid those big sad eyes, like the saddest Andrex puppy ever on a particularly sad day. "I'm working, so even if I wanted to come, the answer's no."

Dee, whose own eyes had been popping like Ping-Pong balls ever since Cal had taken off his celeb camouflage, took pity on him and gave Gemma a prod.

"You're not officially working this afternoon," she pointed out. "You're free to go."

Cal looked hopeful but Gemma wasn't going to be persuaded.

"I'm busy with the gingerbread Lanhydrock, remember?" she told Dee.

"That can wait until tomorrow," Dee insisted. Turning to Callum, who was still hovering awkwardly by the door, she smiled brightly and added, "Why don't you wait in the car? She'll be right with you once she's freshened up."

"I don't want to go for lunch with him," Gemma hissed as her boss bundled her back into the kitchen. "He's a tosser and I can't stand him."

"Nonsense!" Dee whipped Gemma's apron off. "He's Callum South and he might be a few pounds heavier these days but he is still bloody gorgeous." Reaching into her Seasalt bag, she plucked out a comb, which she tugged through Gemma's wild hair before fastening the tresses into a loose knot at the nape of her neck with a glittery slide. "Besides, both my sons are huge Dangers supporters and if you could manage to get an autograph, or even better a couple of tickets, they'd be thrilled."

"You're pimping me out for tickets to the football?"

"Don't be so dramatic." Now Dee was flourishing a mascara wand like Obi-Wan Kenobi's lightsabre. Gemma dodged; things were bad enough without having an eye poked out – although, thinking about it, this would be a great reason to skip lunch. As if not wanting to spend time with a cowardly, lying and egotistical git wasn't enough of a reason.

"Anyway," Dee continued, practically wrestling Gemma into a half nelson and squirting her with No 5, "you said how upset you were with what happened, so now's your chance to let the guy make up for it."

Gemma tried to protest but by this point Dee was busy slicking lip gloss on and she couldn't move her mouth.

"You also keep telling me how much you want to act and to be on the television, so maybe this is a golden opportunity," Dee continued, stepping backwards and admiring her handiwork. "Remember how we talked about putting it out there for the universe to deliver? Well, here's your chance to do exactly that."

Gemma wasn't convinced. "I don't think reality TV is really where I want to be anymore."

"You won't know until you try." Dee put her hands on her narrow hips and gave Gemma a searching look. "What have you got to lose? At the very least you'll have an apology and a nice lunch."

It was a fair point but Gemma was hardly dressed for lunch with an A-lister, even one that was several stone overweight and in disguise. She was wearing her oldest, tattiest leggings and superannuated Skechers. She had some paisley shorts in her rucksack, which she supposed she could put on, but it had been so long since she'd shaved her legs Gemma could have grated cheese with the stubble. Besides, those shorts made her bum look huge.

Or should that be even huger? Oh God, she really ought to diet...

"I look a state," she wailed.

"You look lovely. I do wish you'd stop all these negative comments; they're so self-defeating. Haven't you been practising the exercises in the mirror?"

"I would but I keep cracking them all," Gemma quipped, and her boss rolled her eyes.

"I can see we've still got a lot of work to do on your esteem," Dee sighed. "But that can wait. Now go out there and get those tickets – I mean have a lovely lunch!"

Makeover completed, Dee propelled her back into the shop and handed Gemma her rucksack. Feeling mutinous, Gemma ventured out into the street where Cal was waiting in a white Range Rover Sport that dazzled in the sunshine. With its pimped alloys, private number plates and tinted windows, it couldn't have looked more conspicuous. When he caught sight of her, Cal honked the horn and waved.

"I thought you were supposed to be incognito?" she grumbled as she clambered into the vehicle. "So much for the dark glasses and baseball cap. I don't know why you don't just roar up in a red Ferrari."

Cal sighed. "Because I can't squeeze into it anymore."

"You actually have a red Ferrari?"

He gave her a quick grin and in spite of the fact that she still smarted from his words of a week ago Gemma found herself smiling back. That crescent-moon dimple made his good humour contagious.

"Sure, of course I have a red Ferrari. And don't they make you buy one when you sign for a premier team? And a mock-Tudor mansion? And a giant hot tub?"

"And full of babes in bikinis?"

"WAG soup? Practically compulsory."

At the mention of soup, Gemma's stomach rumbled. It was feeling empty because Angel, who had rolled in drunk at some ungodly hour last night, had eaten the remaining two slices of bread and polished off what was left of the cereal. Skipping breakfast made Gemma feel virtuous, or at least it did until she tended to crack around half eleven and raid the biscuit tin.

"Hungry?" Cal asked.

Gemma flushed. "I didn't have any breakfast."

Cal knocked the gearshift into drive and the car rolled forward, so silently that for a moment Gemma thought he'd forgotten to start it. Wow. This was a bit different to her elderly Beetle, which sounded like a tractor. After the long drive to Rock she'd been contemplating buying earplugs in bulk to hand out to any future passengers.

"I did," he told her as they drove through the town. "I had two egg whites, a wheatgrass juice and a buckwheat pancake. It all came to under three hundred calories."

Gemma wasn't sure what wheatgrass or buckwheat was. They sounded like something her father would feed the cattle. And what was the point of eating eggs without the lovely yellow yolk to dip big fat soldiers in?

"That sounds very healthy," she said politely.

"It was fecking disgusting," Cal said, screwing up his face. "I swear to God my stomach was digesting itself by 10 a.m. Then I went for another run and lifted weights for an hour. This is time off for good behaviour and, believe me, I've earned it. It's good to escape the cameras for a bit. And my management," he added with a grimace.

"So where do they think you are?"

"Truro, seeing my solicitor."

"So, they've no idea you're with the mad cake girl then? I suppose you'll pretend this never happened too?"

They were in Wadebridge now. The small town thronged with tourists wobbling on hired bicycles en route to the Camel Trail. Gemma couldn't help thinking that a bike ride along the river looked like much more fun than lifting weights.

Cal sighed. "I behaved like a total knob, didn't I?"

Gemma wasn't about to deny it. "Yes."

"Yeah, well, it wouldn't be the first time. Breaking my leg falling out of a nightclub pissed and ruining my career wasn't my smartest move either."

Gemma recalled the press going wild the day Callum South had ended his glittering career so abruptly by literally falling out of a nightclub. One fractured femur and a junior doctor who hadn't set it quite right later, and the final whistle had blown for Callum South's footballing career, although the tabloids had written that it was little short of a miracle that this hadn't been caused by a groin strain, so famous was Cal's varied love life. He'd gone from being the Irish Beckham to a bloated, boozing has-been in less than six months, and rarely a day had passed without the red tops running a story about his latest drunken escapade or picturing him looking as though he'd swallowed himself. Without a Posh-style WAG on his arm and a bunch of photogenic children to pose prettily with him for *OK!* magazine, the Callum South brand had been in real jeopardy. Only his reality show had managed to save him from becoming the next George Best.

"But honestly? The knobbiest thing I've ever done? That must be turning down your cake. It looked bloody gorgeous. I haven't stopped thinking about it since. How can I eat Ryvita when all I can think about is cake?"

Gemma couldn't help it. He was making her smile, which was annoying when she was actually very cross indeed.

Sensing that she was starting to defrost, Callum pressed on with his explanation.

"Look, you've got to understand – I really need this gig. What else is a washed-up fat footballer going to do? I haven't got the whole brand Beckham thing going on – I tried to pull a Spice Girl back in the day but even Sporty turned me down – and if I screw up this TV show then that's it for me, game over. They'll just wheel out another fat celebrity, won't they? It's not like we're thin on the ground. Jaysus, or thin anywhere, now I come to think of it!"

"I hear Val Kilmer's looking very porky these days," Gemma offered. To cheer herself up the other day when her size-fourteen jeans had refused to do up, she'd Googled fat celebrities. Cal had featured heavily – no pun intended – as had various once-gorgeous A-listers. It made her feel better and alarmed all at the same time. At least they'd all had the head start of being attractive in the first place, whereas she'd always been average on a good day, wearing Spanx and with her hair done.

"Sure, I remember how ripped he was in that volleyball scene with Tom Cruise in *Top Gun*. Now he looks like he's eaten Tom. Poor bastard. It's hard work keeping the weight off when you love food," Cal sighed wearily as he turned the car in the direction of Watergate Bay. "Every day is like a food war for me. I've signed this watertight contract with Leopard TV, and I have to lose three stone by the end of the summer otherwise they'll drop me, and Claire from Steps will be drafted in before you can say 'Tragedy'."

Now it was Gemma's turn to sigh. "You and me both. I'm an actress but I'm far too fat to get any work, according to my agent. She's refused to put me up for any roles unless I'm a size ten by September."

"That's ridiculous. You're not fat. You're gorgeous, so you are," Cal said gallantly.

Gemma looked down at her thighs, which were spilling over the edge of the cream leather passenger seat. "Thanks, but I think we both know that's patently untrue. I am fat and I do need to lose weight."

"You're curvy and sexy." Cal's eyes were hidden behind his Prada shades, but Gemma felt them flicker over her body and her face grew warm. Instinctively she sucked in her stomach and wished she wasn't wearing a scoop-necked top from which her boobs always fought to escape like scoops of troublesome vanilla ice cream. "I couldn't take my eyes off you in that bakery, so I couldn't."

Gemma was crap at accepting compliments, especially from men, and even more especially from attractive ones. And Callum South, three stones overweight or not, was still a very attractive man. She supposed that if she'd practised the mirror exercises more faithfully she might be better at it. To deflect attention away from any discussion of her looks, she took her usual tack and cracked a joke.

"That's blatantly untrue. You only had eyes for the sausage rolls!"

Cal bantered back, "I was more interested in the baps!" Then, seeing her blushing, he said gently, "Seriously, though. Don't put yourself down. If you're a good actress then you're a good actress. Weight shouldn't come into it."

"Yeah, right. Tell that to all those size-zero actresses. The trouble is I love cooking and I love food. It's a nightmare."

They were whizzing down Tregurrian Hill, the sea a glittering Maggie Thatcher blue before them.

"Tell me about it," said Cal bleakly. "When I couldn't play football anymore it was such a relief to kick back for a bit and enjoy my grub. My grandmammy makes the best sausage coddle in the world and her soda bread's to die for. But I had to earn some money somehow; houses in Brentwood don't come cheap, and have you filled up a Range Rover lately? Jaysus!"

Gemma had to admit that she hadn't ever filled up a Range Rover, lately or otherwise.

"So the reality show was a godsend," he explained. "It pays the bills and the costs for my grandmammy's nursing home back in Cork. My agent was thrilled when I first hit sixteen stone because Peter Andre was off for the summer and ITV2 had a spare slot. Before I knew it, the contracts were through, I'd practically signed in blood and I was on the treadmill, literally and metaphorically. No more making bread and plastering it in mammy's butter; no more cheesy chips and no more cakes. Just rabbit food and diets."

He looked so forlorn at this that Gemma's tender heart went right out to him. She knew from bitter experience just how grumpy she got when she was trying to diet.

"Can't you just give it all up and try something else?" she suggested.

Cal shook his head. "I'm a footballer. What else can I do? I haven't a GCSE to my name, I can't act – although, to be sure, that's never stopped Vinnie – and I can't think of another talent I have apart from making bread. I can't give up the reality show because then the whole fecking house of cards comes falling down. That was why I panicked and pretended that I'd never seen you. If Leopard TV find out I'm cheating, then it's the end of my contract."

Gemma was confused. "But you put on weight before, after the boot-camp show."

"Different show, different contract," Cal explained. Then he shuddered. "The boot camp. Jaysus, that was hell on earth. But at least I was locked up and couldn't get out. This time I have to lose weight through summer sports and exercise. If I don't then there's no show. The fridge is all but padlocked, I usually have a camera crew everywhere I go and then I've got a personal trainer yelling at me. I only gave them the slip that day because Nicky, my trainer, had to have a tooth out and the crew were filming cutaways in town. Sure, but I saw my chance and took it. I could have killed for a cream horn!"

"So when I showed up with the cake I totally blew your cover," Gemma finished for him. "And that would have meant game over."

Cal pulled the car up outside a long building of glass and wood, so close to the sea that it was practically paddling.

"You got it," he said. "Look, I'm not proud about how I behaved. I was a total prick and nothing like a gentleman. I really wanted to apologise. I'm not normally such a moron, I promise. I was also half bloody starved and the sight of your cake nearly sent me over the edge.

Especially after all that running; for the last few months the most exercise I'd had was lifting my fork to my mouth!"

A strange thing had happened: during the distance between Rock and Watergate Bay all of Gemma's anger had vanished like the river mist in the morning sunshine. Now she felt nothing but sympathy for Cal. Like her he was stuck in a body that refused to play ball (literally, in Cal's case) and was a slave to a passion for all things gastronomic. In the metabolism lottery they'd both had a bad time.

In other words they were kindred spirits.

As he killed the engine she turned to him and said, "Look, it's fine. You can stop apologising. I totally understand why you did what you did."

"You do?" He exhaled slowly. "And you don't think I'm a total knob?"

"I wouldn't go that far," Gemma said. She was still sore about being made to feel like some kind of deranged stalker.

Cal laughed. He had a nice laugh; it was warm and ripply like the sand on the beach.

"Fair enough. Now listen, I know we're diet buddies and I am strictly not supposed to be eating anything unless it's on Bugs Bunny's menu, but what do you say to having a spot of lunch now? On me for being such a tosser. We can always start our respective career-saving diets afterwards."

Gemma thought her career was so far gone that even Charlie Fairhead couldn't revive it. One more meal couldn't possibly make any difference.

"I'd love to," she said warmly. "But aren't you worried you'll get spotted?"

He gestured to his wrap-around shades and baseball cap. "I'm incognito. Besides, my mate says he'll give us a private area. He's got it all sorted." Keys in hand, he pushed open the door and smiled at her. "Shall we?"

"Shall we what?"

"Shall we go to lunch?" Cal said patiently.

Gemma was confused. Watergate Bay was a breathtaking sweep of gold and blue, as though a giant with a Cal-sized appetite had taken a massive bite out of the lush green hillside. Breakers rolled in carrying surfers towards the shore and a lone dog bounded across the sand – but restaurants were thin on the ground.

"Where?" she asked.

"Where do you think?" Cal said. He pointed to the long low modern building, all vast windows, wooden cladding and breathtaking views of the Atlantic. "There, of course."

Gemma frowned. "I thought you said we were going to your mate's place? That's Fifteen Cornwall."

He started to laugh. "I know. And it is my mate's place. I called Jamie earlier and explained everything. He said it was no problem to find us a private space. He's sound; he won't give us away."

"Your mate is Jamie Oliver?" Gemma said and then wanted to wallop herself on the head with the nearest copy of *The Naked Chef* cookbook. Duh. *He* was Callum South, one of the most famous faces in Britain; of course he was friends with other celebs. It was just that in the car they'd chatted so easily that she had totally forgotten who he was; he'd just become Cal, a nice guy who loved his food.

"Yep," said Cal, "and he is dying to meet you. Tore me off a strip for being so rude about the cake. Said that to carry a cream sponge up a hill in June meant you were 'pukka'."

She was pukka? Gemma liked that idea almost as much as she liked the idea of tucking into a massive plate of butternut squash and walnut tortellini!

"In that case," she replied, with a huge smile, "what on earth are we waiting for?"

Chapter 24

Andi was beginning to worry about her sister. Truth be told, to say that she was *beginning* to worry was pushing it; she'd been worrying about Angel from the moment her mother had brought home the demanding baby, and nothing much had really changed in the past twenty-seven years. It was probably more accurate to say that Andi was worrying even more than usual about Angel. The endless late nights, rapidly expanding designer wardrobe and uncharacteristic secrecy were ringing all sorts of alarm bells. There was a man involved too, judging by the manic glitter in Angel's eyes and the increasingly elaborate outfits, but who this might be was a mystery: so far Angel was keeping him well and truly under wraps. Usually Angel talked so much her tongue could power the National Grid, so her sudden silence was both unprecedented and disconcerting. Andi hoped that Angel hadn't got herself in a mess. It wouldn't be the first time.

No, Andi had decided yesterday – as she'd looked up from her desk to gaze out over the estuary and caught sight of her bikini-clad sister posing on the biggest, flashiest RIB imaginable – it was time they caught up and talked properly. She had no idea who Angel was spending time with or what she was doing. On the few occasions they had passed one another in the caravan, her sister had mentioned something about working as a beautician, which might explain the money – but when Andi had asked about the tall dark man she'd glimpsed her sister with on the boat, Angel had just shrugged and changed the subject.

Andi was probably just being paranoid, and spending far too many evenings flicking through Gemma's copies of *Take a Break*, but you heard such awful things about young girls getting themselves mixed up in all sorts of trouble and she couldn't help worrying about Angel. Her sister might look streetwise and as though she'd just strolled off the set of *TOWIE*, but in reality she was pretty naive. All the romcoms and pink books had convinced her that there really was a knight in shining armour out there when, as Tom had proven only too well, the disappointing truth was that he was more likely to be a tosser in tinfoil.

"Speak to her," was Jonty's advice when Andi shared her worries with him. She seemed to do a lot of that, because he was just so easy to talk to. They'd fallen into the habit of meeting up most afternoons after work at the boatyard, where Jonty would take a break from slaving over the Glastron to have a coffee and share a bun. Her caffeine levels were probably dangerously high and all the Danish pastries were playing havoc with her waistline, but perching on the engine crane while he worked and they chatted about everything under the sun had quickly become one of her favourite things about living in Rock. London, Tom and her debts seemed a world away when she was hanging out with Jonty.

Tom was a subject that Andi hadn't yet raised with her new friend, partly because it was still too painful and partly because it felt like another life. There was also a sharp edge of humiliation involved; how ever had she been so stupid as to trust him with her heart and her finances? It didn't say much for her judgement. She'd behaved like such a muppet they could probably have given her a role on *Sesame Street*. And then there was the issue of losing her job too, which she had also kept to herself. It wasn't that she didn't trust Jonty or that she in any way thought he'd judge her: it was just that it was good to leave that part of her life behind.

In fairness, Jonty didn't really talk much about his past either. Andi knew there'd been a break-up with the mysterious Jax and suspected from what he *didn't* say that he had been deeply hurt. There had been a business at some point too, but Jonty never really spoke about that either, and Andi couldn't blame him. Like her, he was in Rock to heal, and rehashing the past wasn't the way forward. In fact Jonty often pointed out that if the past was really so great it wouldn't be in the past. Andi smiled; this had become their maxim and they often quoted it at one another. If Jonty had any idea just how messy her past was he'd probably run for the hills and, because Andi was enjoying their uncomplicated friendship so much, she was determined to keep her past well and truly under wraps. Little by little she was starting to pay back some of the debts Tom had run up, and at night she often lay awake racking her brains to come up with ways she could clear her name with Safe T Net, but so far inspiration had failed to strike. Sometimes she was sorely tempted to tell Jonty everything and ask his advice, but the fear of spoiling everything held her back. Andi didn't think she could bear it if he didn't believe she was innocent. No, it was much better to keep things simple.

In contrast, her relationship with Angel was anything but uncomplicated. Angel was more elusive than the Scarlet Pimpernel and Andi had spent days seeking her here, there and everywhere before eventually pinning her down. Finally she'd managed to find a window in Angel's manic schedule to meet up for a coffee – her sister was so busy she made the Tasmanian Devil look chilled. So today, which was her day off, Andi was wandering through the town to meet Angel in The Wharf Café rather than relaxing somewhere with a book.

It was another glorious day, the British summer having come up with the goods for once, and a Selfridges-yellow sun was blazing down onto the town from a sky the bright blue of a child's painting. Holidaymakers crowded the street, munching pasties – steak and Stilton or pollo con pesto, none of the bog-standard meat-and-potato variety here – and pouring into the shops. The beach was smothered with sun worshippers while the estuary teemed with all kinds of boats, from little tenders to flashy RIBs to graceful sailing boats. Andi paused at the slipway and watched for a moment, entranced by the moving picture. It really was a gorgeous day. Jonty was hoping to launch his boat for the first time that afternoon and said the smooth water and warm southerly breeze would make conditions out on the water absolutely perfect.

Andi was no sailor herself – Balham was a little short on places for boating, unless you counted floating paper ones on Tooting Lido – but she was surprisingly excited about this afternoon's watery adventure. She'd enjoyed watching the little boat being coaxed back to life under Jonty's loving care. His attention to detail bordered on perfectionism and when he worked there was such intensity to him that the air practically crackled. Andi had found herself wondering whether he applied the same attention and passion to everything he did, and had to bring herself up short. That train of thought was being derailed right now. The last thing she needed was another set of complications.

So, back to the business in hand, namely catching up with Angel and finding out exactly what her little sister was up to. This afternoon's sailing trip, the picnic Andi was going to buy on her way back down through the town to meet Jonty at the beach, and the strange warm glow she felt whenever she thought about spending time with him – all these things would have to wait until later on. At this point in time her sister was her priority.

The Wharf Café was doing a roaring trade on such a sunshiny morning. As Andi queued for her latte she glanced around at the stylish clientele, all Musto sailing gear, Sebago deck shoes and hundreds of pounds worth of sunglasses perched upon immaculately streaked hair. Oh dear, maybe she was a little underdressed in her cut-off jeans, white vest and old DM sandals? At least she had shades wedged into her red curls (even if they were only a fiver's worth from Asda) and a tan, albeit from tramping up the hills in the Cornish sunshine rather than lolling on a Kensington sunbed. Grabbing a paper and heading out onto the balcony, Andi reflected that it was just as well Jonty didn't give a hoot about status symbols or how his coffee-drinking pal looked, because there was no way she could ever compete with this glamorous summer crowd.

As always, Angel was late, so Andi found herself a seat, ordered coffee and cake, and settled down with her paper. Being in Cornwall and staying in a caravan without a television or Internet access was like living on another planet. Angel and Gemma were suffering from serious Facebook withdrawal. For Andi, too, the outside world had started to retreat: she had no idea how long it was since she'd last read the financial pages or kept up with current affairs. She'd been far too busy working for Simon and spending time with Jonty to even think about buying the *FT*, let alone reading it avidly from cover to cover. Knowing from experience that Angel would be at least half an hour late, she flicked through the *Mail*, bypassing moral outrage stories and bonkers new education initiatives, until she found the financial pages. With her shades firmly in place and her face turned towards the sunshine, she lost herself in the old familiar language of facts and figures.

Andi became particularly engrossed in a piece about Safe T Net – apparently the company's going public had rocketed the CEO, Mr Smug Sports Car, practically to the top of the UK's rich list. According to the *Mail*, which Andi reckoned she had to take with a whole salt cellar's worth of Cornish sea salt, he was now worth over five-hundred million pounds. Five-hundred million pounds? She rubbed her eyes until she literally saw stars. How on earth did anyone contemplate having that kind of money? And whatever would you spend it all on? Although the black hole of her overdraft still caused Andi to wake up in the small hours with a racing heart and an overwhelming sense of doom, she wasn't sure she would like to have that amount of wealth. And almost overnight too. How would you ever know who was genuine? Or who to trust? And what could there possibly be to get out of bed for in the morning when you'd already made a small fortune in interest alone by the time you'd opened your eyes? No, Andi decided as she folded up the paper and turned her attention back to the busy seascape across the road, she was glad she hadn't been burdened with that kind of responsibility. Her sister, on the other hand, wouldn't have had any such qualms. In fact for Angel five-hundred million pounds would probably just about cover her shoe budget. Whoever the mystery man was, Andi hoped he was rich.

"Andi Pandy! I am so sorry!"

Angel flew across the place – a whirling dervish of long blonde hair, jangling Pandora bracelets and flailing LV tote bag that threatened to send assorted teapots and paninis flying – and flung her arms around Andi. She smelt wonderful, of something sweet and suspiciously expensive. This perfume was new. As she hugged her sister back, Andi noticed that Angel's clothes were new too; she'd never seen those Chloé jeans before or the silky white top, and were those real Gucci shades? New outfit or not, Angel looked stunning and the eyes of every male in the place were practically out on stalks. With her smooth Caramac-coloured tan, slim denim-clad legs and waterfall of golden hair, she could have strolled right from the pages of a glossy magazine.

"I've been doing a full body massage and exfoliation for Vanya and two of her friends," Angel explained, folding her long legs under the table and pushing her shades onto her head. "I ache from head to foot but they seemed pleased. Vanya even gave me this bag as a thank you!" She thrust the LV tote under Andi's nose. "It's last season's but, even so, it's gorgeous!"

"You've been working today?" Andi asked.

"Like, duh. Of course I have. In case you hadn't noticed, big sis, you and Gemma aren't the only ones with jobs around here. I'm working for Vanya Alexshov; I told you that before. I'm her personal beautician while she's here. Afterwards, well, who knows?"

"And she pays you in bags?"

Her sister grinned. "Bags, shoes, old clothes she doesn't want. Seriously, she has so much stuff! It's totally worth squeezing zits and waxing fannies!"

Andi wasn't convinced, but then she was more than happy with her ancient rucksack.

"So you needn't worry that I'm on the game or something," Angel continued airily, reaching across and grabbing a menu. She shook her head. "And don't deny that you thought I was up to no good; it's written all over your face. Honestly, Andi, you must have a really low opinion of me."

Andi blushed. Her wild imaginings hadn't quite placed Angel on the corner of Rock Road touting for business, but she had started to worry. She felt relieved now. At least this explained all the new designer gear that her sister could never have afforded otherwise. There was still the mystery man of course, but maybe she'd leave that for a moment?

"This is on me," she told her sister as Angel scanned the menu. "It's payday for me, so the least I can do is buy you a latte and some cake."

But Angel couldn't have looked more horrified. "Just black coffee for me, thanks. I'm cutting out dairy and carbs."

"That doesn't leave much to eat," Andi pointed out, patiently. "Besides, you're looking way too thin."

Angel grabbed an imaginary roll of flab and pulled a face. "Not thin enough. I need to get myself down to a size six at least. Have you seen the girls around here? They're tiny!"

Andi grimaced. She wasn't kidding. The wealthy female summer inhabitants looked as though a puff of Cornish wind would knock them over; they probably lived on a mixture of thin air and Pilates. Jonty and Andi, who enjoyed tucking into carrot cake whenever they visited their favourite café, pitied them on a regular basis. While she went to fetch the drinks (espresso for Angel and a calorific mocha for herself), Andi hoped that her sister wasn't going to lose too much weight or get obsessive. Angel was naturally tiny anyway and really didn't need to diet.

"So where's the odd-job man then?" asked Angel when Andi rejoined her. "Mending boats or mowing the lawn today?"

Andi sighed. Her sister made no secret of the fact that she thought Jonty was a waste of oxygen. "I know he's nice and good company," she'd wailed the last time Andi had mentioned him, "but so's a dog. Rock's crawling with seriously loaded guys, babes. Can't you at least give one of them a chance?"

Andi had tried to explain that she wasn't looking for anything except friendship and, besides, she wouldn't date somebody purely because they were wealthy, but her sister had just pulled faces and tutted.

"Jonty's getting the boat ready for launching this afternoon," she said now, tipping a sachet of sugar into her hot drink and watching Angel wince. At the thought of the afternoon ahead, her stomach flipped. She could hardly wait to feel the wind rip through her hair and hear the growl of the engine as they buzzed up the river. It was probably the closest she would ever get to being a Bond girl!

"I bet it's not as big as Laurence's—" Angel began to say, and then clammed up like the scallops on Padstow quay. She pretended to suddenly be totally absorbed in the activity on the Camel. "I mean, I bet it's not as big as some of the other boats."

Andi's cup was frozen halfway to her lips. Her carrot cake was instantly forgotten.

"Laurence? I take it this is the mystery man?"

"Oh look! Is that a Lotus?" said Angel hastily, but Andi wasn't so easily distracted. As a seasoned elder sister she was well and truly used to getting the truth out of Angel, although now they were in their twenties she'd rather not use Chinese burns or have to sit on her.

"So is this Laurence the reason you've been coming home in the small hours, hogging the bathroom even more than usual and wearing a soppy expression?" she teased.

Now it was Angel's turn to blush.

"Maybe," she said, suddenly fascinated by the polished surface of the table; then, when Andi prodded her with the cake fork, "Ouch! OK then, yes! Laurence is the guy I've been seeing."

"Don't stop now," Andi said. Slowly and deliberately replacing the fork, she settled back into her seat and crossed her arms. "I'm listening and I want to hear everything. Go on, spill!"

So spill Angel did, and for the next half an hour Andi's coffee went cold and her cake untouched while she listened to tales of viscounts and stately homes, exclusive houses at Daymer Bay, fast RIBs and trips to flashy restaurants. Angel scarcely drew breath as she described how utterly gorgeous Laurence was and how much she liked him. Andi was taken aback because she couldn't ever remember seeing her sister so animated about a man. Usually they all chased Angel like crazy while she got bored, leaving Andi and Gemma to field the phone calls, make excuses and pick up the pieces of all their broken hearts.

"So, you see why I can't possibly have him drop me back at the caravan," Angel concluded, once she'd finished explaining why Laurence always dropped her at the Alexshovs' house, where she hid until he'd driven away, before walking two miles back to Trendaway Farm. No wonder she was losing weight and never in until the small hours, thought Andi in despair.

"If he finds out that I live in a caravan and am just a beautician he'll soon lose interest," Angel summarised.

"Doesn't he like you for who you are?" Andi was confused.

"Of course he does, obviously," Angel said with the total confidence of the very beautiful, "but he's a viscount and he's only ever dated aristocrats and wealthy girls. When he's totally and utterly head over heels with me of course I'll tell him the truth. By then he won't care anyway."

Sometimes her sister didn't so much take the biscuit as the entire chocolate-digestive factory.

"But you're lying to him," Andi pointed out. She was shocked by her sister's glib attitude. In Andi's book a relationship had to be based one hundred percent on honesty and trust. She knew from very bitter experience how once a partner lied about one thing it was very hard to trust them. But Angel, the moral equivalent of Teflon, didn't seem at all concerned.

"Technically he's just making assumptions," she said airily. "I've never actually told him I live at Vanya's."

Andi knew there was no point arguing, so she changed tack.

"So, if you found out he wasn't a viscount it wouldn't matter? You'd still feel the same?"

Angel stared at her as though she was crackers. "What are you on about? He *is* a viscount."

"But if he wasn't? Say he turned out just to be an ordinary guy?"

"He isn't an ordinary guy. I Googled him! Kenniston Hall is huge, Andi! It's been in his family for donkey's years. And he parties with Prince Harry and everything. Don't worry, he really is who he says he is."

At least one of them was. Andi gave up. Angel simply didn't get it. When the truth came out this Laurence would either embrace his inner chav or take for the hills. She just hoped her sister didn't get too hurt in the process.

"So it's all on with Laurence then?" she said, returning to her cake and hoovering it up. Honestly, thirty minutes with Angel and she was comfort eating. No wonder poor Gemma had a weight problem. "As far as it can be, of course, seeing as he hasn't really got a clue who you are?"

Angel bit her lip. "Well, sort of. The thing is he hasn't made a move yet. I know he fancies me. I just don't get it."

She looked so concerned that Andi couldn't help laughing. Angel was usually a man magnet, so it must be blowing her mind to encounter resistance.

"Perhaps he's just being a gentleman," she suggested. "Some guys actually like to buy a girl dinner first."

"Hmm, maybe." Angel didn't look convinced. "He invited me back to his last night and I really thought that this was going to be the night it happened. I could tell he really wanted to. The way he was looking at me was so hot my knickers were practically melting."

Andi clapped her hands over her ears. "Too much information already!"

"Don't panic; that's as exciting as it gets. When we arrived back at his house – it's seriously stunning Ands – one of his mates had turned up unannounced. Honestly, I couldn't believe the cheek of it. He was treating the place as though it was his own, helping himself to Laurence's booze and everything. That put the end to any hopes we might have had of being alone together. I had a quick drink and then Laurence called a cab for me. He said he really needed to talk to this guy."

"Maybe his friend was in trouble and needed help? Perhaps he was broke and needed a place to stay?" Andi offered. She'd lost count of the times she and Tom had been about to eat or go out only to be interrupted by her sister in the throes of some crisis. Angel of all people should be sympathetic.

But Angel shook her head. "He's Travis Chumley. Of Chumley's Chunks?" she added when her sister looked blank. "He's the heir to the Chumley pet-food empire and seriously loaded. He and Laurence were at Eton together, apparently, so I don't think he came over for a handout. It's bloody selfish; he could easily stay in a hotel. I hope we're not going to be stuck with him; I'll never get Laurence to myself then. Not if he's got a single mate in tow who's going to want to hang out all summer. Oh, it's so unfair! Why did he have to turn up and interrupt us?"

Andi had no idea. She was just about to offer an explanation along the lines of maybe this Travis was lonely, or just wanted to see his friend, when Angel cried, in the fashion of Archimedes in the bath, "Oh my God! I've got it! I've had a brilliant idea!"

Andi's heart sank because she knew this expression of old. It had last been uttered when Angel was planning how to gatecrash Peter Andre's party – and look how well that had ended. When Angel got an idea into her head, that was normally that. Nothing would move her.

Unfortunately.

"My God!" she was declaring triumphantly. "Am I, or am I not, a genius? I've just had the best idea to keep Travis occupied and sort out all your money problems."

"Oh really?" Since Angel was to finance what Posh Spice was to fast food, Andi wasn't holding her breath. When she lay awake at night, her eyes wide open and her heart hammering with fear, she seldom thought of calling on her sister for fiscal advice.

But Angel was almost bouncing in her seat with excitement. Turning to Andi, eyes wide, she said, "Yes, really. Big sis, this is your lucky day – I'm going to introduce you to Travis!"

Chapter 25

By the time she reached the pontoon Andi had just about stopped laughing at Angel's latest ridiculous idea. Honestly, sometimes she worried that her sister really was a few lipsticks short of a MAC counter. As if she would be interested in dating somebody just because he was going to inherit a few million tins of cat food!

"Do it for me then," Angel had pleaded when Andi told her exactly what she thought of Project Date Travis Chumley. "How will I ever get to have time alone with Laurence if his sad single mate is always hanging around like cheap aftershave? We'll probably never get together; he'll have to marry some titled girl who looks like a horse and I'll die of a broken heart! Can you live with yourself then?"

Andi had said that, on reflection, she thought she probably could, so Angel sulked into her coffee for the next twenty minutes before dashing off to meet Laurence and, she'd said pointedly, probably Travis as well. When she died a lonely old spinster, she would know exactly who to blame.

Andi shook her head. When it came to drama, Angel could give the RSC a run for their money. Living with Gemma must have rubbed off on her.

Heaving her rucksack, now crammed with delicious picnic bits from the deli, onto her shoulders, Andi walked to the far end of the pontoon and stared out across the water. A beach-ball sun beamed across the estuary and she shaded her eyes with her hand, trying to see if she could make out which of the boats zipping over the water might be Jonty, but the light was too bright to see anything much except their lacy wake. She perched on the end of the wooden platform and dangled her legs over the sea, listening to the call of the gulls and slap of waves against the pontoon. The sunshine was sprinkling freckles across the bridge of her nose, Jonty was on his way to pick her up by boat and she had a rucksack stuffed with crusty rolls and Cornish Brie. Did life get any better? And would dating a millionaire make her feel any happier than she felt at this moment? Somehow, she didn't think so. There was no way she was going to get embroiled in any of Angel's madcap schemes. Sometimes her sister made Andi felt like a right old stick-in-the-mud and closer to a hundred and twenty-nine than twenty-nine, but she couldn't help it; she didn't approve of Project Rich Guy. At all. Angel could argue until she was blue in the face that this was no different from what Jane Austen's heroines had been up to, but Andi wasn't buying it. If a relationship wasn't built on the truth then it wouldn't take long before the quicksand of fibs sucked it under. Besides, as far as she remembered, Mr Darcy had never been led to believe that Lizzy Bennet was an oligarch's daughter...

On the other hand, Angel did seem genuinely distraught about not being able to spend time alone with this Laurence, which was most unusual. Normally she played it so cool it was a miracle none of her boyfriends got frostbite. Andi swung her legs thoughtfully. This could mean one of two things: either Laurence Elliott ticked all the boxes on her sister's extensive list, or – and this was an extraordinary possibility – Angel *really* liked him. This idea made her stomach twist nervously. What if Angel was wrong and Laurence ran a mile when he discovered who she really was? Angel might give the impression of being shallower than a flea's paddling pool but Andi knew better. Angel was actually very tender-hearted and once she loved somebody she adored them, no matter what. Years of having to mop up her sister's tears when Alex let them down had taught Andi that much. She just hoped that Laurence Elliott, viscount or not, wouldn't prove to be a disappointment.

"Andi! Hello!"

She looked up with a jolt; she'd been so deep in thought about Angel that she'd failed to notice Jonty had come alongside the pontoon in the boat and was smiling up at her. Gazing down, she saw herself reflected in his mirrored shades, her hair a startling tangle of reds and damsons against the bright blue sky. It hardly seemed possible that she and the always-immaculate Angel were related.

"All ready for the maiden voyage?" Jonty asked, sliding the shades onto the top of his head and reaching out to take her hand. Strong, tanned fingers closed around hers and squeezed gently. "It's OK, don't worry. Just throw the bag down first and then jump down. I've got you. You won't fall in."

Something about him inspired absolute trust and, bag launched first, Andi jumped from the pontoon towards the deck. Jonty caught her waist and lowered her carefully. For the briefest moment she felt the corded muscles of his arms tighten around her and her heart seemed to miss a beat. Then, almost before she could even stop to think, she was safely on board. Although the small boat was lurching like Angel and Gemma on a pub crawl, Jonty barely moved. He was totally at home on the water. Andi shifted her weight cautiously. It felt a bit like being on the Tube; she'd soon get used to it.

"Welcome aboard!" Jonty grinned, scooping up her rucksack and stowing it carefully in the hold. "Well, here she is, on the water at long last. What do you think?"

This sleek little vessel with its jaunty red hull, cream leather seats and gleaming deck was a million miles away from the sad flowerpot she'd seen in pictures. The electronics were state of the art, all the fittings were highly polished and the engine was purring away like Bagpuss. Although this was probably the oldest craft on the Camel and nothing like the flashy RIB Angel had been posing on the day before, Andi didn't think there was a nicer boat anywhere. She might not be the newest or the most expensive, or even the fastest, but she'd been restored with such care that she was priceless. All Jonty's hours had been a labour of love, but it had been worth every second and Andi told him so.

His answering grin could have powered Rock's street lighting for a year.

"That's exactly how I feel," he nodded. "I know she's old but she's got heart. And she's been in a Bond film too. She's sleek and sexy – a true Bond girl. What more could a man want?"

Andi laughed. "So she's the Ursula Andress of the boating world?"

"Wrong film; I think Ursula Andress was in *Dr No*, which was the first Bond film." His brow crinkled thoughtfully. "I've been struggling to come up with a name for her and I think you might have just nailed it. What do you think of *Ursula?*"

"I love it, but don't you want to choose the name?"

Jonty passed her a life jacket, and then helped her secure the ties and tuck them in. His deft fingertips brushed against the bare skin of her arms and, although the sun was hot, she shivered.

"I was half thinking about calling her *Miranda*," he admitted shyly, tugging the straps tight before turning his attention to his own. "But I think your name would be better suited to something more elegant and classy and new; a Princess maybe? Or a yacht?"

Andi was flattered. The way her life had gone lately, *Ursula* had been an exact metaphor when she was rotting and full of weeds. Her, elegant and classy? Really? Was that the impression Jonty had of her? She felt a twinge of unease; would he still feel the same if he knew about Tom and her sacking?

"I think *Ursula* is perfect," she said, trying hard to shove these bad memories back into the dark corners of her mind. "So, Mr Bond, where are we going?"

Jonty opened up the throttle and the boat glided gently away from the pontoon.

"I thought we'd go gently up to Wadebridge, grab some chips and then float back with the tide," he said over his shoulder. "I don't want her maiden voyage to be out to sea, just in case we hit a problem."

"More chips? I'll sink the boat." Andi glanced ruefully down at her stomach. She always had a wonderful time with Jonty but a lot of their activities seemed to involved cream teas, pasties or chips.

Jonty knocked the boat into neutral and turned to face her. Although she couldn't see his eyes from behind the shades, Andi felt the intensity of his gaze and her skin danced with goosebumps.

"You look perfect," he said firmly. "Absolutely perfect."

As they put-putted upriver to Wadebridge, Andi allowed herself to bask in both the glorious sunshine and Jonty's words. Although she knew she quite obviously wasn't perfect – as someone who'd spent most of her formative years being compared to Angel, she was far too aware of her own physical flaws to ever be under such an illusion – it still gave her a Ready Brek glow that he might think so. She stole a glance at him, intently concentrating as he guided the boat upstream, and found herself wondering what the soft skin just below his ear would feel like against her lips.

Right! Stop there! Andi scolded herself. Honestly, thoughts like these were so not the way to go. If she carried on like this she'd be looking at the cognac-hued skin of his strong forearms and the muscular chest sculpted beneath the soft white tee shirt. The heat must be getting to her. Maybe she should just hurl herself overboard into the icy river? There was no way she was going to allow herself to think like this. They were friends and she was not going jeopardise that. Besides, after Tom she was steering well clear of men. Her face felt hot, and not just from the sunshine. She really hoped he couldn't tell what she was thinking.

Luckily for Andi, Jonty might be skilled with all things marine but like most men he wasn't a mind reader. Calling her over, he gently showed Andi how to steer the boat and trim the engine. Before long she was so engrossed in this task that she scarcely noticed he was standing so close to her that their forearms brushed. And if when he put his hand on hers to help guide the steering her heart skittered like the moorhens alongside the riverbanks, then it was from the excitement of driving the boat, nothing more.

As they returned to Rock, heavy from fresh air and vinegary chips, Jonty let Andi take the wheel and guide *Ursula* downstream. While she steered, loving the way the little boat responded to the slightest motion, Jonty pointed out egrets and the blue flashes of kingfishers. At one point he moved to pick up her fleece from the stern and the boat lurched to an abrupt halt.

"What did I do?" Heart hammering, Andi looked over to him in panic. She'd only been in charge of *Ursula* for a few minutes! Surely she couldn't have broken the boat already?

"Absolutely nothing," he assured her. "You're doing it all perfectly."

Reaching down, he carefully unwound a length of what looked like old-fashioned red telephone flex from his knee. He had nice knees and, above his battered deck shoes, muscular tanned legs. She swallowed and looked away.

"This is the kill cord," he was explaining, as he held up the wire. "The driver clips it on and if there's an accident and he takes a spill, the engine stops instantly and hopefully nobody's injured. It's vital and saves so many lives. I just forgot to take it off when we swapped over."

"Phew! I thought I'd broken her."

He grinned, a dimple dancing in his cheek. "No, I was just being very responsible and giving you a safety demo."

"Don't give me that. This is just your way of getting girls stranded out on the water with you!" she teased, and Jonty raised his hands in mock surrender.

"You've got me! What more can I say? Boats are great – lots of girls willing to take their clothes off and wear bikinis!"

Andi thought about her own pale and very bikini-unready body. There was no way she was revealing that any time soon.

"Seriously though, did you enjoy it?" Jonty asked, as he restarted the engine on their approach to the pontoon. The gentle breeze lifted his hair from his strong-boned face as he looked hopefully down at her.

"I loved it," she said.

What wasn't to love? They'd seen stunning wildlife, Jonty pointing out a variety of seabirds she'd never really noticed before, and the stillness of being out on the water had been wonderful. There was so much more to see by water, from the bicycles rolling by on the Camel Trail with their jaunty flags and kiddy carts, to the stunning hidden properties that fringed the riverbanks. They'd even spotted a seal, sleek and sad eyed, popping its head out of the water. The real world, the one where boyfriends cheated and colleagues stitched you up, was a million miles away and like a half-remembered fragment of a bad dream.

If only every day could be this peaceful and this perfect. If she could spend every day boating with Jonty, then Andi thought it probably could be.

Jonty beamed at her, a smile of such delight that her heart melted like butter on a hot jacket potato. "I knew you would. She might not be the flashiest boat but she's done us proud today."

Andi patted the console. "I think she's wonderful. Who needs flashy, anyway? We've seen some amazing wildlife and I've had the best time. Thank you so much for taking me out."

It was one of those moments when time seemed to hover. Sound ceased and the movement of the water slowed in that suspended second. Gradually, Jonty's hand touched her shoulder; his fingers were cool and strong against her sun-kissed skin, and even the blood pulsing through her veins seemed to pause in anticipation.

"You don't need to thank me," he said softly. His hand rose from her shoulder to her cheek, brushing a stray curl away. His shy smile was white against his tan and his stubble midnight dark. His lips were just a kiss away. Tenderly, Jonty tucked the curl behind her ear. "Andi, there's something I need to tell you—"

There was a roaring in her ears, which wasn't her racing heart – and for a moment Andi thought she had lost consciousness. The earth was certainly moving, anyway – and if it dipped and rolled this much at just the mere thought of kissing Jonty, then whatever would the reality be like?

Then she was thrown from her feet and slam-dunked onto the deck with such violence that the air was punched from her lungs so that she lay gasping like something out of *Deadliest Catch*.

"Hold on!" Jonty was shouting. Winded, she watched him leap across the surging deck with the deadly grace of a panther, somehow keeping his balance as he knocked the engine out of gear. With horror she realised that they really were lurching from side to side, the water either side of the hull dangerously high, as the wake from a RIB passing at lightning speed all but swamped *Ursula*. As the RIB zoomed by, shrieks of excitement and the throaty roar of many horsepower filled the air. With legs trembling like a newborn foal, Andi clambered to her feet.

"Are you all right?" Having gained control of the boat, Jonty's arms closed around her as he guided her to the driver's seat. "Have you hurt yourself?"

Above her heartbeat, currently banging like something from a Magaluf nightspot, Andi could hear the concern in his voice. She shook her head. "I'm fine apart from maybe just a few bruises. What happened?"

Jonty's face was tight with anger. "Some total moron just drove his boat flat out past us. He must have been going at about sixty knots, way too fast for this stretch of the estuary. The wake could have sunk us."

Ahead, the huge RIB was still blasting across the river, scattering smaller craft and jet-skiers like ninepins. Jonty pushed his shades onto his head and his eyes glittered with fury.

"That bloody idiot is going to kill someone if he carries on like that," he grated, still holding her so close that she could feel his racing heartbeat against her cheek. "Haven't these boy racers learnt anything? Apart from nearly capsizing us, that pair of three-hundred-horsepower engines could make short work of anyone in the water; the props are nothing but giant blenders. Bloody stupid bastard!"

Andi was taken aback. Jonty was normally so laid back he could double as a hammock; she hadn't seen him like this before.

"Sorry to swear," he added, seating her carefully and checking her legs for cuts, like a racehorse owner at Aintree, "but that kind of behaviour makes me wild. Out on the water accidents can happen in a split second, and when you add some show-off city boy without a clue and more horsepower than brain cells, it's a recipe for disaster. Last summer there was a dreadful tragedy here, and you'd think people would have learnt from it." He frowned. "Apparently not."

"I'm fine," Andi assured him. To be honest she was more annoyed that they'd been interrupted than that by tomorrow she'd look like she'd had an argument with an iron bar. Had Jonty really been about to kiss her? Or was the sun stronger than she realised?

Whatever the moment had been, it had passed. Jonty was businesslike now and the delicious tension of earlier had melted away. "That's lucky for him. I couldn't be responsible for my actions if he'd hurt you." Turning to the console, he clicked the engine into gear and, his face grim, pointed *Ursula* in the direction of the pontoon where the RIB was now moored. Moments later they were alongside the RIB. The legend *Wet Dream* was emblazoned across the hull.

"Says it all," muttered Jonty.

"Want me to catch a rope, mate?" A man with wrap-around Prada shades, a tan the colour of yacht varnish and the most peculiar highlighted hair gelled up into a funky Mohican beamed across at them. Dressed in head-to-toe expensive sailing gear, he looked like a Tangoed cockatiel that had been caught in an explosion in the Musto factory.

"Is this your boat?" Jonty demanded.

The cockatiel glanced at *Ursula* and preened visibly. "It certainly is. Do you want to come on board?"

Jonty threw him an expression of such disgust that, in a just world, it should have laid him out in a heap on his shiny fibreglass deck.

"What I want," he said, in a tone so icy that Andi wouldn't have been surprised to see a polar bear swim by, "is for you not to drive her like a complete cock. Have you any idea of the damage you could have done just then? There's a speed limit on the river for a reason."

"Chill out," said the cockatiel airily. "Nobody's hurt, except maybe your pride." Craning his neck, he looked critically at *Ursula*. "What's that, seventy-five horsepower?"

"Showing off on the water is a recipe for disaster," Jonty said evenly. Andi noticed how his fists clenched as he fought to keep calm. "There's nothing to prove by hooning around."

"I'd say that too if I was in that pile of crap," said the cockatiel pityingly. "You can tell the men from the boys by the size of their toys. This beauty can cruise happily at eighty knots. What do you say to that?"

A muscle twitched in Jonty's cheek. "I'd say you should be wearing a kill cord."

"A kill cord? Am I hearing you right? You don't have a baby like this and strap yourself down." He grinned, revealing toilet-bowl-white teeth. "Don't worry man, I can handle her." He winked at Andi. "I can handle anything!"

"You can't reason with stupidity," Jonty said wearily to Andi, but her attention was suddenly elsewhere. On the deck of the RIB, to be precise, where a stunning blonde in a tiny white string bikini was waving to her.

It was Angel.

"Andi Pandy! Oh my God! What a brilliant coincidence! Travis," Angel said excitedly to the cockatiel, "this is my sister! The one I've been telling you about!"

"The gorgeous big sister?" Travis gave her a wolfish grin. "What are you waiting for, baby? Hop on board!"

Jonty turned to Andi. Confusion was written all over his face.

"Do you know these people?"

Andi opened her mouth to try to explain (although quite how you explained Angel was anyone's guess), but it was as if she was suddenly possessed of ventriloquism skills: her sister's voice seemed to be speaking for her.

"Jonty! It's me, Angel!" she called, blissfully oblivious to the fury coming from him in waves. "Oh, Ands! This is brilliant timing! Laurence has just gone to pick up some champers for a picnic; we're going to blast out to Lundy. Travis has been dying to meet you. You must come with us."

"Yes, you must," said Travis to Andi. He pointedly turned his back on Jonty while his eyes took a leisurely tour of her body. "Any sister of Angel is a friend of mine, especially one who's single and looking for company." He fixed her with that white smile and Andi was relieved she had her shades on, or there might have been permanent retina damage. "Hop aboard, sister of Angel. We have bikinis and sunscreen on board, although both are optional." When he said this he actually winked.

Seriously, was the guy for real?

"Thanks for the offer but I'm busy," Andi said coldly. She would throttle Angel when she next saw her – if Travis didn't drown her first, that was.

"Later then," Travis said firmly. He clearly wasn't used to the word "no". To Angel, he said, "Hold tight then, baby! Let's nip to Padstow and pick up Laurence."

As Travis busied himself with casting off, Angel leaned across the boat, treating the whole of Rock to her best Jordan impersonation, and called to Andi, "See! I said you could find a rich one if you looked harder! Come for dinner with us all tonight. Borrow my green Chloé dress! We'll pick you up from The Wharf Café!"

Before Andi even had the chance to tell her sister exactly what she thought, there was a sudden roar of engines, spray filled the air and the RIB shot forwards like a scalded cat. Angel shrieked with excitement as the boat screamed across the estuary, her long hair flying like a golden banner and with not a thought of life jackets in her head. Actually, Andi thought in despair, with not a thought at all in her head.

Jonty was looking stunned. "That's your sister's friend?"

"Afraid so," Andi admitted.

"My God." He looked disgusted.

Andi couldn't blame him. At this point in time she wasn't exactly proud of her sister. Travis Chumley, pet-food millionaire or not, was clearly not going to be a great influence. Still, Angel was her sister and Andi couldn't help feeling protective.

"He's a friend of a guy she's started dating," she attempted to explain, but the right words evaded her and even to her own ears the reasoning sounded weak. "Angel likes the finer things in life and she's certainly found them here. She's seeing a viscount and it's all very mysterious. I haven't been allowed to meet him yet, but if his friends are anything to go by..." She trailed off awkwardly because Jonty was looking seriously unimpressed.

"So you mean she's a gold-digger?" he said coldly. "She's come to Rock just to trap a rich man?"

"No!" This sounded awful and instantly Andi jumped to her sister's defence. "It's more complicated than that. I think she really likes this Laurence."

Jonty's top lip curled. "No, I think it's simple enough. The world is full of shallow women like that."

"You don't know my sister. You can't judge her," said Andi, needled. Nobody put Angel down. Defending her was second nature.

His face darkened. "I don't need to. Believe me, I've met enough women to know her kind."

"She's just insecure," Andi insisted, but Jonty wasn't having any of it.

"Stop making excuses; she's a user," he said bluntly. "But I guess you already know that if she's out lining up rich men for you too. Maybe you should have joined them rather than wasting time here?"

Andi's vision blurred dangerously. How could he say this? "If you really think that then you don't know me at all."

Jonty shrugged. "You're right. I don't think I do. Not if you've sent your sister out hunting for rich men."

They stared at each other, the mutual sympathy of earlier evaporating like early morning river mist. There was an anger radiating from Jonty and a tension she hadn't seen before, which seemed to her almost an overreaction. Andi stepped back. Time that had seemed so slow earlier now began to accelerate and the distance between them was far more than inches.

"If that's your opinion of me, then fine," she told him. "I won't hassle you any longer."

"Fine," he echoed. "You may as well get off here. I'll moor up and fetch the trailer."

Andi's throat tightened with grief. When she stepped ashore, she wanted to ask him why Angel's words had upset him so much, but there was such a closed look on his usually open face that she didn't dare. His anger was palpable. As he steered the boat away without so much as a backwards glance, she felt so close to tears that she had to gulp fresh air. Their friendship meant so much to her that to contemplate losing it was unbearable.

She pulled her rucksack onto her shoulders and bit back her disappointment. She had absolutely no idea what had upset him so much and, worse still, even less of an idea how to put it right.

Chapter 26

Angel was in a determined mood. Wired from all the excitement on the water and slightly squiffy after drinking champagne in the sun, she was adamant that her plans were going to go smoothly. Nothing, but nothing, was going to stand in the way of her and Laurence finally getting it together. Not a pet-food millionaire, or her own lack of funds – and certainly not her spoilsport big sister. Travis had been really taken with Andi; it was impossible not to be, because her sister was, when she put her mind to it, actually very pretty. Angel had high hopes that in spite of getting off to a bad start they might actually hit it off.

As she heated up the straighteners and ironed the Chloé dress, Angel reflected that Andi could do much better for herself than that miserable odd-job man she insisted on hanging out with. Granted, he was ridiculously good-looking; Angel would give him that much – and when his eyes had flashed with anger her stomach had knotted deliciously – but he was such a killjoy and totally lacking in fun. You only had to see how he drove that ancient boat as though he was some kind of pensioner to know exactly what he was like – about as much fun as a wet weekend in Margate! Whereas Trav, with his sexy boat and love of speed, was much more exciting. He never stopped laughing either, whereas that glowering Jonty could have given Oscar the Grouch a run for his money. No, Angel decided as she shook out the dress and hung it carefully from the curtain rail, her sister had wasted far too much time with useless guys who bled her dry and had no sense of adventure. Andi was gorgeous and deserved to be treasured and spoiled rotten; she should be with a man who could take the financial strains away and give her the best of everything, which was exactly what Travis could do.

This Jonty, living in his sister's garden shed and making ends meet by doing odd jobs, was bound to end up expecting her sister to do everything while he played boats and bummed around. In short, Andi was in danger of hooking up with another Tom and there was no way Angel was going to let that happen again. Not on her watch, as Laurence would say!

Hmm, Laurence. Angel paused in the middle of sorting through her extensive wheelie bag of make-up, lost in thoughts of her eligible viscount. He liked her – she knew he did – but talk about taking it slowly. They were practically going backwards! Today's champagne picnic off the coast of Lundy had been fabulous but Trav had been there too and the closest she had managed to get to Laurence was a discreet brushing of fingertips when he passed her a flute of champagne. Angel's knickers had practically burst into flames at just this, and she was starting to wonder how much longer she could take the frustration. It was all very well his being a gentleman, but at this rate she'd be drawing her old-age pension before they even kissed. No, there was nothing else for it but to make sure that Travis was occupied with Andi. She was doing her sister a favour anyway; it was high time Andi had some fun.

Gemma was certainly having fun. Angel didn't get it personally, but working in Rock Cakes seemed to agree with her best friend. Gemma had just rolled in at half five positively glowing and, amazingly, had managed to bypass both the biscuit tin and the fridge. She'd not stopped for long, muttering something about going into town for an audition, but her sparkling eyes and smiling face spoke volumes. Although it was only for an amateur production, Angel was relieved: during their last few weeks in London, Gemma had been on an increasingly downwards spiral, which could only end with her face buried in a pizza. At that point, Gemma's acting ambitions had only seemed to extend as far as pretending she hadn't polished off Angel's Special K. It was good to see her looking happy and getting excited about acting again. So the Callum South thing hadn't quite worked out, but it wasn't the end of the world. There was always Peter Andre...

Cheered up by thoughts about how she could help revitalise Gemma's reality TV career (she'd be perfect for the whole weight-loss DVD angle), Angel busied herself with selecting the perfect hot-date outfit for her sister. When Andi eventually arrived at the caravan, feeling flatter than week-old only cola, Angel was waiting for her, armed with the Chloé dress, fake tan and her wheelie bag full of make-up.

"You shall go to the ball, Cinders!" Angel declared, the second Andi all but fell through the door. "Go and jump in the shower, borrow my Mademoiselle body lotion and then I'm going to give you a makeover."

Andi looked less than thrilled. The last time Angel had given her a makeover she'd made the cast of *Geordie Shore* look understated.

"You'll look fabulous, really natural," Angel said swiftly, seeing her sister baulk. "Honestly, you won't regret it. Vanya loves the make-up I do for her. I'll do you a fake tan too," she added kindly, holding up a mirror. "See? You look really pale."

Andi felt pale. She glanced in the mirror and her face was white beneath her slight tan, her freckles standing out like foxglove speckles. After Jonty had left she'd sat staring at the river for what had felt like ages, their disagreement playing on her mental DVD like a video nasty. She couldn't bear the fact that he thought badly of her. On the other hand, that he could jump to conclusions so readily made her wild. Jonty didn't know the first thing about her or about Angel. How dare he make judgements?

"A fun evening out with friends is exactly what you need," Angel was saying, propelling her in the direction of their cupboard bathroom. "Laurence has booked a table at The Wharf Café for seven. I said we'd meet him and Travis there."

The thought of an evening with the cockatiel, on top of her row with Jonty, was enough to make Andi want to stick her head in the Calor-gas oven.

"I don't think so," she began, but Angel wasn't taking no for an answer; finally Andi caved in, partly because she was too shattered to argue and partly because there seemed to be no point in protesting. Jonty had already made up his mind that she and her sister were just a pair of fortune-hunting harpies, so staying in the caravan moping wasn't going to do any good. Before long she was showered and wearing Angel's green dress. Still feeling as though her stomach was trying to digest cut glass, Andi let Angel tweak her hair and play with her make-up, although she put her foot firmly down when it came to the fake tan.

"You look gorgeous," Angel declared, spritzing her with a final blast of Mademoiselle. "Honestly, I don't know why you don't make more of an effort." Her hands on Andi's shoulders, she spun her sister around to face the cracked mirror tile they all fought over. A slim girl with light honey-coloured skin and wide eyes stared back, the green dress picking out the deep reds of the hair swept back from her face. For once Angel hadn't opted for the full Lily Savage look, but had dusted Andi's face with the softest of bronzes to highlight her subtle tan and swept mascara across her lashes. Andi stared at her reflection and thought that she preferred the usual version, all tangled curls, cut-off shorts and vest top. Still, Angel seemed thrilled and that was the main thing.

It was a perfect summer's evening, the air so still that the town seemed to be holding its breath. The estuary was a silver ribbon winding its leisurely way out to the milky sea, which seeped into a pearly pink sky. Small boats glided silently across the horizon and even the gulls were quiet for once, as though too tired from the long hot day to squabble and squawk. Cow parsley frothed in the hedgerows and valerian flowers nodded drunkenly from the dry-stone walls. While they walked down into town and Angel texted frantically – the mobile black spot in the caravan being a cause of great anxiety for her – Andi looked down at the perfect view that ended what should have been a perfect day. She still couldn't work out what had gone wrong and why Jonty had been so angry, but she knew she wouldn't find peace until she did. Unlike Angel's mobile, which was buzzing like a swarm of wasps, hers remained as silent as a Trappist monk. Andi sighed.

"An-dee," Angel said, breaking through her tangled thoughts in a familiar sing-song tone that Andi recognised all too well as usually preceding a request. "Laurence has just texted. He says Trav has had to go to Newquay. He's really sorry but he won't make it for dinner, so I was wondering..." She paused and Andi smiled at her. Sometimes Angel was so transparent she could have doubled for a pane of glass.

"And you were wondering whether I would mind leaving you alone with him?" she finished.

Her sister looked sheepish. "I feel terrible because you've made such an effort and you look amazing. And you haven't eaten."

Food was the last thing on Andi's mind. It would be hard to stuff her face when it felt as though piranha fish were chomping on her stomach.

To escape a meal and several hours with Travis the cockatiel was a relief.

"You go and see Laurence." She gave Angel a hug. "Have a lovely time and don't worry about me. I'll pick something up on the way home."

"And hang out with the odd-job man?" Angel sighed. She'd had such high hopes of Travis – his brand new Range Rover was to die for – but her stubborn sister seemed determined not to listen. Much as she was fizzing with excitement at the mere thought of seeing Laurence, she was bitterly disappointed that Andi wasn't spending time with them all this evening. Maybe she could persuade Andi to go out on the boat tomorrow? Trav's RIB was amazing and went much faster than that old wreck her sister had been in earlier. Once she saw the RIB properly, Andi was bound to be impressed with Travis. Pleased with this plan, Angel hugged her sister back.

Alone at long last, Andi turned around and, as though her feet had a memory all of their own, she soon found herself taking the path up to Ocean View. The cobalt-blue pool glimmered invitingly in the evening sunshine, an array of snorkels and wetsuits were strung from makeshift washing lines between the cedars, and the smell of barbecue drifted on the warm breeze. As she walked past the pool house it was clear that the place was deserted. Wherever Jonty had gone once *Ursula* was safely back in her shed, it wasn't home. She was surprised to discover just how bitterly disappointed she was.

"Don't look so sad! He's in the kitchen!" Mel called, crossing the lawn with a basket of washing clamped against her Joules-clad hip. Tucking her arm through Andi's, she steered her gently through the lavender and rosemary bushes towards the house. "You look gorgeous," she added admiringly. "I hope my brother is going to take you somewhere wonderful. Not that he's bothered to change – I think he practically lives in his board shorts and deckies." Mel's chatter was like the Severn in full flood, and before Andi could get a word in edgeways, she continued confidentially, "Jonty's in a vile mood, which isn't like him at all. Hopefully you'll cheer him up. He's always happier when you're around."

Right now Andi doubted this.

"He was grouchy from the moment he got in," Mel confided. "His phone's been beeping non-stop and he was closeted with Simon for hours." Her eyes flashed with anger. "If it's that Jax hassling him again, I swear to God I'll swing for her."

Andi couldn't help herself; she had to know more. "Were they together long?"

"Too long," Mel said darkly. They had paused by the back door and she lowered her voice a fraction. "About three years, on and off, I guess. She's an older woman; she knows what she wants and she goes after it, but she let Jonty down really badly when he had business troubles. He wouldn't allow her interests to be compromised in any way – my brother's a total gentleman like that – but Jax was more than happy to leave him high and dry when the tables were turned. He could have lost everything and she wouldn't have given a toss."

"So they were business partners?"

Mel nodded. "Then she broke his heart and couldn't have cared less." She reached out and deadheaded a rose so viciously that if it had been a voodoo rose the notorious Jax would have been in trouble. "He sold his flat and moved in with us for almost a year, which the boys loved because they could see him every day." She looked thoughtful.

"In fact there's still a Jonty-shaped dent in the sofa from all the Xbox playing, although that's probably with Simon rather than the kids. Anyway, at least things are better now, although she'll know that too of course. No wonder she's been desperate to get back in contact. Jax loves money."

"But he's working for you, isn't he?" Andi was confused. Jonty couldn't earn much more than board and lodging mowing lawns and cleaning the pool for Simon and Mel. Where would the appeal be for the money-loving Jax? Apart from the fact that Jonty was wonderful, of course.

Mel looked flustered. "Well, yes, of course. I just meant that she's probably bored and looking for somewhere to go for the summer." She dropped her voice even further. "I probably should have told him, but she's left several messages on our answerphone. She's renting a place here for a month, to try and worm her way back I guess. I deleted all the messages, obviously." Snap! Another rose met its end. "I just wish I could delete *her*!"

Andi had never seen Mel so ruffled or so angry. Her eyes were bright with emotion and she visibly had to gather herself. "Sorry, Andi, I didn't mean to pour all that out on you. It's just that he's in such a happy space at the moment and I couldn't bear to see that fall apart again. Jax isn't good for him at all, but they have a history and I worry sometimes. I'm probably just being an overprotective big sister."

Andi thought that if Mel had seen Jonty earlier she might reconsider her idea that he was in a good space. She was just about to make her excuses and head home – as interrupting a family evening was not on her agenda – when the kitchen door opened and Jonty strode out. When he saw Andi chatting with Mel he looked taken aback.

"Anyway, enough of me gassing on," Mel said hastily when neither her brother nor Andi spoke. The air crackled with tension. "I've got washing to sort and two revolting children to bath. I'll catch you both later."

She shut the door firmly behind her and moments later they heard her yelling for the boys.

"You're very dressed up," Jonty said quietly.

"I'm not off hunting for rich men, if that's what you think," Andi shot back. His earlier words still stung.

Jonty looked at Andi, his eyes slowly raking the length of her body. She pushed her hair away from her face, unusually shy with him all of a sudden. After talking to Mel, a few parts of the Connect Four of Jonty's anger were falling into place for Andi. If he'd been hurt and betrayed by a woman who had cost him dearly, both emotionally and financially, it would explain his overreaction to Angel and her talk of rich men.

A blackbird trilled in the undergrowth, some wind chimes tinkled and suddenly it was like an evil spell was broken. Jonty exhaled slowly, as though he had been holding his breath underwater for a very long time.

"You look absolutely gorgeous," he said softly. "And I've been vile. I'm so sorry for that. I wish I could wipe all those ugly words away and just go back to our wonderful afternoon."

Her voice caught. "So do I."

He reached out and took her hand. It fitted snugly inside his and Andi looked up at him wonderingly. When he raised her fingers to his mouth and kissed them gently she thought she would dissolve. Oh Lord. This was not good news. She wasn't supposed to feel like this!

"There are lots of things I need to tell you," Jonty said quietly. "Things I should have told you about earlier on but that I've held back." He smiled ruefully. "I guess I was scared it might change what you thought of me and ruin our friendship. That's come to mean a lot to me."

Andi stared at him, wondering what bombshell he was about to drop. She too knew all about holding back through fear. "And to me," she said.

"I should have been honest with you," Jonty continued, his thumb skimming across her palm, "and there have been a thousand times I've been on the brink of saying something. This afternoon when we were out on *Ursula*, I nearly told you then."

Her stomach was a mesh of delicate knots. Only what he said next would untie them.

"You can tell me anything," Andi said quietly. "We're friends, aren't we?"

He squeezed her hand. "The best of friends, I hope. And boating buddies too, of course."

She squeezed back. "Definitely."

He bit his lip. "I know what I'm going to say will change everything, but I need to be straight with you. I have to be."

Jonty looked so stricken that Andi's heart melted like tarmac in a heatwave.

"It doesn't matter to me what might have happened in the past," she said firmly. "If the past was so great it wouldn't be in the past, remember?"

But this time he didn't laugh. "This isn't just about the past, this is about the present too. When I saw your sister earlier, it made me wonder if I could actually trust anyone ever again. Believe me, I've made so many mistakes before."

Andi thought of her emptied bank accounts, finding Tom with Gina and being stitched up at work. "We all have," she agreed. "But unless people tell the truth then I don't see that friendships can work. They have to be based on honesty, surely?"

He nodded. "Absolutely."

"So tell me what's troubling you," Andi began – but her words were lost in the screech of tyres as a scarlet Audi TT scrunched around the driveway, spraying gravel everywhere and shattering the evening stillness.

A door flew open and a pair of Louboutins and long leather-clad legs swung slowly out, followed by a lean gym-honed body and waterfall of dark hair topped with giant bug-like shades. Jonty's hand fell to his side and he looked stunned and horrified in equal parts.

Andi didn't need to ask him why. The Audi's number plate, JAX 1, told her everything she needed to know.

Chapter 27

Gemma was on cloud nine. Not only had she enjoyed the most amazing afternoon with Cal (she'd be dreaming about that lobster ravioli for weeks) and met Jamie Oliver too, but also this evening she'd actually plucked up the courage to audition for *Twelfth Night*.

"You have to do it. It's the perfect way to ease yourself back into acting," Cal had urged her over lunch. They had been tucked into a very private corner where they had spent several mouth-watering hours working their way through the taster menu. Spearing a seared scallop and feeding it to her, Cal had added, "Your friend Dee is right about the surprising amount of influential people skulking around Rock in the summer. You just never know who might see you."

Gemma had licked garlic butter from her lips thoughtfully. "That might just be the kick up the butt my acting career needs. It could be my big break."

Cal had screwed his nose up. "I guess so, although I can't for the life of me think why anyone would want to put themselves up on the stage to be gawped at. Sounds like my worst nightmare."

She'd laughed. "Says you, the reality TV star!"

Cal had shaken his head, the golden ringlets bouncing emphatically. "Sure, but isn't that by accident? I'm a footballer, or at least I was until I ballsed it all up. All I ever wanted to do was play. I never wanted to be famous. That just happened by accident. Believe me, being famous isn't all it's cracked up to be."

Gemma – who'd spent most of her formative years singing into a hairbrush in front of the mirror and going to soul-destroying auditions – thought that, even so, it might be nice to find this out for herself.

"So, apart from football and reality TV, what else would you like to do?"

He'd frowned. "That's a good question. To be honest, I'm not really sure what else I'm good at." Cal had glanced down ruefully at his stomach, which was bulging over his waistband as though on a mission to escape. "Apart from eating, obviously."

Gemma had prodded her own squidgy tummy. "That makes two of us. I really shouldn't eat another mouthful. If I can't get myself down to a size ten by September then that's it, career over. I'll be baking cakes forever."

"Would that really be so bad?" Cal had asked. "You're obviously talented – that sponge looked wonderful. Don't think I haven't been thinking about it ever since."

Gemma had thought wryly that it was the story of her life that her teen hero was thinking about her cake rather than her. "I love baking," she'd said thoughtfully, "but I'm not sure there's a career in it."

"Are you kidding? Tell that to Mary Berry and Paul Hollywood! They bake and are on the telly. And, if we ask him, Jamie will tell you it's possible too!"

At this point they'd both been distracted by the arrival of the sweet trolley. Once a slice of berry cheesecake and a slab of pecan pie had been dished up, Cal had said, in the tone of somebody in confession, "Just between us, I love baking too, but bread's my thing rather than cakes. Sun-dried tomato rolls, olive focaccia and caraway bread. I love it all. Jaysus! It doesn't really go with the macho image though, so maybe keep that to yourself."

Gemma, plopping a big dollop of clotted cream onto her pie, had been impressed. "That sounds wonderful. Don't be embarrassed about enjoying baking."

"The trouble is I don't stop at the baking stage," Cal had admitted. "I just can't resist lathering my bread with full-fat Irish butter, so I can't. And then I tend to eat the lot."

She'd paused, mid-chew. "Oh my God. I do exactly the same with my cakes. Sometimes they don't even make it from the baking tray to the cooling rack."

They'd stared at each other, enjoying the moment of mutual sympathy.

"Maybe we should go into business together," Cal had joked. "With your cakes and my breads we could single-handedly cause an obesity epidemic."

She'd licked the last sticky smears of pecan from her spoon. "I don't doubt it for a minute. I've been a huge success already working on my own obesity."

"You're not obese," Cal had said staunchly. "You're curvaceous."

Gemma had rolled her eyes; she'd lost count of the times she'd heard that cliché.

"Yeah, and I'm a real woman," she'd finished for him. "Which would be fine, except I'm about five real women all rolled into one."

"Which makes me about ten men," Cal had said with a grimace. "But sure, I don't regret a mouthful of today's lunch. The food was great and the company even better."

Now, as she walked through the town and back towards Trendaway Farm, Gemma smiled to herself as she recalled these words. Cal had proved to be very easy to spend time with and their conversation had flowed as effortlessly as the Camel was now flowing out into the Atlantic. Far from the arrogant footballer she'd been expecting, he was funny, self-depreciating and hugely encouraging of her acting ambitions. In fact, if it hadn't been for his enthusiasm, Gemma doubted she would have found the courage to audition for the role of Viola this evening.

"If you can do this," Cal had said, dropping her off at the rehearsal venue, "then I can certainly pluck up the courage to go wakeboarding tomorrow. Jaysus! I fecking hate the water. Do you think I should have told my manager I can just about doggy-paddle?"

Gemma – who'd been looking at the gathering crowd of thespian wannabes, the women all wearing leggings, organic handmade shoes and loose floaty tops which probably cost more than her entire wardrobe – had felt her stomach lurch. What on earth had possessed her to do this? There was no way she could compete with them. Who would want a chubby Viola? She'd probably end up being cast as Sir Toby Belch instead. She'd opened her mouth to tell Cal that she'd changed her mind, but he'd put a finger against her lips and shaken his head.

"Go on, show them how it's done," he'd told her. "Get out there and break a leg. Hopefully, unlike with me, that will start your career rather than ending it!"

So Gemma had dredged up all her courage and, after arranging to watch him wakeboard the following day in return, had gone and auditioned. Although she'd last learned the lines a lifetime, and several dress sizes, ago the words were as fresh as if she'd memorised them yesterday. While she'd waited her turn she'd trembled like a puppy left out in the rain, and the delicious lunch had curdled and churned as her stomach had done its best washing-machine-on-spin-cycle impression.

What little nails she did have had soon been gnawed to stumps; she'd just been making inroads on the skin alongside them when her name had been called. Before she'd even had time to gather her thoughts, Gemma had been propelled onto the stage.

For a moment she'd stood still, blinded by the lights and racked with self-doubt. What had she been thinking?

"Ready when you are!" A voice had carolled. "From the top!"

Her tongue had turned to cotton wool. For a hideous minute it had felt as though her throat was closing up, and there had been a whooshing in her ears. Then, Gemma had taken a deep breath.

"Too well what love women to men may owe," she'd begun and, just like a racehorse catapulting out of the starting gate, she'd been up and running. Viola's beautiful, heartfelt words had tumbled from her lips, the rhyme and rhythm carrying her along in a tide of emotion, until she'd no longer been Gemma, the overweight awkward girl who liked cakes a little too much for her own good, but Viola, young, alone and hopelessly in love with the handsome Duke Orsino, a man as far out of reach from her as Cal was from Gemma. As Gemma had described how she would love him constantly and silently, her heart breaking because she could never reveal her feelings, her voice had caught and her eyes had shimmered with tears.

"I am all the daughters of my father's house, and all the brothers too," she'd finished sadly. She had chosen to end the section here, an unusual finishing point but one which she hoped would have an impact on the audience.

The hall had been totally silent. All Gemma had heard was the thudding of her own heartbeat and her ragged breathing. Oh crap. She must have been seriously bad and shocked them speechless. Silently she'd cursed Dee and Cal for letting her think she was good enough to do this. Could she just sneak out now and hide under a rock? Or, in her case, a whole heap of rock cakes?

Just as she'd been contemplating bolting for it, a slow ripple of applause had spread around the room, quiet at first but slowly gathering in volume and conviction until the whole place had rung with it. Somebody had even whistled. Gemma was stunned. They liked her. They really liked her!

"I don't like to jump the gun, darlings, but I think we've found our Viola," a tall skinny man with sparse ginger hair and thick black-framed glasses had declared. Stepping forward, he'd extended clammy hands, which had clasped hers excitedly. "Derek Vanos, director of the Rock and Padstow Players, at your service! My dear, that was simply divine! I just adore the way you delivered!"

A big Halloween-pumpkin grin had split Gemma's face. Derek's admiration had made her feel a million dollars. By the time she'd left, with a copy of *Twelfth Night* held firmly in her hand, Gemma had felt almost drunk from an overload of praise and excitement. Not only had she plucked up the courage to audition but she'd also been offered the part there and then! She could hardly wait to see Cal again and tell him!

Still buzzing, Gemma wandered through the town. She wasn't quite sure when she would see Cal again – he had a busy filming schedule and found it hard to escape his team – but they'd made a pact to meet once a week to eat something naughty and commiserate about calorie counting. Cal thought this would just about keep him sane and Gemma had agreed that, in the spirit of solidarity, she would do her hardest to watch her food in the interim. It was nice to have a friend who actually understood just how hard it was to resist the biscuit tin and for whom diet really was a four-letter word. Right now she was so excited about being in the play and getting stuck into rehearsals that for once food was the furthest thing from Gemma's mind. Instead, she was reading *Twelfth Night* as she walked along, oblivious to all the delicious smells from the restaurants. Even the piles of chips in the local chip shop failed to drag her away from the pages of iambic pentameter. It was only when Angel waved her hand under Gemma's nose that she left Illyria and returned to Cornwall.

It was a sign of just how engrossed Gemma was in the play that she didn't notice Angel: her best friend was glammed up to the nth degree in a scarlet Valentino number which made her hair stand out like a halo and her skin turn to golden suede. Although she was walking along Rock Road, presumably on her way back to the farm, Angel was inappropriately shod in sky-high silver wedges, in which she wobbled and tottered like Bambi on ice.

"Bloody hell, am I glad to meet you. These shoes are killing me!" Angel grumbled, clinging to Gemma's elbow for support. Her pretty face was screwed up with pain. "Have you got the car? I swear, if I take another step my feet will fall off!"

"I walked," Gemma said. This wasn't strictly true, of course, because Cal had given her a lift, but she didn't want to discuss him with Angel. Apart from the fact that she was looking forward to poring over their lovely afternoon like a miser counting his gold, she'd promised Cal that any lunches they had would be top secret – and since Angel had a bigger gob on her than Zippy, she would be kept firmly in the dark. Luckily for Gemma, she wasn't forced to fib or elaborate because Angel was totally focused on her own predicament.

"Bollocks," she said, slipping off a shoe and bending over to massage her red toes. "I was really hoping for a lift. I can't walk another step. I don't suppose," she added hopefully, "you've got enough money on you for a taxi?"

Gemma shut her copy of the play. "Why are you walking? I thought you were dating a viscount? Can't he afford a cab?"

"Of course he can," Angel said with huge confidence. "He's just dropped me off at the Alexshovs. I have to wait until he's gone and then walk home. I can't have him seeing the caravan, can I?"

Gemma stared at her. "You're still hiding where we live from him? That's madness. Surely you can tell him the truth now?"

"Not yet," Angel said firmly. "Not until I'm sure he really likes me. Until then I'm doing a lot of walking and getting a lot of blisters. So, Gems, can we get a cab? Please?"

Gemma had been enjoying her walk home. It was a beautiful night: the black velvet sky glittered with stars and the air was warm and sweet. Although it was dark, the town was still busy. People were squashed onto benches and tables outside the cafés, and bubbles of laughter and the clinking of glasses filled the air. Unlike Angel, Gemma was wearing sensible shoes – her fat feet would have looked like trotters in strappy sandals – and was more than ready to stomp up the hill.

"Please?" Angel repeated, her eyes wide and sad. "I'll do anything! Lend you my Gina sandals? Introduce you to Laurence's millionaire mate?"

"How about you clean the loo?"

Angel gulped. "You strike a hard bargain, but OK, I'll clean the loo."

"You really are in pain, aren't you?" Gemma teased, since Angel was to cleaning what Cal was to healthy eating. She fished around in her bag, located her purse underneath the detritus of tattered magazines, fluffy Tampax and leaky biros, and tugged it out. Inside was all her worldly wealth until payday; paying the rent and food upfront had wiped out what little savings she did have. Andi was working hard to reimburse her but she'd yet to see a penny from her best friend.

"Oh goody, a twenty," Angel cried, when Gemma opened her purse. "That will get us back easily."

Gemma sighed. There went her last twenty pounds. She had been planning to spend tomorrow in Truro, but no longer.

"Bugger Truro," Angel said cheerfully when Gemma mooted this idea. "I've got a much better plan for you, girlfriend! And it can be a big thank you too. Laurence's pal has got a really cool boat and tomorrow he's promised to take me and Andi out on it. It'll be a blast. You can have a go in the tubes and on the wakeboard."

A bit like Cal, Gemma could think of more enjoyable activities than water sports – like cordless bungee jumping, for example. Besides, there was no way she was letting anyone see her flabby body in a swimming costume.

"He's got wetsuits too," Angel continued, warming to her theme. "You'll love it."

Gemma couldn't think of anything she would love less. Dressed in rubber she would look like a whale. No thanks. She was just about to refuse when a thought occurred to her: Cal would be on the water tomorrow, wouldn't he? If she were out on a boat too then maybe she would bump into him. Somehow the thought of Cal seeing her in a swimsuit didn't faze Gemma in the slightest. Nobody would understand better how she would feel. At the thought of seeing him again, her heart did a cartwheel. Oh dear. She was still a fifteen-year-old in her head.

"OK, then," she agreed.

Angel beamed and brandished her iPhone. "You're going to love Trav and honestly, babes, you'll have the best time. You won't regret it."

And with this decisive comment, she set about calling the cab company, while Gemma kissed goodbye to her last twenty quid and hoped desperately that Angel was right. She had a sinking feeling and, although she was no expert on water sports, Gemma was pretty certain that when it came to boats a sinking feeling was not a good thing...

Chapter 28

It was one of those Cornish mornings when the air was Jif-lemon sharp and the light so clear it almost hurt the eyes. Although it was only seven o'clock, the heat of the day was already intense, ripe with the promise of more warmth from the gold-medallion sun. While Andi, Angel and Gemma waited on the pontoon, the Camel was already teeming with boats as holidaymakers and locals alike prepared for a day out on the water. The concentration of Breton tops, Joules tee shirts and Seasalt gear was probably higher here than anywhere else on the planet, Andi thought with a smile. And as for the rash of designer sunglasses atop perfectly styled hair – it must be really contagious, because here came Travis sporting a monster pair of Guccis and, next to him, a tall lean man with long dark hair and a panther-like grace, who was wearing mirrored wrap-around Pradas. From the way Angel lit up like Harrods at Christmas, Andi guessed this had to be the mysterious Laurence.

"All right, ladies?" Travis carolled, giving them a jaunty wave as he strode along the pontoon. He was wearing a scarlet pair of Rip Curl board shorts and little else, the sun glinting off his smooth waxed chest. He obviously worked out because he was ripped, but it was an oddly sexless look. Andi couldn't help comparing him to Jonty, who was tanned and muscular from all his work in the boatyard and Ocean View garden. Jonty was strong, but not in an airbrushed showy way; she liked the freckles on his shoulders and the sprinkling of hair across his chest.

Andi pushed such thoughts away. Jax probably liked Jonty's features too...

Once Jax had arrived last night, Andi had made her excuses and left swiftly. Jonty hadn't tried to stop her. He'd been rooted to the spot, as motionless as any of the rosemary and lavender bushes beside him, and her last image of him had been of a figure so still he could have been mistaken for a statue. Whether he'd been frozen with horror or amazement Andi hadn't been able to tell, but either way she hadn't felt comfortable staying. Whatever had happened between Jonty and his ex, and whether Mel and Simon's version was biased by affection or not, Andi had no idea. She only knew one thing: Jonty and Jax had a history and she was no part of it. He was her friend but, like her, he hadn't chosen to share many details about his past. Andi wondered whether it was because this was too painful or because he was still in love with Jax? For about the hundredth time since yesterday evening she checked her mobile for a voicemail or a text, but it remained stubbornly silent. Andi sighed, and pushed it back into her rucksack. Life was complicated enough already; she ought to be grateful that Jonty was choosing not to make things even more difficult. Maybe he and Jax had spent last night talking long into the small hours and then making up until the stars faded and a small fingernail of sunshine scratched dawn into the hillside? That thought gave her a nasty twisting sensation, which Andi didn't want to even think about attempting to identify. Instead she shoved all thoughts of Jonty away and concentrated on saying hello to Laurence and pretending to be thrilled to see Travis again.

"Delighted to meet you at last," Laurence was saying in polished upper-class tones, as he took her hand in his. He was attractive, Andi thought, in a severe hawklike fashion, and those dark stormy eyes were definitely compelling. When he smiled down at her it was as though the sun had come out after months of cloudy skies, and she couldn't help smiling back.

"This heatwave is marvellous, isn't it?" he continued politely. "Simply marvellous for boating."

He was still shaking her hand. Andi felt a bit as though she were meeting Prince William at a garden party, and had to resist the urge to curtsey.

"Angel tells me you are here for a few weeks staying with friends," Laurence said. His vowels were so precise and his pronunciation so razor sharp it was amazing he didn't slice his tongue. "Is that for the whole summer or will you move back with your family?"

Over Laurence's Ariat clad shoulder Angel was pulling frantic faces. Andi hadn't a clue what she was on about or what pack of fibs her sister had told Laurence, but the meaning couldn't have been clearer: *don't tell him anything!*

"Mmm, that's right," Andi hedged. Not for the first time, she could have cheerfully throttled her sister. She hated lying, even by omission. In fact, especially by omission; hadn't that been Tom's forte?

"Enough of the touchy-feely bollocks," said Travis cheerfully as he barged past, with armfuls of inflatables and ski lines. "Plenty of time for all that once we're on the water. Time and tide don't wait, even for viscounts."

Laurence laughed. "They might for multimillionaires!"

Travis grinned. "They certainly do! I'd have the lot dredged and a bigger pontoon stuck in!" He leapt onto the boat and whooped. "All aboard the *Wet Dream!*"

Angel, shrieking with laughter, was already jumping down from the pontoon while Gemma, looking very worried, clambered awkwardly behind her. Although they were boating she was dressed in a white floor-length skirt, every inch of her swathed awkwardly – and inappropriately for today's water sports – in fabric. She looked like a prim Victorian sea bather.

Andi shouldered her rucksack. She was half inclined to turn tail and just head back for the caravan. Some time on her own, the calls of wood pigeons and blackbirds the soundtrack to her day rather than Travis's foghorn tones, was a very appealing notion. Only a nagging sense of unease and an unwillingness to leave her sister in the care of the Mr Toad of the boating world prevented her from running for the hills.

"Is he always like this?" she asked Laurence, nodding towards Travis.

Laurence gave Andi an apologetic smile. "Trav's all right once you get to know him. A lot of that bluster comes from having to survive the public school system. You can probably imagine that a bunch of upper-class twits weren't particularly kind to a boy whose pater sold pet food for a living. I class myself as one of those upper-class twits, by the way, but I hope I've grown up a bit since Eton."

"So you're school friends?"

He nodded. "Shared a dorm and then a study. When Pa died he was really there for me. A chap never forgets things like that."

"I felt the same about some of my friends when my mum died," Andi agreed, but Laurence looked puzzled.

"Forgive me, but I had no idea. Angel hasn't mentioned it. I thought she was with your parents now?"

Andi could happily have chucked her sister, presently cavorting around the RIB in the world's smallest bikini – which was more like three of Barbie's hankies lashed together with dental floss – in the water and held her under until the bubbles stopped. Luckily she was saved from trying to invent some plausible tale by Travis yelling for Laurence to move his ass right now. Then the casting off, stowing of picnic hampers and digging out wetsuits began.

"I hope this isn't a big mistake," Gemma whispered to Andi as the girls settled themselves on the boat. Her freckled face was etched with worry and her eyes were terrified saucers. She glanced nervously at Travis, who was more interested in checking out Angel as she sprawled across the front of the boat than in coiling the dock lines, which lay in blue tangles across the deck. "Do you think he knows what he's doing?"

Andi recalled yesterday's trip out on the water with Jonty. Whereas he had moved deftly around the boat, coiling ropes and trimming engines with the ease that came from years of experience, Travis was galumphing about and making a great show of actually not doing very much at all. Apart from writing the cheque for the RIB, she strongly suspected that the closest he had ever come to boats was playing with one in his bath. Still, she decided not to voice her misgivings to Gemma, who was looking worried enough as it was. Fortunately, she escaped having to make false reassurances when Gemma was suddenly distracted by something going on further along the pontoon. Following her gaze, Andi saw a snot-green ski boat casting off, followed by two little RIBs crammed full with camera crew and fluffy boom mikes.

"That's Callum South," Gemma breathed, actually clutching Andi's arm in excitement. "He's filming his new show today. Look! There he is!" She pointed towards a chubby man poured into a wetsuit and surrounded by an entourage. Andi squinted against the light. If it hadn't been for those trademark bedspring curls she would never have recognised him.

"I thought you were over your crush on Callum South?" she said, surprised at just how excited Gemma was. After Cakegate his name had been mud in their caravan.

Gemma didn't meet her gaze. "That was just a misunderstanding. At least, I think it must have been," she added hastily. "He probably has lots of fans doing crazy things all the time."

"You baked him a cake," Andi pointed out. "It was hardly an act of lunacy."

"But it could have had anything in it," Gemma argued. "How was he to know I'm not a stalker wanting to poison him?"

Across the water Callum was being wrestled into a buoyancy aid. One of his entourage was yanking the straps tight in the style of a lady's maid fastening a corset. That reminded Andi of something Jonty had said and she called to Travis, "Have we got life jackets to put on?"

"They're not compulsory, baby," he hollered back. "But bikinis are! Come on, strip off! Don't be shy!"

"Tosser," she muttered. It was going to be a very long day.

Gemma paled. There was no way she was taking her clothes off! Nervously, she backed away to the stern and perched on the side of the tube.

"We can put the life jackets on once we're out at sea," Laurence offered, seeing the look of concern on Andi's face. Coiling a bowline expertly, he added gently, "It's flat calm today, so there's no need to worry."

Andi, recalling how safety conscious Jonty had been, wasn't convinced.

"I'll take one anyway," she said stiffly. "Gemma?"

Gemma – who was busy waving at Callum South, and not doing much to prove she wasn't a deranged stalker – shook her head.

"God, no way. I'll never do it up. Anyway, I'm so fat I'm bound to float."

Laurence passed Andi a life jacket before making sure that Angel, despite her protests, was safely belted up too. Then Travis turned the ignition and the quiet of the morning was blasted into smithereens as massive twin engines roared throatily into life. Travis grinned from ear to ear.

"Let's see what this baby can do!"

"Come and join me up here!" Angel looked up from basting her long limbs in tanning oil. "You've got your bikini on, haven't you?"

Actually, Andi had – but she had absolutely no intention of stripping down to it in front of Travis, who was clearly under the delusion that he was the Hugh Hefner of Rock. Ignoring her sister, she pointed to the kill cord dangling from the console.

"Shouldn't you put that on?"

Travis grimaced. "I don't need to lash myself down. Not while I'm manoeuvring, anyway. The thing's a major pain in the ass. Don't look so worried. This is one of the most powerful boats there is, not like that pile of crap you were in yesterday. She can handle anything."

"It's not the boat I'm worried about," Andi grumbled. Still, everybody else seemed happy enough and it did look as though it was going to be a beautiful day. Perhaps she should lighten up and try to enjoy herself? Jonty and Jax could already be up at the boatyard, hitching *Ursula*'s trailer to his Defender and preparing for a day out on the water. They would have made a big picnic and packed their swimming gear, and perhaps Jonty would even have brought the snorkels? He'd been talking about taking her snorkelling; perhaps he would take Jax instead? Why not?

Andi took a seat and resigned herself to spending the next couple of hours aboard Travis Chumley's floating penis. The RIB glided away from the pontoon, drawing many admiring glances, and headed out into the estuary.

"This is the sexiest boat in Rock," Travis boasted, turning around and flashing his Armitage Shanks white teeth at Andi. "She cost over a mil."

Andi could only imagine what she would do with a million pounds. Definitely not buy a boat, even one as pretty as this and with a Bose stereo pumping out Lonely Island's "I'm on a Boat" at about the same decibel level as a 747 taking off. As far as she was concerned, *Ursula*, despite all her quirks, was far superior. She had class, which was something Travis would never understand. Still, he seemed thrilled, as did Angel and Laurence, who were sunning themselves at the front. Turning around, Andi saw that Gemma – who was perched on the side – was looking worriedly at the boat just ahead. Callum South, a rubber mummy in his wetsuit, was balanced precariously on the stern. Even from here she could tell that his face was pea green.

"Is he OK?" she asked.

"He hates the water," Gemma explained. Her brow pleated with concern. "To be honest, I don't think he's a very good swimmer."

Andi was just about to ask Gemma quite how she knew this when a jet ski whipped past them, heading out towards the horizon in a blur of speed and spray.

"That looks awesome!" Angel said admiringly. "Wow! I'd love to go that fast!"

Travis screwed up his nose. "Think that's fast? You've not seen anything yet. This little baby will whip his ass!"

And then, without so much as even a cry of "Hang on!", he pushed the throttle to flat out and the RIB surged forward like Skippy the Bush Kangaroo. Quite how she stayed on board, Andi had absolutely no idea; bags went flying, screams ripped through the air and Angel's suntan lotion splurted everywhere. The forwards motion shot Travis onto the deck with such a thud that he hit his head hard and lay gasping like a landed mackerel while the RIB hurtled across the river, heading straight towards a small sailing boat.

It was as though the world had turned upside down and the beautiful morning was morphing into a slow-motion horror movie. Out of the corner of her eye Andi saw Laurence holding his head with one hand, blood trickling through his fingers, while the other clung on to Angel with all its might. Andi glanced around wildly for Gemma. Where only moments earlier she'd been sunning herself on the side of the boat, now there was no sign of her. Andi's heart almost rocketed out of her chest with terror. Gemma must have lost her balance when the boat had surged forwards, and shot straight off the stern and into the water! Jonty's comment about how the propellers were little more than blenders was suddenly and dreadfully stark in Andi's mind, and she began to panic. Where was Gemma? And was she all right?

Travis was still sprawled across the deck, and the small boat was getting alarmingly close. Somehow, and with strength she hadn't known she possessed, Andi managed to lurch towards the console and yank the dangling kill cord with all her might. Abruptly the engines were silenced, everyone was jolted forwards and the boat reared to a halt.

With her heart hammering in her chest and her breathing harsh in her ears, Andi sagged against the console. For a moment she couldn't speak.

"Are you all right?" Laurence was asking as he joined her. Taking the kill cord from her trembling fingers he added, "Bloody well done, by the way, for thinking to stop the engines. If you hadn't done that..." He shook his head, freckling the white deck with blood. "Well, it doesn't bear thinking about."

Angel crouched next to Travis. "He's hit his head really hard. I think he needs an ambulance."

If he didn't now, he certainly would when she got her hands on him, Andi thought grimly. What a moron.

"Never mind him; we've lost Gemma," she said. "She must have fallen overboard when the boat took off. We have to find her: she could be hurt!"

Beneath ten layers of fake tan, Angel turned white.

"Oh my God! And she hasn't got a life jacket on either!" She grabbed Laurence's arm frantically. "We have to go back!"

Laurence's face was dark with anger. "We certainly do. Keep your eyes open and see if you can spot her in the water. We can't risk running her down."

Angel was crying now, her mascara running like Alice Cooper's, but Andi was beyond tears. As Laurence started the RIB she scanned the water desperately for signs of her friend. It was only when they were almost back at the pontoon that she realised the film crews were no longer anywhere near the bogey-green ski boat. Instead, their RIBs were out in the middle of the river and she could hear shouts and laughter. Screwing up her eyes against the sun's glare, Andi could just about decipher two shapes bobbing about in the water. One was seal-black and clinging tightly to the second which, from Andi's distant vantage point, looked like a big white blob. Even from this far away it was impossible to miss the flash of cameras.

"Over there!" Angel shrieked, pointing in exactly the same direction. "She's in the water by those boats!"

Without hesitation, Laurence put the RIB into gear and moments later they were alongside. Sure enough, Gemma was floating in the water, her long skirt spread up around her waist, making her look for all the world like a giant jellyfish. She didn't look any worse for her ordeal, but when Andi thought how she must have missed the propellers by inches she felt sick to her stomach. The film crew must have caught the accident frame by frame.

But it wasn't the accident that had captured the attention of the press. As Laurence manoeuvred the boat carefully around to lower the ladder, Andi realised that Gemma was floating easily but supporting in a life-saving position another swimmer, who was thrashing around and spluttering, his eyes wide with fear. Callum South, reality TV star and macho footballing hero, was also overboard – and the press was relishing every second of his terror.

Chapter 29

Angel was beside herself with excitement. What a day this was turning out to be! OK, so the near-death experience on the water was something she could have done without, but the events that had followed completely made up for it. Not only had Laurence been the most demonstrative and attentive so far, holding her close to his heart and brushing butterfly-soft kisses onto her mouth, but now he was sweeping her away from Rock and the trauma to Kenniston Hall.

Angel had Googled Kenniston so many times on her iPhone that it was a miracle she hadn't worn the web pages out. She could hardly wait to see the place in the real world. What she didn't already know about the Palladian mansion, with its landscaped gardens, follies, grottos, lakes and thousands of acres of land, wasn't worth knowing. If she were to go on *Mastermind* her specialist subject would be the Elliotts of Kenniston Hall, and she wouldn't have any problem answering questions about the Capability Brown landscaped parkland or the catalogue of Chippendale furniture. As Laurence's Aston Martin purred along the high-banked Devon lanes, each mile bringing them closer to his ancestral home, Angel thought she would combust with excitement, leaving just a pair of Louboutins (borrowed from Vanya) smouldering gently on the bushbaby-soft carpet.

"You're still shaking," remarked Laurence as his left hand strayed to her knee. He squeezed it gently and her stomach fluttered. "I am so, so sorry about everything that happened earlier. I could murder Travis with my bare hands for what he did to you all."

If Angel was shaking, it was because her nerves were strung more tightly than violin strings at the thought of seeing Kenniston, rather than because she was suffering some kind of post-traumatic stress disorder from the boating accident. To be quite honest she was feeling remarkably chipper about the entire episode. It had all taken place so fast that it had been over before she'd even realised quite what had happened. One minute she'd been sunbathing on the bow, and the next she'd been catapulted into Laurence's chest – which wasn't the worst thing that could have happened – before her sister had somehow managed to stop the RIB. Gemma was fine, if sodden; Andi was furious and Travis concussed, but there was no real harm done. Personally, Angel thought her sister was a bit OTT with all the boat safety stuff anyway, but when she'd seen how concerned Laurence was about her she'd managed to dredge up a few tears – thinking about her overdraft usually did the trick – and before long she was being folded into his arms and treated like glass. Result! Murder Travis? Not likely. In fact, Angel could have kissed him!

"I'll be fine," she told Laurence bravely now. "Honestly. The main thing is that everyone is safe. Gemma's a strong swimmer and she was just a bit soggy, so no harm done there. Andi will calm down eventually too."

Laurence looked doubtful. Actually, Angel thought, given the blast of wrath that her sister had fired at Travis, concussed or not, he was probably right to be wary. Andi didn't have red hair for nothing: beneath her usually calm exterior there was a fiery temper, that was for sure. Once she'd finished telling the two men exactly what she thought of their boating skills neither could have been under any illusion about her opinion of them.

"City boys with more money than sense and toys they can't handle!" Andi had raged, green eyes flashing as she'd helped Laurence moor the RIB. "Showing off like that could have had us all killed! Morons!"

"I'm so sorry," Travis had moaned for the hundredth time, holding his head in his hands and looking as though he was about to vomit. "I never meant any of it to happen. I didn't think the throttle was so sensitive…"

Andi had rounded on him, her curls bouncing in fury. "You didn't think at all! Thank God Gemma was picked up by Cal's film crew and that the propellers missed her, or you'd be up for manslaughter."

Angel, worried that Andi would be the one up for manslaughter if she didn't calm down, had diverted her sister's attention by crumpling into a heap and sobbing. Laurence had been horrified and before long she had been wrapped up in a blanket, had a very good brandy administered by one of the yachters from the sailing club and was being driven back up to Laurence's house in Rock. There she had spent the rest of the day being pampered and tended to, which had been a much better option than doing bikini waxes for Vanya and her friends. By the time Andi and Gemma had decided to go back to the caravan, Angel had been very busy pretending to be fast asleep on Laurence's king-size bed. Of course, nobody had had the heart to disturb her after such a traumatic morning, although later Andi had prodded her very hard and snorted rudely when Laurence pointed out that the stress of it all had really upset her. Angel had nearly frowned but then remembered just in the nick of time that she was supposed to be fast asleep. When Laurence had offered to drive Andi and Gemma home, though, she genuinely had felt stressed, especially when Andi had almost accepted. Now, Angel shook her head as the countryside whizzed by in a green blur. She was going to have to have firm words with her sister. There was no way she was risking having her mystique blown now. Not when she was so nearly there!

Once the house had fallen quiet, Angel had been hoping to finally get Laurence to herself. Draped across his bed with her hair artfully spread out across the pillow, she'd just about managed to make out her reflection in the mirror. With the white Egyptian cotton sheet slipping off her tanned shoulders, Angel had thought she looked just the right blend of delicate and desirable.

God. If *she* were a man she'd have shagged her! What on earth was Laurence waiting for? All this gentlemanly stuff was really starting to do her head in. Still, she'd mused, now that they had the house to themselves, surely he would crack? She'd yet to meet a man who could resist the Angelique Evans magic.

She just hoped that Laurence wasn't the exception to the rule…

In any case, Angel never got to find out, because at this point Travis had returned from Treliske Hospital, wearing a bandage around his head and filled with more regrets than a Shakespearean tragic hero. There had been a murmuring from the drawing room, followed by raised voices, and then the next moment Laurence had been flinging clothes into a monogrammed weekend bag and telling Angel that he was taking her to Kenniston for the night, where he was going to look after her. He hadn't said very much else, but she could tell that he and Travis had fallen out. Angel thought it was very generous of Laurence to be the one to leave, rather than throwing Travis out, seeing as this was his own house – but then she supposed that Trav was injured. It just went to show what a good and selfless person Laurence was.

Anyway, who cared about whether Travis stayed or left? She was off to see Kenniston Hall, ancestral home of the Elliotts! And, if she was lucky, maybe her home too one day?

So now, as the Aston Martin bore left onto a lane hemmed by a high red-brick wall, Angel sneaked a glance at Laurence and her stomach did the most delicious bellyflop. Oh Lord. He really was gorgeous. That stern profile and that commanding air really made her go weak at the knees. Even if he hadn't been a viscount and heir to one of England's most stunning stately homes, she would have fancied him rotten. A girl would have to be practically dead not to feel her pulse skitter just by looking at him. But did he feel the same way about her? For the first time in her life Angel felt uncertain. He had taken her away from Rock, had treated her like she was made of glass and was about to introduce her to his mother. Surely that had to mean something?

She liked him *so much*. Surely he felt the same?

The red wall went on for several miles, following the gentle swell of the landscape. At one point they swept past an enormous gate, topped by a statue of a stag, and Angel craned her neck to peer through, wondering who and what lay within. Goodness, but it looked like the opening section of *Rebecca*, with the wrought-iron gates all bound with rusting chain and tangled with grasses and bindweed. What remained of the drive was long smothered by nature's tenacious fingers and the parkland was little more than a rippling hay meadow. A mile or so later they passed another similar gate, this one topped with a huge stone lion the size of a small car, and similarly neglected. Beyond the wall, land stretched as far as the eye could see.

"What's in there?" Angel asked, intrigued.

Laurence turned and smiled. "Home. That's Lion Wood and we just passed Stag Gate." He slowed the Aston Martin and swung the car to the right and through an even larger pair of gates, wide open this time and guarding a drive that swept across a deer-filled park, towards deep green woods and a glittering lake. "Welcome to Kenniston."

It wasn't often that Angel was lost for words, but she was now. This was Kenniston? OMG! There was no way the Internet did this place justice! It was bigger than Disneyland Paris! As the car juddered and jolted its way along the drive, Angel was too distracted by the breathtaking views to care that her boobs were pinging about like a pair of wallabies thanks to all the potholes. And if the foliage seemed to be encroaching upon the drive with all the determination of the crowds at the Next sale, then she was far too busy staring at the enormous house to think too much of it. Angel didn't really register gardens anyway. In her book, gardening was far too much like outdoors housework. No, she decided as she pulled on her shades to admire the house in the bright rays of the evening sunshine, Andi was the Evans sister with the fetish for gardeners. She, on the other hand, was more than happy to leave the Lady Chatterley fantasies well alone.

"What do you think?" Laurence asked, sweeping the car up before the house in a gravel-scattering arc. The mansion loomed up before them, the graceful pillars and honeyed stone seeming to spring from the earth just like the winding ivy. Windows glittered like eyes, the gardens tumbled away to the lake and years of history, wealth and privilege seemed to bask in the sunshine.

Tooting Bec it wasn't.

"Do you like it?" he pressed.

Did she like it? Angel was just on the brink of shrieking with excitement when she remembered that Laurence was still under the impression that she was used to immense wealth. Vassilly and Vanya's place probably made Kenniston look like a Barratt starter home to him, so jumping up and down shouting "Kerching!" probably wouldn't go down well.

Not cool, Angel. Not cool at all.

She took a deep breath. "It's lovely."

Laurence beamed at her and the genuine pleasure in his smile made her heart melt.

"I can't wait to show you inside. We'll have tea and then I'll give you the tour."

Angel could hardly wait to see inside herself. And the thought of having afternoon tea on the lawn, probably served by a butler, made her very happy. As Laurence took her arm and guided her up the sweeping steps, she had a Lizzy-Bennet-seeing-Pemberley-for-the-first-time moment and had to restrain herself from asking him to jump in the lake. Laurence in a wet shirt would be sex on a stick! Or, more appropriately, sex in a pond! She almost needed to jump in herself in order to calm down.

"The place suits you," Laurence said, taking her hand and raising it to his lips gallantly. "Your grace and beauty enhance it."

Angel goggled at him. Was he saying what she thought he was saying? That he could see her here with him? When Laurence then lowered his mouth to brush hers, his lips skimming her own, she almost passed out from a mixture of desire and joy. Yes! He was! She was certain of it!

Lady Angelique Elliott, she mused to herself as hand in hand they climbed the steps that led to an enormous front door. Yes, that would suit her very well indeed!

An hour later, though, Angel was starting to feel slightly less certain. Whether this was down to the roaming pack of smelly dogs shedding hair over every surface or the icy chill that pervaded the place even in the midst of the hottest heatwave on record, or just a side effect of the overwhelming smell of damp, she wasn't sure. What she did know for certain, as she cuddled the ancient range in the kitchen and pushed the wet nose of a retriever out of her crotch for the umpteenth time, was that she was bloody cold. Her little vest top and floaty wrap might be brilliant for showing off her tan but they were pretty useless when it came to keeping her warm. Brrr. Even her goosebumps had goosebumps. And as for the afternoon tea… rather than having that served on the lawn and in delicate bone-china cups, it was brewed by Laurence in a chipped teapot and in a cavernous kitchen that might have been the latest word in culinary technology when Queen Anne was ruling, but which now left a great deal to be desired. The huge range and chimney, together with the spit, quarry-tiled floor and yellowing butler's sink, were a million miles from the designer kitchen of her dreams. Where were the chandeliers and marble worktops, she wondered as she sat at the huge scrubbed table and sipped her tea (after fishing out several dog hairs), and where was the Smeg fridge? In *25 Beautiful Homes* all the mansions had stunning kitchens. Hadn't the Elliotts seen a copy?

It appeared not.

"Darling, you're cold." Horrified, Laurence shrugged off his beautiful cashmere sweater and draped it over her shoulders. His expensive aftershave and body warmth were a soothing combination, and as his hands skimmed the bare flesh of her shoulders, Angel shivered – and not just from the draught.

"It is always cold here," he added apologetically. "Kenniston was intended to be manned by a small army of servants and every room had a fire going, back in the day. We obviously don't run it like that anymore and the central heating is a little temperamental to say the least."

He wasn't kidding. Angel could see her own breath. In mid-summer.

"Can you turn it up?" she asked hopefully.

Laurence grimaced. "To be honest it isn't working right now. I will have it serviced before the winter but it hasn't been a priority. Ma isn't a fan anyway and prefers to have fires lit in her rooms. Would you like me to lend you a coat?"

A coat? Indoors? Angel wasn't sure she recalled the part of *Pride and Prejudice* where Darcy lent Lizzy his Puffa jacket.

"Why don't you show me around?" she suggested. Surely if they walked around she would warm up a bit?

"Excellent idea," Laurence agreed, and they set off on a tour of the house. It was on a vast scale that Angel had only encountered on trips to Blenheim Palace and Hampton Court. As Laurence showed her around she marvelled at the tapestries and friezes and at the beautiful rooms that streamed with light when he pulled open ancient wooden shutters. The sheer size of the place was incredible, and it would have taken her breath away if the dust hadn't got there first. Where was Gemma's asthma inhaler when she needed to borrow it?

Seriously, this place was so dusty it made the flat she shared with Gemma look clean. Some rooms looked as though they hadn't been opened for years; the furniture was shrouded with yellowing sheets and the antique carpets were pale with dust. Eugh. It needed a good clean.

"We don't use the majority of rooms very often," Laurence explained when he caught sight of the expression on her face. "There's only Ma and myself living here now, so we tend to stick to the west wing where the kitchen is. A place this size costs a fortune to run."

Angel nodded sagely. But didn't he have a fortune? Wasn't that the whole point?

"Come and see the Grand Bedchamber," Laurence continued, taking her hand and guiding her through a chain of apartments until they reached a beautiful room smothered in exquisite hand-painted Chinese wallpaper and crammed full of antique furniture. "This was commissioned by the Fourth Viscount for his favourite mistress. If you look up you'll see the artwork on the ceiling he chose especially."

Angel craned her neck. Plump cherubs and fat goddesses with serious cellulite cavorted merrily over the ceiling, scarlet nipples and dimpled bottoms on full view to leering satyrs with very graphic hard-ons. Good Lord. It was the eighteenth-century version of *Fifty Shades*. She blushed and looked away.

Laurence caught her blush and grinned. "I think a lot of fun could be had in here." He nodded at the canopied four-poster, swathed in moth-eaten yellow silk and balanced precariously on a plinth. "What do you think?"

It was the most suggestive comment he had ever made to her, but Angel was too busy listening to the woodworms chomping away for it to really register. When she did acknowledge him, he looked so proud that she did her best to look enthusiastic. Besides, everyone knew that antiques like this lot were worth gazillions. She must stop being such a pleb.

"Totally," she agreed. If somebody went through the place with a Dyson first and then fumigated the place, that was.

"And this is the Fourth Viscount, famous for his five mistresses who all lived in the house," Laurence declared proudly, pointing to a portrait on the wall. "He's the eighteenth century's Hef! That's him there, painted by Gainsborough."

From within a gilded frame a version of Laurence in a powdered wig and frilly suit stared beadily down at her. Even after centuries there was no mistaking the gleam in his eye. Angel only hoped she could put the same gleam into his descendant's. Still, if fat bums and chubby arms were what did it for the Elliott men, then she was on a hiding to nothing. He'd be better off with Gemma. She wiggled her arm a bit so that the borrowed sweater slipped to reveal the smooth curve of her shoulder and the elegant line of her throat; these were usually sterling weapons in her arsenal, but Laurence was far too busy reeling off his family history to even notice. Angel sighed and tugged the fabric up before she got frostbite, and pasted a riveted expression onto her face. It was all very well hearing about the past but it was the future she was more interested in. While he talked on, Angel entertained herself by imagining just how she could redecorate the entire place. With some white walls, a decent carpet, less tatty furniture and those gross cherubs painted out, the room would look awesome. Surely a viscount's wife got free rein to decorate?

They continued to stroll through the house, taking in endless bedrooms, galleries and even a billiards room. She wondered if Prince Harry had ever enjoyed a game there. It was certainly a house where the rich and titled would feel at home. Everywhere she looked there were wonderful treasures on display, although some shelves and sideboards seemed curiously bare. Now and again Laurence stooped to move a bucket out of the way (the roof, it seemed, could be a menace), and when the sun poured through the freed blinds, bright patches of wallpaper stood out like scars. Paintings must have hung on every surface at one point, Angel realised. Where were they now?

"On loan to various galleries," Laurence said smoothly when she asked him. "One can't be selfish. The nation should enjoy my heritage too. That was one of the first things I did when I inherited."

Angel drew a finger through the dust on the dining table. If she'd inherited Kenniston the first thing she would have done would be to send the cleaners through. Still, aristocrats did things differently, didn't they?

"Ah, that'll be Ma," Laurence added quickly when a car door slammed outside. He gently took Angel's hand and brushed the dust from it with his long slim fingers. She wondered how it would feel to have those fingers dusting the rest of her. She could hardly wait until bedtime. Maybe she would find out at long last. In a house this large they'd be sure to find some privacy.

"Come and meet Ma," he said.

"Really?"

He nodded. "Really. She'd love to meet you at last. She must be sick of hearing me bang on about you."

Wow. He'd told his mother about her? Excitement rocketed through her. In that case he must really like her!

Running a nervous hand through her hair and tugging her vest top up so that she didn't reveal too much cleavage, Angel followed

Laurence through a warren of passageways and out to the back of the house where an ancient shooting brake had pulled up. Several dogs were hanging out of it, panting in the heat and drooling while a tall skinny woman dressed from head to toe in tweed wrestled with Aldi carriers.

Angel stared. *Aldi?* Was this for real? Lady Kenniston was shopping at *Aldi?* Missing pictures? No heating? Dust everywhere? Leaking roofs? Suddenly Angel was full of questions, which she was determined to ask Laurence as soon as they were alone again.

But the first and most important one had to be: *where on earth is the nearest Waitrose?*

Chapter 30

It wasn't often Gemma picked up a newspaper and discovered her backside plastered all over the front page. In fact this had never happened before, so when she arrived at Rock Cakes to see her cellulite featured across the red tops it came as something of a shock.

"Is this you?" Dee asked curiously, looking up from scanning the story, and brandishing a paper in Gemma's direction. "Did you really save Callum South's life?"

Hands over her mouth, Gemma backed away in horror – as though putting distance between her actual self and the pale blobby newsprint image would help to erase the hideous sight. Not that there was any hope of this now she'd clocked it. Her pallid skin and the sodden fabric of her skirt clinging to every dimple and bulge was branded onto her retinas. She'd probably need to be in therapy for years to have any hope of getting over it.

"'Callum South, ex-striker for the Dangers, and reality-TV star, was filming for his new show when disaster struck,'" read Dee, tipping a sugar into her coffee as though she was the one in shock. "'South fell into the water without his life jacket properly fastened and, being a poor swimmer, panicked. At this point a mystery woman heroically dived from her speedboat to save him.'" She looked up. "I won't go on but there's loads more in a similar vein. All the papers are running the story, and *The Wright Stuff* has already been debating whether or not Callum's show sets a bad example of safety at sea and should be pulled. On the *Today* programme, John Humphrys made some very cutting remarks about Callum South's heroic image gravely misleading the public. It's only a matter of time before the Loose Women tear him to shreds."

Gemma felt terrible. Poor Callum. Being carved up by Radio 4 while he ate his bran flakes was probably not the best start to his day.

"That isn't *exactly* what happened," she said carefully.

Dee shrugged. "Since when did the truth ever get in the way of a good story? The press is going mad speculating as to who you might be," she continued cheerfully. "Even though there's a hotline inviting people to call in if they recognise the mystery girl, they haven't managed to identify you yet."

Since all they seemed to have to go on was a picture of her arse, Gemma was extremely pleased to hear it. At least none of her exes had phoned in yet and said that they recognised Gemma Pengelley's cellulite. Stepping closer, she looked at the image and groaned. When on earth had she tipped upside down? Was it when Mike had hauled her into the ski boat? And why hadn't she listened to Angel and started her diet and body brushing months ago? To cheer herself up she took a flapjack from the cooling rack. There might be a thin Gemma inside her, frantic to escape, but right now she was going to silence her with stodge.

Once she was chomping on oats, golden syrup and sugar, Gemma felt slightly calmer. There was no way anyone could really see it was her, she decided as she peered over Dee's shoulder. Her hair was a mass of dark rats' tails, her smeared make-up would put rock legends Kiss in the frame, and in real life she definitely only had one chin, two at the most and only from a really unflattering angle. Nobody could possibly tell from looking at these images it was her.

"It's so obviously you," Dee said.

Gemma crumpled onto a chair. Leaning on the table, she placed her head in her hands and forced herself to take a deep breath. Hopefully

Chloe was out of the country on the annual pilgrimage to Tuscany and the story would pass her by. If Chloe saw how fat Gemma was looking, she could kiss goodbye to her agent. Never mind having a part in *Twelfth Night*. Chloe wouldn't give a hoot about that. Nobody made a fortune from playing Shakespeare in the provinces, but they did from being skinny and getting film roles.

She shoved the paper away. "It's a non-story anyway. *Callum South falls into the River Camel*. Big flipping deal."

"It's silly season," Dee pointed out. "There's not a lot of news anyway except for heatwaves and the royal babies. But you must admit it is quite amusing. Callum South is supposed to be this amazing action hero who loses weight doing all kinds of extreme sports and it turns out he can just about doggy-paddle. It doesn't really go with the image. People are bound to feel a bit cheated."

Gemma took another flapjack. Sod it. The whole of the UK knew she had a fat bum now, so what difference did a bit more flab make? Besides, the papers had got it all wrong: Cal *was* a hero. He'd just misjudged his swimming ability, that was all – which would have been a minor detail, except that he'd seen her thrown from the boat and then hurled himself into the river in an attempt to save her. His heart was in the right place; it was just a shame that his life jacket hadn't been.

"Cal didn't fall in: I did," she told Dee. "I was out on a boat with this total idiot who didn't have the first clue and went flat out without even telling us. I was just sitting on the side minding my own business, and the next thing I knew I was in the water. Cal saw the whole thing happen from his ski boat and leapt in to help me. He's actually a hero."

Even now, over twenty-four hours later, Gemma's pulse still accelerated when she thought about it. Everything had happened so fast: one moment she'd been sitting peacefully on the side of the RIB, watching Cal wiggle out of his life jacket to pose for some cutaways, and the next she'd been underwater with the rushing of propellers in her ears and her long skirt rising around her face, threatening to weigh her down and drag her onto the seabed. The glacial water had shocked her for a few moments before the instinct to struggle for breath had prevailed and she'd kicked for the surface. Gemma might be out of condition now, but in her teens she'd been Bodmin College's swimming champion. Gemma's limbs had taken over, pulling her free and towards the surface. Breaking through the waves, gasping and spluttering, she had seen that the boat was just a distant speck in the estuary and realised she was adrift mid-channel.

"Gemma! Gemma!" A desperate cry had grabbed her attention and, treading water, she'd seen Cal teetering on the edge of the ski boat, waving at her frantically. "Hold on! I'm coming!"

Before she'd had the chance to shout back that she was fine, Cal had hurled himself from the boat and bellyflopped into the sea with an enormous splash. Gemma had watched, horrified, as his head had bobbed beneath the waves while he'd attempted to doggy-paddle towards her. Even above her torn breathing she'd heard him choking and spluttering as the salty water had splashed into his face. Oh God. Cal really hadn't been exaggerating when he'd said he was a bad swimmer. Why hadn't he put his buoyancy aid on first?

The answer was, she knew, because he had been so desperate to reach her that he hadn't given a thought to his own safety. There was a lump in Gemma's throat; it had to be the kindest, most selfless thing that anyone had ever done for her, although definitely the most stupid.

When she'd seen his head go under for a second time Gemma had known that she had to act fast.

Somehow she'd managed to hitch her skirt up around her waist and, striking into a crawl, sliced through the water until she was at Callum's side. He was thrashing wildly in the water and Gemma knew from all the life saving she'd done as a teenager that if she got too close he was likely to push her under.

"Cal!" she'd called, "I know you're Irish but this is no time for River Dance! Just relax, and let me take your weight. The boats are coming – God that sounds like a line from *Titanic*. Talk about 'You jump, I jump'!"

Cal had spluttered, which she'd taken for laughter. Supporting his weight and keeping him afloat, Gemma had been able to distract and calm him by pointing out sea birds and chatting until the film RIBs came alongside.

"Stop taking pictures and help us out!" She'd hardly been able to believe that they were more interested in snapping away than in rescuing poor Cal, who, despite his wetsuit, had been shivering with fear and cold. Just as well she had a good layer of blubber, Gemma had thought ruefully. Whales had about as much chance of getting chilled as she did.

Finally, once the shots were in the can and the pap boat had roared away, Cal's own team had been able to come close enough to haul him onto the deck, where he'd lain shaking and exhausted.

"I couldn't leave you there alone," he'd gasped, as Gemma was being bundled up in towels. "I thought you were going to drown."

Gemma had shaken her head. "But you can't swim. What were you thinking?"

Cal had looked up at her with big mournful eyes. Although she'd been cold, at this moment parts of Gemma had started to grow very warm.

"I wasn't thinking at all, so I wasn't," he'd confessed. "I just couldn't let you be out there all alone."

Gemma had reached out and squeezed his hand. "Thank you," she'd said.

Unfortunately, just as she'd been about to ask Cal what exactly was going on, his entourage had taken over – including Evil Emily, who'd shot her such a look of disdain it was amazing Gemma hadn't shrivelled on the deck. Shoving Gemma out the way, and making sure that Cal had a view of her slim bikini-clad frame, Emily had made a big show of rubbing him down with a towel – all while the cameras were rolling, of course. With a sigh, Gemma had removed herself from shot – no need to alarm Greenpeace unnecessarily – and was relieved when Travis's boat drew up alongside them. Soon she was being whizzed to shore and straight to Laurence's house, where she'd wallowed in deep baths and drunk brandy for the rest of the day. Cal had texted once to make sure she was all right, but after that he had been silent. Now, looking at the media storm blazoned across the papers, she realised why he was incommunicado.

"I just can't work out why Cal would jump in like that. It was a crazy thing to do," Gemma said. Flicking the kettle on to make a coffee, she added over her shoulder, "He knows he can't swim. Jumping in without his life jacket was completely mad. What on earth possessed him?"

Dee grinned. "You really need it spelling out? For a smart girl, Gemma, you can be really slow off the mark sometimes! Callum South likes you, and not just for your baking."

Gemma nearly dropped her jar of Nescafé. "What? Don't be soft!"

"I'm not being soft." Dee looked stern. "Why shouldn't he like you? What about all the wonderful, positive things there are to admire about you?" Holding up her hands, she started to tick them off on her fingers. "Talented cook. Wonderful actress. Sexy, curvaceous figure. Golden hair. Funny. Ambitious. Loyal. Genuine. I could go on, but I'm running out of digits!"

Gemma busied herself spooning granules into the mug so that Dee couldn't see her blushing. This wasn't at all how she saw herself. Fat and lumpy was more like it, and this was a view that unfortunately most of the UK would now share.

"He's a huge star," she mumbled. "He could be with anyone."

"So why shouldn't he choose to be with you?" Dee asked. Since Gemma had confided in her about the trip to Fifteen – it had seemed a waste not to share the details of that glorious pecan pie with somebody – Dee had been convinced that there was more to Callum's friendship with Gemma than a shared love of food. She had even donated several pasties and saffron buns to Gemma to deliver to key points on the running circuit whenever Cal was able to text that he was out alone. She strongly suspected that it wasn't just the food he was interested in. Still, Gemma wouldn't have it, and Dee resigned herself to the fact that they had a long way to go when it came to working on her young friend's self-esteem.

Just as Gemma was about to argue the toss, she heard the tinkle of the Rock Cakes shop bell, followed by oohs and arrahs of excitement as Jean, Dee's other part-timer, spoke to somebody. Moments later an enormous bouquet of flowers burst through the fringed tassels that separated the kitchen from the counter.

"These have just arrived for you, Gemma. Aren't they beautiful!" announced Jean as proudly as if she had grown them herself.

Gemma was speechless. Beautiful didn't even come close. She'd been bought flowers in the past, but they were normally the fiver-from-the-Texaco variety grabbed by boyfriends when they had to try to make up for being knobs. The wilted carnations and hideous blue chrysanthemums she was used to bore as much resemblance to this bouquet as Gemma did to Angelina Jolie. Plump pink and cream roses nestled next to pompom peonies, while fat waxy lilies were scattered like stars throughout and woven into baby's breath and ivy. The entire creation was held together with rustic string, curls of pink spotty ribbon and rustling brown paper. These weren't flowers. These were a work of art.

"See," crowed Dee. "What did I tell you? He likes you."

Gemma's mouth was dry and her heart was racing. The flowers were so gorgeous; of course they had to mean something! Dare she hope that Cal really did feel something for her? Surely, he wouldn't make such a romantic gesture if he didn't?

Gingerly, and with trembling fingers, she drew the card from the small white envelope, only to feel her dreams come crashing down around her ears when she read it.

I am an utter dick. Please, please forgive me.
Travis

The flowers were still beautiful. The sun was a still shining. She was still alive. Nothing had changed at all. So why then, thought Gemma as she bit back tears, do I feel like the world has ended?

Chapter 31

The thumping of fists against melamine dragged Andi out of the deepest sleep she'd had in years. For a moment she lay confused, her eyes gritty with sleep and her heart pounding from being unexpectedly awakened, before the events of the previous day came flooding back and her heart hammered even harder. They could have all been seriously hurt or worse! Bloody Travis and his showing off! Andi hoped the wallop he'd had to the head hadn't just concussed him but had knocked some sense into his thick skull too.

Once the adrenalin of the near-accident had worn off, Andi had felt almost drunk with exhaustion and wanted nothing more than to curl up in the peace and quiet of the caravan and close her eyes. With Travis safely dispatched to Treliske Hospital, Gemma wallowing up to her neck in Floris bath essence and Angel swigging Courvoisier like it was juice, Andi had declined Laurence's offer of dinner and a bed for the night and made her way back to the farm. As luxurious as his house was and no matter how stunning the views, she longed for solitude. Maybe she was in shock from everything that had happened, or maybe she was just antisocial; Andi wasn't sure. All she knew was that she needed time to recharge. Somehow she had managed to stagger back to the caravan, where she'd collapsed onto her bunk with fatigue.

Glancing at her watch she saw that it was now ten in the morning. Good Lord, she'd been asleep for hours! And Angel wasn't here, which could only mean one thing: she had spent the night with Laurence. Andi hoped her sister knew what she was doing. Laurence was handsome and polite and utterly plausible but there was something about him she just couldn't get her head around. He seemed as though he was almost acting a role, which reminded her rather worryingly of Tom. Andi sighed. She hoped to goodness she was wrong.

Thud! Thud!

The fists thumped again and the ancient caravan practically shook.

"Andi! Are you there? It's me, Jonty!"

Jonty? Andi sat bolt upright. What was he doing at the caravan?

"One minute!" she called, throwing off her duvet. Underneath she was still dressed in her shorts and vest. She must have just fallen into bed. Glancing in the mirror tile, she groaned. Just as well it was already cracked! She looked awful. Her hair was a mass of wild curls and her eyes were ringed with shadows and yesterday's mascara; she could have doubled for a panda. An image of the immaculately turned out Jax, with her sheet of straightened hair and perfect make-up, flitted before her mind's eye. Andi squashed it firmly. Jonty wouldn't care that she looked like the undead; he didn't see her as anything more than a friend anyway. Just as, of course, she also saw him as only a friend.

"Sorry, I didn't mean to wake you," Jonty apologised when Andi unlocked the door in her state of disarray. His eyes, brimming with concern, searched hers as he spoke. "I've just heard what happened yesterday and I wanted to make sure you were OK. If I'd known before I'd have come straight over."

Andi couldn't help wondering where he'd been. When she'd walked home the whole of Rock had been abuzz with the episode, especially seeing as Callum South had been involved. Maybe he had been out somewhere with Jax? Yes, that was probably it.

"You didn't answer your phone and I was worried," Jonty added when she didn't speak. "I must have called you about twenty times."

Andi was touched. "You shouldn't have worried; I'm fine, honestly. The phone isn't, though. It went overboard."

"Thank God *you* didn't." His hands were clenched into fists. "Honestly, I knew that guy was a total cock when we saw him on the water. A liability. You could have been killed, Andi."

This thought had already gone through her mind and Andi strongly suspected that the horror of realising that Gemma had vanished and the RIB was careering across the river totally out of control would haunt her for a very long time. She shivered in spite of the heat.

"I know, but luckily it didn't come to that. Anyway, I have you to thank for being able to stop that boat," she told him. While Jonty listened with a horrified expression, she went on to explain how she'd recalled what he'd said about the kill cord and had pulled it to stop the engine.

Jonty's mouth set in a grim line and he shook his head.

"He should never have put you in that position." He took her hands in his and held them tightly. "Andi, promise me you won't go out on a boat with him again."

Andi was certain Travis Chumley wouldn't be in a hurry to go out to sea for a while, if ever again. When she'd last seen him staggering into the ambulance, concussed and bruised, he'd been full of apologies and regrets. Apparently his friend from the boatyard would be selling the RIB and Travis was going to take some sea-safety lessons.

"Don't worry," she said. "My days of boating with Travis Chumley are well and truly over."

Jonty's answering smile was warmer than the sunshine.

"Phew, you have no idea just how happy it makes me to hear that!" he said. Letting her go, he reached down and picked up a bulging carrier bag.

"I've brought some bacon and eggs and the morning papers. I thought it might be fun to cook some breakfast and eat it outside? And you really need to see the headlines! I've brought a selection of the dailies."

At the thought of bacon and eggs Andi's stomach rumbled like Vesuvius. Jonty laughed.

"I'll take that as a yes, shall I?"

She blushed. "I haven't eaten since yesterday!"

No wonder she had slept for hours. Two big tumblers of brandy on an empty stomach probably hadn't been the smartest move. At the mere thought of food, she realised she was famished.

"Then it's high time you did eat," Jonty was saying sternly. "Why don't you go and have a shower and it'll be ready by the time you're finished."

Andi didn't need asking twice. While she lathered herself in Angel's Chanel shower gel – after yesterday's shenanigans she figured this was the least her sister owed her – and smothered her curls in deep conditioner, mouth-watering smells of cooked breakfast filled the place. By the time she was finished and feeling human again, Jonty was sitting outside at the weathered picnic table, drinking tea and poring over the papers.

"Tuck in!" he urged, pushing a plate towards her. It was piled high with bacon, sausages, sunshine-yellow scrambled eggs and big buttery field mushrooms. "I picked those this morning," he added proudly.

"The fields are covered in them. Honestly, you won't taste anything better even if you eat in a Michelin-starred restaurant."

The mushrooms were brown and plump, underneath as pink as ponies' noses. They ate in companionable silence and he was right, Andi decided: the mushrooms were amazing. Not worrying in the slightest about whether or not she looked like a greedy pig, Andi polished off the lot and wiped her plate clean with a hunk of bread and butter.

"That was wonderful." She leant back and put her hands on her full stomach. "I'll probably never eat again but it was worth it. You're a great cook."

Jonty shrugged modestly. "Of fry-ups maybe. Mel says I'll die of a heart attack. It comes of years of living like a student. "

"And asking girls how they like their eggs in the morning?" she teased.

"You've got me! Although, to be honest anything other than scrambled and I'm rubbish. My fried eggs turn to rubber. Jax always had a go at me about my cooking. It drove her demented."

"Jax likes fry-ups?" Andi couldn't help herself; she had to ask. When it came to Jax she was wildly curious. She didn't look as though she ate at all.

He sighed. "Jax wouldn't dream of eating anything so unhealthy. She's a bran-and-wheatgrass person. Besides, her personal trainer would kill her if she so much as looked at a sausage. She doesn't like the same things I do."

Andi thought that bran and wheatgrass sounded vile. Jonty was so chilled and lacking in airs, whereas the older woman with her *look at me* car and groomed appearance was clearly high maintenance. They must have something in common though, surely? Apart from their shared business, of course?

"That's a shame," she said lightly. "She's missing out."

Jonty just nodded. He didn't seem to want to talk about Jax any more so Andi decided not to probe. Hadn't he already told her it was "complicated"? Which in man-speak was shorthand for *we're shagging but not together, even though she thinks we are.* Mel had hinted that she was worried he would take Jax back. Andi sighed. As much as she liked Jonty and enjoyed his friendship, he was still a man at the end of the day and therefore bound to be a total disappointment. Hadn't she learned anything after Tom? She ought to step back.

"Fry-ups are one of life's great pleasures," Jonty said thoughtfully. "As is reading the tabloids when you should know better!"

Andi smiled. This easy banter was familiar ground.

"I won't tell anyone about your *Daily Mail* habit if you make me more tea," she told him.

"Phew," said Jonty. "I thought for a moment my cover was blown. I was only pretending I liked the *FT*! Look, spoil yourself, the *Mirror's* there too. I'll go and find the PG tips."

So while Jonty went to brew some more builders'-style tea – he always made it so strong Andi was amazed the teaspoon didn't salute her – she pored over the gutter press, her chin practically on the newsprint. Poor Gemma would be mortified when she saw the shots of her bottom! And as for Cal – well, the press were having a field day ripping him to shreds, which seemed a bit harsh when Travis was the one to blame for the entire incident. There was only a brief mention of the cockatiel-haired one (a line or two about him being the Moggy Mix Millionaire), and a blurry shot of Laurence, who was apparently one of

Prince Harry's party set – but there was nothing else of much real interest. Andi flicked through the pages, marvelling at how such a non-story had managed to attract so much attention. She supposed it was down to Cal being a household name. Everything he did generated huge publicity.

Andi just hoped that Gemma knew what she was getting herself into...

She was about to give up on the papers and enjoy basking in the sunshine when a headline caught her eye.

Ben J Teague, Safe T Net Founder, donates £20,000,000 to child vaccine charities

Andi leant forward, suddenly captivated. She knew that when Safe T Net had floated it had made a fortune, catapulting its CEO right to the top of the rich list, and even though she'd been ripped from the project in the worst fashion her interest in the company was still strong. Wow. Twenty million pounds. That was some donation. It made her weekly purchase of the *Big Issue* seem a bit puny. Maybe Aston Martin man wasn't such a tosser after all? Intrigued, Andi read on, wondering what her old contact PMB would have made of this story.

Teague made a large charitable donation when he pledged £20 million to develop and distribute vaccines. The Safe T Net founder hopes the money, to be spent over the next three years through his new foundation, will save the lives of more than eight million children in the world's poorest countries.

"We must make this the decade of vaccines," Teague said. "Vaccines already save and improve millions of lives. Innovation will make it possible to save more children than ever before."

Andi leant back and cradled her face in her hands thoughtfully. She couldn't help comparing Benjamin Teague's actions with those of

Travis. Both were worth mind-blowing Monopoly-style silly sums, but whereas Travis spent his on toys, this Benjamin Teague seemed set on doing something worthwhile with his millions. If the work she had done had gone some way towards helping him do this, then she was proud to have been involved.

"What do you think?" Jonty asked, joining her. "Crazy headlines, huh?"

"Bonkers," Andi agreed, nodding. "But to be honest, I wasn't reading about that. This caught my eye."

She turned the paper so that he could see the page she was reading.

"This guy who owns a company called Safe T Net has just donated millions to charity."

"Right," said Jonty. He didn't sound particularly interested. Andi guessed it didn't seem very relevant to him.

"I used to work for Safe T Net," she explained when he didn't respond. "I was part of a team that helped prepare the company for going public. I spent hours of my life emailing a team there, and I probably talked more to this guy, Project Manager B, than I did to my boyfriend."

Tea slopped all over the newspaper and the story dissolved before her eyes.

Andi glanced up. Jonty was staring down at her and there was an expression in his eyes she hadn't seen before. If she hadn't known better, she would have said it was fear.

"Are you OK?" she asked.

Jonty swallowed. More tea splashed onto the table and, collecting himself, he put the mugs down slowly. Then he sat down next to her and sighed wearily. Running a hand through his hair – the short cut Mel had advised against was growing out and Andi liked the way curls were starting to brush his ears – he turned to her. He looked troubled.

"What's the matter?" Andi asked.

Jonty exhaled slowly. "It's complicated."

She smiled. "You're a man. Isn't it always?"

But he didn't smile back. Just as she was about to ask him what the matter was, a small van featuring a florist's logo drew up at the gate. A door slammed and, seconds later, the most enormous bouquet of flowers was walking towards her. It looked as though Kew Gardens was holidaying in Rock.

"Somebody loves you!" announced the florist as he thrust the flowers at her. "Those are the most expensive ones we do!"

Andi opened the card and promptly screwed it up. Travis Chumley. What a surprise. As though a bunch of flowers could make up for nearly killing them all. She shook her head and placed the bouquet carefully on the grass. She didn't want it or anything to do with Travis. Maybe Angel would like them? Or perhaps she could donate them to the hospital?

"Sorry," she said to Jonty. "We got interrupted. What were you going to say?"

But Jonty didn't seem to want to talk anymore. "It doesn't matter."

"Of course it does." She reached out her hand to him. "We're friends."

He didn't take her hand and for a moment it wavered in the air before, feeling foolish, she withdrew it. For once she couldn't read the expression on his usually open face.

"I have to go," he said in a strange flat voice that sounded nothing like him. "I'll leave you to deal with those. Somebody obviously cares about you a great deal."

And without even giving her the chance to explain, Jonty turned on his heel and walked away, leaving Andi staring after him in confusion. Hadn't they been having a lovely morning? What, apart from the flowers arriving, had changed?

She pressed her forehead against the table and closed her eyes wearily. All of a sudden her head hurt.

Nothing made sense. What on earth could have happened to upset him so much? Jonty was proving harder to figure out than *The Times* crossword; he was certainly every bit as cryptic. She sighed and pushed her hair behind her ears. There was no time to sit and stress about it now though, however much she might want to; she was supposed to be working this morning and she was already running late. Although Simon was easy-going and probably knew all about yesterday's trauma, Andi didn't want to be unprofessional. Gathering up the mugs and plates, she headed back into the caravan to get herself ready for work.

Jonty and his issues, whatever they were, would just have to wait.

Chapter 32

Once the morning's baking was completed Gemma often took herself off for an hour to get some fresh air and stretch her legs. Normally she would head into the town and down to the water's edge, where she would kick off her shoes and walk along the beach, loving the sensation of damp sand against her feet and waves tickling her toes. Today though, Gemma decided she'd seen quite enough of the River Camel and the beach for a day or two. Whenever she moved her head, water sloshed around inside her ears. Not only that, but her throat was scratchy with the beginnings of a cold, so a change of scene was definitely in order. Besides, everyone in town was bound to have seen her bum, complete with more dimples than Cheryl Cole's smile, all over the red tops – and Gemma didn't think she could face the sniggers and sideways looks.

"Take the afternoon off and have some 'me time'," Dee said firmly, untying her own pinny and fixing Gemma with one of her looks. Gemma knew those looks; they said quite firmly that she wouldn't be argued with. No wonder Dee had become such a force to be reckoned with in the corporate world. She was scary enough just wielding Cath Kidston oven gloves; in a suit she would be terrifying.

"I won't take no for an answer either," Dee continued, "or any of your protests about how much there is to do here." Hanging her pinny up, she turned her attention to a battalion of scones lined up like a curranty army on wire cooling racks. "These are all ready for the National Trust to collect, and I can decorate the cakes quite happily. Your job is to help yourself to a pasty, go through some of those positive mantras we talked about, then go and sit somewhere quietly to learn your lines."

Gemma, who had been on the brink of protesting, paused. To be honest she could do with going over her lines before this evening's rehearsal. The play was going exceptionally well and she loved every minute, but she really needed to nail tonight's scene. The idea of returning to the caravan and hiding away with her copy of *Twelfth Night* was very appealing. Andi would be at work and Angel had gone away with Laurence, so if things had gone well, which they generally did for her best friend, Angel wouldn't be back for a while. That meant that Gemma would have the caravan all to herself and plenty of time to mull over why Cal had jumped in to rescue her. Err... she meant to study the play. Promising Dee that she wouldn't read another paper and would spend at least twenty minutes in front of the mirror doing her positive-thinking affirmations, Gemma set off for home.

It was a beautiful day and the sun was already hot. The small town thronged with holidaymakers, all intent on getting to the beach or onto the water; luckily for Gemma they were all headed in the opposite direction. Shouldering her bag and pulling out her tattered copy of the play, she set off along the street, eyes glued to the page and desperately trying to believe she was no longer in Rock but wandering through Illyria. With her hair falling over her face, sunglasses wedged firmly in place and her backside camouflaged by a long cardigan, Gemma was hopeful that nobody would recognise her. All she had to do was make it through the hordes surging along Rock Road, and then she could turn up the narrow lane that led past the golf course and head out of town to safety. If she got a few odd looks then hopefully it was because she was crashing into the tourists rather than because her arse was being recognised.

God, she thought as she charged through Rock with her eyes trained on her lines, why had she *ever* thought she wanted to be famous? Cal must be mad. This was no fun at all.

It was at this point, and almost as though she'd conjured him up, that a huge white Range Rover pulled up alongside her. A blacked-out window whirred down and Cal peered out at her. At least, she thought it was Cal; the huge baseball cap, scarf and dark glasses made it hard to tell. It could have been the danger stranger her mother had terrified her with for years. Instinctively she picked up pace.

"Gemma!" hissed Cal from behind several layers of scarf. "It's me!" Leaning across, he flung open the passenger door and pulled down his scarf. "Quick! Hop in before anyone sees!"

Since they were in the middle of Rock, where the pavements were ten deep in tourists, it was probably already too late to worry about this, Gemma thought despairingly. Not that it was very likely that anyone would recognise the hat-and-scarf-swaddled driver, but the facts that these were in Dukes Rangers colours and that his number plate bore the legend CAL 1 were something of a giveaway. Glancing quickly over her shoulder just in case the paps were lurking by the ice-cream kiosk, Gemma took a flying leap into the Range Rover and huddled down into the seat. Cal slammed the door so hard her teeth rattled; then, with the wheels spinning in haste, he was tearing out of the town.

"You've seen the papers then – or are we just in a hurry to get lunch?" Gemma tried to joke, but the tight set of his lips told her that Cal wasn't laughing. Instead, his brow was furrowed and his hands gripping the wheel were white-knuckled. Oh dear. Gemma supposed it was even worse for Cal than it was for her. So what if the whole nation knew she had a fat backside? It was embarrassing but hardly the end of the world, whereas Cal had built his entire career on being an action man. He practically had the swivelly eyes and grippy hands! His watery escapade didn't exactly enhance his image.

"This is a nightmare," he said.

Gemma sighed and stared bleakly down at her hands, still clutching the copy of *Twelfth Night*. "I'm so sorry, Cal."

Cal shook his head. "I didn't mean the press. That's all bollocks. What I mean is this: the whole celebrity circus. Aw feck it, Gemma. I've had it."

She bit her lip. "But if I hadn't fallen off that bloody boat none of this would have happened."

"None of this is your fault," Cal said firmly. "So I was a total plank to try and save you when I can't even swim that well myself, but I don't regret that at all. I couldn't have left you all alone in the water, could I?"

He couldn't? Gemma's heart soared to hear this and, glancing up, she saw he was looking sideways at her. Although the sunglasses hid his eyes, there was an expression on his face that she didn't dare read in case she got it wrong. It wouldn't be the first time. Gemma could translate Mandarin more easily than she could the workings of the male mind.

"In fact I forgot I can't swim," Cal confessed. "I just wanted to help."

Help. Of course. He was a kind person. Thank God she hadn't let herself think it could have been for any other reason. She exhaled slowly. "Well, thanks. That's probably the nicest thing anyone has ever done for me. Don't listen to all that crap in the press. You risked your own life to save mine, and that makes you a hero in my book."

Cal smiled back. "Then that's all that matters."

Gemma doubted this was true. "But what about the press?"

He shrugged. "Of course, it caused a riot when the story broke. My team have gone absolutely ape and Mike was climbing the walls when I left, but to be quite honest I'm almost beyond caring what they think. Feck 'em." And feck the whole TV show too. I don't care about any of that."

They were clear of the town now and driving through the high-banked Cornish lanes, sunshine dappling the roads when it penetrated the tangled treetops above. Cal yanked off his cap and scarf, shoved the glasses onto the top of his curly head and wound the windows down. Instantly, cool fresh air, salted by the Atlantic and sweetened by honeysuckle, filled the car and Gemma took a big gulp. Gosh. She hadn't realised how tense she'd been. She must have been holding her breath pretty much since she'd seen the headlines.

"But what I do care about is that you got dragged into it all," he continued. "I wouldn't have had that happen for the world."

Gemma could have done without it; that was for sure. Still, none of this was Cal's fault. If anyone was to blame it was that idiot Travis. If Gemma ever laid eyes on him again she'd tell him exactly what she thought. And if there was any water nearby she'd have a bloody good go at drowning him and see just how much he liked it.

"It'll all blow over in a day or two," she said gently, because Cal looked so downcast. The chirpy Irish chappie from the telly was nowhere in evidence. To try to cheer him up she added, "Honestly, something else will happen and then this will all be forgotten. It's a non-story anyway."

"I don't give a toss about the story!" Cal said hotly. "I couldn't care less what they all think about me." He shook his head and raked a hand through his golden ringlets. Gemma suspected there had been quite a bit of this already today – the curls were in danger of turning into dreds. The look quite suited him.

"I'm sick to my back fecking teeth with it all," he continued. "Being told what I can eat, where I can go, who I can talk to, what I can wear. Jaysus! It's a miracle I can even go to the bog by myself. Everywhere I go there's somebody trying to shove a camera into my face or sell a story on me. I tell you, Gemma, this celebrity stuff isn't what it's cracked up to be."

Gemma, who had spent the last ten years of her life believing that there was nothing she wanted more than to be famous, was starting to agree. Oh dear. That was seriously going to bugger up her career plans. Maybe she would stick to baking?

"But most of the time it's fun, isn't it?" she asked hopefully.

Cal's usually merry face was drawn and lined, and as he gripped the wheel she noticed that his nails were bitten almost to the quick.

"Most of the time I'm so busy pretending to have an amazing time that I don't really think too much about it," he said. "That's the key to it, Gemma. Don't think, for Christ's sake. Just keep going; pretend everything's great and ninety-nine percent of the time it will be. Jaysus, I know I haven't got anything to moan about but sometimes it's all too much."

"So do something else," she said.

"Like what? I'm a fat, washed-up footballer with a massive house to pay for and a bloody expensive family to support in Ireland. My mammy would be broken-hearted if the family farm had to go." Cal shook his head. "Gemma, I'm a fecking eejit. I'm mortgaged to the gills. I have to keep going."

Gemma wasn't buying this. She'd read *Hello!* and *OK!* enough times to know that footballers were loaded. After all, she'd yet to bump into Posh Spice in Primarni.

"You must have made loads when you were playing?"

Cal looked shamefaced. "Sure, sure, and I spent it too. Big houses, supercars and *Playboy* models don't come cheap. Aw feck it, I'll have to go on *This Morning* and grovel a bit about my hero image being a bit misleading. I'll eat sodding lettuce for a month. I'll let the Loose Women take the piss. I'll really diet hard and not cheat." He paused thoughtfully. "Maybe the show could feature me learning to swim or something? Jaysus, they'll have me in a rubber ring before I know it. And do you know the worst thing of all?"

Gemma didn't.

"All I can think about right now is how hungry I am," Cal said sadly. "There was no breakfast this morning. Mike said the sight of me in a wetsuit was enough to put the nation off its breakfast and practically had the fridge padlocked. I know that I'm shallow but, Jaysus, I am famished."

He looked so miserable as he said this that there was only one thing Gemma could think of to cheer him up. They were on the A30, Cornwall's closest thing to a motorway, which led to a very important place indeed – McDonald's. In Cornwall these were rare, so whenever she chanced upon one Gemma stopped. You just never knew how long it would be until you saw another. Pasties were all well and good but when it came to a really good pig-out there was nothing quite like a Big Mac. As the road began to descend a steep hill and the Golden Arches loomed before them, Gemma knew it had to be a sign.

"Do you see what I see?" she said, pointing.

"Oh my God," breathed Cal. "Are you thinking what I'm thinking?"

"Big Mac meal, large fries and a strawberry milkshake?"

They stared at the vision in front of them. The car drew closer. There were only seconds to make the decision.

"Oh feck it," Cal said, yanking the wheel so hard she nearly fell off the leather seat. "We deserve a bit of a treat after yesterday and all that crappy press. Big Mac here I come. I'll diet tomorrow."

"Me too," Gemma promised, thinking ruefully of the costume she had to wear for Viola. Those tights showed every lump and bump. She really ought to try harder to lose that weight. Thank God Chloe hadn't recognised her bum. Gemma had checked her phone several times but thankfully there were no missed calls or angry messages from her agent. She was safe.

Fully resolved to be good after this final calorific binge, Cal and Gemma headed to McDonald's. While Cal, still clad in his disguise, bagged a corner table, Gemma queued and ordered. She glanced across at him, worried that he was attracting attention, but to be honest this was more likely to be down to the fact that he was wearing a scarf in July and shades inside. He must be sweltering. He was right, Gemma thought. Being a celebrity wasn't much fun at all. While she squirted ketchup into tubs and grabbed as many serviettes as she could, Cal huddled down in his seat and tried his best to look unobtrusive. He wasn't very good at it and several diners were looking over.

"Chill," Gemma told him as she set the tray down. "Look around; there's nobody here except holidaymakers and kids. Try and look normal. That way nobody will notice."

"What's normal?" Cal said bitterly.

Gemma rolled her eyes. "Two overweight people in Maccy D's scoffing fast food, that's what. Just look like it's what we always do and nobody will look twice. Honestly."

Looking nervous, Cal unwound his scarf. The glasses and baseball cap remained intact, though. She plonked herself down opposite him and raised her thickshake in a toast.

"Here's to ignoring headlines and health-food freaks!"

"Amen to that," Cal said, bumping his paper cup against hers. "I don't know about you but I'm starved, so I am! Let's get stuck in."

So get stuck in they did, and Gemma didn't think a burger had ever tasted so good or been so much fun. As they ate they chatted, dunked fries in ketchup and discovered that they both loathed gherkins. They were having such a good time that they failed to notice the man at the table opposite, who was tapping away urgently on his mobile and scribbling notes onto a tattered pad. It was only when he took a photo on his phone and the flash lit up the restaurant that Cal looked up in alarm. When he realised what had happened, the smile slid from his lips just like the relish sliding from the food held halfway to his mouth. Gemma, just on the brink of shovelling in the last of her fries, turned to see what had got his attention – and found herself blinking in the glare of several more mobile cameras.

Their eyes met in horror. The food fell from Cal's grasp and frantically he tried to pull the cap low over his face. Everyone in the restaurant was looking his way, pointing and whispering.

"That's Callum South!" somebody cried, and instantly they were surrounded.

Callum grabbed Gemma's hand and tugged her out of the seat.

"Come on," he said, his head bent low, "let's get out of here while we can."

But even before they'd reached the door, Gemma knew it was far too late for that. Yet more mobiles were snatching pictures, and in a nanosecond Twitter and Facebook would be buzzing. She'd probably be a hashtag before they'd even reached the car. As if things weren't bad enough for Cal as it was... Already his phone was ringing and he was as white as his car.

This was not going to be good.

Chapter 33

Angel didn't think she'd ever been so cold. Even reclining in a ginormous four-poster bed – so high from the worn carpeted floor that a small set of steps was required to reach it, like something out of *The Princess and the Pea* – wasn't enough to compensate for frozen fingers and toes.

Frozen fingers and toes? In the middle of the UK's hottest summer for a decade? This was crazy. Did all the blue blood and years of practice in draughty public schools make the landed gentry immune to the cold or something?

When Laurence had shown her to the guest room Angel had been overwhelmed with excitement. In the rosy rays of the setting sun the large bedchamber had been blushed with peachy light that lent it a romantic glamour and, she realised later on, hid the holes in the carpets and faded Chinese wallpaper. No, these things had bypassed Angel's radar entirely; she'd been far too busy racing to the floor-to-ceiling windows that gazed out over acres and acres of rolling parkland and imagining herself dressed up and watching the carriages trundle up the drive for a ball. OMG! It was like landing in a virtual-reality episode of *Downton Abbey*!

"Do you like it?" Laurence had asked. He'd leant against the doorframe as he'd spoken, the easy posture speaking volumes about how comfortable he was living in a house the size of Buckingham Palace. As they'd wandered hand in hand through the endless maze of corridors she'd worried that she'd need a satnav to ever find her way back down to the kitchen for evening sups, as the Elliotts referred to dinner. He'd looked so perfect framed there, his glossy dark hair falling across his face and his grey eyes bleak with worry, that her heart had turned a slow and most unfamiliar somersault. Suddenly she'd wanted nothing more than to make him happy.

It was a very peculiar sensation.

"It's beautiful!" she'd said, and had been rewarded with such genuine delight that it was hard to say whether his smile or the sunset had been brighter.

Laurence had crossed the room and swept her into his arms. As he kissed her and the spacehopper-orange sun bounced on the horizon, Angel had basked in both the rays of light and his happiness. Kenniston was heaven on earth, she'd decided as she kissed him back. She could happily stay here forever!

Just a few hours on though and it was a very different story…

After a meagre supper of bread, cheese and pickle – eaten at the kitchen table rather than in the sumptuous candlelit dining room of her imagination – Laurence and Angel had huddled up on the sofa in the drawing room, which would have been romantic except for the fact that his mother insisted on joining them. When the viscountess had eventually retired for the night, Angel had hoped that maybe Laurence would make love to her on the rug by the fire; she fancied him so much she was prepared to overlook the fact that it was a particularly moth-eaten lion skin with a suspicious case of mange, but the pack of assorted dogs had already hogged the spot and lay basking in the warmth. There was no hope of snuggling up with Laurence either, because a huge and very smelly Labrador was wedged in between them, panting contentedly and drooling. Much as Laurence melted her knicker elastic and much as she liked dogs, Angel wasn't overly keen on sharing this romantic scenario with a four-legged friend.

Maybe this is just the way aristocrats do things? she'd thought when they'd returned to the kitchen and Laurence had brewed up the weakest-looking tea she'd ever seen, served with value-price digestives that seemed to have passed their sell-by date (even the dogs weren't impressed). After all, wasn't the Queen super stingy, according to rumours, and dog mad? So it didn't quite look like this on *Made in Chelsea*, but that was probably all put on for the show. Gemma was always saying that reality TV was a contradiction in terms. The posh telly totty probably all lived in one wing of their family seats too. Cheered by this thought, she'd perched on the Aga and then Laurence had kissed her again until her tea turned cold and the stars freckled the sky. Then she hadn't thought about much at all, apart from the delicious sensation of his mouth meeting hers.

It had been a bit of a surprise to find herself alone in the guest bedroom, when his touch had turned her entire body to the consistency of Cadbury's caramel, but Laurence was frustratingly old-fashioned; after escorting Angel to her room, he'd kissed her goodnight and left her alone.

That was weird. Men never, ever turned down the chance to stay the night with Angel. Not that there had been a huge amount of them, but the ones she had given the green light to had never backed off. Confused and disappointed, she began to get ready for bed.

The room was bitterly cold. In her thin vest top Angel was soon shivering. This place was Baltic! Rubbing her arms in a vain attempt to keep the goosebumps at bay, she looked around for some source of heat. The enormous marble fireplace, all blue-veined like a giant Stilton, might look the part but it hadn't seen a decent blaze for a very long time. Ashes dusted the grate, speckled with a few twigs fallen from long-ago nests in the chimney, and the log basket was empty. A quick inspection of the bed soon revealed that there was no electric blanket. The huge sash windows, so romantic at sunset, were old and tired. Draughts blew in icy blasts across the room; in an attempt to stop them she tugged at the ancient velvet drapes, only to be practically asphyxiated by a dust cloud.

One thing was for certain: this house seriously needed taking in hand. Maybe if things worked out with Laurence she could have a go at redecorating? Goodness only knew that the place was in need of a makeover.

As she undressed in the light of a small lamp, Angel shook the dust from her clothes and soothed herself by imagining how wonderful Kenniston would look with the walls all painted in neutral tones and with the windows cleaned and fixed. Maybe some of those tatty tapestries could be shoved into the attics? And as for the dogs, they needed to be kicked out of the living space. She'd never seen so much dog hair before. Perhaps as an engagement present Laurence would pay Sarah Beeny to come over and help?

Angel had become lost in a lovely daydream where she and Laurence were planning a wedding, second only to William and Kate's, so it was a horrible shock when the light bulb popped and the room was plunged into darkness. Angel shrieked, but in such a large stately home no one could hear her scream. And neither could they appear with another bulb.

Angel was in despair. What on earth was going on at Kenniston? This wasn't at all what she had imagined. If it hadn't been for the magic of Laurence's kisses and the way her bones melted just at the thought of him, Angel would have been so out of here. As she stumbled through the darkness, bashing her shins on the bed steps, she realised with a jolt of terror that she must really, really *like* Laurence. Maybe even more than like. And not just because he was a viscount, either. To be honest that didn't matter a toss when Travis had nearly drowned them all. All she'd cared about then was that his first thought had been for her safety. Angel was used to guys worrying about her looks. That was a given. She'd been Alex's little princess, adored and paraded about until she'd grown too old and he'd lost interest. Then she'd dated various men who liked to have her on their arms but who soon lost interest when Angel wanted more. It hurt but it seemed to be the way these things went. That was why she'd decided to cut her losses with all the true love stuff and just stick to the serious business of finding a rich man. Gemma could keep the romantic fantasies. Angel felt tired and cynical but she knew the truth: all princes soon turned into frogs once they'd been kissed. And one frog was pretty much the same as another, so the chosen frog may as well be loaded.

Laurence, though, wasn't anything like this. He made her laugh, he protected her when she was in danger and he was so easy to talk to that several times she'd had to stop herself from telling him the truth. The words had been right on the tip of her tongue and she'd had to bite them back or drown them in the champagne that they were invariably drinking. It sounded mad but she almost felt that Laurence would totally understand. He was a kindred spirit. Her other half. Her soul mate.

Was she in love with him? She must be to even contemplate staying the night in this dusty, freezing house. Jewel of Palladian architecture or not, the harsh truth was that Kenniston was a skip. It needed serious work...

Oh bloody, bloody hell; wait a minute, thought Angel, stopping in her mental tracks before she got too carried away with thoughts of design, garden parties and even a TV makeover.

Was she in love with Laurence Elliott?

Maybe.

She sank onto the floor and placed her head in her hands. This was not good news. At all. In her experience, being in love sucked. Just look at how Tom had walked all over Andi, or how Gemma, funny caustic Gemma, had been reduced to a complete sap around her useless ex. And then there was the sad case of her mother who'd been treated like dirt by their handsome, charismatic good-for-nothing bastard of a father. No good ever came from falling in love. Her parents' example said it all.

Angel batted this thought away; bitter experience had taught her that dwelling on her parents never brought her anything except heartache. Thinking about them in the dark and when she was cold and on edge was not going to help.

The drapes had successfully concealed any friendly moonlight and there was no way Angel was going to risk contracting bubonic plague or whatever other dire germs might be lurking in that fabric. Those curtains hadn't been cleaned since Henry VIII was in nappies. If only she knew where to find Laurence. Whether he was gentlemanly or not, Angel didn't care. She would stay the night with him – but there was no way she could find her way to his room without a map. The endless passageways were bad enough, but the fact that all the light bulbs on the corridor had been removed and the place was pitch black was another matter altogether. If there was one thing Angel hated almost as much as being cold then it was the dark. When she was a kid she'd shared a room with Andi, who'd always been there when she'd had a bad dream or not been able to sleep. The night was when thoughts about losing her mother always came, too, and she'd wake with a start, her heart hammering and her skin slick with sweat. Angel would rather bin her designer shoe collection than admit this to anyone but, grotty as it was, she actually enjoyed sharing the small caravan bedroom with Andi. As shadows pooled across the room and a severe-looking Elliott ancestor sized her up with beady grey eyes, Angel's pulse broke into a gallop. She wasn't sure she would last the night alone in here.

Maybe she could call him? Brightening at this thought, she fetched her bag, tipping the contents out onto the threadbare carpet and patting the floor until her fingertips brushed her iPhone. Yes! Almost faint with relief, she swiped the screen, only for her heart to sink when she saw that there was no reception. She couldn't even phone him. It looked as though she was well and truly on her own. With a whimper, Angel scurried up the steps and dived into the bed, tugging the covers up to her ears. Whether her teeth were chattering with terror or cold she really didn't know, but they could have doubled for castanets.

Angel lay in bed with her eyes screwed tightly shut. She shivered. Even her nose was going numb. In an attempt to distract herself, Angel tried to concentrate on adding up the value of the antique furniture and the ornate gilt-framed portraits – but the insistent chill seeped through her skin, into her bones, and froze her very thoughts. She tried burrowing beneath the covers but the scratchy blankets and starchy sheets were about as yielding and snuggly as granite. Besides, the bottom sheet was decidedly damp. Her icy feet had lost all sensation. Would she even make it to the morning? Somehow Angel doubted it. She'd be a blonde ice-lolly by dawn.

Just as she was contemplating jumping out of bed, wrapping herself in one of the blankets and wandering the corridors in search of Laurence like a tragic Shakespearean heroine, there was a soft rap of knuckles on the door.

"Angel?" murmured a voice into the darkness. "It's me, Laurence. Are you awake?"

Angel could have wept with sheer relief. She didn't think she'd ever felt as lonely as she did right then, marooned in the giant bed in the middle of the sea of holey carpet.

"Yes," she whispered.

There was the soft padding of footfalls across the floor. Then the bed dipped to the left and seconds later she felt the solid warmth of Laurence pressed against her.

"Angel! You're frozen!" He pulled her close against him, his hands gently rubbing her arms. His warm lips dropped butter-soft kisses onto her cheeks, her lips and her poor frozen nose. As she felt the warmth of his skin against hers, Angel began to defrost. This wasn't difficult. Laurence's touch turned her blood to lava.

"I'm so sorry," he was saying. "I forget how cold it is here. I guess you get used to it when you've grown up with it."

Angel nodded, but to be honest she didn't really see how you could ever get used to the cold, or why you would even need to when there were giant cast-iron radiators and enormous fireplaces everywhere.

Then again, the way his lips were grazing her neck you could probably heat the whole of Kenniston from the fire igniting deep inside. She closed her eyes and allowed herself to drift away on the blissful current of his touch. The cold forgotten, she twined her arms around his neck and turned to kiss him, long and deep. It was a kiss that promised everything and for a moment Laurence kissed her back before breaking away and sighing. In the darkness she heard his breathing, just audible above the thudding of her own heart.

"I can't do this," he said.

Angel, whose nerve ends were crackling like popping candy, reached out to pull him back.

"Of course you can," she said. "I want you to."

He traced the curve of her cheek with his thumb.

"Oh, I want to, believe me. I want to very much."

"So what are we stopping for?" Angel was beyond caring what he thought of her now. All she knew was that being this close to him, feeling his skin against hers and the promise of his mouth, was enough to make her explode. Stopping was not an option!

Laurence sighed. "We're stopping because, Angel Evans, I like you far too much not to." He dropped a kiss onto the top of her head and then took her hands in his. "If this is going to go any further then there can't be any secrets between us."

Angel's blood chilled in an instant. Oh God. He'd found out all about her. Somebody had told him the truth: that she wasn't a loaded Russian or *MIC* girl, but rather a down-on-her-luck beautician who waxed legs and lived in a caravan.

"Laurence, I don't know what to say," she began, but he placed a finger on her lips.

"Don't say a word. Sweetheart, you don't need to. Just listen." He paused and although she couldn't see them Angel knew those stormy eyes were brimming with concern. Then he took a deep breath.

"Angel, I haven't been altogether honest with you…"

Chapter 34

Spending her working day in the garden at Ocean View had to be one of Andi's favourite things about living in Cornwall. Although she had her spreadsheets and ledgers piled up in front of her, and the MacBook in its shady spot was constantly pinging with urgent emails, this hardly felt like work. Quite the opposite in fact. With every moment that passed, the kaleidoscopic estuary shifted, the waters sparkling like a thousand stars as small boats danced across the waves. Her lightly tanned skin and the freckles that dusted her nose spoke of the weeks spent outside in the fresh air and sunshine rather than the usual pallor courtesy of office strip lighting and city living.

Andi collected up a sheaf of papers that she'd found buried under the newspapers on Simon's desk – Mel was right: he really was utterly hopeless when it came to organisation – and stacked them on her desk in a neat pile. Desk! As she fastened the documents together with a bulldog clip, Andi couldn't help smiling at *desk* as a description of her present working area. Hardly! This was nothing like the hard chair and viewless desk she'd occupied back in the bad old days of Hart Frozer. Here she was seated at a large wooden table on the terrace, an enormous white sunshade opened above her, and surrounded by pots crammed with bright geraniums, waterfalls of aubrietia and psychedelic orange nasturtiums. If the sun wasn't already bright enough, the flowers alone made Andi reach for the Oakleys that Jonty had loaned her. As the gulls called and wheeled above the lichen-speckled rooftops and the bright blue pool shimmered on the level below, she was able to whizz through Simon's accounts and enjoy every second of this Cornish idyll. Working here, with Mel popping over to chat or the boys begging her to join them for a kick about on the lawn, was as far from the pressures of the office as a girl could possibly get, and Andi still couldn't quite believe her luck.

She picked up another folder, smiling when she saw that Mel had slipped a note inside. *Scotch eggs and salad in the fridge for lunch!!* She'd already delivered a pitcher of home-made lemonade and some cookies. Mel was always thinking of Andi and leaving lunch for her and Jonty. Not that Jonty had been in evidence for the last few days. Since Jax had turned up he had made himself scarce, at sea in *Ursula* according to Simon or hiding out at the boatyard. Andi missed him.

Pouring some lemonade into her glass, the ice clinking against the jug, Andi thought that it was going to be a horrible shock when the summer drew to a close and the family returned to the city. She supposed that the locals would be pleased to get the town back to themselves and have some time off after the intensity of the season, but the thought of saying goodbye to Cornwall filled her with melancholy. She'd really miss her life here: the salty air, the walk into the town... She'd even miss the caravan – although bidding farewell to Gemma and Angel's mess wouldn't be quite so much of a hardship. To her surprise, though, Andi realised that she'd miss them both. Angel might drive her round more bends than Lewis Hamilton did his Mercedes, and Gemma had a dreadful habit of leaving crumbs everywhere for the ants to collect, but in the main they were easy to be around – and, after living with Tom, sharing a place with people who actually seemed to like her was like sinking into a warm bath. Yes, she'd miss them both once the summer was over.

But most of all she would miss Jonty…

Andi sighed and pushed her paperwork aside. This was ridiculous. It was still the height of England's best summer for years; even as she worked bees were droning in the lavender, and the balmy morning air held none of autumn's blackberry sharpness. There were lots of days to enjoy yet before the leaves changed their hues and woodsmoke filled the air. She didn't need to worry about what was coming next. All she had to do was live in the moment and enjoy herself.

But Andi had never been very good at living in the moment, or rather she'd never been able to. There had always been something or somebody to worry about and it was probably too late to shake the habit. How hard could it be to just relax and make the most of this golden summer? Already the days were flying by as though piloted by *Top Gun*'s Maverick and Goose. Wasn't it said that it's when we're happiest that time goes the fastest? She just needed to stop fretting and enjoy the weeks ahead.

But then what? asked a small voice that Andi usually chose to ignore. That small voice was proving to be very annoying. It was constantly whispering into her ear at the oddest and most inconvenient times. And it never seemed to take no for an answer, either.

Then I'll have a healthier bank balance and more of a plan, she told it firmly, but the small voice just snorted disbelievingly. She would have a plan, Andi decided, and already the black hole in her current account was looking less like something Stephen Hawking would find fascinating and more like a mere crater. It was still a crater she could have done without, but at least things were moving in the right direction. That dreadful day when she'd lost her job and discovered that Tom had cleaned her out no longer felt like the end of the world. As she rested her chin in her hand and gazed across the river to Padstow, Andi reflected that Tom and Alan Eades had actually done her a huge favour. There was a simplicity to Cornish life that brought with it the mental elbowroom she had always longed for. How ironic that she'd had to let go of everything that she'd held dear in order to find it.

"Liquid! Thank God!" Jonty leaned across the table and helped himself to her glass of lemonade. Gulping back the drink in just a couple of mouthfuls, he exhaled gratefully and smiled at her. "Sorry! That was very ill-mannered of me, stealing your lemonade without even asking."

Jonty's face was flushed beneath his sea-salt tan, and above his powder-blue board shorts he was bare-chested. His skin was fudge smooth, the pecs well defined with just a sprinkling of dark hair tapering down to his taut stomach and the waistband of those shorts. Andi swallowed and looked away quickly. "Help yourself. You look hot."

"I am!" He plopped down on the bench beside her and poured himself another glass of lemonade. Scooping up a handful of Mel's cookies, he added, "I'm starving! I've been mowing the lawns all morning with an ancient push mower."

"Not the old green one with the wooden handles? That was here when we used to stay!" Andi could hardly believe it. Alex Evans had huffed and puffed for about twenty minutes before giving up with the whole idea and calling in a local to do the hard graft. Physical effort wasn't really her father's thing, Andi reflected; nor was any kind of effort, come to think of it.

Jonty grinned, his greenish-blue eyes crinkling. "Yep, that's the one. A relic of a bygone era and one that doesn't make quite such a din or require extension cables. Great for the environment and my fitness but bloody exhausting."

Andi glanced down at her own stomach ruefully. "Flexing mental muscles doesn't have quite the same effect."

"You look great," he said warmly. Leaning back a little, Jonty stared at her through twinkling eyes. Andi felt hot under his scrutiny, which was odd seeing as she was seated in the shade. She looked down at the table rather than meeting his gaze. "You look different to how you did when I first met you in the paper shop."

"Less make-up? More freckles?" she offered.

Jonty shook his head. "No, I don't think that's it. It isn't a physical change. If I had to try and put my finger on it I would say that you looked softer somehow, less tense?"

She laughed. "That's true. It's pretty hard to be stressed living here, isn't it?"

"Sometimes," he agreed.

They sipped their drinks in silent companionship for a while, watching the boats buzz up and down the river and listening to the drone of the bees.

"We'll have to go out on *Ursula* again," Jonty said eventually.

Andi wasn't so sure. "I'm not convinced about boats. Not after the last time I was on one."

"If you must choose to go to sea with Captain Knobhead what do you expect?" he teased. "Seriously, Andi, come out on *Ursula* with me again. I know I've been a bit preoccupied lately but I really did enjoy our last trip and I know you did too. We could go down the coast a bit, see some seals and maybe a basking shark?"

"Sounds tempting," Andi nodded, although she was still a little wary. Jonty's reactions lately had been so odd.

"I'll even throw in a picnic? Pasties?" He nudged her. "Some saffron buns? Go on, you know you want to!"

Andi started to laugh. "Oh, go on then. How can I resist a saffron bun?"

They were just making arrangements to meet at six (when the tide would be high and, according to Jonty, the water would be like silk), when Mel joined them on the terrace. She was looking flustered; like her brother's, her cheeks were pink beneath her tan. Moments later the reason for this became very apparent: Jax, dressed in a floating white halter-neck, floppy hat and huge Chanel sunnies, was hard on her heels.

"Sorry to interrupt your work," Mel said, rolling her eyes at Andi, "but Jax was very insistent she spoke to us all. Apparently she couldn't just leave a message with me. It's almost as though she doesn't trust me to pass it on."

"Darling, it's not like that at all!" Jax declared, catching up and giving Mel a taut-lipped smile. There really was no love lost between Jonty's sister and his ex, Andi thought. The air practically crackled with animosity. Only her good manners were stopping Mel from shoving the older woman into the infinity pool.

Jonty ran a hand across his face. Andi could feel the sparkle and excitement of only moments earlier fizzle away. "You could have just left a message up at the house."

Jax shrugged. "Don't be like this, Jon. If you would only answer your mobile it would make life so much easier!"

Jonty shook his head. "We've had this conversation already."

"And no doubt we'll have it again," Jax said with a theatrical sigh. "Anyway, it makes more sense to speak to you all at once and give you these."

She flicked her hair back from her slim shoulders then delved into her Mulberry bag to fish out two big white envelopes. One she thrust at Mel; the other she pressed on Jonty, leaning rudely across Andi and treating him to a full view of her tanned cleavage. Andi looked away. Knowing that Jax had perfect pert boobs without the help of a bra didn't make her feel any better. Suddenly she found herself wishing that instead of wearing her cut-offs and green tee shirt she'd made more of an effort. Jax's nails, clutching the envelope, were perfect shell-pink ovals, not short and unpainted like her own. She really had let herself go.

"I'm having a party tomorrow night!" Jax explained excitedly when nobody dived into the envelopes as she clearly had expected. "I've invited just about everybody who's anybody in Rock and it's going to be amazing. I've hired the same caterers who Roger Taylor had for his bash on the Helford, and I've got the coolest Cornish bands playing. I just wanted to invite you guys personally, seeing as we're old friends."

Mel snorted. She'd either been watching too much *Peppa Pig* or she really was cheesed off, thought Andi.

Jonty placed his invitation on the table. "I don't really think I'm the partying kind these days."

Jax's perfectly plucked eyebrows shot into her blunt fringe. "But darling, you of all people should be partying! In fact, one of my reasons for throwing the party in the first place was so that you could celebrate selling—"

"That's really kind, Jax, thanks," Jonty interrupted hastily. The sunshine smiles had clouded over now and he stood up quickly. His arm caught the lemonade and the glassed tipped, spilling the drink all over his envelope, the ink bleeding into the cream paper. When he made no move to rescue it Mel scooped up the invitation and laid it out on a sunny part of the huge table. There was something really odd going on here but Andi couldn't work out quite what. Was it just the awkwardness between two exes? It made no sense but it felt like more than this. Even Mel was looking panicked.

Jax's hand flew to her mouth. "Oh! Am I being indiscreet in front of the staff? Sorry, Jonty. I didn't think!"

She turned to Andi and her grey eyes were so glacial that it was like peeking into a fridge. "While I'm here maybe it makes sense to offer you a bit of extra work? I could do with some help at the party, people to hand out the canapés and drinks. Would you be interested? I'd pay above minimum wage, of course!"

That puts me in my place, thought Andi. *The staff.* While everyone else went to the ball she'd be there to collect the glasses and stack the dirty plates. Why not scrub the grate too while she was at it? Then again, Jax's money was as good as anyone else's and every penny that she earned was another step closer to paying off her debts. That was why she was here in the first place, after all. Being proud wasn't going to make Barclaycard and friends happy.

Mel looked furious. "Andi's a PA! Not a waitress!"

"Oh, sorry," said Jax, looking anything but apologetic. "I had no idea. I just thought it might be something she'd like to do."

The words *rather than actually be a guest*, hung in the air like sparkler trails on Guy Fawkes Night. Andi waited for Jonty to say something, maybe tell his ex-girlfriend to stick her invitation somewhere dark and private, but he was silent. The teasing and excitement of earlier had totally evaporated and his hands were clutching the picnic table tightly. Whatever was between him and Jax was obviously unfinished, Andi realised. She had to get a grip. She was in Rock to sort her finances out. There was no point getting involved with anyone and even less point in being proud about what kind of work she would or wouldn't take.

"I'll do it," she said quickly. "Thanks, for the offer."

Triumph flared in those shark's eyes. "Great. I'll let my caterers know to expect you at about four tomorrow." Her gaze flickered up and down Andi's body and her lip curled. "Wear something smart, though, won't you?"

"Sure." Andi thought she'd have to borrow something from Angel, although heaven only knew what she'd find in her sister's overflowing wardrobe. Angel wasn't big on sensible clothes and she didn't think Jax would appreciate her serving nibbles all *TOWIE*d up in a catsuit or bandage dress. Maybe she could belt in a pair of Gemma's black trousers?

Satisfied that she'd managed to put Andi well and truly in her place, Jax turned her full attention back to Jonty. She beamed a dazzling white smile up at him.

"Now, I think you and I need to catch up properly," she said firmly. "And probably better that we do that alone, don't you think? Although, I'm happy to chat here, if you like?"

Jonty said nothing. Even Mel was silent. Andi looked from one sibling to the other, and felt more at sea than the boats beyond Rock. Why didn't they just tell Jax to get lost?

Maybe, said the annoying little voice, because Jonty doesn't really want to tell her that?

"We'll leave you in peace to get on with your work," Mel said finally when it became clear that her brother wasn't about to speak. She jangled her car keys. "I'm popping into town to get some bits for our barbecue later, so feel free to use the house, Jonty."

"Or come to mine? We can be alone there," Jax suggested. Andi was impressed. This woman really was the Velcro of the relationship world. "Shall we?"

"I'll catch you later?" Jonty said to Andi. "For that boat trip?"

But Andi wasn't going to get herself caught up in whatever was going on with him. Lovely as Jonty was, he was clearly a guy with big issues. She had enough of her own crap to deal with.

She shook her head. "Actually, I have a few things I need to do tonight. I'll catch you another time."

Jonty stared at her. The expression on his face was hard to read.

"Fine," he said eventually. "Another time."

Andi watched as he and Jax crossed the lawn back to the pool house. They were talking in low urgent voices and Jax had threaded her arm through his. Feeling like Cinderella, she returned to her work, but the figures refused to cooperate, jumping about all over the page and sticking numerical tongues out at her just when she thought she had cracked it. It was hopeless. Instead of lines of numbers and calculations, all she could think about was Jax winding those slim arms around Jonty's neck and twining her way back into his affections, tenacious and determined as bindweed. She sighed and pushed her work away. The woman was gorgeous, rich and clearly crazy about him. They had history too and it must have worked once between them, so why not again? If Jonty had wanted to, he could have told Jax to leave – but he hadn't. They were probably in the pool house and making up right now.

Andi pressed the heels of her hands into her eyes until stars danced across her vision, but still the image of Jax and Jonty remained. What was happening to her? Was this some kind of weird delayed reaction to the trauma of the early summer?

When the new pay-as-you-go mobile that Simon had pressed on her beeped with a message, it was the welcome distraction she needed. Today's hours at Ocean View were going to have to be made up tomorrow. Unlocking the phone's screen, Andi was taken aback to find a text from none other than Travis Chumley, asking her out to dinner. He'd been pestering for days and Angel must have passed her number on, which was typical – her sister never took no for an answer.

Andi checked her watch. It was almost noon. The sun was out, the town was bustling and she'd decided to give up on work for the day. Jonty was with Jax, Gemma was out and Angel was heaven only knew where with Laurence. Nobody else wanted to spend time with her, it seemed, so why not go for dinner with a keen if dim multimillionaire? At least Travis didn't just see her as somebody to do the sums, scrub the dishes and pass the time until his glamorous ex arrived back on the scene. Travis wanted to spend time with *her*.

She took a deep breath. *OK, pick me up at 7*, she typed. For a moment her thumb hovered over the green send key. If this were Jonty, would she hesitate? The answer to that was pretty obvious.

But it wasn't Jonty, was it? And never would be. He was preoccupied with Jax.

Oh, sod it, thought Andi. It was only dinner. What harm could it do?

Her thumb swooped down and hit the send key. There. It was done. For better or for worse, she was going on a date with Travis.

Chapter 35

"That's it, that's fecking it. I have had enough of this. It's a fecking joke."

Cal's foot pressed down hard on the gas and the Range Rover tore out of the car park and towards the A30. Gemma had barely time to shut the passenger door and buckle up before the tyres were smoking on the asphalt and the speedometer was hitting sixty. The A-Team had nothing on an upset Callum South.

"Are you all right?" he asked as the car shot onto the main road and picked up even more speed. Gemma grabbed the seat and clung on for grim death as they hurtled past the startled holidaymakers in their luggage-laden cars.

"Shit." Cal said. "I can't believe this."

Gemma couldn't find the breath to reply. Cal was much fitter than he gave himself credit for; he'd raced out of McDonald's so fast that she'd only kept up because of his fingers locking with hers and pulling her after him. At one point she'd thought the joints were going to pop, so insistent was his tugging of her from the restaurant and towards the car. So all she could do for the moment was nod and try to slow her racing heartbeat; there was no way she could speak.

"Jaysus, what a nightmare." Cal exhaled slowly, relaxing a little as they put a few miles between themselves and McDonald's. "That's probably the last straw for me. Those pictures will be all over Twitter by now. Mike will freak and ITV2 will probably pull the plug. Leopard TV will sue my sorry arse."

Gemma felt terrible. "Cal, I'm so sorry."

"This isn't your fault," Cal said. "Sure, and wasn't it my idea to go for a burger? It was hardly as though you forced me. Anyway, I loved every mouthful. What's the point of it all if you can't even have a Maccy D's?"

"But your image! The show!" Gemma could have wept. She knew how hard Cal had worked to promote his career and just how much he needed the money. That it could all be swept away just because they'd fancied a Big Mac seemed terribly unfair. "And what will Mike say?"

"That I'm a fecking eejit, probably, and he's right," Cal admitted. "But, Gemma, can you see what it's like for me? I don't think I can handle living like this much longer. I'm going to have to either get my eating under control or give up the telly."

"Your eating is under control," said Gemma hotly. "Cal, you're a six-foot man. You have to eat! What's screwing it up is constantly having to analyse and control it. That's enough to drive anyone round the twist. I should know."

Cal nodded. "But you don't depend on your weight for your living, Gemma. You have a talent. You can act – no don't pretend you can't," he added when she opened her mouth to protest. "I've seen you in rehearsals and you're brilliant. Thin or fat, you will always have your talent – whereas me? I blew it going on the piss and tripping up. The only thing I'm famous for now is my weight and my action sports. That's why I have to keep playing this game. I'm stuck."

"So do something else," Gemma said. She knew as she said it that she was being a total hypocrite. After all, hadn't she had this very conversation with Angel and Andi at least ten times? "What else are you good at?"

Cal gave her his slow and cheeky grin and Gemma felt her heart somersault. All the excess flesh couldn't disguise the pure sexiness of his smile and the glitter in his brown eyes. Oh God, it would be so easy to fall for him…

"Apart from *that*," she admonished, her cheeks hot – and not from the afternoon sunshine.

"Spoilsport! OK then, eating?" he said.

"That's what's got us into this mess," she pointed out dryly.

"Fair enough." Cal turned off towards Padstow. His brow crinkled with concentration. Then, suddenly animated, he cried, "Baking bread! I'm bloody brilliant at that!"

"That's great, Cal, but I think Mother's Pride probably have it covered."

"Not white bread, you heathen. Proper artisan bread. Hey! Why don't we stop off at Tesco, buy the ingredients and I'll show you? My sun-dried tomato and Parmesan loaf is to die for."

He looked so happy at this idea that Gemma's kind heart nearly broke. "Because, Cal, I don't think Mike will be up for the idea of a bread-baking marathon when you arrive back. He'll be wanting to do all kinds of damage limitation and PR work. You'll probably have to run a half marathon with Emily or something."

"Jaysus, take me now," said Cal, and thumped his head on the steering wheel. "I know! Maybe Richard and Judy could meet me at Talland and I could do an interview with them and talk about my food issues? A confessional exclusive? Maybe I could write a book too and they could put it in their book club?" He brightened at the thought. "And Richard's a great cook. He does this brilliant tuna and crisp bake."

But Gemma was too busy scrolling through Twitter to be interested in A-list cuisine. Already Cal was trending and blurry pictures of them both ramming fries and thickshakes down their necks were all over Instagram and Facebook. God, did she really have that many chins? And how come Angel and Andi had never let her know that her legs looked so awful in these denim cut-offs? Weren't friends supposed to tell you stuff like that?

She was seriously going on a diet. At some point.

They continued to drive back to Rock in despairing silence. Gemma looked miserably out of the window as the Cornish countryside sped by in a blur of khaki scrub and crumbling mine workings. Although it was another beautiful sunny day, she didn't think she'd ever felt more miserable. What was it about her that everything she tried to do always ended in tears? She only wanted to make everyone happy. If she'd left Cal in peace none of this would have happened.

"You OK?" Cal asked, reaching across and squeezing her hand.

Gemma was about to reply but at that very second Cal's mobile started to ring. In his car everything was Bluetoothed to the stereo (which was safer than the illegal tucked-under-the-chin technique she usually employed in the Beetle), and the name *Mike* now came flashing up across the dash in accusing neon-blue letters. Cal and Gemma stared at each other guiltily as the call went through to answerphone.

"I'd better listen to that," Cal sighed afterwards. "I'll pop it on loudspeaker; then you can hear me get a bollocking. Share my pain."

Gemma grimaced. She wasn't convinced pain was her thing, but before she could protest, Cal was playing back the message.

"Cal! Why aren't you picking up the phone? I know you're there," barked Mike.

There was a pause and then Cal's manager said wearily, "Look, ignore me if you have to, but I'm telling you, bud, this isn't going away. I've just had a call from the network. Apparently you're all over the social media sites stuffing burgers down your neck. Well done, mate. Sheer genius. I'll have to really grovel to get a good PR team to take this one on. And who was the big bird? Was it the one with the cake? Gemma something? That's what I've seen on Facebook."

Big Bird. Not something yellow and fun from *Sesame Street*, but her. The words hit Gemma like a slap. That was all she'd ever be to some people, wasn't it? A body that was too heavy to fit what was deemed to be perfect. A joke.

"Ignore him," said Cal quickly when he caught sight of her stricken face. "The man's a knob, so he is. You're not fat: you're voluptuous and gorgeous."

At this point Gemma's iPhone decided to join in the debate by pinging into life with a text message. When she saw that it was from Chloe, Gemma nearly hurled her Mac lunch all over the luxurious cream leather seats. With a trembling thumb she unlocked the screen and retrieved the message. When she read it and all her worst fears came true, it was almost a relief. Either from hysteria or from the irony of being dumped for finally acquiring the media attention Chloe had been demanding, Gemma started to laugh.

"What can possibly be funny at a time like this?" Cal asked.

Gemma flung her phone onto the back seat and pushed her hair behind her ears. It was so weird, but now that the worst had happened – she was agentless and her acting career was in the trash can of life – it no longer felt like such a big deal. So Chloe didn't want to represent her anymore? What had actually changed? She was still working with Dee, and next weekend she'd be headlining in the Rock Players' production of *Twelfth Night*. She had the caravan to live in and friends who loved her. All that had changed was that she no longer had to put up with somebody who didn't accept her as she was, didn't support her, and made her feel like crap. This was something to celebrate!

"My agent just let me go," she told Cal, who instantly looked mortified.

"Aw feck, this is all my fault. If you hadn't been papped with me, she'd have never known you hadn't got down to a size zero."

"Cal, look at me! I'm not designed to be a size zero! Chloe knows I can act and she should have seen beyond that and pushed me towards what I'm actually good at. But no, it was easier to try and cram me into the mould rather than look outside it." She took a deep breath. "And do you know what? If she doesn't like me for how I am then I'm better off without her. So I might not be a famous actress but at least I can enjoy myself and live my life."

He whistled. "You really mean that, don't you?"

She nodded. "Totally. The worst has happened and do you know what? It wasn't nearly as bad as I'd imagined. In fact quite the opposite. It's liberating."

"Unlike going back in there," said Cal bleakly, pointing towards his house, or rather where his house would be if they could actually see it for the hordes of people and press milling across the tarmac.

"Bloody hell," said Gemma. It was easy to forget at times just what a big star Cal really was. When they were shooting the breeze and hanging out he was just a regular guy. The fact that he was best mates with David Beckham and regularly partied with A-listers always came as a bit of a surprise.

"Bloody hell indeed," said Cal. "Well, that rules out the going home option."

He put his foot down and shot past the gates while Gemma crossed her fingers and prayed that nobody would notice the personalised number plates. For once luck was on her side: they were all far too busy trying to peer through.

"Great." Cal looked so downcast that it was all Gemma could do not to reach across and hug him. "Now what?"

She smiled at him. "Now you drop me off at Tesco's for ten minutes and then come back to the caravan while this all dies down. It's nonsense, Cal! Look at it from the perspective of the real world. You ate a Big Mac. Nobody died."

"Just my career," he muttered.

"Not necessarily." Gemma plucked her purse from her bag. Twenty quid. Great, Angel hadn't been on a raid, so there was more than enough for what she needed. "I know exactly how to cheer you up."

Again Cal gave her that famous slow, sexy grin that made Gemma feel as though somebody had lit a furnace deep inside of her. Oh no. Not good.

"Chocolate body paint?" he suggested.

She sloshed him on the arm and hoped he couldn't see that her sex drive was dancing a tango. The thought of Cal covering her in chocolate body paint and then licking it off very, very slowly was one that she'd have to save for another time. And she'd have to get a very big vat of body paint too.

"Much better than that," Gemma told him. "Callum South, prepare yourself. We are going to do some baking!"

Chapter 36

Earlier on that same morning, while Andi had already been at work for several hours and before Gemma and Cal had taken their ill-fated trip to McDonald's, Angel had floated out of a heavy sleep and back into consciousness. For a moment she'd lain still, wondering what had happened to shut up the squabbling seagulls and Gemma's endless obsession with Pirate FM. She felt less cramped too: her legs weren't jammed against the melamine of the caravan wall for once, and she seemed to have acres of space. The tip of her nose that poked above the covers was frozen, though, and her fingers could have easily competed with anything from Captain Birds Eye. She yawned and rolled over, burrowing into the heavy blankets before colliding with a solid form: Laurence Elliott, Viscount Kenniston, Lord and master of a huge and crumbling mansion and, as it ironically turned out, as stony broke as she was.

Yes, it was all coming back to her now. Gingerly, Angel reached out with her foot and, sure enough, her French-pedicured toes brushed against solid male calf. Laurence, fast asleep, reached out and pulled her against him, wrapping his arms around her and pulling her tight against his chest. With his touch, Angel's heart raced as memories of the previous night came rushing back like the Severn Bore. Angel had no idea that her body could do *that*. Finally she understood what Jackie Collins and Jilly Cooper had been going on about. Even *Fifty Shades* was starting to make a bit more sense. Penniless or not, she didn't want to let Laurence Elliott go in a hurry!

Angel had heard the expression "gobsmacked" before but until the moment Laurence confessed that he was pretty much penniless, she'd never really understood it. For a moment she simply couldn't speak. What on earth did he mean, he had a *cash-flow* problem? But that was impossible! He was a viscount! He lived in a house that made Buckingham Palace look like a garden shed. He drove an Aston Martin. If this was a posh guy's idea of being skint then bring it on.

"Skint. Brassic. Broke," Laurence said, just in case she didn't follow. He'd looked close to tears as he'd said it. "Angel, I can't pretend anymore; I've got to be honest. You've come to mean too much to me for there to be any secrets." He hung his head. "The truth is, although I might create the opposite impression, I am struggling to be solvent."

She'd stared at him. "I don't understand. You live here, in this huge house! You're a viscount… aren't you?"

Laurence nodded. "The last in a long line of hard-living, hard-spending Elliotts with all the debts and responsibilities that come with inheriting an estate this size." He raked a hand through his hair and his shoulders slumped as though the weight of all those responsibilities was sitting on them. "Can you imagine what the death duties were like when Pa died?"

Angel couldn't – she struggled enough when Mr Barclaycard came knocking – but suddenly the patches on the wall where portraits had been removed, the freezing-cold rooms and the Aldi bags were starting to make a lot more sense. It was like looking at the back of a tapestry, all tangles and knots, before turning it over and seeing the true picture. The lack of ready cash. The cards that constantly got declined. The pennies were dropping. Maybe she should offer them to Laurence?

"But what about your house in Rock?" she whispered, once her vocal cords had recovered. "Your beautiful car?"

He closed his eyes in defeat. "Neither one is mine. They're both Travis's. He's my oldest friend from school; he's been really good about bailing me out but I can't expect him to do it indefinitely. I think he wants his house back too. He's seriously got the hots for your sister."

Personally Angel thought Trav had more hope of flying to Mars than he did of getting lucky with Andi. Her sister was more interested in the moody handyman. Andi might deny it but Angel could tell; her sister used to get that soppy look on her face when she looked at her Busted posters. Still, it was all making sense. No wonder Travis hadn't taken the hint and pushed off to a hotel. Why should he if it was his own house?

"But you've got all this," she said, gesturing at the room and the gardens beyond. "What about all the land? Surely you don't need it all? Couldn't you sell some?"

Laurence looked horrified. "Angel, the estate's been in our family since the conquest; I can't be the one who breaks it up. Christ. I'd be the Elliott who went down in history as losing Kenniston."

Angel gave him a stern look – the kind that Andi often gave her when she pleaded poverty but went out and bought some Gina sandals on her credit card.

Laurence sighed. "Yes, I know it sounds crazy but there has to be another way. Besides, the land's all tied up with all sorts of codicils and entails."

"So it's either sell the lot or nothing?"

The expression on his face said quite clearly that selling the lot wasn't an option.

"What about antiques?" Angel suggested. Having skived off work quite a bit in her time she was pretty much an expert on *Car Booty* and

Cash in the Attic. Since Laurence had a bloody big attic, there had to be something useful hidden there, surely? Maybe a Monet they'd all forgotten about, or a tiara? She herself had often stemmed her overdraft by selling a (fake) LV bag or pair of shoes on eBay, which was practically the same thing.

But Laurence wasn't leaping at this genius idea. "Anything that can be sold has already gone to Christie's. We've closed up most of the house to save on heating and you've seen how frugal Ma is."

Angel certainly had. She'd thought Spam went out at about the same time Winston Churchill left Number Ten. Come to think of it, the dusty tins that Lady Elliott had fished out of the pantry probably dated to around then. Her stomach lurched at the thought.

"I'm in an impossible position," he continued, starting to pace up and down the room in agitation. "I'm the trustee of a priceless mansion and millions of pounds worth of prime land, but I can't release equity from any of it. The roof is starting to fall in, there's dry rot in the grand stairwell and two of the estate cottages have to be renovated. The Munnings has gone, Ma sold two Chippendales last week and I've sent our last Stubbs to auction. It's the law of diminishing returns, though, because once those have gone that really is it. I can't think of anything else that could help."

Angel nodded. This made her maxed-out credit cards look like nothing. Wonga.com wouldn't be much help to Laurence either. Her mind started to wrestle with the problem. Angel might look like a lost member of the *TOWIE* cast but her intellect was straight out of *University Challenge* and she was usually very good at thinking her way out of trouble. While Laurence continued to explain about inheritance tax and insurances and the Lloyd's of London crash, her brain was shuttlecocking the problem about. There had to be an answer; she just needed to find it.

"What about the National Trust?" she suggested finally when Laurence paused. Her mother had loved visiting stately homes; as a child many of her weekends had involved exploring castles and moated manors. Andi had lapped it up but Angel had been bored, wishing instead that they could go to the West End. The National Trust shop was fine but there were only so many tea towels and lavender sprays a ten-year-old could appreciate.

Laurence laughed despairingly. "They're turning people away. There's so many of us in the same boat that they can take their pick now. Besides, they state that the property has to be financially self-supporting, which Kenniston isn't – we're haemorrhaging money."

Angel filed this information away. No to the National Trust then, but there had to be another way. She thought hard and her brain, which hadn't really thought much beyond bodycon dresses and leg waxes for quite a while, started to whirl. A flicker of an idea flashed through her mind like a fish flitting near the surface of a lake; there one second then gone the next. She'd dive for it later when she had a bit of time to reflect. Besides, she had her own cash-flow issues to address now that Project Rich Guy had crashed and burned in such spectacular style.

"Are you angry?" Laurence asked quietly when she didn't speak. His dark grey eyes were troubled and could hardly meet hers. "I wouldn't blame you if you were but, Angel, please believe me when I say that I never meant to deceive you, not seriously anyway. That was never part of the plan."

Angel felt gutted that her gorgeous millionaire had been nothing but an illusion, and a little bit stupid for taking everything at face value rather than stopping to question the disparities that now, with the gift of twenty-twenty hindsight, were glaringly obvious. But a small part of her was also whispering that, actually, hadn't she done something very similar to Laurence? Angel was at heart an honest person and she wasn't afraid to admit that, by leading Laurence to believe that she lived in the Alexshovs' house and cleverly rotating the few designer pieces she owned, she was doing *exactly* the same to him.

But a plan? What did he mean by that? She pinned him with a bright blue stare. "And what exactly was this plan?"

Laurence couldn't have looked more uncomfortable if she'd thrown him face down onto a bed of nails and jumped up and down on his back.

"It sounds really crass now," he groaned. "Oh, who am I trying to fool? It was really crass before, but somehow I convinced myself that it was perfectly acceptable. Travis pointed it out to me actually, so I should have known it wasn't going to be genius."

Angel nodded. Since this was the same Travis who had nearly drowned them all it stood to reason that he probably wasn't the best person to take advice from.

"I've got a title and a stately home," Laurence continued apologetically, "and a family seat that goes back centuries. What I don't have is cash. So Trav thought—" he paused, "or rather, we thought, that if I found myself a rich wife it might solve a lot of problems. There wasn't time to hang about; something had to be done, and done quickly before Kenniston Hall is just a pile of mouldering rubble – or, even worse, snatched up by some footballer and his WAG, who'll paint it pink, lay shagpile all over the mosaic floors and turn the chapel into a fitness studio."

Angel took this in. To be honest, shagpile wasn't such a bad idea, since the house was so bloody cold, and as for the fitness studio… That silver flickering fish idea surfaced again.

"Why Rock?" she asked. "Surely you'd have had more choice in London?"

Laurence looked shamefaced. "There are too many people there who know the truth. Everyone who goes to Boujis or Annabel's knows everyone else. It's actually a very small pond. Besides, you'd be surprised just how many of us are in the same boat. And," he gave her a self-deprecating grin and, in spite of everything, her heart cartwheeled, "I was tired of competing with Prince Harry! Trav had a place in Rock and it's where the new as well as the old money plays for the summer. So I came here. It was either that or sit at home and count the holes in the roof. Rock seemed like the perfect place to start."

Angel couldn't argue with this. Hadn't she already figured that much out for herself? And wasn't she doing exactly the same thing? Then a dreadful thought occurred to Angel, and to her horror her throat grew tight and her eyes began to prickle. Did this mean that Laurence was only spending time with her because he thought she was rich? Didn't he like her just a tiny bit? To her distress, Angel had started to realise that she liked Laurence much more than just a bit, and not because she'd thought he was wealthy, either.

"So you've only been spending time with me because I'm financially viable?" she said, and her voice wobbled. Was she going to cry? Over a *man?* Angel hadn't even been this upset when her LV bag was outed as a fake. What was going on?

"Christ, no!" Laurence strode across the room and swept Angel into his arms. She held herself rigid for a moment but as his grasp tightened, pulling her against his chest, her senses were overwhelmed by his delicious scent and the joy of being so close to his warm skin.

Laurence was pressing kisses into the crown of her head. "I feel like such a shit," he murmured into her hair.

Angel said nothing. She'd decided to let him suffer for a bit. Hadn't the nuns at school said something about suffering being good for the soul? Angel had certainly suffered when they'd said her skirts were too short and had made her lower the hems. But still. The principle was surely the same.

"I noticed you straight away," Laurence said. "Who wouldn't? And, I'll admit, the fact that you're wealthy got my attention too, but if I'm honest that was only an added bonus. I couldn't stop thinking about you. When I bumped into you in the bank that day I could hardly believe my luck." He stepped back and tilted her chin up with his forefinger so that those storm-grey eyes could stare into hers. "Angel, I don't know what I was expecting to happen, but it wasn't this. I never thought I'd feel this way about anyone." He swallowed, his Adam's apple bobbing nervously. "Angel, I've fallen head over heels in love with you. That's why I couldn't let things go any further between us without telling you the truth."

Angel's eyes were blue circles of surprise. "You're in love with me?"

Laurence nodded. His forefinger traced the curve of her cheek, the slight touch enough to make her knees wobble and her pulse break into a canter.

"Totally and utterly."

"Me?" Angel said slowly. "Or my money?"

He groaned. "You, Angel! Funny, clever, gorgeous you! I couldn't care less about your money."

That was just as well, thought Angel – although she had better make certain.

"So if I was penniless, just a girl on holiday in Rock who was renting a tatty caravan and working as a beautician for a wealthy Russian woman, and pretending to look rich herself, you'd still be head over heels in love with me?"

"Of course I would!" declared Laurence and then, as Angel started to laugh, he registered the full impact of her words. His mouth fell open. "Are you saying what I think you're saying?"

But Angel couldn't reply: she was too busy laughing and crying all at the same time. What a muddle! And what a time to realise that in spite of all her very best intentions and stern pep talks to herself she was in love with Laurence too!

"Oh. My. God." Laurence breathed. "We're as bad as each other!"

Half sobbing, half laughing, Angel nodded her agreement.

"But Laurence," she said, when she finally managed to recover enough breath to speak. "I feel exactly the same way about you! In spite of everything, it's you I'm crazy about. I couldn't care less about Kenniston or the title, or even the money. Only you."

Laurence's face was still.

"Do you really mean that?"

All the Aston Martins and designer clothes and handbags dissolved like a dream, but Angel found she no longer cared at all. All that mattered to her now was being close to Laurence. It was very strange and, Angel realised to her surprise, rather nice.

"With all my heart," she said.

Laurence's face, so taut with worry only seconds before, split into a huge smile. Now those eyes weren't battleship grey at all but sparkling like a frosty morning. Exhaling slowly, he raised them towards the ceiling, where the dimpled cherubs and sex-crazed inhabitants of Mount Olympus looked down indulgently.

"I think somebody up in the heavens is having a bit of a laugh right now," he said wryly, his arms tightening their hold.

Angel nodded. What were the odds that they had both been playing the same game and had both inadvertently fallen for somebody penniless? Fate certainly had a sense of humour.

But moments later humour was no longer the emotion on Angel's mind – because Laurence was kissing her, a kiss of such joy and passion and tenderness that she thought she would dissolve. Then he'd picked her up (refusing carbs was worth it!) and carried her up the steps to the ancient bed, where they'd spent the rest of the night making the gods and goddesses on the ceiling blush.

Recalling it now, and in the cold light of day that was seeping through the moth-eaten curtains, Angel's cheeks turned quite pink. Money no longer seemed half as important, she decided as she snuggled into Laurence. She'd found treasure of a very different kind. God, she hoped this hadn't just been some kind of amazing dream!

To make sure, she peeled open her eyes, the lashes still claggy with last night's mascara, and sure enough there was Laurence out cold, with a dusting of dark stubble across his jaw and an expression of utter contentment on his chiselled features. Angel stared at him for a moment and her heart did the most ridiculous twisty-turny thing before deciding to dive into her belly. Oh God! But he was gorgeous. Even fast asleep and with his treacle-coloured hair all tousled and while snoring gently, he turned her bones to jelly. Angel didn't think she'd ever wanted somebody so badly in her entire life. Her fingers longed to reach out and touch him, trace the sharp planes of his face and linger over the smiling curve of his mouth, but she managed to resist.

Angel was not a morning person at the best of times. Unless she had her complete Clarins kit and a good dollop of Crème de la Mer before bedtime she was loath to let anyone see her first thing, especially anyone she might have done *that* with. In the past she had been known to slip out of bed, leaving her partner sleeping and oblivious, to tiptoe to the bathroom and apply the full works – mascara, false eyelashes, foundation, lip gloss – before sliding back into bed. Yet somehow with Laurence this didn't seem to matter in the slightest. He'd already seen her stripped of all her designer gear and the borrowed patina of wealth, and he still liked her. Loved, her even. Angel realised that the concept of love no longer scared her. Laurence too had laid himself bare, both literally and metaphorically, and trusted her enough to tell her the truth about Kenniston. That had taken courage.

Kenniston. Now that was a problem. As she glanced around the room, even the gloom of closed curtains couldn't disguise the mould that was blooming on the ceiling or the peeling paintwork. It would be fitness suites in the chapel in no time if something wasn't done soon. Even Sarah Beeny would struggle to put this one right…

And there it was! A silver fish of an idea flickering through her mind again, and this time Angel wasn't going to let it slip away. Not when it was an idea this simple, this obvious and this bloody brilliant.

Oh my God! Oh course! The solution to Laurence's problems was so easy it was untrue! It had been right in from of them all the time…

When Angel got an idea into her head there was never any time to waste – and this idea needed action. Reaching over, she shook Laurence's shoulder.

"Laurence! Wake up!" Angel said. "I think I know how we can save Kenniston!"

Chapter 37

Andi was having a very surreal day. Not only had she, for reasons she wasn't quite ready to admit, agreed to go on a date with Travis Chumley, but also when she arrived back at the caravan Callum South was baking bread with Gemma.

"Hi, Andi," said Gemma, as though it was the most normal thing in the world to find a Premier League footballer in the caravan.

"Hi, Andi," echoed Cal.

"We're baking," added Gemma, just in case this wasn't evident from the yeasty smell and globs of dough that spattered the tiny kitchen. It looked as though Tesco's bread aisle had exploded.

Baking? For a split second Andi almost asked what on earth was going on, but when she saw the way that Gemma was looking at Cal, as though she could gobble him up and never mind the buns, it all fell into place.

Oh dear; she really hoped Gemma knew what she was getting into. Back in the days of Dukes Rangers, Callum South's womanising had been notorious. Had he changed? Andi hoped so; physically Gemma might look like a robust girl, but her heart was as tough as cotton candy.

"Cal's been demonstrating his bread-making skills," Gemma told her proudly.

Cal, squashed into the galley kitchen and up to his elbows kneading bread, pulled a face. "More like bread therapy."

"Bad day. We got caught in McDonald's," Gemma explained. "If we had any signal I'd show you the pictures on my phone. It's gone viral; Cal's manager is on the warpath and a load of paps are camped outside the house, so we're in hiding till it dies down."

"It's a nightmare, so it is," sighed Cal. His sleepy brown eyes were troubled. "Poor Gemma's been sacked by her agent."

"Oh Gemma, I'm so sorry!" Andi knew just how desperate Gemma had been to lose weight and please Chloe in order to jump-start her acting career. It had been the driving force of her move to Rock.

But Gemma didn't look very upset. "I actually feel like I've been set free. If Chloe doesn't want me as I am, then sod her. I'm loving doing the Shakespeare and there's more to life than pleasing people."

"Good for you," said Andi. If only she herself had taken that tack a few months ago, then Tom and Hart Frozer would have been very surprised.

"I'm in big trouble for breaking my diet," sighed Cal. Leaving the bread to prove, he looked out of the window. "Mike's going to crucify me. I'll probably get the bollocking of me life. He makes Stalin look like a pussy."

"So while all this is going on you're baking bread?" Sometimes Andi wondered if Gemma lived in another universe altogether. Still, it seemed that Cal was from the same planet as Gemma. It was a match made in calorie heaven.

"I love making bread," Cal said happily. "It probably sounds mental but it's a kind of relaxation for me."

"Just like baking is for me," Gemma added, and they smiled at each other, two kindred cooking spirits. Andi exhaled slowly; she hadn't realised that she'd been holding her breath. Somehow she didn't think she needed to worry about Gemma. Angel, on the other hand, was going to be responsible for her first grey hairs. It was evident from the lack of shoes/bags/drama that her sister still hadn't come home. She hoped Angel was all right.

"Here, try some. It's sun-dried tomato and Parmesan and it's bloody gorgeous," insisted Gemma, hacking through a sunshine-yellow loaf blushed with speckles of crimson. She whacked a slice onto a plate and smothered it with butter. Although the smell was wonderful – and so was the taste, judging by the butter smears and crumbs that coated Gemma's bee-stung mouth – Andi didn't have any appetite. Mel's biscuits and lunch had been totally wasted; from the moment that Jax had strutted into the garden Andi had felt decidedly off colour.

It didn't bode well for a dinner date with the heir to Chumley's Chunks.

"I've just eaten," she fibbed.

"All the more for us then," said Cal cheerfully.

Talk about in denial, thought Andi despairingly as she left them exclaiming over a banana loaf. Cal's career was in the balance and Gemma had lost her agent, and all they could do was bake? Mary Berry had a lot to answer for! Still, at least they seemed happy; she could even hear their laughter and chatter above the gush of her shower. Perhaps she was just a miserable cow?

As she towelled her hair dry and rummaged through her clothes to find something suitable to wear for her evening out, Andi gave herself a pep talk. It was a lovely sunny afternoon, her finances were turning a corner at long last, and she was about to be treated to dinner. Travis had suggested driving over to Newquay for a change of scene and Andi was looking forward to seeing Cornwall's famous surf capital for the first time. Jonty often took his nephews there to catch some waves and said that it was a fun place to be, with a really cool surf vibe.

"It's all Beetle vans, guys with long blond dreds and funky twenty-somethings necking Bud and making campfires," Jonty had said, and his voice had been so animated that Andi had been able to picture the scene perfectly. "There's a great chip shop too, just by the beach. We'll have to go there, eat fish and chips out of the paper and watch the sun go down. Then we'll hit some of the bars and clubs – pretend we're students again!"

She'd laughed. "I was far too busy being a swat at uni to ever hit the clubs and bars!"

"So now's your chance to let your hair down," Jonty had told her. "The Boardmasters Festival is on too, so maybe we can watch some surfing? Or even have a go ourselves?"

It had sounded like a brilliant plan, but Jonty would be far too busy with Jax now to go surfing, thought Andi sadly. They had planned to go and find Andi a shorty wetsuit so that he could teach her, but things had changed so much in the last few days that she couldn't imagine this happening now. Andi couldn't see Jax being a fan of Fistral Beach in any case; she looked far more like a Sandy Lane Barbados kind of girl. And as for eating chips out of paper? Jax didn't look like she'd seen a carb since the last millennium.

Andi sat down wearily on her bunk, narrowly escaping being skewered in the backside by a rogue spring. She felt ridiculously close to tears, which was crazy since there was absolutely nothing to be down about. Life was on the up. She hadn't heard from Tom for months, she had enough work to keep up all her repayments and she had her first date for ages – even if it was only Travis Cockatiel, it was still a date – so she really should be feeling cheerful.

But the bad mood that had been shadowing her ever since Jax had dragged Jonty away didn't show any signs of going anywhere. It was such a pain.

Andi sighed and wound a curl of red hair around her forefinger, deep in thought. Maybe accepting this date with Travis wasn't her smartest move? She didn't fancy him in the least and goodness only knew what they would talk about for an entire evening. Perhaps boat safety would be a good starting point.

What had she been thinking of, agreeing to go in the first place?

You know exactly why you said you'd go, said the annoying voice of conscience, piping up just when she least wanted it to, as per bloody usual. *You wanted to show Jonty that he isn't the only person out and about having a good time.*

Well, yes, Andi admitted. But he'd dropped her like a hot brick as soon as his ex appeared. She knew that she and Jonty were only friends but, even so, it was hurtful. One minute he'd been arranging another trip out on *Ursula,* the next she'd hardly seen him for dust. Maybe it was a childish reaction but she'd wanted to show him that she could have fun too. And that was one thing you could say about Travis Chumley: he liked to have fun. He'd also been very persistent in trying to make amends since their boating disaster and, in spite of herself, she was flattered.

Picking out a funky green smock dress which she paired with black leggings and her chunky DM sandals, Andi pinned her curls onto the top of her head with a butterfly clip and, since her own Mademoiselle had mysteriously vanished, borrowed a squirt of Angel's Alien perfume. The bottle looked a bit like a Transformer and the smell was certainly out of this world. Rather than the gentle floral notes she was used to, this perfume was woody and eastern and yelled *I'm Here!* It was about as subtle as a smack in the face and totally unlike her, which was probably a good thing. Going on a date with a millionaire she didn't fancy in the least wasn't much like her either.

Oh dear. Was it too late to back out?

"You look nice," said Gemma when Andi ventured back into the living area. Callum had vanished and she was up to her armpits in washing-up, looking like she was at an Ibiza foam party. "Are you off somewhere?"

Andi grimaced. "I think I'm going to live to regret this, but I gave in and said I'd have dinner with Travis."

Gemma's eyebrows shot up into her blonde fringe.

"But you can't stand Travis! Especially after the other day!"

"I know, I know," groaned Andi. "Not my brightest move ever. But I really fancied a change of scene and when Travis suggested a night in Newquay it seemed like a good idea."

"And it is," said Gemma quickly. "You work far too hard. It's about time you had some fun. And that's one thing I will say for Travis – he is fun."

Andi wasn't convinced. Half drowning your friends wasn't exactly what she would call fun. On the other hand, at least there was no subtext with Travis. He was the definition of superficial and seemed to just live for fun. Jonty, she'd noticed, had shadows in his eyes and a tension about him, like a leopard poised to pounce. There was something on his mind, she was certain of this, but he didn't seem willing to share whatever it was that was burdening him. Not that she could talk. Andi hadn't mentioned Tom to anyone. Sometimes she recalled his threats and felt sick; at other times she would dream about his mocking laughter and wake up with a pounding heart. There was nothing he could do – he didn't even know where she was – but thinking this didn't make her feel any easier. So Andi chose to treat thoughts of Tom a bit like Angel treated her bank balance: if she didn't dwell on them then they couldn't make her feel bad.

"Where's Callum?" she asked.

"I've got a rehearsal at half five and Cal couldn't hide out here forever. He's gone back to face the music." Gemma looked worried. Her top teeth bit her bottom lip. "It doesn't look good. I really think he could lose his ITV2 contract over this."

Andi was about to ask Gemma exactly what was going on with her and Cal, but the sight of a big black Range Rover pulling up outside the caravan halted the conversation. Moments later the horn was blaring; a naff cacophony of notes that Del Boy would have been proud of.

Gemma grinned. "Your knight in shining car awaits!"

Andi shouldered her Quiksilver rucksack and took a deep breath. It was too late to back out now. She really was going to Newquay with Travis Chumley. She hoped she wouldn't live to regret it.

Two hours later and seated at a window table in one of Newquay's premier restaurants, Andi's desire to see Fistral Beach was certainly fulfilled. It was a beautiful golden evening. The sinking sun stroked the sea with liquid gold fingers and turned the surfers into silhouettes against the peachy sky. Although it was growing late, the sand was still teeming with beachgoers, some playing frisbee, others sprawled out on stripy towels and a few happily barbecuing. All the people looked tanned and outdoorsy and just like they'd stepped straight out of a Fat Face advert, Andi thought. She wished that she was outside too, curling her bare toes into the cool sand and breathing in the tang of sausages and charcoal rather than sitting here at a starched white table, trying to decipher a menu written in inaccessible French and listening to Travis berate the maître d' about the cheap price of the restaurant's lobster.

She'd listened to him all the way from Rock to Newquay. On and on he'd gone, showing off about his Range Rover, his expensive watch and his big new house in Spain. She'd listened with half an ear, making sounds of assent at appropriate intervals and wishing more and more with every mile they drove that she'd stayed put. Andi had felt like yelling at Travis to put a sock in it, and telling him that she didn't care how loaded he was or how many houses he owned; she couldn't tell a Rolex from an Omega, and neither did she care much for lobsters and Cristal. Travis was going all out to impress her, that was for sure, but he was going about it the wrong way completely: these things didn't impress her at all. He'd be far better off with Angel.

"So, what would you like?" Travis was asking. His white Boss shirt blended in so well with the tablecloth that it was a bit like talking to a disembodied head. "You can order whatever you like, you know; cost isn't an issue to me. Besides, my father owns this place." He put his menu down and smiled at her. "I thought I'd have the foie gras followed by the lobster with black caviar. Still, I'm not sure about the price. It seems a little on the low side. They'd better not be cutting corners."

If Travis's blatant showing off hadn't already made her feel queasy, the thought of all those poor geese being force-fed until their livers popped certainly sickened her. Andi shut her menu and placed it on the table with a thump. Travis, still moaning about lobster, looked up in surprise.

"I can't do this." Andi pushed back her chair and stood up. "It's a mistake."

Travis stared at her. "What? The food? Are you a vegetarian or something? That's not a problem. My father owns this hotel. They'll cook whatever you want. They'll do anything we like. Just name it."

And this summed him up in a nutshell, thought Andi in disgust. A spoiled, rich brat.

"I couldn't eat a mouthful while listening to you complain and moan and show off," she said coldly. "You should listen to yourself, Travis. Who on earth do you think you are? Just because a quirk of fate means that you were born to a rich father doesn't mean that you're any better than the rest of us. If you didn't have any money what would you actually be?"

Travis's cockatiel crest seemed to wilt under her onslaught. He opened his mouth to speak, but Andi wasn't done yet. Not by a long shot.

"I don't care about your Rolex, or your chalet in Aspen, or how many sports cars you have in the garage, or how fast your speedboat goes," she told him. "And I certainly couldn't care less about bloody lobsters." For a moment she thought about Jonty, how down to earth he was with *Ursula* and his battered Defender. She wished so much that she was here with him, munching chips on the harbour wall and chatting about everything under the sun, that it felt like a physical pain in her chest. Jonty was brassic but she didn't need money to have a fantastic time with him. Just hanging out together was more than enough.

"Calm down, Andi," said Travis, glancing about the restaurant in embarrassment. "You don't have to have lobster. You can have anything you like."

"It's not about the lobster!" Andi cried. I'd rather eat chips out of newspaper than eat here with you. I can't listen to you brag and show off for another second."

Travis looked mortified. "Andi, please sit down! I can explain," he said, and there was a catch in his voice, which would have touched her if he hadn't spent the last few hours being so totally obnoxious. He reached across the table and touched her arm imploringly. "Please? I'm sorry if I've offended you. That was never my intention. I was trying to make up for what happened the other day!"

Now it was Andi's turn to stare. That was his idea of making up? She hoped Travis never applied for a career in the diplomatic service.

"Please?"

In spite of herself, she sat back down and regarded him across the bone china and silver cutlery.

"Thanks," said Travis. Then he exhaled and all the swagger and bounce seemed to deflate him, like air leaving a balloon. He gave her an apologetic smile. "I thought you were about to walk out on me."

She had been, and she still hadn't abandoned the idea entirely. She was sure she could scrape together enough funds for a taxi home. To be honest she'd even walk if it meant escaping this dinner date from hell.

"I'm sorry if you thought I was being a show-off," Travis said quietly. "It's just that I was so nervous of being with you. I wasn't sure quite what to say or do. When I'm nervous I turn into an arse. I'm sorry, I just can't help it."

"Nervous? Of me?" Andi was taken aback. "Why on earth would you be nervous of me?"

Travis coloured. "Apart from the fact that you're probably the most beautiful girl I've ever met and I think you're absolutely wonderful?

Where else can I start? You're obviously blisteringly intelligent, that goes without saying, and highly principled."

Andi, reeling from his opening comment, was totally thrown.

"Principled?"

"Yes, absolutely. I can't claim to understand it myself; I suppose I am a spoiled brat." He shrugged ruefully. "But the way you choose to live in that caravan with your friend and do things the hard way? That's something else. I'm impressed that you do that when you could be living in the lap of luxury with your family. Is it some kind of eco thing?"

"Travis," said Andi kindly, "what are you talking about?"

"You, not living at the big house with Angel," Travis explained earnestly. "Christ, I've seen your family's boat! It's awesome. Even my old man would think twice about shelling out for that. Of course I was nervous. I wanted you to think that I was good enough to take you out. I bet you've been out with some really loaded guys."

Angel. Of course. Andi could have swung for her little sister. Now it all made sense. Travis was best friends with Laurence, for whose benefit Angel had been exceedingly busy all summer creating the impression that she was loaded and lived in the Alexshovs' house. Quite how she explained her lack of Russian was anybody's guess, but Andi wasn't surprised she'd managed it; when Angel put her mind to something she generally got it. No wonder Travis had been showing off all the way to Newquay. He thought she was an oligarch's daughter. Recalling her bank balance, Andi started to laugh.

"What's funny?" Travis sounded hurt. "What did I say? Is it that I can't compete?"

Andi shook her head. She still couldn't stop laughing. The situation was totally ridiculous.

"Why would you even need to compete?" she said, once the laughter subsided.

Travis shrugged. "Habit, I guess. Years of having the shit kicked out of me at public school by a load of sadistic toffs because Dad's in trade and I say 'tea' not 'supper' and have a northern accent. The only thing I had over them was shedloads of cash – most of the landed gentry are broke – and I guess the habit's stuck with me."

"Hence the boat, and the cars and the bling," finished Andi. It all made a bit more sense now. She looked at him, so crestfallen and slumped against the table, and suddenly saw beneath all the swagger and expensive toys the schoolboy who'd been teased. God, kids were cruel. She remembered that much from her own miserable time at boarding school.

He nodded. "Without it I'm just an oik."

"Well, that makes me one too then, because I'm stony broke," Andi said cheerfully.

Travis frowned. "I don't understand. How can that be true, when Angel's so loaded? Do you have different dads or summat?"

If only, thought Andi. Right now she was ready to divorce her sister, but she'd given up on Alex Evans years ago. Andi knew she was about to blow her sister's cover but was way beyond caring.

"Angel isn't loaded," she said gently. Travis, waving away the waiter, looked puzzled. Taking a deep breath, Andi began to explain exactly what her sister's circumstances were. She had to admit, it didn't sound great – and she couldn't help remembering Jonty's scathing comments about gold-diggers. Much as she loved her sister, Andi knew that Angel had been misguided at best and deliberately deceitful at worst, and she felt ashamed. Why on earth hadn't she tried harder to steer her little sister in the right direction? Stopping the Severn Bore in mid-flood was probably easier but, even so, she should have at least given it a try. Mum had asked her to look after Angel and she hadn't done a brilliant job so far. Even to her own ears, her sister sounded selfish and shallow and mercenary.

But Travis didn't look at all upset to learn that his best friend had been totally duped. In fact quite the opposite: with every word that Andi spoke the grin on his face grew wider. By the time she came to an embarrassed halt he was shaking with mirth.

"What can possibly be funny?" Andi asked, put out. She was feeling terrible.

Travis shook his head. "Andi, you are not going to believe this! It's absolutely priceless! Laurence and your sister are a match made in heaven. He's as broke as she is!"

Now it was Andi's turn to be confused. "I thought he was a viscount? And what about his big house here and his car?"

"He is," Travis grinned, "but he's a skint one. The house in Rock and the car are both mine. Loz might have the titles and the estate but he hasn't got a pot to piss in. He's been trying to find ways to make cash, but he's only really any good at being lord of the manor. When *Made in Chelsea* rejected him there was only one solution – he needed to find a rich wife."

Andi couldn't believe it. What were the odds of Angel bumping into the male equivalent of her?

"But what Loz didn't expect was that he'd like your sister so much," Travis was saying, with an even bigger grin. "He's crazy about her and the last I heard he was driving her down to Kenniston to tell her the truth. He was bricking it, the poor bastard. He's terrified she's going to dump him. You don't think she will, do you?"

Andi hoped Angel would be kind to Laurence. She'd better be. It wasn't as though she had a leg to stand on, was it? "I hope not," she said. "She does seem genuinely fond of him."

"He'll be gutted if she does," said Travis.

"He might dump her," pointed out Andi. "She's lied too, after all. Lord, what a muddle."

"When people hide the truth it does tend to make a bit of a mess," Travis agreed. "Sometimes it makes them behave like total cocks too."

She smiled and their eyes locked across the table.

"Start again?" he asked softly. "As friends this time?"

He looked so hopeful, and even more like a cockatiel with his eyes bright with hope and his head on one side, that Andi's heart thawed. Under all the bluster and stupid showing off there might, just might, be a decent guy.

"Sounds like a plan to me," she agreed.

"Great!" Travis jumped to his feet with so much enthusiasm that his chair went flying. "Come on, let's go!"

"Out of here?" Andi asked.

"Absolutely!" Travis told her. "There isn't a minute to waste. The Newquay night scene is waiting, but first we've got a chip shop to get to!"

Chapter 38

"Andi? Andi? Come on! It's time to get up! It's getting late!"

Wake up? Seriously? Although the voice calling to her through layers of fog and dreams was insistent, Andi had absolutely no intentions of obeying it. To be honest she wasn't sure she *could* have done even if she'd wanted to. She couldn't ever remember feeling so dreadful. Her head was pounding as though Miley Cyrus was swinging a wrecking ball inside her skull. She was dying.

There was a swish of curtains being pulled open, followed by the thud of footsteps, and although her eyes were tightly closed she could still sense daylight pressing against the lids, ready to prise them open at any moment and blast her retinas into dust.

Andi winced. If the thought of this was enough to fill her mouth with the metallic tang of vomit then the actuality didn't bear thinking about. With a groan, she curled up into a tight ball and pressed her face into the pillow. Couldn't she be left in peace and lie here all day, to not move until the sun slipped away again and the techno beat in her temples slowed?

She was in agony. Everything hurt. Even the ends of her hair ached.

"Go away, Angel. I'm not well," she mumbled.

"I'm not Angel and you're not ill," replied a cheerful voice, accompanied by the rattle of cutlery and the chink of plates. "You're hung-over. No don't go back to sleep! Wake up and eat up something. Honestly, trust me on this. It'll do you good."

From her foetal position beneath the covers, Andi froze. Hold on. This voice was male and if that wasn't a big enough giveaway that the speaker wasn't her sister, then the aroma of sausages and bacon certainly was. Apart from the fact that Angel wouldn't dream of eating breakfast, she was a dreadful cook and even less likely to make a fry-up for anyone else.

Oh my God. Where on earth was she and, more importantly, what had she done?

With a growing sense of doom Andi opened her eyes. Bright sunshine streaming through a massive bay window walloped her hard, and for an awful moment the world dipped and rolled in a sickening blur of glass, blue sea, an enormous four-poster bed, designer wallpaper and none other than Travis Chumley perched beside her, wearing a fluffy white bathrobe and a smile.

"Morning, sleepyhead," beamed Travis. He waved a glass of Alka-Seltzer under her nose. "I'm on my second of these. Do you want one?"

Andi tried to shake her head but apparently her brain had come loose inside her skull and was sliding about. She didn't dare move again in case she threw up, although she wasn't sure whether this was from too much alcohol or the realisation that she too was in a bathrobe and had nothing underneath except for her underwear...

Oh God. How much had she had to drink last night? She massaged her throbbing temples with her fingers and tried her hardest to recall the events of the previous evening, but it was no use; apart from a raging thirst and a mouth that tasted of stale alcohol, she didn't have a clue what had gone on. This was the mother of all hangovers. Any minute now she'd find a tiger in the bathroom...

"Bloody hell. You can party!" Travis said admiringly. "I could hardly keep up with you. I know you said you wanted to let your hair down, but even so!" He shook his head. "I wasn't expecting that."

What? What wasn't he expecting? Her to party or… something else? Andi felt cold with dread. Lurking beneath her good-girl exterior she knew there hid a wild child who liked to let her hair down from time to time, but Andi normally kept *her* under lock and key. Angel's job was to be the crazy one; Andi's job was to look out for her. Her own partying had always been strictly under control.

She trawled her memory for any recollections of the night before and slowly, like mist clearing over the Camel and revealing little patches of the town below, images began to appear. She'd left the restaurant with Travis and wandered down the hill and into Newquay. Once in the town they'd bought mountains of chips from the kiosk on the harbour and eaten and eaten until they couldn't manage another mouthful. Travis had chatted away and Andi had enjoyed seeing the arrogance and constant showing off vanish; in their place was a sweet guy who was actually surprisingly down to earth and good company. Throwing the remainder of their golden treasure to the squawking gulls, they'd headed into town and straight into Sailors, where Travis had bought them both a Magners and a whisky chaser.

Oh dear. They'd started the night with pints of cider in Newquay's biggest party bar? No wonder her head was hurting and her memory had turned into Swiss cheese.

"You can certainly drink," Travis continued cheerfully. "Respect to you! How many pints did we have, do you think?"

Too many, thought Andi despairingly. She looked at him to try to see if there were any clues as to what may or may not have happened, but it was all a blur.

"At least four, anyway. Then you were stuck into the tequila!" He shook his head. "I couldn't keep up to be honest – and, anyway, one of us had to be relatively sober to try and get us home in one piece. Although getting you off the dance floor was easier said than done."

Oh no. She'd been on the tequila? No wonder she couldn't remember a thing. Kryptonite had a better effect on Superman than tequila did on Andi. And dancing? Seriously? She stared at him in horror.

"Christ, you look dreadful." Travis hopped off the bed and collected a tray. Whipping off a metal dome, like a magician plucking a rabbit from a hat, he beamed at her. "Full English! It's the only cure!"

But Andi was too poorly and too busy having flashbacks of dancing to face food. She vaguely recalled climbing the steps into a nightclub, the sort where the floor was sticky with beer and stuck to your feet, and towing Travis behind her into the gyrating crowd of boho babes and surfy dudes. There had been Jägerbombs too, she distinctly recalled that now, but after this there was nothing but a big blank.

Well, a big blank and waking up in a bathrobe in a plush hotel room with Travis. Nervously, she plucked at her robe.

"It's all a little hazy," she croaked. "What happened? Did we—"

Travis, busy shovelling grilled tomatoes into his mouth, paused mid-chew.

"Did we what?"

Andi felt her face turn the same colour as the food on his fork. She motioned at her robe. "You know. Did we do… *that*?"

For a moment Travis looked totally perplexed. Then he started to laugh.

"Do you mean did we shag, baby? Yeah?" he asked in a dreadful Austin Powers imitation, waggling his eyebrows up and down. "Do I make you horny, baby? Oh behave!"

Oh God, thought Andi in despair. Just how pissed was I?

"Chillax," said Travis, seeing the horrified expression on her face. "Of course we didn't. I'm not such a bastard that I'd do that when you were totally hammered! And anyway, I'd like to think that any woman I do sleep with remembers the experience and doesn't need to drink Newquay dry first!"

Andi slumped against the pillows with relief. No disrespect to Travis, but she was very glad to hear this.

"Besides," said Trav, spearing a sausage and plunging into sunshine-yellow yolk, "all you talked about last night was that annoying Jonty. I know I'm not the smartest bloke on the planet, Andi, but even I can tell when a girl's head over heels with another guy."

Andi closed her eyes. She couldn't bear the sight of food. Nor could she bear to think that she'd been drunkenly spilling her soul to Travis. God only knew what she'd said. It was all nonsense anyway. She didn't have any feelings for Jonty apart from friendship.

"I was drunk," she croaked. "Whatever I said, I didn't mean it."

"*In vino veritas.* Or, in your case, *in cider veritas*," he teased. "Hey, don't look so worried. Your secrets are safe with me. Just ask Laurence."

"So how come, if nothing happened, I'm in a hotel bed and in a bathrobe?" Andi asked. He had to admit, this didn't look good.

Travis gave her a stern look. "Because, young lady, you were so rolling drunk there was no way I was going to be able to get you into a taxi and back to Rock. No taxi driver would have risked you throwing up in his cab, even if I could have paid him ten times the price. So somehow we managed to stagger back to this hotel; Dad owns it so they weren't going to turn us away. I sorted us a couple of rooms – only then you thought it might be a right laugh to jump into the outdoor pool. With your clothes on. Down you sank, of course, like a stone, and I had to jump in and fish you out. I'm sorry if you're offended, but I had to get you out of your wet things or let you die of cold. It made sense to wrap you in a robe." He smiled. "Don't worry. We had a chaperone. The concierge was very helpful too."

Andi buried her face in her hands. Suddenly it was all flooding back. An icy splash, hands reaching for her, the world spinning around and then nothing.

He winked. "Nice underwear, by the way! Red and white spots are very sexy."

She groaned. "I am never drinking again."

"Don't say that. You're a lot of fun when you drink. I haven't had such a good night out for ages. It makes Annabel's and Boujis look tame. And as for Prince Harry playing naked pool? Compared to you, he's a pussy! Wait until I see him next!" He exhaled happily. "Andi, that was a wicked pub crawl. Or should I say, stagger?"

Andi held out her hand. "I think I'll have that Alka-Seltzer."

Travis passed it over. "Good idea. Try some food too, if you can. It really will help. Then I guess we should head back. Aren't you working today?"

Oh crap. She was. Andi was supposed to be putting a few hours in for Si – and then it was Jax's party, where she'd have a starring role tugging her forelock. Maybe Travis should have let her stay in the pool and drown? The way things were going it would have been a happy release.

She took a big gulp of the drink, gagging at the salty taste. Bubbles fizzed up her nose and she spluttered.

"Not as much fun as tequila?" asked Travis, looking sympathetic.

Andi grimaced. "No fun at all. In fact I may not make it back to Rock."

Travis might have thought this was a joke, but by the time his Range Rover crunched up the drive to Ocean View he'd seen enough to realise that Andi was serious. She'd spent most of the journey with her head stuck out of the window gulping back tidal waves of nausea. A couple of times she'd looked ready to leap out and launch herself under a lorry.

"Are you sure you're really up to working?" he asked, opening the car door and helping her out. "I can't imagine that you'll be much good at adding up figures today."

With legs that felt about as sturdy as soggy string and a stomach doing cartwheels, Andi wasn't convinced that she'd be much help to Simon either, but she hated to let him down. Besides, he'd been so accommodating when she'd phoned and said she'd be in late that she felt she owed it to him to at least try. What had she been thinking, getting roaringly drunk with Travis? Andi was furious with herself. She hadn't gone on a bender like that for ages. She'd thought her inner wild child was well and truly locked away. The last time she'd drunk so much that she'd gone blank had been back in the heady early days with Tom…

Another wave of nausea swamped her at this memory, although possibly not from her hangover this time, and Andi pushed it away quickly. She was doing her best not to think about Tom and his threats.

"Mel's bound to have some strong coffee on the go and I'll mainline that for a few hours," she told Travis. "I'll be fine. Anyway, there's not a great deal left to do. The accounts are practically tied up."

"As long as you're sure," said Travis, doubtfully. "Give me a ring if you change your mind and I'll come back and run you home."

Rising onto her tiptoes, Andi kissed his cheek. "Thanks for being a gentleman."

Travis's hands rested on her waist and he stared down at her with a half smile.

"Let's just say that may go down as one of my biggest regrets."

She stared up at him, surprised. In his mirrored shades she saw her reflection, wild red curls bright against the blue sky and yesterday's clothes all creased and dishevelled. Goodness, but she looked like a girl who'd been out partying all night and then some. Maybe she should have gone home and changed first?

Travis winked. "I'll leave you to go and show those numbers who's boss."

Andi laughed at this, before a movement from the shrubbery caught her eye. She stepped back swiftly when she saw that it was Jonty. The water running in rivulets down his golden torso and glistening in his dark hair spoke of a morning swim, and now he was on his way from the pool to Mel's kitchen for his usual breakfast. When he saw Andi and Travis he'd stopped in his tracks.

For a split second the three of them were frozen in a tableau; Travis lightly touching Andi's waist as she laughed up at him and Jonty, statue-still in the greenery, the light dappling his face and making his wet skin glitter like one of Stephenie Meyer's vampires.

Travis's hands fell away. For the briefest moment Jonty and Andi stared at one another. There was an expression in Jonty's eyes that she couldn't fathom before indifference slipped over those finely carved features and masked his thoughts.

"Andi. Travis." Jonty nodded a curt greeting before turning on his heel and walking back into the shadows.

Andi watched him go with a horrible sense that something fragile had been broken beyond repair. Their easy friendship of the weeks before seemed almost an impossible dream and his unspoken disappointment with her quivered in the air. Andi wasn't a fool. She knew exactly what this looked like; her with wild hair, wearing yesterday's crumpled clothes and kissing Travis Chumley goodbye. Yet who was Jonty to judge her? Jonty, who seemed to go running whenever Jax clicked her fingers?

There was a knot in her throat. Why was she filled with the strongest urge to tear after him and explain exactly what had happened? Although the sun was still high in the cloudless sky, Andi felt suddenly cold.

Chapter 39

Gemma was a nervous wreck. So far she'd totally ballsed up a chocolate cake by using plain flour by mistake, dropped a mixing bowl (and splattered the entire kitchen with sponge mix in the process), and spelled the name wrong on the birthday cake she'd been icing. It was hardly surprising. She was so busy checking her phone to see whether Cal had texted that she couldn't concentrate on anything else. Her hands were shaking so much that it looked as though the three-year-old the cake was intended for had taken matters into his own hands.

Gemma sighed. The way she was performing today, a three-year-old would probably have done a better job. Dipping a palette knife into hot water, she began the soul-destroying task of scraping off the frosted *In the Night Garden* scene that she'd just spent the last twenty minutes struggling to perfect. She really ought to focus on Igglepiggle and Upsy Daisy, but all she could think about was Cal.

Why hadn't he called? Gemma put the knife down and checked her phone for the umpteenth time, but the little flame of hope that maybe the iPhone had beeped so quietly to itself that she'd missed it died quickly when she saw that the screen was stubbornly blank. Was Cal angry with her? Did he blame her for what had happened? Was he at this very moment wishing he'd never met Gemma Pengelley? Or, even worse, was he so upset and broken by the events of the day before that he was unable to even face talking to her? Gemma hated to think of this scenario even more than she hated to think that maybe he was avoiding her. Cal was such a big personality, in all senses of the word, and she couldn't bear to think of him being alone and miserable. Knowing Mike and the rest of the entourage, he'd be punished by having to pound on a treadmill or gnaw endless celery sticks like a masticating Sisyphus.

The press had been savage. Dee's copies of the tabloids lay in a well-thumbed, chocolate-fingerprint-covered pile on the shop counter. After reading several of the red tops, Gemma had felt queasy and unable to face sampling the saffron buns and fairy cakes. Most of her formative years had been spent longing for fame and press exposure, so it was a shock to finally be handed it on a plate – or in this case in a Big Mac box. Headlines like *I'm Loving It – too much*, *Cal-ories* and her personal favourite *Who's Fat Girl?* were doing things for Gemma's appetite that Weight Watchers could only dream of.

Angel, who'd reappeared ridiculously loved up with an adoring Laurence in tow and babbling on about some brilliant idea, had been weirdly delighted by the press attention.

"We must get hold of Cal!" she'd shrieked, bounding around the caravan like a demented creature. "Oh my God! Talk about timing! This is perfect!"

It was the oddest definition of perfect Gemma had ever come across. She'd ignored Angel's plea for Cal's phone number and stomped off to rehearsal, where she'd fluffed her lines and generally made a total mess of the part. She had to get a grip, Gemma decided. The first performance was only days away and after all the effort that had gone into it she couldn't blow it now. So it might only be an amateur production in a small Cornish town, but everyone had worked so hard and there was no way Gemma could let them down. As she mopped up congealing cake mixture, Gemma thought that just as Viola "sat like patience on a monument", eating her heart out for Orsino, it was ironic that she'd be doing the same for Cal. Her only consolation was that it would hopefully make for a stellar performance. What she'd do when the play, and indeed the summer, was over was anyone's guess.

She'd worry about that later.

Angel, on the other hand, didn't seem at all concerned about the future. Gemma had, to her amazement, heard the story about Laurence being as stony broke as her friend – and although there was a certain poetic justice in the situation, she couldn't help being alarmed. After all, hadn't the whole point of Rock for Angel been Project Rich Guy? She would have expected her best friend to be furious and straight back to the drawing board, but instead Angel seemed thrilled and unable to let go of Laurence's hand for a nanosecond. It was all very unusual and, quite frankly, disconcerting.

Angel's behaviour was nearly as peculiar as her sister's, Gemma decided as, placing the iPhone out of reach, she returned to the sink and started to rinse out bowls of bilious green and pink icing. Most uncharacteristically, Andi had stayed out all night with none other than Travis Chumley, he of the ridiculous hair and dubious maritime skills. In a million years Gemma would never have pegged the bumptious northerner as Andi's type. With his flashy cars, ludicrously expensive watch and bulging wallet, she'd have placed her last penny on him being far more Angel's cup of tea. Andi was brainy and sensitive and, with her gorgeous figure and cloud of tumbling red curls, she looked just like a girl from a Rossetti painting – albeit one who wore jeans and a worried expression. Stacking the empty bowls to drain, Gemma decided that she would have staked her life on Andi carrying a torch for the dark and brooding Jonty. He might not have two pennies to rub together but he had an undeniable presence, and when he looked at Andi his eyes seemed to light up from the inside. Gemma smiled in spite of her misery. Oh, who was she kidding? Jonty was bloody gorgeous: he looked as though he'd stepped straight out of a Calvin Klein advert, with his Gillette-sharp cheekbones, striking eyes and slow sexy smile. She'd seen how other women followed him with their gaze (even while they were seated with their wealthy partners), as he strode across the pontoon. She wouldn't have blamed Andi in the slightest for falling for him. But no, it seemed that Travis Chumley had mysteriously found his way into Andi's heart.

Gemma paused, tea towel in hand. After Tom she'd really hoped Andi would have found a man who was worthy of her. Maybe Travis had hidden depths, although from what she'd seen of him so far they were very well hidden indeed!

Still musing on the intricacies of her friends' love lives, Gemma turned on Pirate FM, fished out her battered copy of *Twelfth Night* and began to measure out icing sugar, butter and drops of colouring to begin again. While she beat the mixture she propped her lines against the packet of Silver Spoon and went over her scenes, determined that at tonight's rehearsal she'd be word perfect. Wow. It was amazing just how well rhyme went with beating buttercream into submission! Soon she was deep into Act Four, the creamy icing was rising into emerald peaks and Cal's lack of communication was almost forgotten.

Gemma was so lost in Shakespeare that she didn't hear the shop bell tinkle or the tap tap of designer shoes tripping across the tiles and into the kitchen. It was only when a harsh sob interrupted Viola's conversation with Olivia that Gemma looked up and realised she was no longer alone.

Emily, stick-insect model and Cal's co-star, was standing at the far side of the kitchen.

The spoon clattered into the bowl and Gemma's heart skipped a beat. Lord, how on earth had Emily crept up on her? It was like something out of *Fatal Attraction*.

"My God! You made me jump!" Gemma put her hand on her chest and stared at the other girl. "What on earth are you doing here?"

But Emily didn't speak. Instead her eyes narrowed and her mouth set in a tight line. Gemma felt a prickle of unease. Rather than being her usual arrogant self, all glossy straightened hair and perfect make-up, today Emily looked as though she was fraying around the edges. Her eyes were red, her hair was a mass of tangles, and a crop of spots had appeared on her chin. She looked awful.

"How could you let this happen to Cal?" Emily spat.

Gemma felt sick. Was Cal all right?

"Has something happened to Cal?" she whispered.

"Of course it has, you stupid bitch," snarled Emily. "As if you don't know! It's all your fault! If it hadn't been for you, Cal would be fine!"

Everything stopped. Gemma was afraid to move. The radio chattered away to itself. Emily seem poised to spring at her; every sinew in the girl's body was coiled and tense. Gemma gulped. She hoped there weren't any stray knives lying around. Never mind boiling bunnies. From the expression on Emily's face, Dee was quite likely to come back and find Gemma bubbling away on the hob.

Abruptly Emily stepped forward and swept her arm across the table. Gemma shrank back as a rush of utensils, bowls and packets flew upwards, crashing onto the tiles and the opposite walls. Icing sugar clouded the air, tingling against Gemma's teeth and dusting everything. Green buttercream smattered every surface as though Shrek had sneezed, while sharp ceramic shards littered the floor like broken shark's teeth. Gemma couldn't believe this display of violence, and for a moment she was afraid to move.

My God! Who would have thought that skinny Emily had that much strength?

Emily crossed the room in a couple of strides, halting only inches away from Gemma. Although she knew she was bigger and stronger, Gemma was afraid because the other girl seemed to have totally lost control. She shrank back against the cooker, little caring that the heat was burning into her calves.

"It's all your fault!" hissed Emily. Fury twisted her face, blurring those pure lines that sold products and graced magazine covers, until she was unrecognisable. "You've ruined everything, you stupid fat cow! If it hadn't been for you everything would have been fine!"

Gemma felt sick. She didn't know what had happened, but it must have had something to do with the McDonald's fiasco.

"Is Cal hurt?" she whispered. Something inside her died at the thought.

"He's ruined! That's what he is! All because of you!" Emily jabbed a bony finger into Gemma's shoulder. He's going to lose everything and it's all your fault!"

And then a tide of invective was unleashed as Emily hurled accusations at Gemma about how Cal had lost all of his TV contracts, then his lucrative sponsorship deals with sportswear companies and Weight Busters, and finally about how Emily's big break, the chance she'd been working towards for years to really make it into television, was well and truly over.

"All because you couldn't stop stuffing your big fat face!" she finished, concave chest heaving and eyes bright with spite. "My God, look at you! With your cakes and your burgers and your revolting fat body! Don't you realise what a joke you are? Didn't you know that was all you ever were to Cal, just a laugh? He probably thought you were the only person who could make him look thinner!"

"That's not true," whispered Gemma. Cal was her friend. She knew he was.

Emily's eyes raked her body scornfully. "Of course it is. You're a joke. Don't kid yourself that he ever really took you seriously. You were just somebody to scoff a pie with. And look where that got him. Hanging out with you has cost Cal his career. It's cost him everything! He wishes he'd never met you! And so do I!"

A burning wave of shame swept over Gemma, but not from Emily's cruel personal attack. No, Gemma knew she had body issues, but the weird thing was that since she'd arrived in Rock she'd started to make peace with those. Rather, she felt ashamed that she'd supported Cal's quest to break his diet – encouraged it, even – and guilty too. No wonder Cal hadn't been in touch. He must be desperately upset and worried. He'd told her how precarious his finances were.

"You know I'm right," said Emily, when Gemma didn't respond. "You've ruined Callum South's career and mine. I know you won't care about me, but I hope you're proud of yourself for wrecking his life! No wonder he wishes he'd never met you."

Gemma flinched. She didn't want to believe this, but Cal's silence since yesterday spoke volumes.

"I never meant any of this to happen," she said. Her voice was faint.

"Well it has. You've ruined everything." Emily stalked from the room, pausing in the doorway to survey the devastation. "Everything!"

She spun on her heel. Moments later the shop bell tinkled and Gemma was left alone. The kitchen was quiet again apart from the radio.

Gemma stood still for a moment. Then her eyes filled and the ruined kitchen swam. The truth hit her with gale force. She was a laughing stock and she really had ruined Callum's career, however unintentionally. No wonder the iPhone had been silent. Callum couldn't bear to speak to her because he blamed her too. He wouldn't be calling in a hurry. Emily was right: she'd spoiled everything.

With tears spilling down her cheeks Gemma bent down and began to pick up the broken bowl. The broken pieces of her heart would have to wait.

Chapter 40

"You're late," were Jax's opening words when a breathless Andi knocked on the door of the elegant Victorian townhouse the older woman had rented for August. "You do realise I won't be paying you for the time you've missed?"

Andi, still out of breath from running most of the way from Trendaway Farm to Rock, glanced down at her watch. It was three minutes past the hour. Oh dear. She feared this set the tone for the evening.

"I'm really sorry," she apologised, following Jax through into a stunning glass and chrome atrium, filled with white fairy lights, lush potted palms and tables covered in neat rows of sparkling champagne glasses. The caterers were already hard at work unloading food onto trestle tables. Glancing over, Andi saw helpings of pink prawns swimming in garlic mayonnaise, glistening black caviar piled onto blinis and, to top it all, several large lobsters standing guard over steaming vats of bisque. Goodness, Jax was really pushing the boat out to impress.

"It's been a really busy day," Andi attempted to explain when Jax didn't reply. She actually thought she'd done incredibly well to make it at all. Her hangover had really kicked in. No amount of coffee had been able to revive her and it had felt as though Cornwall Council's road gang were using pneumatic drills inside her skull. Mel had taken one look at Andi's green face and packed her off home straight away. She'd spent most of the day tucked up in her bunk sleeping it off. Now, after lots of water and Nurofen, she was feeling slightly more human – but her temples were still pounding and the sight of all the food made her feel queasy.

Jax gave Andi scathing a look, which suggested she could see through the neatly tied back hair, white smock top and agnès b. trousers to the hung-over wreck beneath. Dressed in a stunning black dress slashed so low that it showed both kinds of cleavage, and with her hair straightened to within an inch of its life and her face beautifully made up, Jax looked the antithesis of how Andi felt.

"There's a lot to do," she said curtly. "The guests arrive at half seven. I need you to take their bags and coats when they arrive and then pass around the canapés. I'm expecting most people to walk through and be on the terrace, so make sure you're there and on hand to refill their glasses too. Afterwards you can wash the dishes and glasses so they're clean to return."

Andi waited for a *please* but it didn't come. With a sinking heart she followed the older woman through the atrium and out onto the terrace where once again it seemed no expense was to be spared. Citronella torches were already lit to keep the midges at bay and a string quartet was warming up by a forest of potted bay trees. Jax was going all out to impress her neighbours; that was for certain. As well as Andi there were several other local women she recognised, dressed in waitressing attire. Surely she was surplus to requirements?

Or was Jax putting her very firmly in her place? As she busied herself pouring champagne, the thought of alcohol making her stomach lurch alarmingly, Andi had to admire Jax's logic. She wanted Jonty back, that much was obvious, and she hated and was threatened by his friendship with Andi. However misplaced this insecurity was, to be the beautiful queen bee at an elegant party while Andi looked dowdy and served the drinks was a stroke of genius that would have impressed Machiavelli. While Jax barked orders, Andi gritted her teeth and thought that if it hadn't been for all her debts she'd have told Jax exactly where she could shove her lobsters. Not for the first time, she cursed Tom.

At about half seven the first of the guests started to arrive and Andi was busy collecting pashminas and more designer bags than the ground floor of Selfridges could boast, as the great and good of Rock arrived for the free Taittinger and food. Before long the terrace had filled with guests and she was rushed off her feet offering drinks and canapés while Jax drifted from guest to guest, feigning interest but with her eyes always sifting through the crowds. In between asking people if they wanted a drink or a canapé, Andi amused herself with some people spotting. It was like a who's who of Rock's high society. So far she'd spied two celebrity chefs, somebody who looked very much like Martin Clunes and, believe it or not, Angel's old nemesis Mr Yuri. With a gulp and hoping desperately that he'd visited Cornwall for a holiday rather than to fit her sister out with a pair of concrete boots, Andi concentrated on pouring champagne and being generally invisible.

Finally, and much champagne-pouring later, Simon and Mel arrived. Relieved to see friendly faces, Andi left her work for a moment and joined them in the garden.

"Champagne? Canapé?" she asked.

Mel looked taken aback to see her. "Andi? What on earth are you doing serving drinks for Evil Edna?"

"Earning some extra pennies," said Andi with a grin. "Beggars can't be choosers. I didn't expect to see you here though. I thought you weren't a fan of Jax?"

"Believe me, I'm not." Mel took two glasses of Taittinger. Draining one and then the other in swift succession, she added, "That's better. Now I can face the next hour."

"My wife only came because she wants a nosy at Jax's house," grinned Si. "It's one up from watching *Come Dine With Me,* for her!"

Mel walloped him. "Don't be a bugger. You know full well I've come to make sure Jonty isn't eaten alive. I don't trust that woman an inch." She waved her hand in the direction of the atrium, lit up now by the candles and fairy lights as dusk had fallen. "I mean, just look at her!"

Andi followed Mel's gesture and her stomach slowly looped the loop when she glanced into the atrium and saw that Jonty had arrived. He stood framed in the glass of the atrium, a slim but powerful figure dressed in a white Quiksilver shirt and faded jeans. In his simple yet stylish surf dude's outfit, Jonty stood out from everyone else in their Armani and Ralph Lauren. Jax had cornered him already and even from a distance it was clear that they were deep in conversation. Jax had her hand on his chest and her head was tilted up at him, giving Jonty the full benefit of her tanned cleavage. Jonty, though, was too busy saying something back, in between much head shaking and waving of hands, to be distracted by the barely-there frock. His attention was one-hundred percent focused on whatever it was he was saying.

"I can't believe he came," Mel said. She looked upset and two spots of colour bloomed above her achingly familiar cheekbones. "Has he flipped?

"Course he hasn't." Si put his arm around his wife and drew her close. Dropping a kiss onto her dark hair, he added, "You know why he came. Jonty wants to make sure Jax doesn't—"

"Darling, look: there's Alice and Hugo!" interrupted Mel. "We'd better go and say hello! We'll catch you later, Andi!"

"See you tomorrow," said Si as his wife towed him away. Over his shoulder he added with a wink, "Unless you go on the lash again, that is!"

Andi poked her tongue out at him and went back to the serious business of refilling glasses. Although she was busy – even if they were some of the UK's wealthiest citizens Jax's neighbours seemed determined to make the most of all the free booze – Andi's gaze kept returning to the couple framed in the window, lost in conversation and oblivious to everyone around them. Maybe they were sorting things out? Jax had stepped even closer to him now and was doing this weird thing where she kept tossing her hair about and struggling to keep her dress on both shoulders. It was as though her skin was made of Teflon. Jonty's arms were crossed and he kept shaking his head, although he made no move to leave. Quite the opposite. He looked as though he had an awful lot to say. Then he glanced away from Jax and out of the atrium towards the garden. For a split second his eyes locked with hers and they stared at each other. Although it was a warm evening, goosebumps rose on her arms. He raised an eyebrow and mouthed, "Where's Travis?"

Andi looked away, hot with embarrassment. Although it was none of Jonty's business what she did, the idea that he believed she'd spent the night with Travis irked her.

Ignoring him, she concentrated on filling glasses, deciding that it was actually a relief to be invisible amongst the guests. They weren't at all interested in her and as she served the drinks Andi let their conversations drift like dandelion seeds on the breeze. When she did attempt to sneak another glimpse at Jonty and Jax they were nowhere to be seen. Perhaps they'd gone somewhere more private? They probably had plenty of things to discuss. Whatever was going on it was their business anyway. Maybe she should just concentrate on topping up glasses, seeing as that was what she was being paid to do?

The night was falling in earnest now; the air was thick with the scent of evening stock and the river below the terrace was just an inky void. Strains of Vivaldi drifted on the breeze, while the chatter of the guests grew louder as they consumed more alcohol. Andi's headache fluttered again near her temples and she was almost felled by a wave of exhaustion.

After several hours she was losing track of how many trips she'd made carrying trays laden with dirty glasses. Her head was thudding intensely and she felt giddy. Moving as cautiously as she could through the crowd of drunken and excited partygoers, she was attempting to make a return journey to the kitchen when the room pitched and rolled like a boat driven by Travis. Andi wasn't quite sure how it happened, but the next thing she knew she was sprawled on the floor surrounded by broken glass and gawping onlookers. She tried to get up but the room was spinning. Putting her hand out to steady herself, she yelped in pain.

"Oh my God!" Andi heard Mel cry. "Andi! Are you OK?"

"She's bleeding!" somebody else gasped.

"I'm so sorry everyone!" Jax's voice, bright with false good humour, was as welcome to Andi as nails scraping a chalkboard. "I hadn't realised we were having Greek night!"

Andi attempted to sit up. Whoa! That wasn't very nice. Why couldn't everyone stand still?

"Andi? Hey, take it easy. Don't try to move."

From the whirling mass of faces Jonty's voice was like a lifeline. She tried to reach out for it but instead all she saw was Jax, rising like a cobra about to strike. "What the hell are you playing at?" she hissed. "Have you any idea how much the deposit on these glasses was? That can come out of your wages."

"Jax!" Jonty admonished. "She's passed out. Have some sympathy. Mel, fetch some water."

"Passed out?" Jax snorted. To Jonty she said, "She's hung-over to shit, you mean. Didn't you tell me that she was out until all hours with the local playboy?"

Even though she felt horribly dizzy and her hand was in agony, these scathing words, which had clearly come from Jonty, really hurt. God, but he was quick to jump to conclusions. A sense of injustice tightened like a vice around her ribs.

"I'm fine," Andi said. Somehow she managed to sit up. Mel crouched down next to her with a glass of water.

"Have a drink," Mel urged. "And could you manage something to eat? I bet you haven't eaten all day, have you?"

Andi hadn't. With her stomach insisting on doing a trampoline impression, eating had seemed a high-risk activity. While Mel went to fetch some leftovers and Jax stomped off in disgust, Jonty helped Andi to her feet and supported her to the sink, where he gently rinsed her cut hand. Neither of them spoke. Andi leaned into him, feeling his solid strength as he held her, and her heart twisted. He was her dear friend but as far away from her right now as the stars shining above Rock. How had it come to this?

Finally, once the wound was clean, Mel returned with some dressings.

"Maybe I should do that?" said Jonty. His arms still held Andi against his chest at the sink, where crimson droplets feathered the white ceramic.

Mel wrinkled her forehead. "I think this needs more than you or I can do, Jonty. It looks deep. I think it's going to need a couple of stitches."

Andi was horrified. Apart from the fact that this would mean even less wages – if indeed there would be anything left over after she'd repaid Jax for all the breakages – it was miles to the nearest hospital. For a moment she thought about telling them it was fine and just giving up the evening as a bad job, but the blood dripping into the sink didn't show any sign of abating.

"Can you call me a taxi?" she asked.

"I'd take you myself but I've had far too much to drink." Mel grimaced. "And Si's had a skinful too. Jonty?"

Jonty shook his head. "I've had several drinks, otherwise I'd drive. What a nuisance." Then he said, with deliberate care and as though the thought had just occurred to him, "Can I call anyone for you? Travis?"

Mel, who was wrapping Andi's hand in a tea towel, shot her brother a warning look – but Andi was too exhausted to worry about Jonty's issues with Travis. If he wanted to jump to conclusions and judge her, then fine. That was up to him.

"Do you need somebody to come with you?" Mel asked. Jonty said nothing. In the gloom of the kitchen his face was shadowed and his eyes were great pools of blackness. Once, not so long ago, Andi knew he would have offered to come with her, but not now. Something had changed.

"I'll be fine on my own," she said firmly. Blood roses bloomed through the tea towel and Andi moved her hand so that nobody could see. She didn't want a fuss and she certainly didn't want Jonty feeling obligated to come with her, not when he'd once given his friendship and time so freely and joyously.

No way. Let him drink bubbly and eat blinis with Jax. For a guy who professed to love the simple life, he was certainly taking to his ex's privileged world with ease.

"You bloody well won't go alone," Jonty said. He was already scrolling through his mobile for a taxi number. "I'm coming with you."

"No thanks," Andi snapped. "You go back and enjoy the party and spend some time with Jax. I'm fine on my own, but if I need anyone I can give Travis a call."

Jonty stared at her for a moment. The expression on his face was hard to read. Then he shrugged.

"You know what? I think I'll leave you to it in that case. Good luck at the hospital, Andi."

As he walked away Andi stared after him. Without Jonty's arms holding her up she felt strangely untethered, as though she might float away. For a couple of seconds she listened for his footfalls on the wooden floor to return, part of her hoping that he'd come back and accompany her after all; but no, he'd gone, just like that. Back to the party and back to Jax. She felt ridiculously let down.

"What?" she said to Mel, who was looking at her and shaking her head.

"If you don't know then I won't spell it out," Mel replied wearily. She reached into her pocket and pulled out her BlackBerry. "Let's call a taxi, shall we? Si can pop it on his account – don't go scrabbling for money while your hand is gushing blood."

Andi swallowed back her disappointment and nodded. Jonty wasn't going to change his mind. And why should she want him to? She was better off just relying on herself. Hadn't she learned that much from Tom? She took a deep breath. From now on she was doing things on her own. It was better that way.

Two hours, five stitches and several very bad cups of hospital coffee later, Andi was feeling exhausted and starting to wonder whether she'd made the right decision. It might have been nice to have somebody to chat to while she waited in the bleak A&E reception. It would have been even better to have had somebody there to tell her that everything was going to be fine and to hold her other hand while the nurse stitched up the wounded one. The hospital staff were kind enough but she could see how run off their feet they were. Andi felt bad for taking up time that could have been better spent on somebody who was genuinely sick rather than clumsy. Whatever had she been thinking, to get so blindingly drunk like that? Hadn't she learned from her past mistakes? Andi felt utterly appalled with herself.

She hadn't intended to return to Jax's house. Once the doctor was happy with her hand and she'd been discharged, Andi's only thought had been to get back to the caravan, dive into her narrow bunk and sleep for as long as she could, possibly for at least a day. The thought of being able to close her eyes and put this horrendous day behind her was a very welcome one. The only problem was that she'd left her bag in Jax's kitchen with her keys, purse and mobile in it. The hospital receptionist had called a taxi for Andi but had looked so pained as she went about it that Andi had started to feel that this one call would be to blame for the collapse of the NHS. Andi had had no means of getting back to Rock via public transport and no desire to be stranded in Truro at this time of night. So she'd had little choice but to request the taxi and then persuade the driver to take her all the way to Jax's place and wait outside while she fetched her bag.

It was a beautiful August night and, although it was sweet with the scent of lavender and stock, there was crispness in the air that hinted of autumnal days to come. The Virginia creeper around the front door had already turned a deep crimson, although in the darkness it looked like a reddish-brown smudge, and Andi could feel the last days of summer sighing in the light breeze. She had the profound sense that something was drawing to a close and, in spite of herself, Andi shivered.

Jax's rented house was beautiful, a double-fronted Victorian villa with big bay windows that looked out onto an immaculate garden. It was late now, almost midnight, and as she crunched up the path Andi steeled herself for another tongue-lashing. The guests must have all gone by now but hopefully Jax would still be up and not too put out. Closer investigation revealed that the light was on in the sitting room. Andi felt relieved. Jax had to be awake; maybe she was chatting to the last stragglers – or perhaps, and far more likely, she was ordering the other helpers about. The sash window was up and the curtains fluttered. Andi couldn't resist peeking in; at least this way she'd know what she was in for.

Shadowing the brick wall, she edged along – skirting the flowerbed – until she was right next to the window. Reaching up onto tiptoes, Andi peered around the edge and into the room. When her eyes adjusted to the light she realised exactly what she was looking at and her heart twisted.

Jonty and Jax were alone in the room. His broad back was against the window but it was as clear as the moonlight outside that Jax's slender arms were twined around his neck.

Feeling like a voyeur, Andi crept back to the taxi as quietly as she could. She'd have to wake Gemma or Angel to let her in and borrow the fare, because there was no way she was disturbing whatever was going on inside. All she wanted to do was hide away and never see either of them again.

Andi closed her eyes in defeat as a cocktail of emotions raced through her nervous system: shock and embarrassment and anger, but most of all jealousy.

Chapter 41

Angel was beyond frustrated. It was all very well having an absolutely *genius* idea, but if every time you tried to get it up and running people wouldn't co-operate then what was the point? Honestly, she could have screamed with annoyance. Normally she couldn't move in Rock for practically tripping over Andi or Gemma or Cal, but now, just when she had the solution to all of their problems in the palm of her hand, they all decided to go AWOL. Andi was uncharacteristically out late and then sleeping in; Gemma had locked herself in her small room and was refusing to come out, and Cal was presumably in hiding from the tabloid press behind his very high gates.

Angel's chin had a determined tilt to it as she worked the idea backwards and forwards in her mind. There had to be a way she could reach Cal and pitch her idea to him. He'd love it, she knew he would, and it was only a matter of time before she found a way to talk to him.

"Maybe you should just let it go?" Laurence sighed as they pulled up outside the Alexshovs' mansion in Trav's Aston Martin. The roof was down and it was a glorious day. Not that Angel noticed such details: her head was far too full of schemes to be distracted by sparkling waves and cotton-wool clouds. "I agree that it's a marvellous idea but it all seems very complicated."

"It really isn't! It's actually very simple. I just need to talk to Cal," Angel said, with great confidence. "He's the key to all of this, and Gemma too if she ever comes out of her room. Seriously Laurence, if I can get Cal on side then I know we're onto a winner. Kenniston will be saved. Better than saved!"

Laurence covered her hand with his large, strong one and in spite of the warmth of the sunshine beating down on her head, Angel shivered. Those hands of his worked some kind of magic; that was for sure. Laurence only had to touch her with a brush of his fingertips and she was jelly. Since they'd got together she'd hardly been apart from him and it was proving very tricky to keep focused when all she wanted to do was drag him back upstairs! But after two delicious days of scarcely moving from the big four-poster in the master bedroom of Travis's house, it was time to take control of circumstances again. Project Rich Guy may have gone slightly pear-shaped but this was an even better idea! Laurence had taken a little persuading at first, but he'd done the figures and some research and could see the potential. He was firmly onside now – which may or may not have had something to do with those two days in the master suite!

"I won't be very long here," Angel told him. "Vanya's mother's come to stay and she only wants a couple of manicures." Leaning across, she brushed his mouth with hers. Wow. How could just a simple kiss send all her senses spiralling out of control?

Laurence glanced down at the plain diver's watch Angel had bought him in Padstow. The borrowed Rolex had been safely returned to Travis.

"I'll see you at half eleven," he promised. "Wish me luck at the bank."

"You have a copy of our business plan: you won't need luck," said Angel.

As she sauntered up the drive to Vassilly and Vanya's, the KGB-style security guards on the gate waving cheerily when they saw her, Angel felt buoyed up with determination. Unlike Andi and Gemma, both of whom seemed to be doing more than their fair share of moping lately, Angel was a firm believer in grasping Fate by the short and curlies. Callum South might think that his reality TV career was dead in the estuary, but if her hunch was right this was just the start of bigger things to come...

"Angel! Darlink!" Vanya cried when Angel entered the opulent sitting room. Today the Russian woman was channelling her inner Joan Collins and sporting more leopard skin and flowing mane than London Zoo's big cat area. As they air kissed, Angel nearly had her eye put out by one of Vanya's Sky-dish sized earrings. More was definitely more in Vanya's book.

"Vanya! Wonderful to see you," Angel replied, dodging the second earring and smacking her lips somewhere above the Russian woman's razor-sharp cheekbone.

Vanya stepped back and regarded Angel thoughtfully. "You look different, darlink. Radiant! Haff you had hair done? Hmm? An oxygen facial? I know! A leetle filler?"

Angel laughed. In her dreams! No, odd as it seemed, wearing no make-up and spending half the night doing terrible things to Laurence Elliott was proving far more effective than any beauty treatment. The glitter in her eyes and inner luminescence hadn't come for Clarins, that was for sure. That was all House of Elliott.

"Anyway, you look beautiful," Vanya decided, stepping back and clicking her fingers at one of the servants. "Now, some champagne?"

Champagne at nine thirty in the morning was the norm at the Alexshovs'. They drank the stuff like Angel drank Diet Coke. Probably bathed in it too. Accepting a glass, Angel followed Vanya from the drawing room and along echoey corridors filled with priceless works of art and countless photographs of family members, lined up with military precision on mahogany sideboards. Enormous chandeliers sparkled above. The whole place screamed money. It was a long way from the shabby and faded elegance of Kenniston Hall.

"My mama is visiting for a leetle holiday," Vanya explained as they traversed a marble hallway, their heels clicking on the polished floor and then padding over thick Turkish rugs before they climbed the sweeping staircase. "She has been unwell and is staying for a rest. I think haffing nails done cheer her up."

"There's nothing like a manicure to perk you up," Angel agreed. She glanced down at her own nails. Oh dear, they were looking a bit neglected. Making a mental note to give herself a French manicure that evening, she followed Vanya into a large bedroom where, sitting in a big chair by the window, all ice-cream-cone hair and boot-button eyes, was none other than Mrs Yuri.

"You!" cried Mrs Yuri. Her bright red mouth fell open. "You!"

It was one of those awful moments when time seemed to free-fall. Suddenly, Angel was right back in Blush, where she had been screamed at in both Russian and English and sacked with such speed her head had spun for days.

Mrs Yuri rose to her feet. "My husband, he haff been looking for you!"

Angel's mouth was dry. Vanya was Mr Yuri's daughter? Did Fate really hate her this much? Suddenly, now she was in the heart of the Alexshovs' house and surrounded by the kind of security that made the Kremlin look slack, all those stories about concrete boots no longer seemed quite so far-fetched.

"Mrs Yuri, I—"

"He haff searched everywhere but nobody could find you!" Mrs Yuri interrupted. She was pulling herself up to standing now, her hands clutching the armrests of her chair until her knuckles were white. "Everywhere! But nobody knew where you go! The salon, they no tell me!"

"Mama? You know Angel?" Vanya asked, looking from her mother to Angel in confusion.

"Ya, ya!" Mrs Yuri nodded. "This is the girl I tell you about? Angelique? The one who didn't like my mole?"

Angel groaned. She would never, ever try to do anyone a good turn again. "It wasn't that I didn't *like* it. I just thought it looked a bit suspicious and I was worried. I never meant to insult you or hurt your feelings!"

But neither Mrs Yuri nor her daughter was listening to a word Angel was saying. The older woman was gabbling away in frantic Russian and gesticulating wildly, while Vanya's eyes grew wider by the second. Angel tried to work out what her chances of escape were. Pretty slim, since she was on the second floor and Rottweilers prowled the garden.

"It was you?" Vanya gasped finally. "You are the girl who didn't like my mama's mole?"

Angel opened her mouth to try to explain, but before she could speak the words were literally knocked from her as Mrs Yuri engulfed her in a massive bear hug. Kisses were smacking against Angel's cheeks and hey! Was the older woman crying?

"Sank you! Sank you!" gasped Mrs Yuri, in between sobs and kisses. Stepping back so that Angel could see her properly, she pointed to her chin. "Has gone, ya?"

Angel's eyes widened. Where only weeks ago there had been a large mole, there was now a faint scar. Mrs Yuri had had the mole removed? After all the fuss she'd made about ignoring it? God, weren't people odd?

"I explain," said Vanya, after yet more machine-gunfire Russian from her mother. "My mama, she go away after she see you and she think very hard."

Mrs Yuri added something else in furious Russian and her daughter nodded.

"OK, I tell her! Angel, Mama say that nobody had ever dared to mention her mole before. You first one. She very hurt by it."

"Sorry, but—" Angel began, but Vanya held up her hand.

"I not finish! Mama very cross at first but then she think, ya, mole is sore and maybe she need to see doctor? Has got bigger too. Maybe you right? So, Papa take her to see specialist and is bad news. Very bad news. Is cancer. Mama, she has to haff operation very quick. Doctor say that if she left it longer, pah!"

"You save my life!" Mrs Yuri cried. "If you not say about mole, nobody else brave enough. I die!"

"If you not mention it, maybe Mama not get treatment and get better," Vanya agreed. "Angel, you save her life. Papa he haff looked everywhere for you. He not know how to thank you."

Angel was stunned. Not about the mole – she'd seen enough of those to know when one was suspicious – but at how the circumstances of the past few months had all come together to this point. This was beyond weird. It was like something from one of Gemma's cosmic-ordering books.

"You save our little Dmitri too, when he hurt foot," continued Mrs Yuri, tears sending her mascara down her cheeks in sooty rivers. "Our family, we owe you so much."

"Honestly, you really don't," said Angel. She was a bit embarrassed at this outpouring of gratitude, to be honest. "Anyone would have done the same."

"No," said Mrs Yuri firmly. Her fat hands clutched Angel's. "They would not. They too scared. They coward! But you? You really are angel!"

There was no way a manicure was taking place now, Vanya told Angel firmly. They were going to celebrate! Did Angel have any idea just how hard her papa had been searching? Angel didn't, but she was very glad Mr Yuri hadn't found her; she would have died of terror if she'd run into him. Before long she was sitting in the opulent drawing room with an excited Dmitri on her lap and a glass of very expensive vintage Krug in her hand, while Mr Yuri – still managing to look terrifying even clad in a Hawaiian shirt and board shorts – clasped her hand and thanked her over and over again.

Gradually, in between bouts of exuberant broken English and even more glasses of Krug, Angel managed to piece the story together. After the episode at Blush Mrs Yuri had returned home, where she'd fumed for a while and told her husband everything. Then on her iPad (a present from Vanya, iPads were marvellous, ya? She had five, all in different colours and one with diamonds, so pretty), she'd Googled melanoma and had instantly spotted an image of something very similar to her mole and labelled cancerous. Frightened, the Yuris had gone straight to Harley Street where an oncologist had diagnosed malignant melanoma. Mrs Yuri had been operated on the very next day and then undergone an emergency course of radiotherapy. So far things were looking good, the specialist had told her, but if she'd left the mole much longer it could have been a very different outcome.

"If you hadn't spotted it," Mr Yuri concluded. "My wife would haff died."

Everyone fell silent. Angel couldn't argue. She'd seen her own mother die of skin cancer and maybe if somebody had spotted her mole in time…

She swallowed back the knot of grief. Even all these years on it was always lurking and threatening to choke her. "I'm glad I could help," she said.

Mr Yuri beamed at her. It took every bit of self-control that Angel had not to recoil: it was a bit like being smiled at by Jaws.

"So, now I find you, Angel Evans, I want to say thank you. What would you like? Just name it and it is yours."

Once upon a time Angel would have leapt at this. A designer bag? A week on the superyacht? Trolley dash in Prada? Her only problem would have been whittling down the list. Now, though, things were different. Bags and baubles were still nice but Angel had different priorities. She'd tried protesting but Mr Yuri was adamant.

"To refuse thanks is an insult to us," Vanya explained gently. "Papa is a very proud man."

Mr Yuri crossed his arms across his barrel chest and nodded. He looked just like a Bond villain. If it came to a choice between tanks of sharks with lasers on their heads and choosing a reward, then Angel knew what side she was coming down on.

"Anything?" she asked.

"Anything," said Mr Yuri firmly.

Everyone stared at her expectantly. They were probably waiting for a request for a supercar or maybe some diamonds, thought Angel. Well, nothing so clichéd for her.

"In that case," she said thoughtfully, "maybe there is something you could help me with…"

Chapter 42

"You look awful," Gemma said to Andi. "Are you coming down with something? Is your hand hurting?"

It was mid-afternoon and the girls were sitting outside the caravan, drinking tea and enjoying the warmth of the late summer sun. Although Andi's skin was now a subtle golden shade, Gemma thought she looked drawn and pale beneath her slight tan. She held out a Tupperware box. "Would the last of Cal's banana bread help?"

Andi attempted a smile, but it didn't reach her eyes. "I'm fine for banana bread, thanks."

Gemma glanced down at the container and then at her rippling midriff. "Yeah, me too actually. I can't face a thing. Maybe it's nerves about tonight?"

She put the tub down, picked up her copy of *Twelfth Night* and flicked to the final scene. Not that she really needed to go over it again; she was word perfect. Last night's rehearsal had gone brilliantly, the director had been thrilled with her and for those few wonderful hours on the stage Gemma had forgotten all about Cal's silence and Emily's horrible words. Now, though, the other girl's invective buzzed around in her head like acid-tongued hornets. No wonder she couldn't face eating.

"You'll be great," said Andi warmly. "I'm really looking forward to seeing the play tonight."

At the word *tonight* nervous fingers traced a shiver up Gemma's spine. Bloody hell! In less than six hours she'd be on the stage, for the first time in two years, and performing in front of a live audience. God, she hoped she still had what it took. Gemma supposed that at least this pressure took her mind off Cal and his lack of communication. There was still no word from him, and if it hadn't been for the banana bread and lack of baking ingredients Gemma would have thought she'd imagined his visit to the caravan.

And what about the electricity that had crackled between them like Space Dust? Had she imagined that too?

"I hope I pull it off," she said to Andi.

Andi tucked her curls behind her ears. "Of course you will."

Gemma hoped she was right. "Are Simon and Mel going to come and watch? And Jonty? Is he coming with you?"

Andi suddenly seemed fascinated by the daisies growing by the caravan steps. Her slim fingers plucked at them agitatedly. Ouch, thought Gemma. If those were voodoo daisies then the hot handyman was in trouble!

"I doubt it," Andi replied, her gaze still fixed on the flowers. "He's probably busy with his girlfriend."

Gemma was surprised. Since when had the quiet Jonty, he with depths as dark and rich as Thorntons' truffles, had a girlfriend?

"His ex is back on the scene," Andi explained when Gemma looked confused. "She had the big party last night down in the town. Where I was working?"

Gemma shook her head. "Sorry, Andi. I don't know what's the matter with me at the moment. Of course I knew: I let you in and paid the taxi driver. I just didn't realise she was back with Jonty."

"I'll pay you back as soon as I collect my bag," Andi said quickly, choosing to ignore the first part of what Gemma had said. She hated owing people money. She would go down into town later on, maybe on the way to the play, and fetch her bag back. It was just that she couldn't face seeing Jax right now. Even worse, what if she bumped into Jonty?

The image of Jax entwined with Jonty was branded in her mind's eye and the very thought of them being together made Andi feel as though her stomach was clenched up in knots. Honestly, it was ridiculous. There was nothing between her and Jonty anyway; there never had been and never would be. He was free to get back with his ex if he wanted to, just as she was free to go out partying with Travis Chumley.

If she wanted to.

The problem was that, as much fun as Travis was, Andi knew in her heart that didn't want to spend time with him. She wanted to hang out with Jonty, out at sea in *Ursula* watching the sea birds and munching hot pasties, or sitting in the garden at Ocean View and chatting easily until the sun slipped into the sea and the shadows lengthened across the lawn. She wanted to hear his stories of travelling and watch as he tried to teach his nephews to surf. All she wanted to do was spend time with him. They didn't even need to talk; it was enough just to be near to him.

Andi buried her face in her hands. How had this happened? She hadn't come to Rock intending to become close to anyone, but somehow Jonty had slid beneath the radar and his warm friendship had become a part of her life. Andi didn't think she'd ever been able to talk to somebody so easily or met another person with whom being was as simple as breathing. Jonty *got* her and she thought she had *got* him. So what had changed?

"No rush for the money," said Gemma. For a moment she looked as though she was going to say something else, but then she seemed to think better of it. Standing up, she brushed crumbs from her lap and threw her pasty crust to the beady-eyed seagulls staking out the caravan from the tin roof. "I'm off to work for a couple of hours and then I'll be up at the town hall getting ready. I guess I'll see you later?"

"Try keeping me away," said Andi.

Gemma picked up her rucksack and swung it onto her shoulders. "If anyone comes looking for me," she added nonchalantly, "could you just tell them where I am?"

She looked so hopeful that Andi's heart ached for her. Honestly, she could throttle Callum South. He might be an A-list celebrity but what was he thinking, blowing hot and cold with Gemma like this? If Cal couldn't see what a treasure Gemma was then he was an idiot.

"Of course," she assured her friend. Andi decided that she'd also give Callum a piece of her mind if he showed up, but maybe she wouldn't share this sentiment with Gemma.

Looking satisfied with this answer Gemma set off for Rock Cakes, her nose deep in Shakespeare, which left Andi alone in the meadow. It was so peaceful that she closed her eyes and listened to the lazy drone of fat bumblebees and the endless calling of the gulls. Before long the events of the night before and stresses of the past few days began to recede and she drifted away into sleep. It was only when a shadow fell across her face, blocking out the warmth of the sunshine, that she opened her eyes, crying out in surprise when she saw the figure looming over her.

"Hello, Andi," drawled Tom. "Hard at work I see."

Andi shot up; sleep scattered in a heartbeat. For a moment she hoped that she was in the middle of a horrible dream, but no matter how hard she rubbed her eyes, grinding her knuckles into the sockets until stars flared across her sight, Tom was still there and grinning down at her like a Halloween pumpkin. There was no waking up from this nightmare.

"What the hell are you doing here?" she demanded.

"What a charming way to greet me," said Tom, in the cut-glass tone Andi knew he practised in front of the mirror. Hugh Grant had nothing to be afraid of. "And I've come so far to see you as well. A kiss hello would have been nice."

Andi scrambled to her feet. Tom was only a couple of inches taller than her; she was well aware that his lack of height bugged him, and she was not going to let him look down on her. Whatever he'd come to say, he could say to her face.

"What do you want?" she demanded, hands on her hips. "Why are you here?"

Tom didn't reply. Instead he just smiled a self-satisfied smile and Andi's heart plummeted. Tom wouldn't have made the long journey down to Cornwall just on a whim or to say hello. That would have been hoping for far too much. He'd have some ulterior motive in mind, and she had a nasty suspicion she knew exactly what it was.

She exhaled slowly. "How did you find me?"

"Sweetheart, it hardly took the detective skills of Sherlock Holmes." Tom slid his Oakleys onto the top of his head and fixed her with a stare. His eyes were such a cold blue that goosebumps rose on Andi's arms. He looked scruffy, she thought. The collar of his white shirt was grimy and his shades were scratched.

"Who told you where I was?" she demanded. If this was the result of Angel's social media obsession then Andi would kill her sister.

"Ands, you were all over the press the day Callum South nearly drowned. And obviously I recognised Gemma. I'd know that fat bum anywhere."

Another black mark in Travis's book, thought Andi darkly. If it hadn't been for his showing off, Tom wouldn't know where she was.

"So there I was, reading the paper and without a job on, so I thought it might be fun to come and find you and have a little summer hol," Tom continued. A lock of lank blond hair flopped over his eyes and he brushed it away impatiently. "Come on, babe, we were together for ages. Aren't you just a little bit pleased to see me?"

"The last time I saw you, you were shagging the neighbour, so no, quite frankly, I am not pleased to see you."

"How harsh." Tom shrugged. "Well, play your cards right and I won't stick around here for very long. I'd hate to interrupt the nice little number you've got going on."

Unease crawled down Andi's spine. What did he mean by *play your cards right?*

"Bit of a grotty caravan though," Tom remarked, glancing around with a critical expression. "I'd have thought you'd be living somewhere a lot flashier, seeing as you're working for Simon Rothwell. He's worth a fucking fortune. Bet he pays you really well? And what about the boyfriend? I hear he's worth a fortune too. It would be a shame to upset him."

Andi gritted her teeth so hard that she thought they might shatter. "I don't have a boyfriend."

"Really? That's not what I hear in the town," grinned Tom. "Come on, Andi, I know you. There's always some cash squirrelled away. Would it hurt to lend me some, for old time's sake?"

Andi was close to screaming. "In case you don't remember, *somebody* ran up loads of debts in my name. I've got shedloads of debts to pay off! Every penny I earn goes on doing that. I don't have anything spare!"

"Jesus, you always did harp on about money." Tom grimaced. "Well, let's not change the habit of a lifetime, baby; let's talk cash." He exhaled slowly. "Let's keep it simple. Why don't you just give me a couple of thousand and we'll call it quits?"

Andi stared at her ex, totally lost for words. His once handsome face was etched with petulance and his mouth was set in a sulky sneer. He looked grubby and down at heel. Life, it appeared, was not going Tom's way.

"You honestly think I'll give you some money?" she said slowly. "After what you've done?"

"I was hoping you'd be reasonable," Tom said. "But if you prefer, we could always make it a business transaction." He reached into the fake LV manbag slung over his shoulder and pulled out some photos. "You can buy these from me, if you like? Or maybe we could call it insurance? It would be tragic if any of these pictures found their way onto the Internet, wouldn't it? Hardly the kind of image that Mermaid Media would want associated with their brand. Or any reputable accountant, come to think of it."

This was it. All of Andi's worst fears came swooping down like vultures, clawing at her throat and yanking at her heart. The murky threats he'd made before were now as clear as the Cornish rock pools on the beach. Feeling sick, Andi took the pictures from him and stared down at them with a growing sensation that gravity was reversing.

"Don't go thinking about tearing them up, either," warned Tom. "I've got the JPEGs anyway, so it would be pointless."

Andi closed her eyes in defeat. She didn't even need to look to see what these pictures were. She knew that the glossy paper would show a sun-dappled day, a bit like the one she had been enjoying until Tom arrived, and a wide deserted beach in Norfolk. A wicker picnic basket spilled pork pies and fruitcake onto a tartan car blanket and several empty bottles of wine were testament to a hot and boozy lunch. Opening her eyes and looking at the images, Andi felt again the prickle of the rough blanket beneath her back, the gritty sand between her toes and the silken whisper of the breeze dancing across her skin. Her bare skin. A little drunk and a lot loved up, it hadn't seemed like such a big deal to let Tom take a few pictures. After all, they were only for him and he was Andi's boyfriend. He loved her, and if she loved him she'd trust him. She did love him, didn't she?

Andi wished she could leap into the picture and give the drowsy, naked girl draped across the blanket a good hard shake. How had she ever been so stupid?

"I think you look great," said Tom conversationally, peering at the picture over her shoulder. "If they went viral at least you could be proud of your tits. You ought to check your emails a little more often. I've cropped out your head – for now – but wouldn't it be awful if that email went to everyone you know? And even a few you don't? You'd be an Internet sensation, sweetheart. Trust me."

"Are you blackmailing me?" Andi whispered. Like duh, as Angel would say. Of course he was.

Tom put his hand on his chest and pulled a hurt expression. "I'm offended. What an ugly word to use! I just thought that if I had a couple of grand I'd be more likely to *forget* I had them. Just like I've *forgotten* to mention that you were sacked from Hart Frozer. It's funny; Mel Rothwell never mentioned that. Have you *forgotten* too?"

There was a whooshing sound in Andi's ears. "You've been to see Mel?"

"How else was I to find out where you live? Honestly, Andi, you can be stupid. They seem such a nice couple too. They were thrilled to hear that you had a visitor. Your boyfriend wasn't so happy."

Andi's head was spinning. "Boyfriend?"

"Rich guy? Nice car? Orange tan?" Tom shook his head. "He seemed so keen on you. Loaded too, I bet. Nice work."

Travis. Who else had Tom been to see? Suddenly, Andi felt the life she'd started to build in Rock sway as precariously as a sapling in a gale. All it needed to fall completely was one little push – and Tom, she knew, wouldn't hesitate to give it a shove. In an instant her job, her friends and her recovering bank balance would be destroyed.

"I tell you what," said Tom, all false cheer and smiles, "why don't I give you some time to think it all over? I'll give you until tomorrow morning before my finger slips on the keyboard and those pictures find themselves in all kinds of odd places." His eyes widened. "Not really the image for a smart accountant, but then what would you expect from an accountant who was sacked for stealing her colleague's work? I'd say two grand was a bargain for keeping all that quiet on its own, never mind the pictures. Don't take too long to make up your mind though. The price may start to rise."

It might as well have been two million pounds. Andi knew that even if she paid Tom now, he'd only be back for more. She'd never be rid of him. A tear slid down her cheek and she turned her head away, determined not to give him the satisfaction of seeing her cry.

"Presumably you still have my number," Tom said. "Give me a call by this time tomorrow. I'm staying in Padstow, so you can meet me there; I'm not trekking back here again. You can buy dinner in Rojano's, if you want. I recall you're partial to a nice glass of wine."

And with this parting shot and a complacent grin, Tom sauntered across the meadow to the stile. He scrambled over it and moments later the sound of a car starting up echoed across the valley. Blinded by tears Andi sank onto the grass, defeated and despairing. Whether she was weeping because of Tom or over Jonty Andi wasn't sure, but one thing she did know: she had no choice now but to hand in her notice with Si, pack her things and leave quietly. Quite where she'd go was anyone's guess, but there was nothing here for her. Not now.

Whether she paid him or not it didn't make any difference: Tom had won. Rock was over.

Chapter 43

"The captain that did bring me first on shore
Hath my maid's garments: he upon some action
Is now in durance, at Malvolio's suit,
A gentleman, and follower of my lady's."

Gemma could hardly believe it; she had just delivered her final lines of the play and, in spite of feeling more nervous than she could have ever imagined possible, she hadn't fluffed a word or missed a cue for the past two hours. Quite the opposite in fact! From the moment she had stepped onto the stage her nerves had melted away and she'd ceased to be Gemma, worried about her weight and even more worried about Callum South, and become Viola, lost and lovesick in a foreign country.

Hmm, maybe it wasn't such a leap of imagination after all?

On the stage the lights were glaringly bright and the audience just a black and faceless mass. Gemma found it easy to forget that they were there and when there was a ripple of laughter or a chorus of groans it jolted her for a moment. Now though, as Feste sang his final song and the cast prepared to take their bows, room erupted into a roar of applause. Whistles and cheers and the stamping of deck-shoed feet on the floor threatened to raise the entire roof.

As the leading lady, Gemma stepped forward to take her bow first, together with her co-star. While she drank in the cheers and smiling faces, her heart felt the lightest it had done for a very long time. So what if this wasn't a long-running soap opera or a reality TV show? The audience had enjoyed every second, and so had she. *This was why I went to stage school,* Gemma realised with a jolt, *to act in the theatre! Not to model stupid pants or lose weight!* The thought was enough to make her feel euphoric with relief. No more trying to force herself to be something she wasn't. From now on she'd act because she loved it, not because she had to.

Once the rest of the actors had taken their bows, the entire cast joined hands and walked forward for a group curtain call. As the house lights came up Gemma was able to scan the audience properly. Much as she hated herself for it, there was only one face she was looking for: a round freckled face with sleepy laughing eyes and a crooked grin. She searched the crowd hopefully, only to feel bitterly disappointed. Of course Callum wasn't there. Why should he be at an am-dram production starring the stupid fat girl who had trashed his career quicker than you could say "cheeseburger"? Swallowing down the misery, Gemma stitched her brightest starry smile onto her face and took another bow. Now she really was acting her socks off, and nobody would ever know.

Who needed Callum South anyway? She had plenty of friends who'd shown up to support her. Look, there were Si and Mel, right in the front and clapping; over there Dee was standing and whistling; and on the left of the hall, and to her enormous surprise, even Travis Chumley had turned up. When he saw Gemma's look of astonishment Trav grinned and gave her a thumbs up. Of Andi and Angel, though, there was no sign, and Gemma felt another stab of disappointment. Angel was as flaky as a hot sausage roll, so her missing the performance was hardly a surprise, but Andi's being there she would have put money on. When Andi said she would do something she always did it. The girl was as reliable as Greenwich Meantime; it was a wonder people didn't set clocks by her.

Gemma hoped Andi was all right. She hadn't looked so great earlier on.

"We rocked!" cried Derek, joining the cast on the stage and bowing with gusto. "Especially you," he added sotto voce to Gemma. "I didn't want to say anything, darling, in case it jinxed tonight, but one of my friends who directs for the RSC popped in – he's got a divine place over near Daymer Bay – and he's blown away by you! How about a late din-dins to meet him?"

Lord! Wasn't this exactly what she'd been hoping and praying for? Gemma was just wondering why she didn't feel more excited and considering her reply when the doors of the hall flew open with a crash and Angel hurtled in, closely followed by Laurence, a posse of security guards and a squat man in a Hawaiian shirt who looked the spitting image of a Bond villain.

"Oh no!" Her blue eyes wide, Angel's hands flew to her mouth. "Have we missed the play?"

Gemma started to laugh. This was so typical of Angel. If Andi was GMT then her sister was her own time zone entirely. Then her laughter stopped abruptly and her heart began to race when she saw who was behind her best friend.

Cal.

It seemed like somebody had slowed down space and time, *Doctor Who* style. To Gemma the noise of the clapping audience faded away and all she could hear was a rushing in her ears as though somebody had diverted the Camel to run upstream, through the town and into the hall. Her legs, rather unflatteringly clad in Viola's tights, started to move forwards of their own volition. To be honest though, they could have danced a jig or performed the cancan for all the attention Gemma was paying them. All she knew was that Cal's eyes were holding hers like superglue and that she never wanted him to look away again.

She dropped Derek's hand – the play, the curtain call and the RSC director all forgotten. All that mattered was that Cal was running towards her now, sprinting down the aisle with the same powerful gait that had seen him score goals at Wembley and made Beckham look slow. The extra pounds didn't seem to matter a jot anymore and he leapt onto the stage with such athleticism that if the England coach had been present Cal's football career would have been totally rejuvenated. With her heart racing as though she'd just climbed the hill out of town, Gemma paused just inches away from him. There he was, he really was! There was no mistaking the halo of crazy ringlets, strong stocky body and those melting Malteser eyes. Cal. Lovely, funny, sexy, daft Cal. The only man who understood her. The only man who ever would.

Oh bollocks, thought Gemma as the truth suddenly smacked her on the nose.

Cal. The only man she would ever love.

She was in love with Cal. Not Callum South the TV star, football hero and ITV2 golden boy, but the chubby, bread-baking, exercise-skiving Cal. The Cal who got excited over banana bread, who'd sneaked them into Jamie Oliver's and Maccy D's; the man who loved his mammy and worried about paying the bills. That Cal.

How on earth had this happened?

"Gemma, I'm a fecking eejit," said Cal, reaching out and taking her hands in his. They were trembling, she noticed. Cal was trembling? "I know I've ruined your career with my antics, and your diet too, and I really should do what everyone says and stay away from you but I can't. I really can't. It's killing me, so it is."

Gemma shook her head.

"I've ruined *your* career you mean," she corrected. "Emily told me how ITV2 have pulled the contract. She said you were broken-hearted."

"Sure, and will that be the same Emily who told me how gutted you are that your agent dropped you and how you blamed *me*?" asked Cal. He gave her his lopsided smile and Gemma melted like buttercream in the sunshine.

"I would imagine it is," she whispered. Emily had played her beautifully.

"And like an eejit I believed her," Cal sighed. He reached forward and pushed a curl from Gemma's forehead, tucking it tenderly behind her ear. As his fingertips brushed her skin, Gemma thought she would pass out with longing. All this from just touching her ear. Imagine what it would do to her when he…

Get a grip Gemma! Focus!

"It nearly killed me, so it did," Cal confessed. "Gemma, I don't care about ITV2, or diets or any of that crap. I've lost my contracts, I'm out of a job and the Loose Women probably want my balls on a plate. I don't have anything to offer you, but there's one thing I do know for certain, and that's how much I care about you. Aw, feck it, Gemma! I *have* to be with you. I *need* to be with you. Can't you guess why?"

If her pulse got any quicker, thought Gemma, they'd need to call an ambulance. Unable to speak, she could only shake her head. Was he going to say what she thought he was going to say?

"Why?" she whispered.

"Because I can't live without your sponge cake," Cal said, and his laughing eyes crinkled down at her. "And," he whispered, so softly that she had to strain her ears to catch his words, "cake aside, I can't live without you for a second longer."

Before she could tell him off for making her believe he was about to declare undying love, his lips, softer than any sponge that Gemma could ever bake, met hers. As Cal kissed her, Gemma felt everything else fall away. And when he slipped his arms around her waist and pulled her close she kissed him back, while the delighted audience rocked the town hall with cheers of delight. Breaking apart, Gemma and Cal smiled at one another, suddenly shy.

"Jaysus! I'd never have thought it," he said wonderingly. "But there is something you do even better than baking!"

He lowered his head and kissed Gemma again, at which point Derek motioned hastily for the curtains to be closed. While the cast traipsed into the wings and the stagehands dismantled Illyria, Cal and Gemma kissed and smiled and kissed some more until their cheeks and mouths ached. He had a lot of explaining to do, Gemma thought as she threaded her fingers through his, but that could keep for another time. Right now she could think of better things to do than talking...

"Oi! Stop snogging, you two!" Angel burst through the curtains, towing an awkward Laurence in her wake. "This is Shakespeare, not the stage play of *Fifty Shades*!"

"Do you mind?" said Gemma. "We're trying to make up for lost time here!"

Cal's arms tightened around her and he pressed a kiss against her temple.

"If Angel hadn't read me the riot act then we'd still be wasting time," he said.

Gemma was confused. "What's Angel got to do with you coming here?"

Angel grinned. "Go on, Cal. Tell her what happened."

"Aw, it's a long story," he began, "but let's just say there I was minding my own miserable business and eating Wotsits in peace. My TV career was in meltdown, Emily had convinced me that I'd ruined Gemma's career and life, and the press were at the gate trying to get a shot of me comfort eating. Mike doubled security and I'd told him nobody was to come anywhere near. It was death by Wotsits for me."

"So how did you get in?" Gemma asked Angel. Then a thought occurred to her. "Was it like when you tried to gatecrash Peter Andre's barbie?"

"What's this?" asked Laurence.

"Nothing, nothing!" said Angel airily. "Just a bit of a misunderstanding!"

"But how did you get past everyone? Cal has serious security." Gemma had seen enough of the cameras and guards and barky dogs to know this much. How on earth had her friend managed it?

"Ah, this is down to me, I think!" The squat man in the Hawaiian shirt stepped forward. Beaming at Gemma, he held out a meaty paw and added proudly, "I am Vladimir Yuri. I own VY Security – vorld's biggest security agency – so I able to tell all the guards to step aside or, tch – they in beeg trouble with me!"

Mr Yuri? Husband of Angel's nemesis? Gemma was suddenly hugely disappointed. Of course. This was all a crazy dream, wasn't it? Cal wasn't really in love with her and she hadn't really just given the performance of a lifetime; she was actually in bed. This crazy dream was nothing more than the outcome of eating too many slices of Cal's cheese bread before bedtime. Pretty soon she'd wake up in her narrow little bunk with Cal still behind razor wire and with her stomach full of knots about the play.

Bollocks.

She closed her eyes, counted to three and then opened them again. Mr Yuri was still there, his smile looking a bit pained now, and with his hand still outstretched. Oh Lord! This really was happening. Still dazed, Gemma stretched out her hand too and had it practically crushed as he pumped her arm up and down. How he moved his arm with a Rolex that big was anyone's guess. It looked like he'd strapped Big Ben to his wrist.

"It was like something out of a movie," Cal told her. "There I was, festering in my trackie bottoms and working my way through a family pack of Wotsits, when your sister and Mr Yuri marched in, with all my security guys trailing behind like puppies. We thought it was an armed robbery. Mike was fecking terrified."

"People are," said Mr Yuri, looking thrilled to hear it.

"Not of you, sir! Of Angel!" Cal shook his head. "She gave me a right dressing-down, so she did. Told me to get off my fat arse if I knew what was good for me and to come and find you."

"You left a family-sized bag of Wotsits for me? I'm flattered," Gemma teased.

"Sure, they'll still be there when I go back," he deadpanned. "Maybe I'll even share them?"

"You must really like me," said Gemma.

Cal squeezed Gemma's hand and smiled down at her with such love that she thought her heart would burst.

"I can't thank you enough," she said to Mr Yuri.

"I owe Angel great debt," explained the Russian. "But you! You are *the* Callum South! I only help my son in law buy Dukes Rangers because I massive fan of yours. When Chelsea for sale I say, 'Pah! Roman, you have eet! I only want to buy team Callum South play for.' You are legend."

In his baggy trackies and grubby tee shirt, and with his curly hair sticking up like a crazy halo, Cal looked more like a tramp than a legend, but Mr Yuri didn't care. He was far too busy recounting a match where Cal had apparently shown Rio Ferdinand a thing or too.

"Yes, yes," said Angel impatiently. She'd never got football, unless you counted the WAGs and their fashion; then she found it fascinating. "That's brilliant and everything, but Cal, there's something Laurence and I really want to talk to you about. We think you'll love it and it could be the solution to—"

"Angel! There you are!"

Simon Rothwell burst through the faded velvet curtains, stumbling across the boards in haste to reach Angel. His usually sunny face was clouded with worry and he was waving his mobile phone about like a Hogwarts first-year pupil in a wand lesson. Thrusting it under Angel's nose so that she could see the screen, Simon said frantically, "This can't be right, can it? Is she joking?"

Colour drained from Angel's face as she gazed at the screen. Surely not? It didn't make any sense. Why on earth would Andi do such an out-of-character thing? Angel was filled with a deep and certain sense of dread. Something very bad must have happened.

Si exhaled slowly.

"You didn't know either, did you?" He looked around at the others. "I guess you may as well find out from me. It's Andi. She's only gone and left Rock!"

Chapter 44

The strap of the holdall dug into Andi's shoulder but she was beyond caring whether or not it hurt. There was something about the physical discomfort of the webbing strap biting into her flesh that was preferable to the savage despair of realising that everything she had worked for and come to treasure was about to come crashing down around her. At least while the strap pinched and the heavy bag thudded against her hip she could pretend that the tears blurring her vision were from pain.

She paused to swing the bag onto her opposite shoulder and to unwind the carrier-bag handles that were twisting around her fingers and making them glow an unearthly green. It was incredible just how much stuff you could accumulate in only seven weeks, and even harder to believe just how awkward it was to carry it all around without the help of a car. Even leaving heavier objects behind like welly boots and accountancy books didn't seem to have made that much difference; she was still bent double under the weight of her worldly goods like some kind of mutant hermit crab.

It was getting late. The evenings were starting to draw in and the scent of woodsmoke in the air spoke of autumn and melancholy. Lights shone from the town, snatches of music drifted on the breeze and, somewhere amongst the higgledy-piggledy rooftops, Gemma was acting her heart out. How Andi wished she'd been able to keep her promise to watch the play. She hated to let Gemma down. But she wished even more that she'd never met Tom, never been stupid enough to trust him...

There was no point staying: Andi had known from the moment she'd seen her ex looming over her that her life in Cornwall was over. Tom would never let her know a moment's peace now that he'd found her. Yes, she could have given in and paid up, but she knew Tom inside out and once he'd had a taste of money he'd be back for more. How could she possibly work for Simon when she would be terrified that every new day might turn out to be the one when Tom decided to reveal that she'd been sacked from her last job? The thought of just how let down Si would be didn't bear thinking about. There was, of course, the option of standing up to Tom and telling Si everything herself, but how disappointed would he feel? Or she could tell her ex exactly where to stick his threats, but then he'd be sure to circulate those pictures out of sheer spite and ruin things anyway. The humiliation would be too much to endure. And how would she ever be able to explain herself to everyone?

No, there was no option. She had to leave Rock and soon, before Tom could cause any more trouble. The moment he'd vanished over the stile, she'd raced into the caravan, stuffing her belongings into her holdall and a collection of Tesco carrier bags, trying to suppress the growing feeling of panic. A quick note to Angel and Gemma was left propped against the kettle with a promise to call them as soon as she could. Then Andi had walked into Rock in an attempt to pick up a mobile signal.

Where she was going, Andi didn't have a clue; she only knew that she had to leave. There was a bus to Bodmin soon and once she was in the small town she would be able to catch a train to London. When she was back in the city she could rent a cheap room somewhere and regroup; her meagre savings wouldn't last forever, but if she was really careful she might have a couple of weeks' grace while she looked for a job. Any job. It wouldn't be like working for Simon – Andi had loved every minute she'd worked for him – and it certainly wouldn't involve feeling like part of a family.

She swallowed. How come she hadn't realised before just how much she missed that sense of belonging, the teasing, the laughter and the easy companionship? Was it because it had been missing from her own life for so long, even before her mother had died? Alex had never been one for close father–daughter chats, and boarding school had been a chilly, sterile experience. The nuns had liked to talk about love but in practice they hadn't been big fans of it. The Rothwells, though, were always hugging and laughing and having fun. Andi had worked hard but there had always been somebody to chat to: Mel with a cup of coffee and a biscuit, Angel with some hare-brained plan, the boys wanting to kick a ball about, Jonty…

Andi's vision blurred dangerously and she bit her lip hard to gain control.

Was it just the strap of the holdall pulled tightly across her chest that was causing this sharp pain, or was it the thought of never seeing Jonty again? The memories of the time that she'd spent with him were stored safely away in her head, and even before she'd even left Cornwall Andi knew that she'd pore over them in the weeks and months ahead like a miser with his money. The day out on the boat, drinking tea up at the boatyard, sharing chips down by the pontoon; all simple enough, but already tinted golden in her mind's eye with the sunshine of this perfect summer and the glow of pure happiness.

The stop for the special summer bus was on the edge of the town, just opposite the same general store where she'd tried to buy the *FT* all those weeks ago. Letting her bags slide through her fingers and bump to the ground, Andi wondered why she still felt so weighed down. Wearily, she closed her eyes in defeat. If the timetable was running to plan then she was only minutes away from leaving Rock, and her heart, behind. She wondered if she could ever summon up the energy to start again.

Or even if she wanted to.

She checked her watch. Almost five past nine – and that sweep of lights headed straight towards her had to be the bus. How typical that just when she longed for a few more minutes it had decided to be on time for once. As the bus hissed to a stop, Andi took one last look around her. If this were one of Gemma's pink books, Jonty would come screeching up now in his Defender to beg her to stay.

Andi sighed and hauled her bags onto the bus. It was just as well she was leaving if she was starting to think along these lines. Of course the road was empty: Jonty was with Jax and probably eating dinner in Rick Stein's right now. This was just another sign, as if the big Tom-sized one wasn't enough, that it was time for her to move on.

Ticket purchased, Andi wedged herself into a seat and pressed her forehead against the cool window. Then the bus lumbered forward, away from the town, away from the friends she'd made there and away from the man who, against all the odds, had somehow managed to steal her heart. With the lights of the town growing ever fainter, Andi closed her eyes – and when the tears trickled from beneath her lids she didn't try to stop them. Even if she'd wanted to, she didn't think she could.

Bodmin Parkway, an old-fashioned wooden relic of the golden age of railways, was marooned in a sea of dense trees and a mile or so down a very dark lane. Apart from the tail lights of the departing bus and the orange glow of the platform, the place was filled with an inky blackness that city dwellers seldom see. The car park was empty save the odd car that had been left behind like a leftover tooth in a gummy mouth. An owl's call scraped the stillness and as Andi lugged her bags towards the ticket office her footsteps sounded unnaturally loud on the gravelly path. It was as though she'd alighted from the bus straight into an American slasher movie, and she shivered.

Maybe this hadn't been such a bright idea?

And maybe she shouldn't have just assumed that there were sure to be trains to London passing through at this time of night? She bit her lip and tried to ignore the little knot of dread tightening in her tummy. There'd be a train at some point. All she needed to do was wait – easier said than done when the waiting room was locked and the ticket office closed for the night. It seemed that she had no choice but to stand alone on the gloomy platform. Hoisting her bag up onto her shoulder, she was about to head towards the small bridge that crossed the tracks to the Paddington-bound line when a sweep of bright headlights cut through the dark with dazzling intensity. A white Range Rover Evoque with registration plates declaring the legend MEL 1 swished to a halt alongside her and, as Andi stood blinking the stars from her vision, the car window hissed down.

"Andi?"

The voice from the car almost bowled her over. Squinting into the gloom she made out a figure buried deep in the shadows with eyes as dark as the night that had now wrapped its grasp around the Duchy.

Jonty.

Her gaze met his and she stared, unable to believe it. Jonty leaned across and pushed the door open, casting a pathway of light straight to him.

"I don't know what this is all about," he said, "and I'm not going to pretend that I think it's a good idea to run away, but there's no way I'm leaving you on an isolated railway platform this late at night."

Andi bristled at his tone. She was just about through with the men in her life thinking they could call the shots.

"I'm fine." She raised her chin a little. God, it was terrifying just how happy she was to see him. The way her insides were seesawing could only be very bad news indeed. "I'm waiting for the London train."

Jonty laughed. "You'll have a very long wait. The sleeper won't be here until gone eleven and there's no way I'm letting you stay here until then."

Gone eleven? Andi glanced at her watch. That was almost an hour away. A whole hour of waiting on a deserted platform listening to the trembling hoots of owls and jumping every time there was a scuttling in the undergrowth really didn't appeal. She tightened her grasp on her bags.

"Look," he said, a note of impatience in his voice, "there's only a few weeks of the summer left. Why don't you just come back and enjoy them? The place will be empty soon – there'll be tumbleweed blowing past The Wharf Café – and I know for a fact that Si will give you a bonus. You can't quit now."

"It's not quitting!" She almost spilled the truth then and there; only her pride stopped her.

"So what is it? For Christ's sake, Andi! If you don't tell me, how can I help?"

The clenched jaw and the tension in his face spoke volumes. Andi wanted nothing more than to tell Jonty the truth, for him to help, but she knew it was impossible. Why would he believe her?

She stood her ground. "I'm not going back to Rock."

Jonty exhaled slowly. "That's fine. You don't have to. If you're really set on doing this then I'll drive you to Plymouth. You can catch a Paddington train from there. But I'm telling you now, Andi Evans, I'm not leaving you here alone. No bloody way."

The vehemence in his voice settled the matter. Andi may have only known Jonty for a few months but she recognised his *I won't be argued with* tone. She'd heard it when he'd made sure that they'd been safe on the boat, when his nephews had been playing up and when Travis had nearly swamped them. She could stand here and argue, Andi knew, but it would be pointless. When it came to being stubborn she'd met her match in him.

"You'll take me all the way to Plymouth?"

He nodded. "If it means you'll be safe, I'll drive you to London, but Plymouth's a good start. There's a connection there for the last train before the sleeper. You'll be fine from there."

Andi doubted very much she'd ever feel fine again, but the idea of being able to make some headway into the journey and put as much distance between herself and whatever bomb Tom chose to drop was appealing. As though in a dream she stepped forward and, as she crossed the few yards between them, Jonty's eyes never left her face. They were tired, she thought with a pang, and so sad. Her emotions were suddenly a whirlpool of despair and fear and, most frightening of all, hope. Why was he here? Why had Jonty come?

"So what's going on?" he asked as Andi placed her bags on the back seat. "I know women don't travel light but this looks very much like you're going away and not intending to come back. And you didn't even think to say goodbye?"

Andi couldn't bear it. He sounded so hurt.

"I couldn't." Andi sagged into the leather seat; she didn't think she'd ever felt so utterly defeated.

Jonty sighed. "Andi, I don't know what's been going on and I'm not going to pretend I understand, but we're friends, aren't we?"

She nodded.

"And I would have hoped that because we're friends you could have told me that you were unhappy in Rock. You didn't have to sneak away like this."

"I'm not unhappy in Rock!" Andi cried, stung. "I've loved every minute of living there!"

"So why are you leaving?" Jonty shot back. The night cast his face into shadows but, even so, Andi could see how upset he was. The skin was tight over his high cheekbones and his eyes glittered in the glow of the interior light.

"Because… because…" Her voice tailed off. How could she possibly tell him the truth? He'd probably turf her out of the car when he knew how she'd lied to Simon.

The car surged forward and moments later they were hurtling along the main road. Andi gripped the armrest tightly and, seeing this, Jonty eased off the gas.

"Sorry. I didn't mean to upset you," he said. "And of course you don't have to tell me. Sometimes people have secrets. God knows, I should be the last person on the planet to criticise anyone for that. If you want to get away then I'll respect that – I'm not saying I like it – but I'll not try to change your mind. I can see you've made a decision."

Andi thought this was ironic. She'd change her mind in a heartbeat if she could. With every mile that drew them closer to Plymouth, the city now a Tango-orange smudge on the horizon, she was feeling sadder. They travelled in silence for a while; the only noises were the sound of the tyres on the tarmac and the ticking indicator when Jonty changed lanes. By the time they crossed the Tamar Bridge, where the lights of the traffic ahead were strung out like jewels above the velvet blackness of the river, Andi was close to telling him everything. There was something about Jonty's still presence that inspired absolute trust. This was it: her last chance to level with him, to tell him about Hart Frozer and Tom and how she felt about him. With every second that passed she knew they were drawing closer to the station. Terraces replaced cottages, cats' eyes were chased away by bright street lamps and soon the traffic juddered to a standstill at the red lights. She took a deep breath, but just as she was about to summon the courage to speak, Jonty got there first.

"I don't want to pry," he said, "so forgive me if that's how it feels, but, Andi, I have to know – is this because of something I've done?"

She shook her head. "No! Of course not! Whatever makes you think that?"

He shrugged. "I behaved like a prick yesterday. I should never have let you go to the hospital on your own. Not when your hand was bleeding like that."

Her hand. Andi had almost forgotten about that and, glancing down, it was almost a surprise to see a dressing. If only the damage Tom was causing could be dealt with so easily.

"It's fine," she told him. "You were a guest at the party. I wouldn't have expected you to leave."

But Jonty wasn't prepared to be forgiven so easily. "Don't make excuses for me," he grated. "I know when I'm behaving like a cock. Whether or not you're with Travis Chumley, it shouldn't make the slightest difference; I should still have been a gentleman and gone with you."

"I'm not with Travis!" Andi laughed out loud at the very idea. "That's you jumping to conclusions!"

The red changed. Pea-green light spilled across the road but the Range Rover didn't move. Jonty stared at her.

"But you spent the night with him! I saw him drop you off the other morning."

He looked so put out that Andi took pity on him. "I'd had far too much to drink in Newquay," she explained. "Travis had to let me sleep it off at his dad's hotel; not that I need to justify myself! He was very proper. When you saw me, I was dreadfully hung-over and I only made it into work by the skin of my teeth."

Jonty was still staring. An impatient blast from the car behind snatched him back to the present and hastily he let up the clutch and had to focus on the road. It may have been dark in the car but it wasn't so dark that Andi couldn't make out his smile.

"What?" she asked.

He shot her a sidelong look. "The station's just here, but how about we keep going until Exeter? We're making good time and you can easily catch a train there. What do you think?"

Exeter. Forty-three miles away. Andi did a rapid calculation and worked out that this meant at least another hour with Jonty. One more hour before a lifetime of never seeing him again? It was a no-brainer.

"Exeter sounds good," she said.

"I'll pull in at the petrol station and get us some coffees," Jonty decided, as he pointed the car back in the direction of the A38. "And you look like you need some food. When did you last eat?"

Andi had no idea. Breakfast maybe? Before Tom had appeared, in any case. There had been no way she could stomach food once he'd issued his ultimatum.

"I'm fine," she insisted, but Jonty wouldn't hear any protests and before long she was sipping a latte and working her way through a very plastic cheese and ham sandwich. While she ate, and the tors of Dartmoor sped by dark and unseen, neither Andi nor Jonty spoke. Only when the last wrapper was screwed up and the cruise control set did the atmosphere shift from companionship to something more charged. A shiver stroked her skin.

"So," Jonty said slowly, "Travis isn't to blame. And you say that it wasn't the appalling way I behaved yesterday. So, is it Si? The work? He's horrified that you've resigned. He called me straightaway and asked if I knew anything about it."

"No! It's none of you! Don't ever think that!"

"So what happened?" Jonty's voice was full of concern. "Andi, I know how happy you are working with Si and I know he thinks the world of you too. He's thinking of offering you a job at Mermaid Media when the summer ends."

Andi closed her eyes in despair. When Si knew she'd lied about being sacked he wouldn't want her anywhere near his company.

Still keeping his eyes on the road, Jonty reached out and took her hand. "Andi, what's happened?"

It was hopeless. His briefest touch was enough to breach the dam of her self-control. To her utter despair Andi burst into tears and her body was racked by huge sobs. Suddenly all the burdens that she'd carried for so long – the financial strains, losing her job, Tom's threats, Jax – were too heavy to bear for a second longer. She was so tired of struggling. She didn't think she could carry on.

Jonty didn't say a word; he just let her cry. Releasing her hand just so he could turn off the main road and park up, he sat quietly and waited. He didn't probe or try to pry but just let her be. When the storm of emotion had passed, he unclipped their seatbelts and pulled her into his arms. She was limp with weeping, and it was a relief to be held.

"Whatever it is, we can sort it," he murmured into her hair. "I promise, Andi. There's nothing so bad that we can't make it better. Just tell me what it is. Let me help." His hand brushed the tears from her cheeks and smoothed the curls away from her face. "Oh, Andi, don't you realise? There's nothing I wouldn't do for you."

And when Jonty lowered his head and kissed her Andi felt everything fall away. She tasted the salt of her tears on his lips and felt the warmth of his arms holding her close. Finally they broke apart and smiled wonderingly at one another. Tilting her face upwards with his forefinger he said, "Do you know how long I've wanted to do that?"

Actually Andi didn't, but the way his eyes were lit from the inside told her everything she needed to know.

"Me too," she whispered. Being wrapped in Jonty's arms felt so right and so safe; she never wanted to move away from that circle, never wanted to be far from him again.

"Now she tells me! So whatever stopped you?" he teased. "Christ! There were so many times when I thought we might be getting closer. Remember that day in *Ursula*?"

Andi knew she'd never forget it. This was one of the memories she'd been treasuring up for the bleak days ahead. Then a thought occurred to her.

"What about Jax?"

Jonty looked genuinely confused. "What about her?"

Andi gulped. Much as she hated to ruin a perfect moment, she had to know the truth.

"You two are back together, aren't you?" When he shook his head, she added, "Jonty, it's OK: I saw you together in her house when I came back from Treliske. I was looking for my bag and I saw you through the window."

His eyes widened. "Now who's jumping to conclusions? You saw that? Jax threw herself at me. I was so shocked. I didn't see that one coming. I thought she'd well and truly moved on." He paused. Didn't you see me push her away?"

Andi rolled her eyes. "I didn't exactly stick around."

"And is that why you were leaving? Because you thought I was with Jax?" He looked down at her, visibly distressed – so dark and square-jawed and gorgeous that her heart twisted. Reaching across, she kissed him again and time seemed to dissolve. How much time had passed? Andi had no idea. When they broke apart she touched her lips wonderingly.

"Too much?" Jonty asked.

She shook her head. "Never." She wanted to pause and make sure this was real, freeze this perfect moment before she told him everything. Maybe when he knew the truth Jonty wouldn't want to hold her any longer. When he knew what ammunition Tom had he might well not want anything to do with her. Just the briefest thought of this almost floored her with loss, but she knew it was a chance she had to take. There could be no more secrets.

She looked up at him, overwhelmed with emotions.

"I really need to tell you everything," she said slowly. "There's so much about me that you don't know."

He laced his fingers with hers. "There are things about me I need to tell you too. Things I probably should have levelled with you a long time ago."

Andi doubted that any secrets Jonty had could compete with being sacked, accused of fraud and having your ex blackmail you with private and personal images, but she loved him even more for trying to make her feel better.

Hang on. She loved him?

"There's so much I need to tell you," she said.

He dropped a kiss onto the top of her head.

"There's no rush."

"But there is!" Andi cried. She sat bolt upright in her seat. With Tom at large, who knew how long she had to tell Jonty the truth before Simon called him and revealed everything? The idea filled her with dread. "Jonty, I—"

Jonty placed his finger on her lips.

"Tell me as we drive. If you still want to go to London we'll have to step on it to make the train," he told her gently. "We can talk in the car."

Panic clawed her throat. London now? After this?

"But if you don't," he continued, "I know the perfect place we can go."

"Back to Rock?" Andi felt exposed and raw at that idea. Would Tom be waiting for her already? Or maybe he'd heard that she'd left and was already emailing Simon? She felt sick.

"No, not Rock." Releasing her, he started the engine. "A place I know not far from here where it can just be you and me in peace."

She looked at him with questions in her eyes. "Where?"

"Somewhere just for us," he said. "Are you ready to talk?"

Andi nodded. The time for secrets and hiding from the truth was over. She was exhausted and the pain of maybe losing him all over again was lurking, but this time she knew that she wasn't going to run away.

"I'm ready," she said.

Chapter 45

The Kingfisher Inn was a small hotel set on the banks of the River Dart, which wound its slow way through the heavily wooded valley like a midnight ribbon. When Jonty threw open the French windows to the balcony, light spilled from them and trembled on the water while the muslin drapes whirled and danced in the breeze. The scent of the roses that wound their way around the balustrade and tumbled from the crumbly brick walls filled the room like a Jo Malone fragrance.

Andi looked around and her heart lifted. Jonty was right: this was a healing place. The inn was set well away from the road, so the only sounds were the slapping of the river against the shore or the odd call of waterfowl. She stepped onto the balcony, breathed the sweet night-time air and felt the tension begin to slide away. The sky arcing above the black smudges of woodland was inky and dusted with stars; Tom and Rock and all of her fears seemed very far off.

It was a good feeling.

"Is this OK?" Jonty joined her on the balcony. Although she couldn't see him, Andi sensed his shy smile in the darkness. His hand came to rest lightly on her shoulder, his thumb gently caressing her skin, and her whole body suddenly came alive.

"It's perfect," Andi said, because it really was.

If there was ever a place that spoke of peace and mental freedom, then this was it. The room was simple but filled with elegant and understated luxury in every detail, from the stripped and waxed floorboards to the huge bed swathed in snowdrifts of linen and plump with pillows, to the billowing curtains. Andi's brow creased; Jonty had just passed his card over to the concierge as easily as though checking into a Travelodge, but this boutique hotel was clearly in another league altogether. This was a guy who lived in his sister's pool house and eked out a living fixing boats and doing gardening for the minimum wage. She couldn't expect him to pay for all this.

"I don't expect you to have to—" she began, but couldn't speak any more because he pulled her into his arms and kissed the words away. The world dipped on its axis and time stood still. It was enough just to be there; nothing else was important.

Finally they broke apart and, slipping his hands around her waist, Jonty brushed his lips against her temple. She could feel the drumming of his heart racing in tandem with her own.

"Do you feel ready to tell me about it all?" Jonty asked. His breath fluted against her skin and she shivered, partly from nervousness and partly from desire. Out on the balcony, wrapped in the darkness and his arms, she felt safe. Inside, where the lamps threw puddles of honeyed light, was just a few steps away – but in another sense it was miles. Her glance fell onto the bed, an island of white goose-down duvet floating amid a Berber-rug sea, and her mouth dried. Everything was going to change.

Following her glance, Jonty said quickly, "I promise I'll be every bit as gentlemanly as Travis Chumley! I'll sleep on the couch tonight; you needn't worry."

At the thought of this, all of her apprehension vanished in an instant. Jonty would sleep on the couch? That seemed like a dreadful waste! She wanted him to pull her close, bury his mouth in hers and love her until the sun rose above the trees and the sleepy stars slipped away, not sleep on the couch!

For a moment they stared at one another; then Andi reached up on tiptoes to kiss him and everything else fell away. She didn't think she'd ever wanted anything so much in her life as to sink into him and then to drift off to sleep with his face in her mind and his skin pressed against hers. The time for hesitation was over.

"I'd rather you lay down too and held me," she whispered. "I don't want to let you go."

Jonty's face broke into a smile of such joy that Andi's heart crumbled like one of Gemma's vanilla sponges. Hand in hand they left the balcony.

Once they were indoors and wrapped up in each other, with the lamps off and only the moon's pale smile lighting the room, Andi watched the drapes dancing in the breeze and then closed her eyes. Jonty's arms tightened around her.

"What's been going on?" he asked gently, his lips brushing the nape of her neck.

She took a deep breath. This was it. Just as the last days of summer always bore the hint of crispness, so her time with Jonty was sharpened by the fear of the truth coming out. She had to tell him everything or this would all be over even before it had begun.

It was easier somehow to speak in the dark. In the circle of Jonty's arms Andi found that the words began to flow; at first a trickle, then a steady stream before a torrent. The riverbanks of silence were well and truly breached and her story tumbled out. The sacking, Alan's taking the credit for her work with Safe T Net, Tom's betrayal, the debts and the emptied account: all these things that had made macramé of her emotions for months were finally out there. The more she told him the more Andi found she wanted to tell him.

Blimey. Catholics were really onto something with confession!

All the way through her rambling tale, half sobbed and half laughed, Jonty said nothing, but the gentleness of his touch and the tension she felt shudder through him when she told him how Tom had threatened her that morning spoke volumes.

"So that's why I've had to leave," she finished quietly. "And do you know what the worst of it is? It's my own fault. I should have levelled with you all from the start. If I'd told Si the truth about losing my job then at least he would have had an option whether or not to take a chance on me. That would be one less thing Tom could threaten me with."

Jonty's arms tightened around her. A human safety belt, she found herself thinking. "That wasn't your fault, Andi. This guy at work, Alan, was totally plausible. It seemed to make sense that he was in charge. He covered his tracks and made sure that he sung his own praises to all the right people. It didn't help that you shared the same initials. He certainly capitalised on that coincidence."

"How on earth do you know that?" Andi was amazed. "Are you psychic or something? That's *exactly* how Alan operates!"

"Hardly! If I were a psychic I'd have made a move long ago. No, Andi, I just know how hard you work and how much you must have deserved that promotion. You held that project together."

She blushed. It was sweet of Jonty to be so vehement.

"I still should have told you and Simon the truth about how it all ended," she admitted ruefully. "That was the right thing to do. I should have been honest."

Jonty thought about this for a moment.

"Andi, you didn't know either of us from Adam. How were you to know we could be trusted to listen and to understand? For all you knew Si might have kicked you out instantly. After all you'd been through with Tom—" He practically spat the name and although it was dark Andi knew that his face was tight with fury. "After that, how were you to know who to trust?"

He understood. He really understood. She felt every muscle in her body loosen with relief. Keeping her sacking a secret hadn't been a deliberate deception, more an act of self-preservation. And it had been worth it, too, because hadn't she worked hard and done Si proud?

"And now he's threatening to circulate emails with personal pictures of you unless you pay up?" Jonty whistled. "Jesus. What a piece of work."

Andi couldn't agree more.

"I feel such an idiot," she said sadly. "I can't believe I was ever stupid enough to trust him. I'll never be that naïve again."

Jonty pulled her around to face him. They were standing so close together that their eyelashes almost brushed. Andi stared into his eyes, no longer turquoise but as dark and full of shadows as the wooded valley beyond.

"Trust is a wonderful quality," he said firmly. "You are a decent and kind and trusting human being. Don't beat yourself up on account of what Tom did. Anything that you did between the two of you was part of your relationship and as such was private and personal. A decent man would treasure that and leave it there, not be looking for an opportunity to exploit it." His jaw tightened and Andi had the strong impression that if Tom ever bumped into Jonty he'd be very sorry indeed.

"But if I hadn't—"

"There's absolutely no point in blaming yourself. Christ! What kind of man would betray someone he once loved, like this? For God's sake, this isn't your fault! The guy's a shit, Andi."

"Tell me something I don't know," Andi agreed. "Not a day goes by when I don't want to kick myself for ever being involved with a creep like him. But unfortunately he's a creep who holds all the cards. If I don't pay up then those images will be everywhere and he'll put posts about my being sacked all over the Internet." Her eyes filled with tears of frustration. "Now do you see why I had to go? My professional reputation's going to be ruined and my personal one won't be far behind it. "

"Not if I have anything to do with it," Jonty said darkly. "I promise you, that is not going to happen."

Andi was touched. But unless Jonty was able to either magic Tom off the surface of the planet (unlikely) or have a chat with Bill Gates (even more unlikely) then she didn't hold out too much hope.

"So what should I do?" she wondered aloud.

"Come back to Rock in the first instance," Jonty said firmly. "You've done nothing to be ashamed of."

Andi thought of the pictures and her stomach turned a horrible slow loop-the-loop.

"I don't know," she said.

Jonty held her tightly against his chest. "We'll sort this out, I promise. It will be fine."

"How will it?" Andi couldn't see a way.

He dropped a kiss onto her temple. "I'll figure that bit out. There's talking to Si for starters, and I promise you that he'll understand. The rest will follow. Trust me."

The weird thing was that she did trust him. After everything Tom had thrown at her, Andi thought this was little short of a miracle. Sinking onto the bed, Jonty held her in the circle of his arms and rested his chin on her head.

"It really will," he promised. "Trust me on this one. Everything really will be all right."

"Maybe," she said, thinking out loud. "I'm so sick of lies, Jonty. It's exhausting. I'm tired of people hiding the truth. Why can't people just be straight?"

Jonty was so quiet for a while that Andi wondered whether he'd fallen asleep. The lapping of the river against the banks and the calls of owls were enough to lull anyone into a slumber, and she felt her own eyelids grow heavy. The window drapes fluttered in the breeze and suddenly she wanted nothing more than to slip under the fat goose-down duvet and drift…

"Sometimes people don't mean to lie." Jonty's voice dragged Andi back from the brink of nodding off. He'd not been asleep but rather deep in thought, she now realised.

"Sometimes they want to tell the truth but they're afraid, or they can't find the words," he continued. "Then, as time goes on, it becomes harder and harder to backtrack. Like you not telling Simon about what really happened at Hart Frozer."

Andi didn't recall mentioning Hart Frozer. She'd still been holding back from revealing the full details, but she must have said more than she realised. What was in that garage latte? The truth drug?

"I kept quiet about being fired because I was ashamed," she said. "I had no way to prove I was innocent, not without having access to my work computer. Why would anyone believe me?"

He reached out and took her hand, lacing their fingers together.

"I know, and I understand all that. And I'm telling you now that you don't need to be ashamed. You've done nothing wrong. You did everything for the right reasons."

"But what I don't understand is how people can lie to people they're close to," Andi said in total bewilderment. "Si was a stranger when I arrived in Rock, I didn't know you either and I wasn't intending to deceive anyone. But Tom and I… we were… we…" She paused, searching for the right words to try to explain. Jonty raised her fingers to his lips and kissed them, and for a blissful moment she totally lost her thread. Moments later he was kissing her again and all other thoughts vanished.

"Sorry," Jonty said eventually, once they broke apart. "I totally interrupted you."

Andi laughed. "I can live with that. You can interrupt again if you like."

His lips skimmed the skin of her throat. "Believe me, I fully intend to do a whole lot of interrupting later on! But go on, what were you saying about Tom?"

Andi lassoed her stampeding thoughts. "It wasn't going so well; I know we should have called time on it months before, but even so I'll never understand how Tom could keep so much from me. I thought I knew him but all along he was living a double life. I knew he was imaginative – all part of being an actor, was how I tried to explain it away to myself – and I thought it was harmless. But I was wrong. The small lies he used to tell about the rent money getting mysteriously lost or not having had a drink weren't harmless at all: they were part of a much bigger picture." She shook her head. "Well, I've learned the hard way now. If somebody lies to you once then they'll do it again."

"Once a liar, always a liar?" Jonty asked.

Andi shrugged. "All I'm saying is that once there's doubt how can you ever trust somebody again?"

"Maybe they would have to prove themselves?" he suggested. "Show beyond all doubt that they were genuine?"

This was all getting a bit too metaphysical for Andi. Besides, all she could think about was the fact that she was lying next to Jonty, skin against skin, and with his lips just a kiss away from her own. It was dark and her senses were heightened; she didn't think she'd ever been so aware of another person's presence in her entire life. Her every cell felt as though it had been plugged into the mains.

"Maybe," she agreed. "But they'd have to really prove it. Anyway, enough of me going on. You said earlier that there were things you wanted to talk about too."

Now it was his turn to shrug. "Did I?"

"Yes," said Andi. She wondered what it was he'd wanted to say. Was it more details about Jax? The very thought of the older woman felt like a knife wound in her heart. Holding Jonty in the darkness, with the sweet river air dancing over them, she never wanted to let him go again. She dropped a kiss onto his collarbone. "And I've banged on and on about my own problems. Now let me be a listening ear for once."

"It can keep for another time," Jonty said firmly. "Right now I can think of much better things to do than talking."

And when he pulled her hard against him and lowered his mouth onto hers Andi was in total agreement. Talking could wait. Moments later words were no longer needed.

Chapter 46

Jonty pulled the Evoque up outside the pool house and killed the engine.

"Are you going to be all right to stay here for a couple of hours?" he asked, looking worried. "There's a few things I need to do with Si this morning – it won't take long, I promise. There's a comfy bed if you want to get some rest." He grinned at her, a slow sexy grin that made Andi's stomach flip like a year's worth of Shrove Tuesdays. "As I recall you didn't get much sleep!"

Andi's cheeks grew warm recalling the night that had so recently dissolved into sunrise. The memories were as fresh as the salty Cornish morning and she could still feel the heat of Jonty's mouth hard on hers, his kisses urgent and demanding as they clung to one another.

"I'll be fine," she said. "But honestly, I'm more than happy to go back to the caravan. I'm not afraid of bumping into Tom. In fact, I think I'm more than ready to deal with him."

But Jonty shook his head. "No way. Not until I've—"

"Until you've what?" Andi was suddenly worried. Just what exactly did he have in mind? She wasn't a fan of her ex but the last thing she wanted was any trouble for Jonty.

"I've got a couple of ideas but they'll take time. Don't look so worried. I'm not about to go and break his legs or anything. This is Rock, not *Reservoir Dogs*! Just trust me, Andi. It's going to be fine."

He reached out to stroke the curve of her cheek and Andi's fears melted like butter. She did trust him. There was no doubt in her mind that whatever Jonty planned to do it was for the best. Besides, how could she not trust him after the night they'd spent together?

Where had that night gone? She had never known time fast forward like that. One moment they had been talking and the sky had been jet black; the next thing dawn was finger-painting the world with rose and gold. She and Jonty had lain in their nest of tangled duvet and sheets holding one another tightly, unable to believe the intensity of what they had shared, and talking endlessly. It was amazing, beyond amazing; it was incredible. Andi didn't think she had ever felt like this.

As the sun had scrambled up its climbing frame of trees and blushed the couple's skin with rosy light, Andi hadn't wanted the moment to end. She only wanted to stay cocooned in their own magical world, and asked for nothing more than to feel his skin against hers, his breath warm against her cheek. Everything else had melted into nothingness. Tom, Jax, and her finances – none of it mattered any more.

Jonty had kissed her as the sun filled the room. "I knew it would be good with us, Andi, but I never imagined just how good."

"So you've been planning the big seduction?" she'd teased. "This hotel? Rescuing me? Was that copy of the *FT* a part of it too?"

His lips twitched. "You've got me! I was playing a long game!" He reached in and kissed her again. "No, I guess that what I'm trying to say – and failing dreadfully – is that there's something about you that's always felt right. Talking to you, spending time with you, it's just so easy. Does that make sense?"

She'd nodded. It felt exactly like this to her too. Waking up with him, with her hair a wild riot of tangles and last night's mascara probably plastering her cheeks as though she was channelling some kind of eighties rock band, Andi had felt none of the awkwardness of being with somebody new. Andi hadn't been with many guys – she rarely slept with somebody without being in a relationship – but with Jonty it felt so natural to throw her inhibitions to the wind. To be honest she wasn't sure she could have been any other way. There was no game playing or point scoring here, just honesty.

They'd enjoyed a simple breakfast of toast and tea on the small terrace and talked quietly about all the events leading them to that point. Andi had told Jonty everything: about her finances being destroyed, about her boss's antipathy and even about the day she caught Tom cheating.

"And that," she told him finally, "is it. You now know everything about me. I feel I know nothing about you in comparison."

"There's nothing really to tell," Jonty said with a shy smile. "I'm just a regular guy, a bit of a geek really, who likes to play computer games, fix boats and spend time with his family. Ask Mel. She's sick of the Jonty-shaped dent in the sofa. I'm pretty boring."

Andi hadn't pressed him further. There was more to Jonty, she knew there was, but he was also very private. His relationship with Jax, for example, filled her with curiosity. Had he been so hurt that he didn't want to open up? This wasn't the impression she got but you never knew. And what had drawn a woman like Jax, so status-symbol obsessed and driven by money, to a guy so down to earth and ordinary? Gorgeous yes, heaven in bed definitely, but a far cry from the millionaires that she could imagine the older woman associating with. Instinct told her there was more to it than Jonty had so far told her. He'd tell her in his own time, she knew he would.

"So, back to Rock," he'd said, interrupting her thoughts by placing his cup onto the saucer with a rattle.

"Can't we just stay here?" Andi sighed. The thought of returning to their haven of a room and losing herself in Jonty's blue-green eyes was far more welcome than that of going back and facing whatever music Tom had been busy composing.

Jonty had reached across the table for her hand. "Tempting, but there are a few things I have to sort out this morning. No hiding. We're going to sort this, OK?"

She'd nodded and gulped back her unease. It sloshed about in her tummy with the toast and Earl Grey in a very unpleasant way.

The nerves that had slipped away the night before had returned with all of their mates in tow from practically the moment the car had crossed the Tamar. With every mile that had brought her closer to Rock, Andi had felt less and less at ease. Not with Jonty, but with the idea of facing up to her demons. Now, outside the pool house, she felt quite sick with dread.

"There you are, Jonty!" Mel called from the kitchen window as, hand in hand, they made their way to the pool house. "I was wondering where you'd been all night but judging by the looks on your faces I don't need to ask!"

Jonty rolled his eyes at Andi. "I'm in my thirties and my big sister is still checking up on me."

"Bloody right I am," Mel agreed. She grinned at Andi. "Last time I let him out alone he ended up with that dreadful Jax! She's been here looking for you, by the way, Jonty, and she didn't look very happy either. In the words of Arnie, she said she'd be back."

Jonty sighed. He squeezed Andi's fingers. "I'll speak to her again. Make her understand that it really is over."

His sister looked delighted. "That would be a big relief. Her face was enough to curdle milk when I said you hadn't come home last night." She grinned. "It's high time – I thought I'd die of old age before you two woke up and smelled the coffee. I knew you were made for each other."

"Ignore my sister," Jonty said to Andi. "It's very sad but I think she's morphing into Cilla Black in her old age."

"You can mock all you like," huffed Mel, "but I am never wrong. Just ask Simon."

Andi laughed at this. Si never dared disagree with his strong-willed wife. He might run one of the biggest media conglomerates in the UK, but Mel decided how many roast potatoes he was allowed and had banned the Xbox for the summer. In the house Mel was most definitely the CEO.

Leaving Mel to gloat about always being right, Andi and Jonty made their way to the pool house. While he filled the kettle Andi curled up on the big squashy blue sofa. The pool house had to be one of her favourite places. A little version of the main house, it was painted white and contained a bed, the sofa, a kitchenette and piles of books. Jonty loved to read and his collection was eclectic; the unevenly stacked piles contained everything from Dan Brown to Ernest Hemingway to JK Rowling, and all were well thumbed and had clearly been read from cover to cover. Arty posters tacked to the wooden walls and scattered rag rugs were splashes of colour in an otherwise empty space. A wakeboard was propped against the wall and a pair of deck shoes had long dried out next to the wood burner. It was simple and comfortable, and Andi felt her eyes grow heavy.

"Nap for a bit," Jonty said, dropping a kiss onto her forehead. "I'll be a few hours with Si."

She smiled up at him. "And then you'll be back?"

He grinned. "Try keeping me away!"

Jonty placed a chunky mug on the table next to her. Steam spiralled heavenwards. "Have some tea and then sleep if you can. OK?"

Andi nodded. Sunlight streaming through the glass bathed her in gilded warmth and renderd her limbs heavy. Before Jonty had even shut the door, she was asleep.

It was the click of the same door closing that woke her. For a moment Andi still drifted, cocooned in warm dreams and the honeyed sunlight, before awareness of a presence dragged her into consciousness. How long had she been sleeping? An hour? Two?

Andi yawned and stretched. "You were quick, Jonty."

A shadow blocked the sunshine.

"Afraid not," said a voice that sounded horribly like Jax's. "Just me."

Sleep fled from Andi faster than money through Tom's fingers.

Her eyes sprung open and, sure enough, there was Jax silhouetted in front of the window. Dressed from head to toe in designer gear, with her hair beautifully blow-dried and make-up that looked practically airbrushed, she couldn't have looked more out of place in the simple room. Car keys on a Montblanc fob dangled from her manicured fingers and she stared at Andi disdainfully. She was wearing a purple Diane von Furstenberg dress and towering purple Louboutins. Andi wondered for a hopeful minute if she was actually having a dream about a giant, walking, talking Quality Street.

In terms of unpleasant ways to wake up, this one was right up there with having a bucket of ice-cold water thrown in your face. "Jonty isn't here," she said, sitting up as fast as she could and hoping that she hadn't been snoring or, even worse, dribbling. "He's with Simon."

Jax swung the key ring backwards and forwards as though trying to hypnotise them both. Her eyes never left Andi's. "I'm not looking for Jonty. I was looking for you."

She was? For a moment Andi wondered if she really was still asleep and having a very bizarre dream. What on earth could Jax want her for? Some emergency waitressing? A last-minute extra pair of hands to pass around the hors d'oeuvres?

"You see," Jax continued, the key fob swinging in time with her words, "I think it's about time you and I had a little chat, woman to woman."

"I don't think there's anything we need to talk about," Andi said firmly. Whatever Jax's problem might be, whatever the history between her and Jonty was, she didn't need to be involved.

"That's where you're wrong," Jax said. There was a pitying tone in her voice, which made Andi bristle. "I think it's high time you and I had a heart to heart."

Jax had a heart? This was news.

"Whatever you want to talk about, it can wait until Jonty's back," Andi told her. "Your relationship with him really isn't any of my business."

Jax laughed. It was a brittle sound, more of a bark than an expression of mirth. "Believe me, there's nothing I'd like more than to have him here too. Besides, my relationship with him is business and pleasure, believe me, and in more ways than you could ever imagine. Do you really think you're the only one? When he could have any woman he wants?"

Andi and Jax stared at one another. She saw that Jax already knew, with that primitive female intuition, exactly what was going on between herself and Jonty. She was jealous and had come to make trouble, that much was obvious.

"You need to speak to Jonty," she said again. "This is between you and him."

Jax smiled. "I think we both know that isn't true anymore. Besides, where is he now when we need him to explain himself? Nowhere to be seen, as always. Good old Jon Benjamin Teague doesn't like to stick around when things get uncomfortable, I should know that. Why do you think he's hidden away here for the summer?"

Andi stared at her. The room seemed to shrink like something out of *Alice in Wonderland*.

"What did you just call Jonty?"

"Jon Benjamin Teague?" Jax raised a perfect eyebrow. "What's so odd about that? It's his name, after all. Benjamin Jonathan Teague. Jon T to his friends. He hates Ben."

Andi's mouth fell open.

"To the rest of the world, of course, he's Mr Safe T Net, the Internet security mogul," Jax continued airily. "Come on, Andi. You read the *FT*, don't you? You're supposed to be smart? Surely you'd figured it out by now? Jon T? The guy whose company went public and made him one of the richest men on the planet?"

It was just as well Andi was still sitting down because her legs had turned to rubber and the room was starting to whirl around like some kind of horrible fairground ride. Suddenly all the pieces of the puzzle, a puzzle that she hadn't even realised she'd been trying to figure out, fell into place.

Jonty was the guy in the sharp suit with the Aston Martin that Cally had been drooling over.

Jonty was a multimillionaire.

Jonty was PMB. Project Manager Ben. No wonder she had felt as though she knew him. But this was all an illusion. He'd been playing her for weeks.

Jonty was a stranger.

Grief clawed her throat. It was worse than him being a stranger. Jonty was a liar. A liar just like Tom. A liar just like her father.

Jax widened her eyes in fake surprise. "Oh dear! Did you really have no idea? And you such a clever girl too by all accounts? I would have thought seeing how *close* you two are he would have trusted you enough to tell you the truth? Clearly not."

Andi didn't reply. She couldn't. Grief and shock had stolen her powers of speech.

"I can't blame him, mind you," Jax confided. "Jonty has a lot to lose if the wrong kind of woman made a play for him. Can you imagine the gold-diggers he dates? Why tell his holiday fling the truth? That would totally spoil the fun and ruin his Marie Antoinette style escape from reality. And that's all you are to him, Andi, a bit of fun while he kicks back from the pressures of the business world. Don't kid yourself that any of this is real. Rock is just a playground for the summer to Jonty, somewhere he can play at being a regular guy and sleep with regular girls. In a week he'll be back in London, where he belongs, and back with me. You see, Andi, unlike you I know the real Jonty. I understand him better than anyone else and he can be himself with me."

Jax might have been in the room, pouring poison into Andi's ear like a Shakespearean villain on speed, but Andi was miles and weeks away. Jonty's overreaction to Angel's pursuit of Laurence, his hasty departure when he'd seen her reading the article about Ben Teague's donation to charity, his accidental slip when he'd revealed Alan's name... No wonder he seemed to be so sympathetic and understanding of her. He'd known for ages who she really was! Their online conversations had revealed everything he needed to know about her. He'd played her like a fool for weeks.

And what had he told her in return?

Nothing.

They'd just spent the night together, the most incredible night of her life. She thought they'd been close, that this was the start of something really special, and she'd laid her soul bare. Jonty had taken down, brick by brick, all the careful walls she'd built around herself since Tom had betrayed her, taken them down so carefully and quietly that she'd not even realised. Neither had she noticed that while her defences were breached, Jonty's were firmly in place with the drawbridge up and the portcullis slammed down. Right now he was probably boiling the oil and arming the cannons.

"Somebody needed to tell you the truth," said Jax, who, bombshell dropped, was prepared to be sickly with faux sympathy. "You're making a fool of yourself and it's embarrassing. I would have thought Mel or Simon would have said something but, then again, they're having a free holiday in Jonty's house, aren't they? Why jeopardise that to save the hired help from looking like a lovesick teenager?"

Ocean View belonged to Jonty?

Everything was back to front. It was like looking in one of those distorted funfair mirrors. The house, the boat, the flash cars... These weren't Simon's, as he'd led her to believe, but Jonty's. So why was he wasting his time living in the pool house and pretending to be a gardener? And what was he doing tinkering about with *Ursula* when he could have had millions of pounds' worth of powerboat moored in the estuary? None of it made sense. It was the most elaborate and cruel deception she could have imagined.

The Jonty she knew and loved, the man who had held her against his heart all night and promised that everything was going to be all right, had vanished like the remnants of a dream. He had never even existed. The whole summer had been nothing but a pack of beautiful lies.

At this moment it felt as though somebody was dragging barbed wire through her heart, but there was no way Andi was prepared to let Jax know all her hopes and dreams had splintered into a million painful pieces. Her pride was all she had left; there was no way she was letting it go.

"Sorry to be the bearer of bad news," Jax said, looking nothing of the sort. The expression on her perfect face was closer to triumphant. "But as one woman to another, you should stay away from a man who's got so much money and power he can do what he like. Women are disposable to men like Jonty. I should know because I've seen enough of them come and go. But do you know something, Andi? It will always be me he'll come back to in the end. Me, because I understand him: we share the same world and without me he would never have made it in the first place. I'm his equal and he knows that. You? You're just some shag. A casual screw. He didn't even trust you enough to tell you who he really is."

Andi felt sick. Had she just been a casual thing to him? It hadn't felt like that at all but then what did she know? She was clearly a crap judge of character. Tom and Jonty both proved that.

"Stick around by all means if you want to be another plaything for him, but bear in mind the summer's nearly over. It'll soon be time to return to London." Jax threw the keys into the air and caught them neatly. "Still, it's your call. I just thought that it was time one of us told you the truth and stopped you making a total idiot of yourself."

"You're all heart," Andi told her.

Jax shrugged. "It's up to you, darling. I just thought you should know."

"And now I do, you can leave." Andi wasn't sure how she kept her voice so calm and level when inside her heart was hammering but there was no way she was going to crumble in front of Jax.

"He'll come back to me; he always does." Jax paused in the doorway and stared pityingly at her. "We go back years and he owes me. I know him, the real him, and he needs that. Ask his sister or Simon. They might hate it but they know it's true."

Jax stalked down the path, still swinging her keys. Andi didn't move a muscle until she heard her car roar into life. Then and only then did she allow herself the luxury of tears.

Jonty had lied to her, played with her emotions and proved beyond all possible doubt that men were not to be trusted. And she *had* trusted him, with every beat of her heart and every breath she drew. She had loved him with every cell of her being and every touch of her lips and her hands. Loved him more than she'd ever thought it was possible.

What an idiot she was. Had she learned nothing over the past month? Men lied. Men let you down. Men weren't to be trusted. Tom, her father, Jonty: everyone was a disappointment.

Andi dashed her tears away with the heels of her hands and drew a shaky breath. There was one thing she now knew for sure: this time she really was leaving Rock and she this time wouldn't be coming back. Her summer escape was over.

Chapter 47

Andi stumbled away from the pool house. How was it possible to fall from heaven to hell in just minutes? The speed of her descent from bliss to utter grinding despair was dizzying. Jonty, Project Manager B, Benjamin Jonathan Teague or whatever he liked to call himself owed her some answers. She might not be a millionaire or a captain of industry but she still didn't deserve to be treated with such cruel contempt. What might have been just a bit of holiday fun for a multimillionaire had actually meant something to her and she'd been stupid enough to think it had meant something to him too. She'd actually trusted Jonty.

Well, that was a mistake she wouldn't repeat in a hurry.

"You're awake!" Mel, pegging wet swimming gear out on the line, beamed at Andi. "We were wondering when you'd surface. Si and Jonty finished up ages ago. Shall I put the kettle on?"

Andi wasn't in the mood for chatting, especially not to a woman who had just spent the best part of two months concealing the tiny fact that her brother was the British Bill Gates. She was so hurt that she could hardly bring herself to look at Mel. So much for thinking she'd made friends here. "Where's Jonty? I need to talk to him."

"He's just strolled down into town. He said something about getting some bits together for a boat trip." Washing line full, Mel turned her attention to Andi and her smile faded. "Is everything OK? You look terrible."

This wasn't really surprising because *terrible* was exactly how Andi felt. Mel and Simon had known the truth all along. Had they been laughing at her all summer?

"I've seen Jax," she said. It was amazing that her voice actually functioned when misery was strangling her every cell. "You don't have to pretend anymore. She's told me everything."

"I doubt that very much," Mel said. Her face was ashen. "Jax and the truth aren't particularly well acquainted."

"A bit like the truth and your brother?"

Mel shook her head. "Andi, you don't understand—"

Andi's eyes filled with tears and she blinked them away furiously.

"You're right, Mel, I don't understand. How could you all have lied to me? You must have thought it was so funny, that I didn't have a clue what was really going on. Have you any idea how it feels to suddenly find out that everything you thought was true is actually a lie? That job with Si – Jonty lined it all up because he felt sorry for me, didn't he? I was never really working for Si at all. And this house, it isn't even yours, is it? It's Jonty's holiday home."

It wasn't only Andi who looked close to tears: Mel's heartbreakingly familiar sea-hued eyes were also suspiciously bright. Andi looked away. The very sight of Mel felt like a slap in the face.

"Shit, shit, shit," whispered Mel. She clutched the peg bag to her chest as though seeking comfort. "I told him this would happen. Look, Andi, I can explain everything. It really isn't what you think."

Andi stared at her askance. "Mel, I'm not stupid. I know you've all been lying to me for weeks. It's exactly what I think. Nobody thought enough of me, or trusted me enough, to tell me the truth."

But Mel shook her dark head vehemently. "No, it wasn't like that at all. Shit, Andi, I wanted Jonty to tell you the truth about himself. I told him enough times that no good was going to come of this. Christ knows Si and I didn't like having to pretend either, but it wasn't our secret to share. And believe me, if you knew what my brother's been through in the past, how he's been treated and betrayed, you'd totally understand why we were happy to help him. He's a good man and I'd do anything to protect him."

"Protect him?"

Mel grimaced. "Rock's full of gold-diggers – you've met Jax for heaven's sake – all I wanted was for somebody to love my brother for himself, not his bank balance. He's been hurt enough in the past."

"I'm not like that!" Andi cried, hurt beyond words. "And Jonty should know me better. We were supposed to be friends! He should have trusted me, like I trusted him." Her voice cracked, "But then again, I don't really know him at all, do I? The man I thought I knew doesn't even exist. He was just playing at being a normal guy."

"You're wrong! The man you know is my brother! He is exactly the person you think he is," Mel cried. "The Jonty you've spent the summer with is genuine, I promise! The rest of it is just crap. Why do you think he drives that ancient car and lives in the pool house? He enjoys the simple things. Even that tatty old boat of his, which he's had since he was at uni, means more to him than a powerboat penis symbol. He's just Jonty. The rest of it all happened by accident."

Jonty. Board shorts and bare feet. Happy eating chips down on the quay. Jonty who had made her gasp and cry and cling to him. Or JB Teague with his smart suit and bright red supercar? With millions in the bank and an army of women frantic to fall at his tanned feet? Andi's head spun. Mel could gush like an oil well all day long about how he was just a regular guy, but how many regular guys made JK Rowling look skint? Andi's brain was a kaleidoscope of confusion. She didn't know what to believe.

"I know my brother and he really doesn't care about the money; that was just an accident." Mel promised. "He really is just a geek who got lucky. Ask Si if you don't believe me. He has a heart of gold and he's still the same guy you know. What he feels for you is real, Andi. You have to believe me. I have never seen my brother the way he is when he's with you."

Andi wanted to believe her, so much that it was a dull ache. When she thought of Jonty and the night they'd spent together, she still felt fuzzy and warm inside. Or she did until she remembered that he was no longer just Jonty, beach bum and chip-eating, *FT*-reading friend. She recalled the guy featured in *Cosmo*, all designer clothes and champagne flutes, and it was like staring into a shattered looking glass.

"You have to believe me," Mel pressed when she didn't reply. "He isn't a liar or a fake. He's just the same person he's always been. Don't listen to Jax. She just hates the fact that now he's worth a fortune, she can't have him. Believe me, she didn't want him when the business nearly folded. We couldn't see the bitch for dust. We've only tolerated her here because Jonty didn't want her to tell everyone who he is and wreck his summer. Being here is the poor guy's only hope of anything like a normal life. You've got to try and understand why he's been so secretive."

This was easy for Mel to say, Andi thought: she'd known the truth all along, whereas the Jonty she knew had been obliterated in seconds.

"He's lied to me, Mel," she said sadly. "And I don't think I'll ever be able to get over that. I'm sick and tired of people lying to me."

Mel nodded miserably. "I understand. I did try and warn Jonty you might feel like this but he was terrified if you knew the truth you'd feel differently about him." She paused. "I guess he was right about that, wasn't he?"

"It isn't the truth that's upset me," Andi said. "It's not being told it to begin with."

Leaving Mel standing in the garden, Andi made her way from Ocean View and down into the town. She knew she had to find Jonty and close their chapter. She needed to hear his explanation for why he had played her for a fool, not his sister's well-intentioned interpretation. Maybe then she would be able to forgive him?

It was early afternoon in town. Tourists clutching sweating paper bags full of hot pasties crowded the streets, and the cafés were doing a roaring trade with people determined to enjoy the last days of summer sunshine. Across the estuary and out to sea the horizon was bruised purple with heavy clouds, while a breeze was whipping white horses into a canter. Inland the air was soupy and the sunlight was a sickly lemon hue. Andi paused to catch her breath and felt sweat trickle down her back. A storm was brewing.

She passed Rock Cakes, peering through the window just in case Gemma might be inside. Andi felt a pang of guilt for missing Gemma's big night. She hoped it had all gone well. When she managed to charge her phone she'd text Gemma an apology.

"Andi! Hey! What are you doing here? I was just on my way back. I've got us some lunch."

Jonty was striding towards her, a brown paper bag from the deli swinging from his hand, and his face was aglow with pleasure at the sight of her. Andi's treacherous heart lifted before it came plummeting down to earth again. She wanted nothing more than to turn time back, to not have heard Jax's ugly words and seen that triumphant sneer.

How could he look like her Jonty, still have that smile that made a flutter of butterflies take flight in her stomach, and yet be a total stranger?

Her head ached. It just didn't make sense. Just being close to him was overwhelming. She wanted nothing more than to step forward and feel his arms close around her, and it took every ounce of self-control she had to step back when he went to kiss her. The expression of hurt on Jonty's face took her breath away.

"What's wrong?" Jonty said. Concern was written all over his open features. "You look really upset. What's happened?"

Andi was silent for a moment. She simply didn't know what to say.

Jonty's eyes searched hers. "You can tell me, whatever it is, Andi. You can tell me anything."

Andi's patience finally snapped. "Like you can tell me anything, you mean?"

Although tanned from the sun and the wind, Jonty paled.

"You've spoken to Jax." It wasn't a question.

She nodded. "She's told me everything."

"I doubt it," Jonty said. He ran a hand through his hair, looking lost for words. "Jesus, Andi, I didn't want you find out like this."

"You didn't want me to find out at all!" The words flew from her lips like bullets. "Why didn't you tell me the truth, Jonty? Why did you lie to me? Couldn't you trust me? Or is it true, I'm just a bit of summer fun for a bored rich guy?"

"Of course that isn't true!" Jonty shot back. "How can you even say that? You know me, Andi, *me!*"

She stared at him. "Do I? The man I know lives in his sister's pool house and fixes boat engines or mows lawn for money. He has an old boat and loves watching the wildlife on the river. That's the man I know. The other one, the CEO of Safe T Net, is a stranger."

"Hardly a stranger. You were talking to me for months when I was managing the floatation," he pointed out. "PMB? Andi, that was me! It's amazing. We were already friends in cyber space before we even met!"

"And just when were you planning to share that piece of information with me?"

Jonty looked stricken. "I wasn't deliberately *not* telling you. I didn't realise for ages that you were the person I'd been talking to at Hart Frozer. You never mentioned that you worked there, remember?"

"I hardly think not telling you where I once worked is the same as totally lying about my entire identity! I don't know you, Jonty. I haven't a bloody clue who the real you is. How do you think that makes me feel?"

"This is the real me!" Jonty's bright eyes flashed, like the darting wings of the kingfishers in the reed beds. "That's the whole point of this. You have seen the real me. *This* is whom I am, me here right now, holding a bag full of brie and grapes and trying to convince the most amazing, wonderful, sexy woman I've ever met not to walk out on me. The rest of it is bollocks."

Tears stung her eyes.

"It might all be bollocks to you but it isn't to me. You lied to me, Jonty. Not just once but for weeks and weeks and weeks. At what point did you just happen to forget you were a multimillionaire and businessman? And Mel and Simon lied too. Simon probably only gave me the job because of you."

"No way! He gave you that job on your own merits." Jonty stepped forward to try to hold her but Andi raised her hands to ward him off.

"I can't believe a word you say," she told him. "How can I when it's all been a lie? How could you have spent last night with me and still not told me the truth?" Her voice caught in her throat and tears threatened to blur her vision. "You had every opportunity to tell me the truth but you didn't. You're as much of a liar as Tom."

Jonty looked as though she'd slapped him.

"If I told you that I've tried a hundred times to tell you, would it make any difference? I've lost count of the times I've almost told you. But Andi, I loved the way things are with you, the way that I can just be myself – my real self – when we're together. You see me, the real me, and I can't tell you just how wonderful that is. I couldn't bear the thought of spoiling it. It sounds wanky I know, but my life has turned upside down. One minute I was renting a room from a mate and writing a computer program; the next the whole deal went mental and I was richer than God." He pulled a wry face. "I'll confess it turned me into a bit of a prick for a while, but I was still the same guy."

Andi said nothing. She didn't think she would ever get over the fact that he'd lied to her. In her mind Jonty's deceit was interwoven with Tom's.

"You didn't trust me," was all she could say.

Jonty looked bleak. "If you'd been through what I've been through you'd find it hard to trust too. Jesus, you've met Jax. It crucified me when she left and it was a million times worse when she came back just because I was rich. But Andi, I was going to tell you about me; you have to believe that."

Did she believe him? Andi wanted to but right at this minute the pain of being deceived, even by omission, was too much to bear.

"I'm so sorry I didn't tell you sooner," he said. "I wanted to but it never seemed the right time and, stupid as it sounds, I was scared."

"We all get scared," Andi said bitterly. "But this is something else. I don't know who you are, Jonty, and I don't think I ever did. "

He looked at her long and hard. "Nothing I can say is going to change the way you feel about me now, is it?"

She shook her head. It was over before it had even begun. This was probably a good thing. At least he'd never hurt her again and she'd never face the pain of being abandoned when Jax next clicked her fingers or a stunning model type came along. It was probably for the best. Jonty was, and always had been, way out of her league.

"I don't think so," she whispered.

The fight seemed to seep from him.

"Fine," said Jonty defeatedly. "You can't handle the truth, I get it."

"The truth I could handle; being lied to and made to look like an idiot I can't," she said softly. "Goodbye, Jonty. Enjoy the rest of the summer."

With her shoulders back and her head held high, Andi walked away. Tears stung her eyes but she knew she was doing the right thing. Of course she was. Men lied and cheated and only let you down. Why waste any more time on Jonty? He was the worst of the lot. Stepping away now was going to save her a whole world of pain a few months down the line when he got bored or decided that the chilled-out life in Cornwall was no longer quite so exciting.

No, this was definitely the right thing to do.

Which just raised one thorny question: why then did it feel so totally and utterly wrong?

Chapter 48

The champagne cork exploded from the bottle with a loud pop and a hiss of foam. All eyes in The Wharf Café swivelled to the furthest table at the end of the balcony, where a group of people were toasting each other and laughing. It didn't really need the opening of the champagne to grab the attention of the other customers: the presence of a major TV star – who'd been splashed across the papers all week long – was quite enough to make them whisper behind their menus, and the stunning blonde pouring the bubbles into glasses was already attracting glances. Add to that an oligarch who looked as though he'd be more at home torturing Bond, an ex-City trader turned cake-maker to royalty, a genuine viscount, plus the heir to one of Britain's biggest pet-food companies, and the eclectic mix was bound to draw attention.

Partying at lunchtime and midweek, the group were certainly having the time of their lives. Even the infamous TV star didn't look very sad about his public humiliation; instead he was smiling at a girl whose tumbling blonde curls and eye-watering curves would have had *Playboy* sign her on the spot.

Their good mood was infectious. Lashings of sunshine were pouring down from the sky in celebration with them while the dark clouds on the horizon stayed firmly in the distance, as though reluctant to spoil the festivities. Even the seagulls strutting along the edge of the rooftop didn't interrupt with their usual squawking.

Angel raised her glass and grinned at the others. She was so over the moon that they had not only listened to her idea but liked it, she was practically in orbit. It had taken all the courage she possessed to visit each one and put her plan to them. Even though Laurence had assured her that she was onto something good, and she was convinced that this was the biggest stroke of genius since the invention of the wheel, everything depended on the other parties agreeing to it. After arranging to meet everyone here she had been on tenterhooks all morning and had almost driven Laurence to distraction. Combined with a late night worrying about her sister's whereabouts that had only ended once Andi had texted to say she was with Jonty, it was amazing that Angel hadn't started to gnaw her new acrylics all the way to her elbows. The last twenty-four hours had been beyond crazy.

"So, we're all agreed, then? You really want to give it a shot?" Angel gazed at them all nervously. As, one by one, they nodded, her heart began to thud with excitement. Call it instinct, call it business acumen, call it psychic powers, call it whatever you wanted – Angel knew with every fibre of her being that this was something good. Something huge.

Mr Yuri, resplendent in a tight white suit that made him look like an obese version of the man from Del Monte, slammed his glass down on the table while his wife nodded like the Churchill dog.

"I have not ever given my backing to a project that fail! With my team to help, it will be beeg, beeg success. Is very good idea. I tell Abramovich and he say, 'Yes, is very good.'" Already he was tapping away on his BlackBerry with his sausage fingers, and when he looked up Angel could almost see pound signs in his eyes. Phew. The concrete boots could go right to the back of the metaphorical shoe cupboard.

"I second that," agreed Dee. "The business plan that Anton and I will put together will help to make some forecasts, but my gut feeling is that this has the ingredients to do very well indeed." Holding up her hands she began to tick them off on her fingers. "Baking is huge business at the moment, the nation still loves reality TV, we've got an

A-list celebrity on board as a big name – and throw into the mix a dilapidated mansion—"

"Steady on," said Laurence, looking hurt. "Kenniston isn't that bad."

"It bloody well is," Angel said firmly. "Babe, I'm still thawing out! But that's the whole point. It's kind of *Downton Abbey* meets *TOWIE* meets *The Great British Bake Off*, with a dollop of Sarah Beeny and *Made in Chelsea* thrown in."

"Which is what makes it such a fantastic pitch," Cal added. His brown eyes were bright with excitement and it said everything about Angel's idea that he was more interested in discussing it than reaching for the breadbasket. "Mike and I had a preliminary chat with ITV2 and they made some very positive noises. They like the idea that this could cash in on my latest escapade and actually turn it into a positive for us. Jaysus, who'd have thought it? Being papped stuffing me face could be my best career move yet. And it's all thanks to Gemma."

Gemma blushed. "I don't think I can take the credit. They also loved the idea of being able to give the BBC's *Bake Off* a run for its money." She entwined her fingers with Cal's and smiled at him adoringly. "Paul Hollywood had better watch out. There's a new sexy TV baker in town. The female viewers will go crazy."

Cal kissed her. "I only have eyes for you, Gemma me darlin'!"

God, I must be going soft in my old age, Angel thought, because her eyes were going all misty. It was wonderful to see how happy Cal and Gemma were together. Since the night of the play when he'd declared his feelings in such a dramatic fashion, Cal hadn't let Gemma out of his sight; they were like Siamese twins joined at the lips. No wonder Gemma was losing pounds: she was far too busy snogging to eat!

"And you're really happy about this?" Angel turned to Laurence. Kenniston was his ancestral home and she knew just how much it meant to him. Would he really want to fling open the doors and invite the world inside? Although the Elliotts were only months away from finding themselves in serious danger of losing the place, she knew that the changes she had in mind would alter life at Kenniston forever. Lady Elliott had been surprisingly thrilled; she was a massive fan of Cal's apparently, and an even greater fan of Travis, who had leapt at the chance to be involved and invest a chunk of his inheritance. Angel knew that he was still riddled with guilt from almost running Gemma over with his speedboat and, naughty as it was, if this was his way of atoning then she wasn't about to tell him that Gemma had long since forgotten about the incident.

Laurence just raised her hand to his lips and brushed his mouth across the soft skin. Delicious shivers of desire dusted her limbs and suddenly she longed for everyone else to vanish so that it was just the two of them again. It was little short of miraculous that she'd actually managed to drag herself out of bed to put her idea into action.

"It's the answer we've all been looking for," he said firmly.

"Even you, Gemma?" Angel was worried. She'd sat down with Gemma and Cal, since he was the key to her idea succeeding, and they'd both been very enthusiastic. Gemma, who'd been inundated with rave reviews following her performance in *Twelfth Night*, had since turned down a plum TV role. Her ex-agent, Chloe, had called the day before, frantic to make amends and convince Gemma to sign a contract, which Gemma had flatly refused to do. Angel hated to think that Gemma might yet again be putting her own dreams on hold. She gave her friend a hard and searching look. "I don't want you stepping away from your acting because of this. I don't want anything else to get in the way of all your dreams."

But Gemma shook her head. "It's the weirdest thing, Angel, but when Chloe called yesterday I was horrified. It was a real case of 'be careful what you ask for'. I've spent years dreaming of getting a part in a soap and then when I do I find it's the last thing I want."

"But you love acting. And you're so talented. Why quit now?" Angel was confused. How many hours had she and Gemma spent trying to devise a master plan that would launch her friend into stardom? From control pants to bumping into Callum South – they had tried everything.

"Because I've only just rediscovered just how much I love it!" Gemma said. "I'm never going to give up acting but I don't want the crap that goes with doing it professionally. All that bollocks about dieting and having to look a certain way; look at how Chloe treated me – she dropped me like a hot brick when she thought that I looked wrong."

Cal looked at her with adoring eyes. "She's a silly cow, so she is. You're gorgeous and talented."

"Thanks," Gemma blushed.

Dee clapped delightedly. "Accepting compliments at last! There's hope for you yet, Gemma!"

Gemma grinned at her. "I'm a work in progress. Seriously though, doing the play here has been brilliant and I've loved every minute of it, which has made me realise how I didn't love it when I was trying so hard to succeed. I'll keep on acting, I can't imagine giving it up, but I'll do it for fun. I've found that I love baking just as much and I can't wait to try something new." She smiled at Angel. "Your idea is brilliant. And spending more time with Cal is an added bonus too."

Cal leaned across and kissed her.

Angel rolled her eyes at Laurence. "This could go on a while!"

He laughed. "In that case, may I propose a final toast? To the team behind *Bread and Butlers* and our new production company, Seaside Rock! To us!"

"To us!" they chorused. Amid the chinking of glasses and excited chatter their food arrived, and before long everyone was tucking into moules frites and tearing off chunks of oven-warm baguette to dunk in the white-wine and garlic sauce. Their enthusiasm and energy for her idea could have powered Rock for a year.

It was a simple plan, as all the best plans tend to be, but once it was in her head Angel hadn't been able to ignore it. From the second she'd learned that Kenniston was in such financial dire straits her agile mind had been whirling back and forth to try to find a solution. When the idea finally landed it was so obvious that she had laughed out loud. What had she been dreaming of for so long? Reality TV, that was what! And what did she have at her fingertips? Only a mansion that needed saving, complete with dotty aristocrats, Laurence and his loaded blue-blooded pals, and a disgraced reality TV star whose career had to be rescued – and there it was, the perfect hit formula. Lots of talking with Laurence, Cal and Mike and a huge cash injection from Mr Yuri and Travis later, and the pitch for *Bread and Butlers* was ready to be turned into a treatment. Angel was so excited she could hardly breathe, although this could just be from being close to Laurence. Minted or moneyless, it didn't make the slightest bit of difference. Just the sight of him turned her into a puddle of longing.

As she watched her friends, both new and old, chat and excitedly discuss their plans, Angel felt a warm buzz of pride that was bigger and better than anything she'd ever felt in her life. Seeing her idea start to take shape was a thousand times more satisfying than buying a new handbag or the latest must-have shoes. Only one thing could have made her happier and that was knowing that Andi's problems were over.

Angel had been distraught. *Andi was running away?* It hadn't made any sense until she'd spotted that total and utter tosser Tom swaggering through the town as though he owned the place. It hadn't taken long to put two and two together after that, and in a blind panic Angel, with the help of Travis's Aston Martin, had torn through the town like the Tasmanian Devil on tyres until she'd enlisted the help of just about everyone they knew.

Angel sipped her champagne thoughtfully. Interesting that it had been Jonty who'd managed to find her sister and persuade her to come back to Rock. Perhaps she should give Jonty a chance? After Tomgate Angel had been ready to strangle any man who treated her sister badly and all she'd wanted was somebody to take care of her sister; was that so bad? How could a guy who earned only pennies possibly manage that? But he if genuinely did care about her sister then perhaps Angel could make an exception?

Maybe there could be a job for Jonty on *Bread and Butlers,* Angel wondered as she stared out into the street. He seemed pretty practical. He was also very easy on the eye, with that taut ripped stomach, smooth golden tan and summer-sea gaze, and he would look great on camera. Not that she was being mercenary or anything! She crinkled her brow in concentration. Maybe he could help with the renovations? Or set-building? Or even the grounds at Kenniston – although he might need more than a Flymo to cope with several hundred thousand acres. And Andi too could be an asset to the team as Seaside Rock's accountant.

Angel was just drifting into a wonderful dream where, several months down the line, she was attending the BAFTAs (dressed in something slinky and designer, obviously, and posing on the red carpet with Laurence, who was jaw-droppingly handsome in his tux) when a slumped-shouldered figure passing by the café caught her attention.

It was Andi.

Angel leaned forward. Surely not? Andi was with Jonty. She must be. Angel had sent her several texts already and none of them had been answered, which she'd taken as a very good sign indeed – when she was lying in Laurence's arms her iPhone could chime and beep itself silly, but there was no way she was going to answer – so she hadn't worried about the silence in the slightest. Now though, a cold hand squeezed Angel's heart. Something was up. She knew it.

Excusing herself from the party, Angel tore down the steps and out into the street. Sure enough the slender red-headed figure walking out of town was her sister.

"Andi!" Angel cried, kicking off her heels and sprinting through clusters of surprised tourists. "Andi! Wait up! Ouch! Shit!" The gritty tarmac bit into her soles and she winced with every step she took. Angel took her hat off to the Little Mermaid. Personally she'd have said *sod the prince* and reached for her Uggs. "Ow! Andi! Stop, before my feet fall to bits!"

Her last agonised yelp caught the attention of several holidaymakers and her sister. Slowly Andi turned around, as though she'd been plucked from her own world. When she saw her sister's face, Angel stopped in her tracks. She was shocked beyond words.

Andi, strong and sensible Andi – the sister who'd carried her, who'd helped her through the horrors of school and loss and crappy boyfriends and even crappier finances, the sister who never moaned or made a fuss – wore an expression so bleak that it took Angel's breath away.

But even worse than this? Her sister, her strong and clever sister, was crying. Angel's hands balled into tight and angry fists.

If this was Jonty's doing, then she was going to kill him.

Chapter 49

Andi had been so deep in gloomy thoughts that she hadn't even noticed Angel until her sister grabbed her arm. Before she could even so much as protest, Angel had frogmarched her up the road and into the Mariners pub. Once the sisters were ensconced in a window seat and nursing halves of scrumpy, Angel began an interrogation that would have made the Spanish Inquisition look like amateurs.

"You can cut out all that 'I'm fine' bollocks," Angel told her. She leaned back in her seat and folded her arms. "I know you, remember? You can't fob me off. What's happened? Is it something to do with Jonty?"

Andi stared down at the table. Condensation ran down her glass like the tears she had wept from the moment she'd walked away from him. Every step she'd taken had felt like a knife through her heart, and it had taken all the willpower she possessed not to turn around and fling herself back into his arms.

"He's a liar," she said bleakly. Was that really her voice? It sounded really odd. She caught a glimpse of her reflection in the window and winced. She looked dreadful: her face was ashen and her eyes were red from crying so hard. It was ridiculous; she hadn't even cried this much when she'd caught Tom cheating. What was the matter with her? She'd only spent one night with Jonty.

Angel's perfect brows drew together. "Jonty? What on earth can he have to lie about?" Then a thought occurred – Andi could almost see the cogs in her sister's mind turning – and she gasped, "Oh my God! He's not married?"

In spite of her despair, Andi laughed. "No, of course not!"

Angel exhaled. "Phew. That's a relief! So, he's not married and I presume he's not murdered anyone, so what's he lied about?"

Andi smiled sadly. "Just about everything, Angel. I hardly know where to start. Let's just say he's not the person I thought he was."

Her sister shrugged. "I suppose Laurence could say the same about me?"

"That's different."

"I don't see how. Lies are lies, surely? Laurence wasn't exactly truthful with me either. I like to think we cancelled one another out, a bit like a minus and a minus is a plus!"

Angel's moral compass was certainly interesting, Andi reflected. But she didn't see how a few fibs about where her sister got her shoes from or the state of Laurence's bank balance equated to lying about your entire life and enlisting the help of your family to spin the untruths even further.

"He was beside himself when he thought you were leaving," Angel told her. "Whatever he's done, or said, that's upset you I can promise that his feelings for you aren't a lie." She took a sip of her drink. "Look, Andi Pandy, I'm not the greatest fan of Jonty; I think you could do a lot better than an odd-job man with no focus and who's scabbing off his sister for the summer, but I do know that he's crazy in love with you."

Andi rolled her red eyes. "You sound like a Beyoncé song."

"Don't take the piss; I'm being serious. He was frantic when he thought you'd run away. He went straight after you. I hardly saw him for dust. Whatever he's done to upset you, the guy is mad about you and I know you're pretty keen on him yourself."

A tear rolled down Andi's cheek and splashed onto the table. "You don't understand."

Angel reached across the table and grasped Andi's hands. "Then make me understand."

So Andi did. Word by painful word, she choked out the story. While Angel listened, saucer-eyed, she repeated the whole tale, from her friendship with PMB, to Jax, to Simon and Mel being party to Jonty's secret. When she got to the part where Jonty was actually the CEO of Safe T Net and one of the richest men in Britain, Angel's jaw dropped. The only parts that Andi left out where those magical, dreamlike hours they'd spent together at the inn on the riverbank. Whenever she closed her eyes she was right back there with his lips trailing kisses across her skin while the night breeze lifted the curtains. The jolt of loss she felt was unbearable.

"So you see," Andi finished sadly, "there's no way I can ever trust Jonty again. He's completely lied to me in every way a person can. He's no better than Tom."

Angel drained first her drink then Andi's. "Bloody hell."

Andi gave her a sad smile. "Exactly."

The sisters sat in thoughtful silence for a moment.

"OK," Angel said finally. "So that is a pretty big secret to keep but I kind of understand why he did it. I mean, you would have seen him in a totally different light wouldn't you?" A sheepish expression flitted across her pretty face. "Even I might have started to find him attractive if I'd know what he was worth. And from what you've told me, that bitch Jax gave him a good kicking."

Andi stared at her in disbelief. "Are you seriously sticking up for him?"

Angel shrugged. "I guess I am. Look, of course he should have trusted you and told you the truth, especially after you slept together—"

"I never said that!" Andi's cheeks flamed. Did she have the word *slapper* tattooed across her head or something?

"You didn't have to. I can always tell and I'm never wrong," said Angel smugly. "But look at how you've reacted. You've basically proved the poor guy right. Now you know the truth you don't feel the same way about Jonty. He was right to be worried."

"Yes I do!" Andi shrieked. Several diners looked up from today's special of organic sausages and sweet-potato mash, and she lowered her voice. "Of course I do, but I don't know him, do I? He's not the person I thought he was."

"Of course he is," Angel said patiently and as though Andi was thick. "Like duh! Weren't you always going on about how much you liked that Project Manager B guy? How much you clicked with him and liked chatting to him? He was your online soul mate. It's Fate, babes: it was meant to be. My God! It's like a movie."

"Some movie. He lied about everything." Andi just couldn't get past this fact.

"Crap! He just didn't tell you about the money!" Angel insisted. "Get over it! He's still got the most ripped body in Rock and a sexy bum – not that I've been looking – and I bet he still likes to pootle around in that knackered old boat and eat pasties. He's still the same person. He just happens to have shedloads more cash than we ever imagined. Lucky you! Laurence was the total opposite."

"But he lied, like Tom!"

"This is nothing like cheating, wanker-features Tom," Angel said firmly. "Tom lied to rip you off and cheat you. Jonty lied so that you could get to know the real him. And if you love him, really love him, then all that matters is that he's the person you've spent the whole summer with. The guy who's put the first real smile on your face for ages, welcomed you into the heart of his family and made you eat more chips than I'd have thought humanly possible." She reached forward and took her sister's hands. "He's the one who came after you when you thought there was nobody else. He's *exactly* who you thought he is. He's the man who loves you with all his heart. The rest of it is just nonsense."

Andi stared at Angel. Was this really her shallow, materialistic, fashion-obsessed sister talking?

"Since when did you get so wise?"

Angel put her hand over her heart. "Since I realised that what really matters is in here. Laurence could have a million pounds or minus a million pounds; it wouldn't matter. I'd still love him. And he'd still love me. I loved what I thought he was but when that vanished I realised that it really didn't matter at all. It's the same with Jonty. Mel's right: he's just a regular guy who got lucky."

Andi's thoughts were whirling like a washing machine on spin. With the blinkers of Tom's betrayal removed and her own hurt at being deceived starting to fade, she began to understand things from Jonty's point of view. If she was totally honest with herself she knew it would have changed everything between them if she'd known the truth. Would she have seen Jonty, or the groomed guy leaning against the flash car who'd featured in Cally's *Cosmo*?

The answer was so clear that she felt ashamed. She would have written him off as a rich tosser, in the league of Travis and Laurence and all the other wealthy people who holidayed in Rock. She'd have judged him straight away.

She was just about to reply when her phone rang from the depths of her bag.

"So it is working!" exclaimed Angel. "Have you any idea how many times I've called that today?"

Actually, Andi did – but she'd been busy ignoring it just in case it was Jonty. Looking at it now she saw that there were eleven missed calls from a variety of mobile numbers. That was odd. She didn't recognise any of them.

"Answer it!" Her sister urged. "It's bound to be him."

Andi delved into her bag and retrieved her phone. When she saw an unknown number flashing she sank back into her seat. The despondency she felt because this wasn't Jonty was awful.

Oh God. What had she done? Had she allowed all her issues and hang-ups to get in the way of something really good? With a leaden heart, she pressed the green button.

"Hello?" A male voice reverberated down the line. Strong and authoritative, but sadly not Jonty. "This is Detective Inspector Jones. Am I speaking to Ms Miranda Evans?"

"Yes." Andi glanced at her sister. *The police*, she mouthed at Angel, whose eyes widened.

"Ms Evans, I'm calling to let you know that we've apprehended an individual in conjunction with fraudulent activity involving several bank accounts and credit cards. I believe that some of this activity was regarding your finances?"

Andi was staggered. "Apprehended? That means arrested?"

"Yes, indeed. The individual concerned is under further investigation and is forbidden from contacting you. We also believe he intended to extort money through blackmail, and certain images and computer equipment have been confiscated. Our team will be in touch shortly to let you know what happens next. In the meantime, I'm told that at least some of the funds that were taken from your accounts are going to be credited back to you as a goodwill gesture – so I'd suggest that you check your balance within the next twenty-four hours."

DI Jones gave Andi some further details, which she managed to jot down on a napkin. Once the call had ended, she was just about to explain to Angel what was going on when her phone shrilled again. Angel pulled a face and gestured to the bar. When she arrived back with two more ciders, Andi was looking shocked.

"What?" Angel demanded. "Don't tell me. It was Jonty and he's bought you a Caribbean island to say sorry?"

Andi didn't even respond to her sister's teasing. She was too dumbfounded.

"The first call was the police," she said in disbelief. "They've arrested Tom."

"Yes!" Angel punched the air. "Brilliant. Porridge here he comes! And who was the second call? Jonty? With a Ferrari filled with roses?"

"Not quite." Andi shook her head. "It was the MD of Hart Frozer offering me my job back, with a promotion to head of department level and a much higher salary. Apparently things have come to light that prove beyond all reasonable doubt that Alan Eades stole the work I'd done and that I was sacked without any justifiable cause."

"Well we all know that," Angel agreed, loyally.

"Yes, *we* do – but how do they? And how did the police suddenly manage to trace the frauds and blackmail back through the Internet?" Andi and Angel's gazes met across the table.

"It's almost like a computer genius who created the world's most powerful Internet security system was involved," breathed Angel. "Do we know anyone like that?"

Andi was trembling like a leaf in a storm. "May I borrow your iPhone?"

Angel scooted it across the table. "Be my guest."

With shaking fingers Andi somehow managed to log into her bank account. When she checked the balance she reached for her drink and gulped back a huge mouthful. Then she looked again just in case she had been mistaken. Nope. That was no error.

"What is it?" Angel was practically crawling across the table to try to peer at the screen. "What's happened? You've gone ever such a funny colour."

Andi felt a funny colour. Silently, she passed the iPhone to her sister.

"All the money Tom stole is back. And the credit cards have been refunded too."

"Bloody hell!" Angel looked stunned as she studied the screen. "It really is! Oh my God! You've got your money back! Git Face has been arrested and you can even have your job back! Isn't it brilliant? Andi?" She gave her sister a stern look. "You should be up on the table dancing. What's wrong?"

"It was Jonty. He did this." Andi felt as though the floor was moving underneath her, which couldn't just be from half a cider on an empty stomach.

"Duh!" said Angel. "Of course he did. That's obvious. Didn't he tell you he was going to help?"

No. He hadn't said a word. When she'd thrown her accusations at him, accused him of deceiving her and of being a liar, Jonty had just stood there, bleak faced, and let her have her say. When she'd told him that she couldn't be with him, that she didn't know him at all and that he was just as much of a liar as Tom, he could have so easily flung back at her all these wonderful things that he'd done for her. But he hadn't. He'd let her hurl accusations and never once tried to change her opinion of him. He'd left Andi to make up her own mind, and in doing so had granted Andi her independence. He hadn't made her feel that she owed him or was beholden to him in any way.

How had she let her prejudices and fears get in the way? She'd got him totally and utterly wrong. He wasn't manipulative or a liar. He was just a kind and genuine man who wanted to make sure she was taken care of and safe. Jonty was still the man who'd let her have his (she now realised) *FT* and who had been her friend all summer. He hadn't changed. He still had the kindest and most generous heart in the world, and arms in which she wanted to be held forever.

He was still the same guy in frayed board shorts and deck shoes.

He was still the same man she'd slowly and gently fallen in love with.

The pub dipped and spun around her and for an awful moment Andi thought she was about to throw up. She'd sent him away thinking she despised him when nothing could be further from the truth.

Angel waved her hand in front of Andi's face. "I hate to interrupt your chain of thought but what exactly did you say to Jonty?"

Andi took a deep breath, exhaled slowly and told her. With every word she spoke her sister looked even more dismayed.

"And do you still feel like that?" she asked gently.

"No!" Andi's eyes brimmed. Goodness, how was it possible to cry so many tears? "Of course I don't!"

"Then you've got to tell him," Angel said firmly.

"After what I said before?" Andi hung her head. "He'll never talk to me again. I've blown it."

Her sister curled her lip. "So you're just going to give up? Throw in the towel? Jesus, Andi. I thought you had more balls than that. What about all the lectures you've given me over the years about facing up to responsibilities and doing the right thing?"

"Like you ever listened!"

"You'd be surprised. I listened more than I let on." Angel stood up and swung her bag onto her shoulder. "Come on, let's go."

"Go where?" Andi had never felt more defeated in her life.

"To find Jonty," said Angel patiently. "At least you can try to put things right with him, which has to be better than not trying at all, I'd have thought. If you love him half as much as I think you do you'll try to give it a go."

She was right and Andi nodded. Even if Jonty never felt the same way about her again she had to tell him she was sorry. Maybe he could forgive her? She didn't dare hope for anything more.

With a heart that was slowly filling with hope she followed her sister out of the pub and into the sunshine. There would be no more hiding in the shadows. From now on Andi was going to tell Jonty exactly how she felt.

Chapter 50

"Just go easy on the gas – she's very sensitive – and remember to watch for the front grill! The car's much longer than you think." The last of a long list of instructions issued, Travis handed the key fob to Gemma. He looked very worried, as well he should. Gemma hadn't driven anything except her ancient Beetle for years and the chassis' many dents and scratches were testament to her less than perfect spatial awareness. If cars could tremble, the Aston Martin would have been shaking in its boots.

"Chill," said Angel cheerfully, hopping into the back seat and coiling her long legs under her. "Gemma's a fab driver. Besides, it's just a car."

"It's a car that's worth nearly as much as a house," Gemma pointed out nervously.

"It still has wheels and some brakes, doesn't it?" Angel declared with enormous confidence. "And anyway, it goes like shit off a shovel, doesn't it Loz? You got it up to almost a hundred and ten on the Wadebridge bypass!"

Laurence couldn't quite look Travis in the eye. "Err, I think that's an exaggeration. Maybe just a hundred?"

Andi, strapped into the front seat, felt increasingly alarmed. Gemma was a crazy driver at the best of times; even in the stodgy London traffic and limited by a car that was older than she was, Gemma still drove as though in a bumper car and one with absolutely no sense of preservation. If they made it to Ocean View in one piece it would be a miracle. Andi could only hope somebody would tell Jonty she'd been on her way to find him.

Gemma jingled the key fob. "I'll enjoy every minute of this."

"I'm sure you will," said Travis grimly. "Just bring her back in one piece, that's all I ask."

"Like you did me when I was in your boat?" said Gemma sweetly.

Now it was Trav's turn to look awkward. "That was totally different."

"Chillax," said Angel. "It's a car."

Travis mounted his high horse. "This isn't some little hatchback, you know. This is a machine engineered for racing. See the 'S' button? That switches it into sports-car mode."

"Don't touch it, baby," Laurence said quickly to Angel. "That's way more power than you can handle."

"Oh sexist ye of little faith," said Angel airily. "Do you think just because we don't have willies we can't handle a supercar? I watched *Top Gear* once, I'll have you know, and Gemma can drive a tractor. And a forklift."

Travis didn't appear comforted by this. When Gemma failed to find the start button and was totally thrown by the lack of gears he looked almost ready to weep. Finally, after some confusion, the car burst into life.

Gemma grinned. "Believe me, this is nothing compared to Dad's combine harvester. And the engine's in the front, right? Just kidding!"

"If I hadn't had so much champagne I'd have driven you myself," Travis said sadly.

"And if you weren't such a show-off and had to drive it down the hill just to pose in, then we wouldn't have had it here to borrow in the first place," Angel teased. "But such is life! Andi owes you a big favour."

"Another one?" Travis gave Andi a rueful smile. "I wish I could call them in but I'm not an idiot, in spite of giving everyone lots of evidence to the contrary. It was obvious in Newquay that you were in love with Jonty. I hope you find him."

It was? Andi wished that somebody had pointed it out to her. It could have saved a lot of trouble.

Broom! Gemma touched the gas and the engine roared like Simba on speed. She revved it again, her eyes widening at the power. Angel reached forward and pressed a button, and the roof hissed down.

"Now we're in business," she said, blowing Laurence a kiss. "See you later, boys! Don't look so worried!"

Andi was glad that her sister and Gemma were having such fun but she wanted nothing more than to get going. Every second wasted channelling their inner Jeremy Clarksons was another second that Jonty thought she didn't care about him.

"Maybe it would just be easier if I walked?" she said.

But Angel was having none of Andi's protests. It suited her sense of the dramatic to screech through town in a supercar with her blonde hair flowing in the breeze and all eyes on her. Her sister was up to something; Andi could tell from the way her eyes were wide and her cheeks flushed, and if she wasn't more concerned about Jonty, Andi would have been alarmed. This was Angel's *crazy idea* face, and the last time she'd seen it a threatening letter from a security firm had followed shortly afterwards. Still, there was no time to worry about Angel now, because the car suddenly bounded forward like Tigger and Andi found herself clutching the dashboard for grim death. Was it too late to say she wanted to get out?

"Blimey!" Gemma gasped, her knuckles white on the wheel. "It's got a bit more oomph than my car!"

"Babes, a lawnmower has more oomph than your car," Angel said kindly. "Now press that 'S' button Loz was on about and let's turn this into a race car!"

Gemma didn't need asking twice. Moments later the car was quivering and dancing beneath them like a racehorse lined up at Aintree, equally explosive and equally likely to bolt. After the long journey to Rock Andi had never thought it would happen, but all of a sudden she was longing for that Beetle. What were a few carbon-monoxide fumes compared to death by Aston Martin?

Andi hardly dared to look as the car tore along Rock Road and roared up the hill. Tourists and seagulls scattered, the scent of burning rubber fought with the stench of oniony pasties, and even the growl of the engine couldn't drown out Angel's squeals of excitement. As Gemma swung through Ocean View's gates, narrowly missing one of the granite posts and spraying gravel everywhere, Andi's stomach lurched. Would Jonty even want to talk to her? Or had she hurt him so much that he'd send her away? That thought was like a knife through her heart.

While Gemma parked, Andi gathered up every ounce of courage she possessed, and went to knock on the pool-house door. The Defender, parked at an acute angle having left deep skid marks in the gravel, suggested that Jonty had returned home in a hurry. An upset hurry? Andi bit her lip. She hated to think of him hurting because of her. She was going to make it up to him for the rest of his life, if he'd let her.

Her knuckles stung from rapping on the door. There was no answer. She knocked again and pushed the letterbox open to call through it.

"Jonty? Are you there? It's me, Andi. I'm sorry about earlier. Can we talk?"

There was still no reply. She squashed her face to the glass, squinting against the reflection of the sunlit garden. Inside, the pool house was dark and there were no signs of life. Maybe he was at the boatyard? Or out on *Ursula*? When he was in need of time to think Jonty had said that boats always gave him headspace. As he took engines apart, peering into carburettors or unblocking fuel lines, he said he found that his own thoughts were similarly pulled to pieces and examined.

"There's nothing that an hour or two in the workshop can't solve," he'd explained. "I've had a lot on my mind this summer. Working on the boat helps."

At the time Andi had assumed that he was talking about Jax and that tinkering with *Ursula* had been a way to work through his heartache, but now she understood that there was so much more to it than a broken relationship. How did a down-to-earth guy who loved his family and his boats and the simple life come to terms with having the kind of wealth that made the royal family look hard up?

It wasn't just life changing, Andi realised, so much as ending life as he'd known it, forever. She wished she'd understood that when he'd told her, rather than being blinded by hurt. If only she'd seen beyond that.

"He's not here." Mel, her face puffy and her eyes red rimmed, joined Andi by the pool house. "He's gone, thanks to you. How could you say those things to him, Andi?"

Andi swallowed the knot of grief in her throat. "I was upset, Mel. I felt like he'd lied to me in every way a person could."

"But he was honest with you!" Mel's mouth trembled. "He let you in, Andi. He trusted you enough to let you get close, something I never thought he'd be able to do again after Jax took him for almost every penny. For the first time in far too long my brother had a smile on his face again. He was happy…" Her voice broke and she turned away.

"I'm sorry!" Andi stepped forward and touched Mel's shoulder. "I was shocked, and angry. I've been deceived in the past and it seemed like it was all about to happen again. I panicked and I just wanted to run away rather than be hurt all over again."

Mel spun round. Her eyes were a startling blue-green against the reddened lids.

"He'd never hurt you! For Christ's sake, Andi! Don't you realise? Jonty would do anything for you. He adores you. He loves you!"

"I know." Andi hung her head. She knew now just how much Jonty did love her; he loved her so much that he would never ask her to stay out of guilt or obligation but would rather set her free no matter what it cost him. "I'm going to the boatyard and I'll find him, I promise."

"The boatyard?"

Andi nodded. "He's there, isn't he? That's where Jonty always goes when he's upset."

Mel exhaled slowly. "He's a bit more than *upset*. He's devastated. I don't think that fiddling around with a boat will cut it this time. Si offered to take him out wakeboarding with the boys but Jonty didn't want to know."

'But his car's here!"

"That's the Cornish car," Mel said bleakly. "Jonty took a cab."

Andi felt an icicle of dread trace her spine. "Where is he?"

"On his way to Polzeath."

"Polzeath?" He'd gone surfing? At a time like this? It was official. Men were odd.

"He keeps a helicopter there at a private airfield," Mel explained, in between dabbing her eyes on her sleeve. "He's going away, Andi. Really going away. He's leaving Cornwall. He said there was nothing to stay for now and that he had to get away. I've never seen him so upset. You should have seen him let rip at Jax when she so *conveniently* turned up to pick up the pieces. She won't be back, that's for certain. He even threatened to sue her for the part of her company he helped set up unless she got out of his way. That had her shaking in her Louboutins, I can tell you. She practically ran back to her car. We won't see her again, thank God."

But Andi didn't register any of this. Jax no longer mattered. None of it did. All she had heard was that Jonty was leaving. The word gave Andi the sensation that she was sinking downwards very, very fast. Jonty couldn't leave.

"Where's he going?"

Mel looked utterly defeated. "I've no idea; he wouldn't say. I don't think he even knows himself but, knowing my brother, it'll be somewhere very far away indeed. And let's face it; he's got the means to go wherever he wants for as long as he wants. What's he got to stay for?"

But Andi wasn't sticking around to answer Mel. There wasn't a second left to spare on explanations. Jonty couldn't fly out of her life thinking that she despised him. The thought was enough to make her feel close to desperation. Mel was right: once that helicopter took off Jonty could go anywhere he wanted to. Safe T Net had floated and, with him no longer needed at the helm, an entire world of possibilities had opened up. No wonder he'd been so quiet at times. What did you do when you could do anything you desired?

And if there was nothing left that you desired? Then what did you do?

"Did you find him?" Angel demanded when Andi returned.

"Obviously not," said Gemma as Andi threw herself into the car.

Andi gasped out the story, her throat tightening with panic at the thought of Jonty flying out of her life, goodness knew only where, thinking that she really didn't care.

"Can you get us to Polzeath?" she asked.

Gemma didn't pause to reply. Instead, she pressed a button on the dash and, in true Bond style, a satnav system arose from the smooth walnut. Crikey. What was next? An ejector seat?

"Let's go," she said.

Andi had never been the type of girl who was impressed by fast cars, but as Gemma floored it out of Rock she began to see the point of them. The smooth Aston Martin ate up the miles like Cal and Gemma gobbled cake. Glancing at the speedometer, Andi was horrified to see that they were nudging one hundred miles an hour.

"Don't worry," said Gemma, following her gaze. "If we get pulled over we'll just tell the police I'm having a baby." She patted her stomach. "After eating all that French stick I look like I'm about to give birth anyway."

"They'd have to catch us first. I bet we'd be faster," said Angel smugly.

Andi buried her head in her hands. If they didn't die then they were bound to feature in one of those *Police, Camera, Action* type shows. Was this Angel's latest reality-TV plan?

Andi's nails scored crescent moons into the butterscotch leather seats as Gemma swung the car through the twisty lanes linking Rock and

Polzeath like tangled shoelaces. The car made light work of the steep hills, devouring the miles until they crested one final summit and all that lay ahead was the endless stretch of the Celtic Sea.

"There's Polzeath!" Angel, leaning forward, pointed to the higgledy-piggledy cluster of rooftops below. The fine weather was finally starting to break. The sky was the hue of an old galvanised bucket and for once the beach was empty; the windbreaks had been packed up and the pink bodies had decamped to the cafés and pubs. The place was certainly a lot quieter than Rock.

Gemma stopped the car and looked questioningly at Andi. "This is Polzeath. Where to now?"

"Is there an airfield?" Andi wondered.

Gemma shook her head. "Not according to the satnav. Do you think it might be nearby?"

Andi had no idea where Jonty kept his helicopter – she was still trying to get her head around the idea that he owned a helicopter, for heaven's sake – but surely it shouldn't be too difficult to spot one? Polzeath was just a tiny seaside town with a scattering of shops and a golden sweep of beach that was surfing Mecca to a bevy of tousle-haired and funky tattooed twenty-somethings. VW campers freckled the pavements. Helicopters not so much.

"I hope so," she said. If not, then Andi wasn't sure quite what she would do. The tide of despair that threatened to swamp over her was terrifying.

"According to Mel, Jonty took a cab – so he's had a head start, fast as we are," Angel said. She frowned. "Would that be enough time for him to have left already, do you think? Or would he have to fuel up or something?"

"Well, the last time I travelled by helicopter..." deadpanned Gemma.

Andi gulped back the rising fear that he might have already left. Surely not? Wouldn't she know? Feel it?

The girls scanned the landscape for a few moments. Andi wasn't sure what she'd expected. A helpful windsock blowing in the wind perhaps, or a signpost?

"What's that over there?" Angel pointed to a small building on their left where a blue smudge blurred the green of a pasture several cornfields away. Shading her eyes against the glare of the sky, Andi made out the form of a helicopter.

"That's it!" she cried.

The car surged forward but this time Andi wasn't complaining. Instead she was willing it to go faster and faster. Gemma did her best, guiding the vehicle through the high-banked lanes in the direction of the field, but she met a series of dead ends and at one point a herd of sheep meandering along the road, all trembling bleats and newly shorn bodies. When the sheep finally poured into a field, only for the girls to meet yet another chained five-bar gate, Andi could have screamed with frustration. Only two huge fields stood between her and Jonty but it might as well have been two hundred miles. She could try to run across, Andi thought, but would she be fast enough and even going in the right direction? What if she only got halfway and then the helicopter took off? Jonty would never know she'd been there at all. When she heard the whir of blades Andi knew there wasn't time to hesitate.

There had to be another way! Another way she could show him how she felt. Make him see that she loved him.

Hang on! That was it! The idea darted through her mind, quicksilver as the mackerel fishermen hauled up on their lines.

Make him see…

"Turn the car round! Drive down to the beach!" she cried to Gemma.

Without even questioning her reasoning, Gemma reversed back up the lane. Foliage scraped against the car's glossy paintwork and its high-performance wheels bounced against the Cornish bank. It was too late to worry about the Aston Martin though, especially as minutes later the car was making its way onto the beach and racing across the sand. When the tyres began to spin, spraying sand onto the windscreen and through the open roof, Andi flung open the car door and continued on foot. Kicking off her shoes, she sprinted across the beach until she reached the flat, wet sand closest to the breaking waves. All the time she ran she watched the sky, dreading the sound of the helicopter. Too soon and he'd be gone.

Not yet, Jonty, she almost sobbed, *not yet!*

Crouching down, little caring that her jeans were soaking up the brine lying in the ripples, Andi scooped her hand through the wet sand with swift and definite strokes. When she heard the unmistakable whir of a helicopter she doubled her efforts, her breath coming in short half-sobs. She had to finish in time! She had to!

The second that her fingers scored the wet sand for the final time Andi sprang to her feet. Done! Was it visible from above? Did it make sense? Could Jonty see it? Would he even fly over the beach? There were a million and one questions racing through her head and, for once, she just didn't have the answers. It was such a long shot but it was the only shot she had.

It was the only *hope* she had.

Then she heard it: a noise like the soft purr of a kitten, growing to the throaty burr of a cat and finally to the full-bellied roaring of a lion. The sound came first, divorced from what was making it and carried by the salty wind. Seconds later a blue helicopter swooped over the beach, its shadow darkening the sand as it hovered above, seemingly poised to strike like a bird of prey.

"Stop! Stop! Stop!" screamed Andi, leaping up and down and waving her arms about wildly. "Jonty! Stop!"

The wind from the blades whipped her hair from her face and slung stinging handfuls of sand against her cheeks. For a moment she hardly dared to hope – had he seen it, and would he stop? – before the helicopter circled lazily and flew away back over the town.

Andi watched it go and her heart went with it. Broken and bereft, she sank to her knees. That was it. She'd given everything she had to give, laid her soul bare and declared her feelings in plain view, and it still hadn't been enough to make him stay. She'd blown it.

Jonty was lost to her and the future suddenly seemed as grey as the pewter sky.

She was on the brink of making her way back to the car – heaven only knew how they would manage to dig it out of the sand – when a sharp blast of air and a shower of sand announced the helicopter's return. It loomed over the headland for a moment as though undecided, before it sank slowly down onto the beach, as graceful as a ballerina dropping into a curtsey. The blades spun in hypnotic circles and she gazed at them mesmerised. Was this really happening or had her longing for him sent her over the edge and off on some wild hallucination? Only when the engines stopped and the only sound was once again the pounding of the surf did she dare to believe that this was real.

The helicopter door opened and a familiar figure leapt down onto the beach. His dark hair lifted in the breeze and even from a distance Andi could see the sadness etched into his face. Her heart twisted. She had done that to him, and she wanted nothing more than to hold him close and kiss away all the hurt.

He was wearing aviator shades. She saw herself reflected in them, a small figure with wild red curls, marooned on the vast beach. Jonty pushed them onto the top of his head. In his faded jeans and white tee shirt, riding up to show a hint of the ripped flat stomach she knew lay beneath, he looked as though he'd stepped straight from a movie. And she knew exactly which one!

"Very *Top Gun*," she teased.

"If you make any cracks about Maverick or 'Take My Breath Away', I'm jumping straight back in," he warned.

Andi couldn't help herself. "Not even, Jonty, you big stud. Take me to bed or lose me forever?'"

Jonty's lips twitched. "Now that one I might have to take on board. Although, it does depend."

It did? Andi was surprised he couldn't hear her heart; it was thudding so loudly.

"On what?"

Jonty stared at the words she'd written so frantically in the sand, and when he looked up at her his turquoise eyes held none of the despair she'd seen earlier but instead they were flooded with hope.

"Do you mean it?" he said quietly, indicating the words and turning back to look at them. "Is that really true?"

Andi followed his gaze. Scrawled across the beach in the biggest letters she'd been able to manage in the few crazy minutes she'd had, were the simplest and most honest words she'd ever had to say.

Project Manager B. I love you. A

She nodded, unable to speak. Everything about Jonty robbed her of breath and flooded her with love. Those blue-green eyes that crinkled at the corners, the waves of dark hair curling against his neck, the strong arms that had held her close – but most of all his kind and generous soul. That was what was truly wonderful about Jonty; *he* was all that mattered. The rest of it was just wrapping. Looking at those simple words she wondered what had ever been so difficult.

"I mean it with all my heart," she said.

Jonty didn't move to close the distance between them but instead held her with his eyes. "And the other things? The secrets I kept? Being Project Manager B? Safe T Net?"

"I don't care about any of that," Andi told him. "I only care about you." Oh sod it. It was time to lay her heart on the line. She'd already written it all over the beach, so there was no point hiding it. "I love you, Jonty. Nothing else matters apart from that."

For a moment they just stared at one another. Then a smile lit his face just like the sun that was punching through the leaden clouds, and, stepping forward, he folded Andi into his arms.

The relief she felt was incredible. This was where she was supposed to be. Her harbour. Her home. Her Jonty. As though it had been waiting all day just for this very moment, egg-yolk yellow light spilled onto the beach, burnishing Jonty's skin and turning his freckles to gold dust. Suddenly the whole world was filled with sunshine.

"I feel exactly the same way," he said, tightening his arms and pulling her close so that she could feel every ripple of his body. Delicious shivers of desire Mexican-waved across her skin.

"You love me too?" The words fell from her lips before she could stop them.

Jonty brushed the hair away from her face. "I love everything about you, Andi Evans. I love the Andi that PMB bantered with. I love the Andi who learned to drive a boat. I love the Andi who worked like a maniac to make herself solvent and refused to give up." He kissed the tip of her nose. "Actually, I think I've loved you since you first tried to wrestle the *FT* from me!"

"The cheek! I was there first—" Andi feigned indignation, but her protests were soon silenced because Jonty was kissing her and she was kissing him back, softly at first but then with ever-increasing urgency as time seemed to slow and transport them to a place where there were no more misunderstandings.

"About what you did for me," Andi began when they broke apart.

Jonty laid a finger on her lips. "I did it because I wanted to. There was no agenda. Can we leave all that for now? How about you and I forget about Tom and Jax and all the rest of the crap and just think about us for a change? And I mean absolutely nothing else. We can go away somewhere quiet where it's just us, somewhere with no exes, sisters or interruptions."

The way he said this, with those eyes holding hers, made Andi want nothing more. The images of a dark river, a soft breeze and billowing white curtains flashed through her memory and her pulse quickened.

Jonty held out his hand. "Do you trust me?"

She took it in hers, lacing their fingers together. "Of course I do."
She always had, Andi realised. From the moment they'd first met she'd
instinctively trusted him. If she had only listened to her intuition she
could have saved them both a lot of heartache.

He raised their linked hands, dropping a kiss onto her knuckles. "So
you'll come on a mystery flight?"

She squeezed his fingers. "Try stopping me."

Hand in hand they retraced Jonty's footsteps towards the helicopter,
their two sets of prints in the sand side by side and closer than words.
Just the way it should be.

"Ready to spread your wings and fly?" Jonty asked, and Andi
nodded, knowing she would follow him to the end of the world if he
asked. It didn't matter where they went. All that mattered was that they
were together. And with Jonty Andi knew that she would fly, in every
way a person should.

Up into the sky rose the blue helicopter, hovering high above the
beach and the two miniature figures next to a matchbox-sized car
waving and cheering. It banked left and flew low over the Camel
Estuary, where two small boys rode the wake of a boat while their
father sounded the horn in greeting. Then it swooped towards the
town, circled Ocean View and headed towards the limitless horizon...

Jonty smiled at her. "Ready?"

Andi smiled back. Her heart was so full of love and excitement that
she could have flown without the helicopter. With Jonty beside her she
knew she was more than ready for whatever might come next.

"Ready!" she replied firmly.

And bidding Angel, Gemma and their Cornish escape a silent *thank
you*, Andi Evans flew up and away into the bright blue sky of her future.

Chapter 51

One Year Later

The National Television Awards

"And the award for Best Reality TV Show goes to..." the famous comedian paused for dramatic effect while the cameras panned across the audience, settling on the expectant faces of the UK's most celebrated household names, all of whom were trying their hardest to look nonchalant. When the floor manager gave the nod, the comedian peeled the envelope open with painstaking slowness, before fixing the cameras with a blinding white grin. "I bloody love this show! Best Reality TV Show – it's *Bread and Butlers*!"

"Yes!" Angel, Lady Kenniston, shot out of her chair and punched the air, a dangerous activity that threatened to bounce her from her stunning strapless Stella McCartney gown. Beaming at all the *TOWIE* stars, celebrity chefs and ex glamour models pretending to look thrilled for her, Angel tossed her golden mane back from her flushed face and flung her arms around Laurence.

"Oh my God! We did it! We really did it!"

In her wildest dreams – and Angel's dreams were pretty wild, it had to be said – she had never imagined that her idea would be anywhere near this successful. Almost from the second the first episode aired, the nation had gone crazy for *Bread and Butlers*. With Callum South's popularity, the stunning setting of Kenniston, an eccentric cast and constant disasters, the ingredients had been as successful as Cal and Gemma's fledgling bakery business that the show followed. Sprinkle into that Angel's stunning looks, Laurence's blue blood and the ongoing stresses of trying to save a crumbling mansion, and it made for compulsive viewing. The everyday dramas, the rows, and the excitement that had built after Laurence's dramatic on-screen proposal for the *Bread and Butlers* summer wedding had all raised the show high in the ratings.

Mr Yuri had been right. It did not fail. As the cheers rang out, the oligarch beamed. He'd already seen Joanna Lumley and had chatted to Katie Price; he was having the time of his life!

"We certainly did do it!" Laurence kissed his wife back while the room erupted. Since the episode where they'd been married amid the half-restored splendour of Kenniston and with three beribboned Labradors and a bemused Gemma as flower girls, Laurence and Angel had scarcely been out of the press. The British public had gone crazy for them; a week rarely passed when they weren't featured in a tabloid or in *Heat* magazine. Apart from Angel being voted *FHM*'s sexiest woman of the year (take that, Kelly Brook) and regularly bumping into Peter Andre (she was far too busy now to attend any of his barbecues, no matter how many times he invited her), the high point so far had probably been when Tom, fresh from his community service and suspended fraud sentence, had sent his CV to Kenniston. As if! Was ever a man so deluded? Angel had filed it in the bin.

"Jaysus, you two! Snog later," Cal said to Angel and Laurence. His DJ strained a little at the buttons, but this was no longer an issue now that he was the face of a successful artisan bakery and more famous for focaccia than football. His brown eyes twinkled. "This is your big moment."

"Go on!" urged Gemma. Unlike her partner she seldom appeared on the show, preferring to support Cal from the wings. Her recipe book, however, based on the show, was proving to be a huge bestseller – and she was already being hailed as the new Nigella. Although Gemma was still curvy, happiness and (judging from all the early nights they had, thought Angel with a smile) lots of good sex had slimmed her down to the size fourteen she'd always longed to be. Gemma still acted in an amateur group but most of her time was spent behind the scenes, running the business and helping with Kenniston. Walking from one end of the house to the other non-stop was also a workout in itself. Angel reckoned that Gemma must trek miles every day. Maybe she should buy her friend a Segway? That could be great TV material! And Laurence's ma, who'd turned out to be a most unlikely star of the show, would be an absolute hoot on it. She made a mental note to look into it as soon as the award ceremony was over and text the production team. Honestly! Her brain hadn't had a minute off since she'd first thought up *Bread and Butlers*.

Claridge's ballroom was still ringing with cheers. On the huge VT screen Angel saw a close-up of her smiling face, interspersed with clips from the show: Cal covered in flour kissing an equally floury Gemma, Laurence in a morning suit waiting nervously at the church, Angel in her underwear talking to the blushing builders, the dogs eating the cupcakes for a society soirée... Scene after scene flickered across the screen, a celluloid record of the best year of her life.

The cameras were panning back to her now. This was it, the moment where she would sweep through the gathered TV royalty and stand on the stage. It was the moment she'd dreamed about for so long; yet now it was here Angel was frozen. She glanced around the table, from face to face, and a knot formed in her throat at the thought of just how dear these people had become. Even Mr Yuri – although he still looked a bit like a pig in a suit – had been an invaluable ally, and Travis too had turned out to have quite a flair for television production. She couldn't have done it without any of them, but there was one person without whom Angel knew she would never have made it this far. One person who had always supported her and looked out for her.

Applause rippled though the auditorium as Angel glided across the stage. The comedian dropped a kiss onto her cheek and tried to squeeze her backside, yelping when her sharp elbow caught him in the ribs. Angel smiled sweetly at the camera. She'd learned a lot this year. Clutching his chest, the comedian stepped back so that Angel could take the podium, and the audience fell silent.

"I'm not going to make you listen to a long speech," Angel promised them. "I just want to say a big thank you to everyone who's voted for us and supported the show. We love every minute of sharing our lives with you all. Although, I must admit that I could do without everyone seeing me without my make-up on such a regular basis. Laurence doesn't have a choice – he married me – but the rest of you don't deserve it!"

There was laughter at this. Angel always looked amazing with or without her foundation.

Angel clutched the award to her chest. "This is the part where I could do a Gwyneth Paltrow; there are so many people that deserve thanks, from my gorgeous husband right through to the fantastic crew. But before I do finish, there is one very special person I want to thank tonight. This is the person I owe everything to. She's always been there, always believed in me and encouraged me. When our mother died she put her own grief aside and looked after me. I guess she's been doing it ever since in one way or another. She's always put me first."

The auditorium was silent. On the big screen Angel's eyes shimmered with emotion. "She can't be here tonight because she's in Mumbai with her partner, Jonty Teague, and working with the Safe T Net Safe Sight charity, but I want everyone to know just how much she means to me and how much I love her." She raised the golden trophy and spoke directly to the camera. "Andi Evans, sister, best friend and fellow Rock chick, this is for you!"

The room erupted into applause and Angel's heart swelled with pride as she rejoined her table.

"That was wonderful," said Gemma, hugging her tightly. "Didn't I tell you that going to Cornwall was the start of amazing things? And just look at how it turned out for all of us."

Nodding, Angel hugged her back. Three girls, two hundred miles and one golden summer. Gemma had been right all along: their escape to Cornwall had been the start of wonderful adventures – and as she smiled at her friends, Angel knew for certain there were plenty more to come.

The End

Ruth Saberton is the bestselling author of *Katy Carter Wants a Hero* and *Escape for the Summer*. She also writes upmarket commercial fiction under the pen names Jessica Fox, Georgie Carter and Holly Cavendish.

Born and raised in the UK, Ruth has just returned from living on Grand Cayman for two years. What an adventure!

And since she loves to chat with readers, please do add her as a Facebook friend and follow her on Twitter.

www.ruthsaberton.co.uk

Twitter: @ruthsaberton

Facebook: Ruth Saberton

Printed in Great Britain
by Amazon